# Peter
# LOVESEY

## DOWN AMONG
## THE DEAD MEN

sphere

SPHERE

First published in Great Britain in 2015 by Sphere
This paperback edition published in 2016 by Sphere

1 3 5 7 9 10 8 6 4 2

A CIP catalogue record for this book
is available from the British Library.

ISBN 978-0-7515-5889-0

Typeset in ITC New Baskerville by Palimpsest Book Production Limited,
Falkirk, Stirlingshire
Printed and bound in Great Britain by
Clays Ltd, St Ives plc

Papers used by Sphere are from well-managed forests
and other responsible sources.

MIX
Paper from
responsible sources
FSC
www.fsc.org   FSC® C104740

Sphere
An imprint of
Little, Brown Book Group
Carmelite House
50 Victoria Embankment
London EC4Y 0DZ

An Hachette UK Company
www.hachette.co.uk

www.littlebrown.co.uk

# Acknowledgements

Martin Baggoley supplied me with expert advice about sentencing procedures and I am grateful to him.

Sentencing in another sense is my responsibility as the writer, but I wish to pay tribute to the many valuable contributions made in this series of books by my editors in Britain and America, Thalia Proctor and Juliet Grames. And for longer than they would wish me to reveal, my literary agents, Vanessa Holt and Jane Gelfman, have provided creative support as well as keeping me employed in the career I love. Finally, Jax, my wife, is always the first to see the novel in its raw, unedited state and help to make it readable. I am truly fortunate to have these five brilliant women in my life.

P.L.

# 1

*Brighton, September 2007*

'Are you sure this thing works?' Danny asked Mr Singh, the gizmo man.

'You want demonstration?'

'I'd be a mug if I didn't.'

'No problem. Where did you leave car?'

'A little way up the street.'

'What make?'

'It's the old white Merc by the lamp post.'

'Locking is remote, right?'

Danny dipped his hand in his pocket, opened his palm and showed the key fob with its push-button controls.

'Very good,' Mr Singh said. 'We can test. Go to car and let yourself in. Step out, lock up and walk back here. I am waiting on street with gizmo.'

Danny was alert for trickery. He wasn't parting with sixty-odd pounds for a useless lump of plastic and metal. But if it really did work, he could be quids in. Thousands.

The gizmo, as Mr Singh called it, looked pretty basic in construction, a pocket-sized black box with two retractable antennas fitted to one end.

No money had changed hands yet, so the guy had nothing to gain by doing a runner. Danny stepped out of the little coffee shop and did exactly as suggested. Walked to the

Mercedes, unlocked, got in, closed the door, opened it again, stepped out, locked using the smart key and walked back to where Mr Singh was standing outside the shop with the gizmo in his hands.

'You locked it, right?'

'Sure did,' Danny said.

'Where is key?'

'Back in my pocket.'

'Excellent. Leave it there. Now go to car and try door.'

Danny had walked only a few steps when he saw that the lock pins were showing. Just as promised, the car was unlocked.

He was impressed. To be certain, he opened the door he'd apparently locked a moment ago.

'Good job, eh?' Mr Singh said when Danny went back to him.

'Nice one. Who makes these things?'

'Made in China.'

'Wouldn't you know it?'

'Simple to operate. You want to buy?'

'How does it work?'

'OK. You know how key fob works?'

'Using a radio signal.'

'Right. Sending signal from fob to car. Programmed to connect with your car and no other. But this gizmo is signal jammer. Breaks frequency. You think you lock up, but I zap you with this.'

'Let me see.'

Danny held the thing and turned it over. 'All I have to do is press this?'

'Correct. All about timing. You are catching exact moment when driver is pointing fob at car.'

'Hang on. There's always a sound when the locks engage. And the lights flick on and off. If that doesn't happen, the driver will notice.'

'Did you notice?'

Danny hesitated. 'There was traffic noise and I was thinking of other things.'

'So?' Mr Singh flashed his teeth.

'In a quiet place the driver would notice.'

'Don't use in quiet place. Street is better, street with much traffic.'

Danny turned the jammer over and looked at the other side, speculating. 'How much are you asking?'

'Seventy, battery included.'

He made a sound as if he'd been burnt. 'Seventy is more than I thought.'

'Fully effective up to fifty metres.'

Danny handed it back. 'I don't suppose it works with the latest models.'

'Now I am being honest. Very new cars, possibly no. Manufacturers getting wise. Any car up to last year is good. That gives plenty choice. To you, special offer, not to be repeated. Sixty-five.'

Danny took a wad from his back pocket, peeled off three twenties and held them out.

Mr Singh sighed, took the money and handed over the jammer.

'Before you go,' Danny said. 'There's something else. This gets me into the car, but it doesn't let me drive it away. I was told you have another little beauty for that.'

Mr Singh's eyes lit up again. 'Programmer. Which make? BMW, Mercedes, Audi?'

'I need a different one for each make, do I? How much will it cost me?'

'Two hundred. Maybe two-fifty.'

Danny whistled. This was getting to be a larger investment than he planned, but he thought about the top-class cars he could steal. 'Let's say the Bimmer.'

3

'BMW three or five series I can do for two hundred.'

'Is it difficult to operate?'

'Dead easy. All cars now have diagnostic connector port. You plug in and programmer reads key code.'

'Then what?'

'Code is transferred from car's computer to microchip in new key. You get five blank keys gratis as well.'

'So I can drive off using the new key? Have you tried this yourself?'

'No, no, no, I am supplier only. Supplying is lawful. Driving off with some person's car is not.'

'But you can show me how the thing works?'

'You come back with two hundred cash this time tomorrow and for you as special customer I am supplying and demonstrating BMW 3 series programmer.'

Next afternoon special customer Danny drove away from Brighton with the programmer and the pride of a man at the cutting edge of the electronic revolution. In his youth he'd used a wire coat hanger to get into cars. He'd graduated to a slim Jim strip and then a whole collection of lock-picking tools. But the days of hotwiring the ignition were long gone. In recent years anti-theft technology had become so sophisticated that he'd been reduced to touring car parks looking for vehicles left unlocked by their stupid owners. For a man once known as Driveaway Danny it had become humiliating. The Mercedes he was driving was twelve years old. He'd liberated it in July from some idiot in Bognor who'd left it on his driveway with the key in the ignition.

Everything was about to change.

He would shortly be driving a BMW 3 series.

It wasn't easy to nail one. For more than a week he patrolled the streets of the south-coast town of Littlehampton (which isn't known for executive cars) with his two gizmos in a Tesco carrier bag. The new technology called for a whole new mindset. He wasn't on the lookout for a parked car, but one that happened to drive up while he was watching. He'd need to make a snap decision when the chance came. *If* the chance came.

Late Sunday evening it did. After a day of no success he was consoling himself with a real ale at his local, the Steam Packet, near the red footbridge over the River Arun. He lived in a one-bedroom flat a few hundred yards away and liked to wind down here at the end of a long day. The pub was said to have existed since 1840, trading under a different name because the cross-channel ferry that departed from there hadn't come into service until 1863. welcome aboard the steam packet, announced the large wooden board attached to the front with a profile of a paddle steamer – and in case the maritime message was overlooked, the north side of the pub had a ship's figurehead of a topless blonde (in the best possible taste, with strategically dangling curls) projecting from the wall. With a little imagination, when seated in the terrace at the back overlooking River Road and the Arun you could believe yourself afloat. This was a favourite spot of Danny's, nicely placed for seeing spectacular sunsets or watching small boats chugging back from sea trips. But at this moment, alone in the half-light at one of the benches around nine thirty on a September evening, his thoughts were not about sea trips or sunsets. He'd just decided he'd wasted his money on Mr Singh's gizmos. How ironic then that this was the moment when a silver BMW drove up and came to a halt in the parking space across the street.

Danny almost knocked over his beer reaching for the carrier bag. He tugged out the jammer and extended the antennas. Its first use for real. He couldn't have been better placed, all but hidden by the chest-high terrace wall.

The car's plates weren't visible from this angle. He couldn't tell from the design of the thing which year it had been manufactured, if it was too recent to respond to the jammer. If the trick didn't work, so what? It was worth the try.

The door opened and the driver got out, no more than a youth, slim, in a dark blue hoodie and jeans. He pushed the door shut. He didn't immediately use the key.

Danny's right forefinger was poised over the switch. As Mr Singh had said, this was all about timing. *You catch exact moment.*

With a springy step and a bit of a swagger, the kid started walking in the direction of the footbridge. No one else was about. He hadn't used the smart key yet. As if in an afterthought, about three paces from the car, he turned his head and glanced back.

Danny's view was masked. All he could see was the youth's back half-turned. It was impossible to tell for sure if the key was in his hand, but reasonable to assume it was. Drivers habitually took a few steps from their vehicle and then turned, pointed the key and pressed.

Now or never. Danny brought his finger down and instinctively ducked out of sight behind the terrace wall.

Nothing happened.

He had to remind himself that the whole point of the jammer was to get a negative result.

When Danny put his head above the wall again, the kid was halfway across the bridge, moving briskly. Danny stowed the jammer in the carrier and hurried out, leaving almost half a glass of real ale behind. On his way through the lounge he raised his free hand in a farewell to the barmaid and stepped out of the building and round the side to where the BMW was parked.

A thousand blessings on Mr Singh. The pins were up. The car was unlocked, begging to be liberated.

But not yet.

He needed to use the second gizmo, the programmer, to make his own key before he could drive his free gift away.

After checking to make certain no one was about, he stepped round to the driver's side and let himself in. The interior was still warm and smelt faintly of body odour. He left the door open. He dumped the carrier bag on the passenger seat and lifted out the programmer. Now it was a matter of locating the onboard diagnostic system and plugging in the sixteen-pin connector.

Should be simple.

Danny had been given a demonstration by Mr Singh, who was as wiry as a strip of three-core flex. Danny was overweight. Grovelling under the dashboard of a car wasn't easy. On his knees and breathing hard, he made more room by pushing the seat back to its fullest extent. Just above the pull switch for the bonnet he found the cover with the letters OBD on it. He opened up, plugged in, watched the programmer light up, used the controls to collect the key code and then remembered he would need something else. He reached for the carrier and scrabbled inside for one of the blank fobs, found one and pressed it against the programmer.

All done in under three minutes.

Relieved, he unplugged, extracted himself and stood up. His hands were shaking and his knees were wobbly. He looked towards the footbridge and saw no one.

The next job would be more familiar: driving the thing away to get the registration plates changed. A guy called Stew was the local specialist, always relocating to outwit the fuzz and currently on a trading estate in Chichester, not more than twelve miles away.

Danny got in, slotted in the key and yelped in triumph as the dashboard lit up. The fuel tank was three-quarters full.

Bridge Road, the main road to Chichester, went past the front of the Steam Packet. Danny drove off as sedately as if he was taking his mother shopping. He didn't want to get pulled over for speeding. The good thing was that the young owner was still unaware his car had been driven away and with any luck he wouldn't return for a couple of hours. You couldn't have much sympathy. He was probably some rich kid whose father had bought the thing for him. Dad would shout the odds and then buy him another.

The Bimmer handled well and was a smooth ride. Danny didn't object to driving an automatic. Not much over two years old, he reckoned. No need for a respray when there were so many silver saloon cars out there. Once this had the new plates, he'd dump the old Mercedes. Selling wasn't an option in the stolen-car game. But it was all very satisfactory, and for not much outlay so far. Stew would be more expensive than Mr Singh, but that had to be faced. New plates were essential.

Now that he was clear of the crime scene, so to speak, Danny needed to check with Stew that he was willing to take delivery. The guy had never been known to turn down a job, but he liked to be contacted first. Only reasonable. Generally he was in his workshop until around midnight.

Out in open country, after the A259 had changed its identity from Bridge Lane to Crookthorn Lane to Grevatt's Lane, he found a field entrance with enough room to pull off the road and make the call on a cheap mobile he'd bought specially for this job.

'You working?'

Stew answered and he knew Danny's voice right away. 'Yep. Got something to show me?'

'If you got time.'

'When were you thinking of?'

8

'Now if you want. Say twenty minutes.'

'See you then.'

Having made the call, Danny wedged the phone under the back wheel of the car so that it would be crushed when he drove off. Technology is a two-edged sword to anyone in a high-risk occupation. He was tempted to do the same with the gizmos, but they'd been an expensive buy.

Before leaving, he thought he would also clear the glove compartment of the manual and any documents. It's common sense to remove everything that can reveal the owner's identity. The seats and door panels were free of obvious clutter, which was a help. For a young owner, it was all incredibly tidy. He leaned across and clicked the latch. The flap pushed against his hand.

An avalanche of banknotes tumbled out. Masses of them, mainly twenties.

The thump, thump wasn't the money hitting the floor, it was Danny's heart. Either the young guy who drove this car didn't believe in using banks or he robbed them. There must have been more than a couple of grand here.

Alternately swearing and thanking God, Danny scooped up handfuls and stuffed as many as possible into his pockets. The rest went down his socks. How glad he was that Stew hadn't found this lot.

What a turnaround in his luck. If it wasn't so late in the day he would have bought a lottery ticket.

Fully ten minutes passed before he calmed down enough to drive again. Even then he was mentally spending the money. Good thing the route was obvious. He was through Felpham and Bognor and on to the Chichester Road without registering that he'd passed anywhere.

Concentrate, he told himself. The job isn't done yet.

The last stretch of the A259 was a dual carriageway leading to the A27. Two roundabouts and he would be at Stew's.

He could safely go up to seventy here and test the acceleration. Watch the speedo, but feel the power.

Faintly over the engine sound he heard the twin notes of a police siren.

Can't be me, he thought. I'm inside the limit.

In the mirror he saw the blue flashing light. Do what any law-abiding motorist does, he told himself. Pull over and let them pass.

He eased his foot off the pedal. Hardly anything else was on the road and they could easily get by, but he did the decent thing.

Instead of overtaking, they closed in behind him and flashed their headlights. What now?

He pulled over, braked, lowered the window and switched off.

Bluff this out, he thought. They can't possibly know this quickly that the car is stolen. It's got to be some minor infringement like a faulty rear lamp.

He grabbed the bag of gizmos and pushed it out of sight under the passenger seat.

They were taking their time, probably checking over their radio that the car wasn't on their list.

Finally a figure appeared at the window. Heavy black moustache. 'Evening, sir. Are you the owner of this car?'

'I am.'

'Step outside, please.'

What was this? The breathalyser? He hadn't finished his pint of real ale. He'd be well under the limit. 'Is something up?'

There was a second officer, a policewoman.

The male cop said, 'Place both hands flat against the car roof and stand with your legs apart. I'm going to search you.'

'What for? I've done nothing wrong.' As he said the

words, he thought of all the banknotes stuffed inside his pockets.

He did as he was ordered and felt the hands travel down his body. What the fuck was he going to say?

'What's your name, sir?'

'Daniel Stapleton.'

'Date of birth, please.'

'Ninth of October, nineteen seventy.'

'Mind if I call you Daniel?'

'Danny will do.'

'What's this in your pockets, Danny? Keep your hands exactly where they are.'

'Some cash.'

'Quite a lot of it, apparently. What's all this money doing in your pockets?'

'I, em, did some business. Cash transaction.'

'What sort of business?'

'In Littlehampton. I sold a boat.'

'Is that where you came from – Littlehampton?'

'Yes.'

'And where are you travelling to?'

'Only Chichester. Bit of a night out.'

'Spending all this money?'

'Not all of it.'

'You said you own the car. It's been reported as stolen. That's why we stopped you.'

'This car? Stolen?' He was able to say the words with genuine disbelief. The young guy had disappeared across the footbridge. He'd been on his way somewhere. He couldn't have returned so soon and got on to the police.

'Do you have any proof of identity? Your licence?'

'That's at home.'

The search had been progressing down his body. 'Do you normally keep banknotes in your socks?'

11

The cop didn't seem to expect an answer, so Danny didn't attempt one.

A large amount of cash might be suspicious, but it wasn't necessarily illegal. They hadn't found drugs or a weapon. They were probably disappointed. Danny was wondering if the comment about the stolen car had been a bluff.

The cop said to his female colleague, 'Let's have a look in the boot, shall we?'

Danny heard her open it.

She said, 'God help us.'

# 2

'You won't believe this,' Jem said.

'Try me,' Ella said.

'The Gibbon has gone.'

Shrieks of amazement and delight from the group. Miss Gibbon was the most disliked teacher on the staff. Her idea of teaching art was endless exercises in perspective.

'Gone where?' Ella said. Always primed for excitement, she was the perfect foil to Jem, the information gatherer.

'I don't give a toss where. Up her own vanishing point, for all I care. She didn't tell anyone in the staffroom she was going at the end of last term. I expect the head knew, but none of the others did, so there wasn't, like, a leaving present or a farewell drink or anything.'

'Who cares? At last they found out she was a crap teacher. I still haven't got the faintest idea what she meant by the golden mean and she never stopped talking about it.'

'Golden section.'

'Golden balls. Was she kicked out?'

'A scandal? Touching up the year sevens?'

'Not the Gibbon. She was sexless. More like pinching the art funds to go on those cultural cruises she was always on about,' Jem said, and her opinion always triumphed. 'The

13

thing is, what happens to us in our final A-level year? They'll have to bring in someone new.'

'That's *all* we need, some new teacher straight out of college.'

'Could be a bloke.'

More shrieks. Jem, shorter than anyone, had a big personality. She was like a conductor controlling the highs and lows of excited chatter.

'You wish!'

'Jem, you're joking . . . aren't you?'

Clearly she had more to tell. She waited for the noise to stop. 'When I came in I happened to notice a sweet little vintage MG in the staff parking. And then I copped the back view of this tall young guy going into the head's office.'

'Get away! What's he like?'

'Like an artist. Dark, wavy hair to his shoulders, leather jacket and black chinos, Cuban heels—'

'Stop – I'm getting the hots.'

'*You*'re getting the hots? Think about the head. He was in with her for twenty minutes.'

Everyone was rendered helpless. Even the coy Naseem got a fit of the giggles.

'Did he stagger out all shaky at the knees?' Ella said.

'I waited and waited, but I'd have been late for French conversation.'

'Wouldn't it be bang tidy if he was our new art teacher?'

'Please God!'

'Dream on.'

'We've only got to wait till third lesson to find out.'

Mel, a pale, watchful girl who didn't often trust herself to speak, went to the window and looked out.

Jem saw her move and joined her. 'Em, sorry about this, people.'

'What? What have you seen?'

'The MG isn't there any more. Dreamboat has gone.'

'Aw, shoot!'

'The head must have put him off.'

'She'd put anyone off.'

'Or . . .'

'Or what?'

'Or he was only a computer salesman and she was like, "While you're here, young man, how about checking my software," and he panicked and legged it fast?'

A ripple of amusement, tempered by sighs all round.

'Back to normal, then,' Mel said, but she wasn't heard.

The mood was even more subdued in the art room at eleven, when no teacher appeared. Genuine anxiety surfaced about their exam prospects. Some hoped Jem had got it wrong for once and the boring Miss Gibbon would shortly put her head around the door. She at least knew the syllabus and was capable of getting most of them a grade of some sort.

Naseem said, 'We ought to tell someone. We're way down on where we ought to be at this time of the year.'

As usual, it was Jem who took the decision. 'That's it, then. Why don't you go to the staffroom, Ella, and say we're in urgent need of an art teacher?'

'I knew you'd ask me. Why don't you go yourself?'

''Cause you're always on about your future and that.'

'I was hoping, like, someone else would do it.'

'I don't mind going,' Mel said. She stood, refastened her hair, and left the room.

'I feel bad,' Ella said, 'leaving it to Mel.'

'Don't,' Jem said. 'She's a peasant. Let her run the errands.'

'You asked me first. Am I a peasant, too?'

'Course not. Your parents pay for you to be here. You're just a pain in the bum.'

In under ten seconds Mel was back. 'He's coming this way.'

'Who is?' Ella asked.

'The new teacher, with the head.'

'Dreamboat? Never.'

'It's true. His car's back,' Jem said, from beside the window.

'Tell me I haven't died and gone to heaven,' Ella said.

No time to tidy hair, make-up, anything.

The head entered first, gowned as always, followed by Dreamboat, except he wasn't dressed as Jem had described. He was in a pinstripe suit, white shirt and tie that made him look like a bank clerk, apart from the long hair.

'I have an announcement,' the head said, although no one was looking at her. 'Through circumstances beyond my control, your art teacher, Miss Gibbon, has taken an extended break from teaching and left the school. However, Mr Standforth will be taking over. He is an accomplished artist and an experienced teacher who will guide you ably through this critical last year of your A level and I have assured him he will have your total cooperation. Because Miss Gibbon left at short notice, I am not entirely sure how much of the syllabus she covered with you. I am confident you girls will be only too pleased to inform Mr Standforth, so that he can effect a smooth transition.'

That was it. A swish of the gown and they had Dreamboat to themselves. The hush was total.

'Forget the "Mr Standforth" stuff. It's Tom,' he said, revealing a set of gleaming teeth. 'Sorry about the late start. I was here in good time, but stupidly I misjudged the dress code, so I had to nip home and change. Can't say I'm too comfortable in a suit. If nobody objects, I'll take off the jacket.'

Take off whatever you want, the dumbstruck class was thinking. Not one of us will object.

His shirt was short-sleeved, revealing muscular forearms and tattoos. He loosened the tie as well and undid the top buttons of his shirt. Thrills in plenty.

'It will help to know your names,' he said, perching his breathtakingly cute bum on the front desk. 'Can't promise to remember them all right away, but let's make a start. Who are you, for instance?'

His brown eyes were on Ella. She managed to speak her name in a strangled voice.

'And is there any topic that excites you, Ella?'

Now she could only blink like a patient with locked-in syndrome.

'Any topic in art.'

Her mind had gone blank. 'The golden mean.'

The rest of them spluttered.

'Well, that's an answer I didn't expect.'

'Golden section, then.'

'Still surprising to me. I'm impressed. Can't say I know a huge amount about either, but no doubt you'll all be able to tell me.' He raised his hand. 'Not now. Who are you, next to Ella?'

'Melanie, sir.'

'Leave out the "sir". I'll let you know when I get my knighthood. What have you been doing with Miss Gibbon, Melanie, or should I call you Mel?'

Jem muttered, 'The smell,' and there were sniggers.

'What was that?'

'I said she's Mel,' Jem said.

'I expect she can speak for herself. I asked you a question, Mel.'

'We did exercises in composition. Lots.'

'Composition. Right.' He didn't sound thrilled. 'The young lady who just spoke, what's your name?'

'Jemima. Everyone calls me Jem.'

'So will I, then. I take it you, too, are well up on compo-sition and the golden mean. Has it helped you creatively, Jem?'

'Like in my photography?'

'You're a photographer?'

'I wouldn't say that. I take pictures.'

'You don't have to be modest about it. You have a camera, you take pictures, you're a photographer. Jem the shut-terbug.'

Smiles all round, except for Jem, who wasn't too sure if it was a compliment.

'I expect the rest of you do some snapping with your smartphones, don't you, all in the name of art? I'm joking, but your phone can be a useful aid. You've all got one, I'm sure.'

'We're not allowed to get them out in class,' Ella said.

'School rule, is it? Well, I'm not going to report anyone I see using hers as a camera. For one thing, you should all keep a record of your work as it develops, and for another you should always be on the lookout for visually stimulating images.'

This was becoming unbearable. At the mention of stimu-lating images sounds like cars starting up came from around the room.

'But here's a warning,' he added. 'I draw the line at video games. Anyone caught playing *Dumb Ways to Die* can expect more than just a telling-off. Who's next to give me her name?'

In lunch break, there was only one topic: the man of the hour, the day, the week and probably the year. Eat your heart out, Prince Harry. Everyone agreed Tom Standforth was a perfect ten regardless of how he would shape up as a teacher. The art group were the envy of the school. People

18

who hadn't yet clocked him made sorties to the staff car park to see the red MG.

For a time the art students were incapable of doing anything except replaying the lesson in their minds.

Jem, a good mimic, had his voice already. '"If nobody objects, I'll take off the jacket."'

Peals of laughter.

'"And is there any topic that excites you, Ella?"'

Ella squeezed her eyes shut and said, 'Don't.'

'She goes, "The golden mean." Anything that excites you, and she's, like, the golden bloody mean.'

'It's all I could think of. Oh my God, I wish he'd ask me again.'

'"Anyone caught playing *Dumb Ways to Die* can expect more than just a telling-off." What did he mean – a spanking? Bags me first.'

Naseem had been using her smartphone. She put an end to Jem's miming with, 'I've found his website.'

Gasps.

'You what? He has a website? Yoiks.' They almost bumped heads trying to see.

'They must be his paintings. Cool.'

'Genius. Those colours.'

'Such energy.'

Active fingertips moved Tom's output at speed across the small screen.

'It isn't only abstracts.'

'What's that? She's starkers. He paints nudes.'

Shrieks.

'Let's see. Hold it higher, Nas. The size of those boobs.'

'They look normal to me,' Jem said.

'They would . . . to you.'

'I'd rather have mine than your pathetic pair. D'you think he paints these from life?'

'Of course he does, pinbrain.'

'Is it, like, his girlfriend? Oh, I hope not.'

'How would I know? I expect she's just a model. Look, this one's blonde. She's gorgeous.'

'They can't all be girlfriends.'

'Why not? With his looks he could pull whoever he wants.'

Naseem navigated back to the home page and found some pictures of Tom in his studio. The place looked large and cluttered, the walls and easels spattered with colour. 'Why does he do teaching when he has his own studio?'

'Maybe he can't sell anything. All the great painters were like that, living in poverty.'

'Poverty?' Ella said. 'He owns a vintage MG. They're not cheap.'

'He's a proper teacher. The head told us.'

'And she's in the best position to know.' Jem grinned.

'Who, the head? What position's that?'

Amid the laughter, Jem said, 'Ask her. I dare you.'

By the end of the afternoon, the excitement had scarcely abated. The A-level group were watching from an upstairs window when the young man returned to his zippy sports car at the end of the day.

'There's only one question left,' Jem said.

'Only one? I can think of hundreds. We know sweet FA about him.'

'Yeah, but this is the one that counts: who gets to ride in the MG first?'

# 3

Tom was shaking up the school. In the first week, his pinstripe suit got so paint-spattered that the head gave him special dispensation to wear whatever casual clothes he liked. And the girls were permitted to bring T-shirts and jeans for art lessons, and change in the dressing room behind the stage.

He'd told year eleven that creating a portfolio sounded boring until you realised a portfolio wasn't a flat case for carrying a mass of drawings, but an opportunity to create exciting things that would never fit into a flat case. He'd taken them to see landscape artworks at Petworth and West Dean. They'd visited the sculpture park at Goodwood and come away with wholly different ideas about creativity. Inspired, they started on projects of their own. Jem worked on a big scale with a leaping dolphin made from driftwood. Mel was collecting pieces of glass worn smooth by the sea and making an exquisite mosaic no bigger than a dinner plate. Naseem was building a Neptune figure entirely from seaweed. Ella's was a big abstract fashioned mainly from broken lobster pots.

Some afternoons Tom would drive them in the school minivan to one of the pebble beaches – Bracklesham Bay and Selsey being only ten miles away – and get them scavenging for materials. On these trips he was relaxed about smoking and swearing and he always fitted in a visit to the beach café. He'd chat about almost anything except himself. His personal life seemed to be off-limits. And of course the girls took this as a challenge.

'Ever come down here at weekends, Tom?'

'Far too busy, Jem.'

'What – painting and stuff? How do you relax, Tom?'

'I'm always relaxed. Haven't you noticed?'

'Except you've got to be sharp when you're driving. Have you had it long, your MG?'

'Some time.'

'Who chose it – you, or your girlfriend?'

'That would be telling.'

'Go on – tell us.'

'I've always liked sports cars. Most guys do.'

'And your girlfriend, does she like it?'

'Who are you talking about?'

'Just now you seemed to be saying there's someone.'

'I'm pretty certain I wasn't – and if there was, I wouldn't.'

Laughs all round.

'Spoilsport. Is she an artist like you?'

'Talking of artists, Ella, give the others a shout, will you? They seem to be chatting up those skateboarders outside the café and I don't think we can justify it as performance art. It's time we started back.'

In the van, the interrogation started all over again.

'Do you have a long drive home, Tom?'

'No more than anyone else.'

'We were wondering where you live.'

'I wouldn't worry about that if I were you. There are more fascinating topics.'

'Such as?'

'Unit three of your A-level art.'

Groans.

'I mean it,' Tom said, and started telling them about the

personal investigation element of their coursework. The prospect of writing up to three thousand words scared even the boldest of them. A neat way to head off the questions about his home life.

With so many girls desperate to know, it was inevitable that someone would find out. Ella came into the art room one morning and said, 'It's Boxgrove.'

'What is?'

'Where Tom lives. One of the year nines saw him drive out of the gates of some major estate outside the village.'

'Is he rich, then?'

'Got to be a millionaire, hasn't he?'

'What's he doing teaching if he's as rich as that?'

'It's a vocation.'

'Come again.'

'Like a mission, making the world a better place through art. He wants to spread the word.'

'You think?'

'Or he fancies schoolgirls.'

'If only.'

'I've been thinking,' Mel said suddenly.

'Listen up, people,' Jem said. 'The Chosen One is going to tell us something amazing.'

Everything went quiet in the art room. Mel was the odd one out, the only girl whose fees were paid by a trade union. She would have been given an even harder time if she hadn't been an original thinker.

'I didn't say amazing. I was thinking about the Gibbon.'

'Groan. That's a thought wasted.'

'I know she wasn't popular, but it's weird how she, like, went off suddenly without even saying goodbye to anyone. Even useless teachers get some kind of leaving present. The head didn't seem to know where she'd gone.'

'Does it matter?'

'All kinds of stuff could have happened. She could have got knocked down by a car and lost her memory.'

'Or been kidnapped by Somali pirates,' Jem said.

'No one better pay the ransom, then,' Ella said.

'Yeah, she goes on about the golden mean and the pirates think she's super rich.'

Mel was still being serious. 'It's just a mystery how a teacher can vanish and no one seems to care.'

'Obvious,' Jem said. 'She did something the school wants to hush up, like running a knocking shop.'

'The Gibbon?' Ella said.

'I didn't say she was on the game. I said running it, like a madam.'

'I can't picture that.'

'The head would have a blue fit in case it got in the papers and no one wanted to send their kids here any more.'

'You're all being ridiculous,' Mel said.

'Now we've got Tom, we don't want the Gibbon back. She was the pits.'

'I don't want her back either.'

'Shut up about her, then. She's history.'

Tom didn't seem fazed when they told him they knew where he lived.

'OK.'

'Aren't you bothered, Tom?' Jem said. 'You wouldn't tell us when we asked.'

'Because it has bugger all to do with why I'm here, which is to show you lot how exciting art can be. Now you know where I live, perhaps we can talk about something useful, like unit three, your personal investigations – and that means being curious about some topic in art and not my totally

24

boring private life. Remember, this is twenty-five per cent of your course mark.'

They'd been told before and they were ready. 'I'm doing mixed media and new materials,' Jem said.

'Elephant dung?' Ella said with a grin.

Jem was unamused. 'And much more, like fabrics, cardboard, wood, porcelain.'

Tom nodded. 'Sounds promising. How about you, Mel?'

'I was thinking of postage stamps.'

'Not another bloody mosaic,' Ella said.

'Typical,' Jem said. 'Always something small.'

'Hold on,' Tom said, 'let's have some respect for each other. What is it about stamps you want to investigate?'

'Like how the designs are done and how they've changed. There was a man in the paper last week, an artist who's just had his first pictures accepted by whoever decides, and there's masses of stuff on the internet.'

'Good thinking,' Tom said. 'Stamp design has come a long way since the penny black. It's unusual and it could be a fascinating study. Yes, go for it, Mel. And you, Ella. What's your area of investigation?'

'The nude.'

'OK, OK,' Tom said over the laughter. 'Get it over with. I take it you are serious, Ella? How do you propose to make this your special study?'

'Like the history from ancient Greece to Lucian Freud.' Sarcastic coos.

'That's good – but it's a huge sweep of history. You might want to come at the subject in a slightly different way, like the nude in landscape, thinking of artists such as Cranach, Giorgione, Monet and Cézanne.'

'I suppose.' She didn't sound convinced.

'Or you could look at why the naked human form has such an enduring appeal for artists. Maybe interview some people who draw and paint from life. Credit is always given for original research.'

'She could interview you, Tom,' Jem said, ever ready to exploit an opening. 'We've all seen your website.'

'I don't know if that's such a good idea. The external moderator might not like your own tutor being involved. Better, really, to talk to artists who are nothing to do with the school.'

'But how will she meet them?' Mel asked.

'Pose for them,' Jem said.

Everyone enjoyed the prospect while Ella turned pink and said, 'Thanks a bunch.'

Tom said, 'Some friends of mine join me most Saturdays for a session in my studio.'

The level of interest rose several notches.

'I'm thinking it would help you guys a lot to meet a bunch of serious artists and see how they work. It would be time out from your weekend, of course—'

'No problem,' Jem said at once. 'We're up for it, aren't we, people?'

They made it obvious she'd spoken for them all.

'I was thinking three at a time,' Tom went on. 'You could sit beside anyone you like and watch, or do some work of your own.'

'Cool,' Ella said. 'Is it all day?'

'A couple of hours in the morning, starting about eleven, and a couple in the afternoon. I provide soup and a roll or salad.'

'Are they, like, guys?'

'A mixed group, men and women, some my age, some older. I'll need to clear it with them first, but they should be OK with it.'

'Do you have a model?' Mel asked.

'Sometimes. Other days we'll do still life or just work at

our own projects. Being together is the main thing. So is it on?'

'How will we get there?' Naseem asked.

'That's up to us, obviously,' Jem said. 'Tom's not going to collect us in the minibus, are you, Tom? I don't mind giving two of you a lift in my Panda – that's if I'm picked.' An offer that seemed to some of the others like a gun at Tom's head.

Jem, Ella and Naseem were the lucky first three. Intense debate followed over what to wear, this being an out-of-school activity. Ella had no problem. She was a goth at weekends, with white foundation and dark eyeliner, black leather and fishnets. Naseem would be sure to come in a gorgeous sari. Jem, with a free choice, was given so many suggestions that in the end she told no one what she'd decided – and on the Saturday put up her hair to make herself taller and wore a favourite red dress with lots of sparkle and spaghetti straps. Also platforms she needed to change into after driving the car. Not one of the outfits was suitable for art, but that hadn't entered their heads.

They arrived late, at Jem's suggestion. 'They'll think we're only a bunch of schoolgirls if we get there on time.'

So at eleven twenty they drew up at the gate of Fortiman House, a mile along a small road out of Boxgrove, and turned down the car radio.

High walls surrounded the property and there was a double gate of wrought iron.

'Awesome,' Ella said.

'Are you sure this is the place?' Naseem said.

'Positive.' Jem was checking her face in the rear-view mirror.

'Shall I see if I can open it?' Ella said. They were all nervous.

Just then, a middle-aged man in a Barbour jacket, jeans and wellies approached the gate from the other side. He was carrying a trug. 'Morning, young ladies. Are you visiting?'

'We're artists,' Ella said, 'here to join the Saturday group.'

'And liven it up,' Jem said, becoming bold again.

'They do their art in the stables. Drive straight up to the house and leave the car where you see the others. I'm Ferdie, by the way. I'll open up.'

'Cheers, Ferdie,' Jem said, as they drove through, and then asked the others, 'Was he after a tip, do you think?'

'Some hopes, from three hard-up schoolgirls,' Ella said.

'Students.'

'Still hard up.'

Along the gravel drive all chatter stopped. Ella's first reaction of 'awesome' was the only word for Tom's house, a massive flint building with seven gables along the front and a pillared entrance. Several cars were lined up, including the red MG and a yellow Lamborghini. Tom was waiting nearby and waved them into a space.

'Trouble finding us?' he said, opening the car door. 'I was wondering if you'd decided to go shopping instead.'

'I must change my shoes,' Jem said.

'Good thinking,' Tom said. 'Comfort is the name of the game.' But when he saw the platforms going on, it became obvious comfort wasn't high in Jem's priorities. Tom didn't comment. Neither did he say anything about the others' outfits. Naseem was in a peacock blue sari and Ella's goth outfit was little more than a basque over black lace.

'Did you bring sketchbooks?'

None of them had – not even Naseem.

'Ah, well, I'm not short of paper. We have a model today, so we got started on time.'

The stables weren't recognisable as a place where horses had been kept. The building must have been gutted and reconstructed with large picture windows and a raked roof with dormer windows.

'If you're wondering how a teacher can afford a conversion like this, I can't,' Tom told them. 'All of this belongs to my old man, Ferdie.'

There was a moment to take in the name.

'We just met him,' Ella said. 'We thought he was the gardener.'

'Dad grows orchids. They're in all the shops. Been lucky in life, and so have I, by association. Let's go in. Don't open the door too wide or there's a wicked draught.'

They edged inside, where a surprise awaited. The model was male.

Ella mouthed, 'Oh my God!'

Artists and easels were ranged around the nude man, hairy, dark and with a beer belly, who faced the door in a standing pose on a table, his arms held high, hands clasped behind his neck.

Tom handed boards, sheets of paper and charcoal to his students. 'Why don't you move about and decide where you'd like to be?'

All three made straight for the rear view.

Twenty minutes in, the model was given a break. He did some twisting and flexing before stepping down from the table. An unnerving moment. What if he came over and struck up a conversation? Relief all round when he picked up a black silk gown and pulled it on.

Tom had been doing some drawing of his own. He came over to Ella. 'How're you getting on?'

Even she could see hers was a poor start.

'Come and see some of the others. You may get a different take on life drawing.' He walked over to a black man in a Rasta beanie hat who had been working in a sketchbook

29

and had moved position several times during the session. 'Do you mind, Manny? I'd like Ella to see the sort of thing you do.'

Manny gave him a suspicious look. 'You kidding, man? I'm just having fun.'

'That's the point. Ella isn't . . . yet. If she sees your work, she'll loosen up a bit.'

'You think so?' With a shrug and a sigh, Manny handed the sketchbook to Tom. To Ella, he said, 'This is how I get found out.'

Tom opened the book and flicked over some pages. 'Was this today's effort?'

'Today's, sure,' Manny said. 'Effort, not so sure.'

The page was filled with small cartoon figures drawn in ink with a minimum of strokes that captured the essence of the characters. He'd drawn just about everyone in the room except the model. Ella recognised Tom straight away from the mop of unruly hair over an exaggerated nose and chin.

'Is that allowed?' she said, smiling.

'It is here. Anything goes.'

'Is this me with my friends?' Ella asked, pointing to three young females pictured in a huddle looking furtively over their shoulders.

Tom grinned. In a few skilful lines, Manny had caught the girls' embarrassment.

'You must be a professional cartoonist,' Ella said.

'No way,' Manny said. 'Just the dogsbody round here.'

'Manny's employed here keeping the garden under control,' Tom said. 'Mowing, hedge clipping, leaf blowing and tree surgery. Damned hard work.'

'Anyone ask,' Manny said, 'I'm the estate manager. Saturdays he let me hang out here. Say it's good for my soul.'

Tom moved on to the next artist. 'This is Geraint. He works with a palette knife.'

Ella managed a twitchy smile at Geraint, a tall, gaunt man wearing a butcher's apron marked with paint. Sunken, blood-shot eyes looked at her over half-glasses. Geraint didn't return the smile.

'See how the form is starting to emerge on the thighs,' Tom said. 'The slashes of blue and brown are bringing the lighter areas forward. It's so much more than simple shadow.'

'Fantastic.'

Geraint wiped the paint from the knife and she thought she heard him say, 'Bloody liar.'

More knives of various sorts, from table cutlery to what looked awfully like a stiletto, were ranged on the donkey bench beside Geraint.

Ella took a step away.

'There's just time to look at Drusilla's work,' Tom said, moving on to the next easel, a pencil drawing difficult to interpret.

Drusilla came over from the window, a willowy woman in corduroy trousers and an ethnic sweater that looked as if it was made from an unwashed fleece. She was more gracious than Geraint. 'There isn't much to show for my efforts, dear,' she said. 'It's a slow process. I don't draw the model. I look at the shapes the background makes against his outline and if I get them right the figure will emerge. We all have fixed ideas about the way the human shape is formed, arms, legs, torso and so on. By ignoring all that, I trick my brain into producing a more honest image, if you understand me.'

'I think so.'

'Have you drawn from life before?'

'Only other students in their clothes.'

'Much more difficult.'

31

Tom said, 'The headmistress would have a fit if they worked from the nude.'

'It was the same in my day,' Drusilla said. 'All I ever got to draw was a vase and I was the despair of the art teacher. I could never get the ellipse right.'

The model had mounted the table again.

'Is the model always male?' Ella asked Drusilla when Tom had moved away.

'Davy? We draw him more than anyone else. He's good at it and he's been coming for years. But we also have women from time to time. By the way, don't let Geraint get to you. He's a pussycat really.'

With another posing session under way, Ella checked the other artists. An overweight woman opposite, her hands black from charcoal. The man to her left wearing a clerical collar. Another man looked about eighty. Next to him was a tall woman in expensive designer clothes.

In the lunch break, there was a chance for the Priory Park trio to take their tomato soup and apple juice to a bench outside the barn and talk about the experience so far.

'I nearly had a fit when we walked in,' Jem said. 'I didn't know where to look.'

'Haven't you seen a willy before?' Ella said.

Hoping she sounded nonchalant, Jem said, 'Of course I have. It was just, like, so unexpected. Be honest, Ell, you were embarrassed, too. I thought they wore a posing pouch.'

'Why should they? Women don't wear anything. My sister went to a hen party where they were all given pencils and paper and supposed to draw a buck naked model. She said he was a hunk who worked out at the gym and he had a good laugh with them. Not like this guy. He's gross.'

'That's mean.'

'It's true.'

'You want a chunky model. Better for drawing.'

'Listen to the expert.'

'I was shocked, too,' Naseem said. 'I hope my parents don't ask to see what I drew when I get home.'

'Don't,' Jem said. 'My dad would be round the school Monday morning. We can say we watched the artists at work, which is true. Let's agree on that, shall we?'

'But we can tell the others at school,' Ella said.

'We absolutely must. This is too good to waste. What did Tom say to you in the break?'

'He was introducing me to some of the artists. Geraint, the one with the serial killer face. If you get a chance, take a look at his collection of knives, all laid out on the bench beside him. I said his work was fantastic and he called me a bloody liar, the only words he spoke.'

'Charming!'

'So who did you start up a conversation with?' Ella said as if she'd been socialising all morning.

'No one in particular,' Jem said. 'One looks like a vicar. I heard Tom call him Bish.'

'A bishop?'

'I expect it's a joke.'

'Someone's coming.'

It was Ferdie, pushing a bag of compost in a wheelbarrow. Now that they knew he was Tom's dad and the owner of the house, he would get more respect.

He stopped to speak. 'Will you be coming every week, then?'

'No. Some others will get a turn next Saturday. Tom says three at a time is best.'

'How many of you are there?'

'In our A-level group? Twelve.'

'That's not many. And will you become better artists by coming here?'

'Tom reckons,' Jem said.

'Seeing how real artists work is a big help,' Ella said.

'You're real, aren't you? You look real to me.'

'You wouldn't call us artists if you saw our stuff,' Jem said.

Ferdie wagged a grimy finger. 'Never undersell yourselves. From what I've seen of the art world, there are no rules about how it has to look. It's more about persuading people your product is special, and you won't persuade anybody if you talk like that.'

'We have to persuade Tom and an external examiner.'

'No problem. It's a matter of confidence. Those artists in there have got it. They believe in themselves.'

'Be nice if some of that rubs off on us,' Ella said.

'It's not for me to interfere,' Ferdie said, 'but I don't see why you have to take turns to visit here. You could take your drawing boards outside and draw the scenery. If the weather's bad you could do interiors in the house.'

'I don't know if Tom would agree,' Jem said.

'Never mind Tom. Would you find it useful?'

'Incredibly useful.' Jem was beginning to think they had an ally in Ferdie.

'I'll put a word in,' he said before wheeling his barrow away.

The girls returned for the afternoon session feeling more relaxed about life drawing, a state of affairs that didn't last. Tom announced that Davy the model would take up a new pose. Davy disrobed and stepped up with a wobble and a grunt and some minutes were spent deciding what was required. He was turned left and right and finally square on to the girls with legs astride and his member quivering.

'OK for everybody?' Tom asked.

The girls were incapable of speech.

'Couldn't he do something different with the arms?' Drusilla said. 'It's too Neanderthal from here.'

'Try it with hands on hips,' Tom said to Davy.

More movement. More embarrassment.

Drusilla shook her head. 'That's camp.'

'Hands clasped behind your back.'

'That's one of the royals on a visit.'

Each adjustment brought an extra disturbance to Davy's person and to the trio from Priory Park School.

Finally, arms folded got the nod from Drusilla and everyone else.

# 4

The whole class were invited to the next Saturday session at Fortiman House. Mel and two others, Anita and Gail, were to have their turn in the studio with the artists. The rest would work on landscape outside.

Jem said to Ella, 'I'd give a lot to see Mel's face when Davy strips off.'

'She knows what to expect. We told her.'

'Yeah, but you know Mel. Remember how she fainted when the condom was passed round in that sex lesson?'

'That was ages ago.'

'And we're not going to let her forget it.'

Mel was an open goal for teasing. Her father had been a humble workman – a 'hole-in-the-road' man, as Jem had categorised him. The fact that he'd been killed when his drill had hit an electric cable hadn't met with much sympathy from her schoolmates. In the eyes of the group, people who worked outdoors knew they were taking risks. Mel's mother had married again – to a bricklayer – and they never attended parents' evenings.

On this fine, clear morning, it was warm enough for Jem and Ella to set up their easels on the lawn in front of the house.

'Are you doing the whole building?' Ella asked.

'No.'

'It'd take too long, wouldn't it? I was thinking of making sketches of bits of it, like those weird chimneys.'

'Good idea.'

'So what are you going to draw?'

'Tom's MG.'

They worked steadily until the mid-morning break, when Mel and the others emerged from the studio. Tea and coffee were being served from the kitchen at the back of the house.

'So?' Jem said when they'd managed to corner Mel.

'So what?'

'Come off it, Orphan Annie. You know what we're dying to hear about. What did you think of Davy?'

'Who do you mean?'

'The model, dorkbrain.'

'There isn't a model. We're doing still life, a big Chinese vase and some drapes.'

'Really? What a let-down.'

'Not for me. I'm enjoying myself. It's amazing how everyone in there is dealing with it. Tom lets us move about and talk to the artists and they're really friendly – well, most of them are.'

'Except Geraint?'

'The man with the knives? He's a bit strange, yes, and he goes at the canvas like he's paintballing. A dollop of red carried right across the room and hit the woman opposite on the cheek. She wasn't pleased. I don't think he said sorry.'

'What did Tom do?'

'Didn't seem to notice. I think he admires Geraint's work.'

'Did he tell you to look at it, then?'

Mel nodded. 'To me, it looked a mess. I couldn't see it had anything to do with the vase. I didn't say so to Tom.

He thinks I'm too careful anyway. He says I've got to break out, whatever that means. Like, there's a guy in there drawing cartoons of us all.'

'Manny,' Ella said. 'He's fun. Have you spoken to him yet?'

Mel shook her head. 'You know me. I find it difficult going up to people.'

'Tom's got a point,' Jem said, winking at Ella. 'You've got to break out.'

'He was talking about my art.'

'Are you working in charcoal?'

'Yes.'

'Try smudging. That ought to please him.'

'Maybe I will.'

'I mean really make a dog's dinner of it, don't just blur the lines. Go for it like that woman who gets black all over her face and clothes. Charcoal Charlotte. He'll say you've found your inner genius.'

Ella butted in. 'Yeah, and he might say she's taking the piss and doesn't deserve to be doing A-level art.'

'Bet you he doesn't,' Jem said. 'That's the kind of thing the Gibbon would've said – not in those exact words, but the message would be the same.'

The mention of their former teacher triggered Mel into saying, 'Hey, did you know there's a missing persons bureau and Miss Gibbon is on it? I found her on the website. It gives a date in July when she was last seen.'

'Never! . . . Really?'

'Honest. There's a picture of her, quite a nice one actually.'

Ella and Jem had both started navigating their smartphones and, sure enough, there was an official police website showing a photo of Miss Gibbon in a pink top against a background of fruit blossom.

'Almost human,' Ella said.

'What a handle,' Jem said, reading on. 'Constance Gloria Gibbon. Thirty-nine? That's a laugh. She was well past forty, in my opinion. Who would have reported her missing, do you think? The head?'

'She must have family. Does it say?'

'Just some number to call. That'll be the police.'

'What if they find her?' Jem said, eyes popping at the thought. 'We could lose Tom.'

'She'll be in no state to teach again,' Ella said. 'Not right away. She'll need time to get over it. She wouldn't come back before we've all left.'

'We can hope,' Jem said.

Any more talk about Miss Gibbon had to be put on hold because one of the other artists joined them. 'Right,' she said in a business-like way. 'I'm Anastasia. Are you young ladies actually finding this helpful, joining in with us?'

All three made positive sounds.

Anastasia was clearly the woman who had been hit by Geraint's blob of paint, because there was quite a smear of red to the left side of her face, even though she'd wiped most of it away. Good thing her clothes had escaped, because they were of designer quality, a blue and white striped top, tight-fitting jeans and calf-length light brown boots. 'The reason I asked is that if it were me looking at all the different styles, I'd just be confused.'

'It's what we're supposed to do for our exam,' Jem said. 'Studying different ways of dealing with a subject.'

'And responding in our own way,' Ella chimed in.

'Good for you,' Anastasia said. 'In my day everyone tried to draw like Holbein and of course we couldn't and got deeply depressed. The way art is taught now is so much better for one's self-confidence.'

'It is if you get a good teacher,' Jem said. 'Tom took over this term and we're improving in leaps and bounds.'

'He's a charmer, for sure,' Anastasia said. 'Perhaps I shouldn't say this, but he gives amazing parties.'

'Why shouldn't you say it?' Mel asked.

'Because they're not the kinds of parties schoolgirls attend.'

'We're students, not schoolgirls,' Ella said. 'We could be at sixth-form college. We'll all be eighteen next year.'

'My dear, I can see you're wonderfully mature. In fact, I wouldn't have dreamed you were still at school if Tom hadn't mentioned the fact.'

'What do you get up to at these parties?' Jem said.

Anastasia had turned so red that the paint mark barely registered. 'Oh dear, I'm getting into deep water here. Maybe modern schoolgirls – sorry, students – do attend such events, but I doubt whether your headmistress would encourage it. Tom might find himself out of a job.'

'Are they, like, orgies?'

Anastasia laughed. 'If they were, I'd stay away. No, we're artists. All we do is let our hair down, so to speak.'

'Smoking pot?'

'Not to my knowledge. Listen, I'm not saying any more and I'm going to ask you, please, to forget everything I said under pain of death. And now I see them returning to the studio.' She turned about and moved off as if she'd disturbed a swarm of bees.

'That's something Tom's been keeping to himself,' Jem said to the others.

'Probably quite innocent,' Mel said. 'A poker school or something.'

'Strip poker?' Ella said.

'Not much joy in that when they see models stripping off for them every other week,' Jem said. 'You'd better get

40

back to the studio, Mel. They're definitely going in. Oh, and Mel?'

'Yes?'

'See if you can find out when the next party is.'

Back in the studio, Mel took a tissue and started smearing the charcoal she had so carefully outlined before the break. Jem had been right. At once the picture had a freer look. She rubbed a few of the lines away completely and was pleased to see that they hadn't been needed. When she stood back, her brain filled in the missing bits.

'What's happening here?' a voice said in her ear.

Tom.

'I'm trying something different.'

'It's good. Go for it, Mel. You can use a rubber to lighten some areas if you want, but add some more charcoal first.'

He moved on.

She was pleased to get approval, but she felt disloyal to Miss Gibbon. All those exercises in perspective must have had some purpose. Her own sense of order had rather welcomed the analytical approach. The idea that there was a golden mean, an aesthetically pleasing formula for designing a picture, had given her something to aspire to. Last year hadn't been a total waste of time, as the others believed.

If, as now seemed inevitable, she 'broke out' and disregarded those principles, she felt a strong urge not to disregard Miss Gibbon herself. The others seemed happy to dismiss her from their minds. They'd never had much respect for her. 'Almost human' Ella had said about the online photo. The knowledge that their former teacher was on the missing persons list didn't trouble them. Their only concern was whether she'd be traced and get her old job back.

Mel had decided she, at least, would make an effort to find out more.

Now was an opportunity.

Tom was still on her side of the room giving advice to Gail, one of the other A-level girls. He'd have to edge past Mel to return to his own easel because Anastasia had built a barricade with two donkey stools to separate herself from Geraint. No one liked to get close when he was wielding the knife.

'Tom, mind if I ask something?'

'Ask away.'

'When you took over from Miss Gibbon, did you get a chance to talk to her?'

He shook his head. 'She left suddenly during the summer break.'

'I was hoping you might have learned what her plans were, like where she was going next. We didn't give her a goodbye present or thank her for teaching us or anything.'

'She's on your conscience?'

'In a way.'

'I wouldn't worry about her. From all I heard, she was rather a private person. She may have decided she needs a break from teaching, a sabbatical. You might laugh at this, but teaching a lively group of students can be really demanding. Doesn't the school have a forwarding address?'

'I don't think so. Miss Gibbon is officially a missing person.'

He raked his fingers through his hair. 'Are you sure?'

'I've seen her picture on the police website.'

'That's really disturbing. I hadn't heard.' Shaking his head, he moved on.

Out on the lawn, Jem had completed three good pastel drawings of Tom's MG by mid-afternoon. She didn't feel like starting another or indeed anything else, so she went for a stroll instead. The grounds weren't vast or particularly beautiful, but there were some wonderful old trees. She found a kitchen garden at the back and a swimming pool with a tiled surround and two larger than life black and gold masked figures in bronze with spectacular headgear and cassock-like garments.

Across another stretch of lawn she spotted Ferdie with his wheelbarrow emerging from a walled garden. He was coming in her direction, so she waited to speak. He seemed surprised when she gave a friendly, 'Hi. Is that where you grow the orchids?'

A slow smile of recognition dawned. 'Didn't recognise you for a moment.' He grounded the barrow. 'Yes, I'd offer to show you round, but they're in controlled conditions.'

'Humidity and stuff?'

He smiled. 'That's about right. Some of them are extremely delicate. How's the art coming along, young lady? Going to show me? I've been handling compost but I won't touch.'

She opened her sketchbook and showed the pastel drawings of the MG.

'Ha, the passion wagon. You've caught it perfectly. Tom will approve, I guarantee.'

'D'you reckon?' she said. 'He'll be like, "You've spent too much time getting a likeness when you should have made it more dynamic."'

'Like a streak of red to show it doing a ton on the motorway? Call me old-fashioned, but I prefer it just as you've drawn it.'

Jem had no thought of calling him old-fashioned. 'If I'd had my head straight when I got here this morning, I could have drawn those amazing figures near the pool, or their reflections in the water, which would have been even better.'

'You like them? I'm pleased to hear that.'

'They're awesome. They set it off incredibly.' Without pause she added, 'Is that where Tom holds his parties?'

'Someone been telling you about the parties, have they?' Ferdie said.

'One of the artists mentioned them as if they're rather special.'

'Not all that special, unless I missed something. Just a social get-together for his art friends. In the summer they gather round the pool and he has some loud music going. Or they sometimes hold it by the lake.'

'You've got a *lake*?'

'We call it that. Others might describe it as a pond. You should take a stroll down there. It would make a nice picture. Of course in cold weather they use the studio for the parties.'

'They're all year round, are they?'

'Night of the full moon.'

'Go on.'

He grinned. 'I kid you not.'

'Cool. D'you think I might get an invite?'

'I can't speak for my son, but I doubt it.'

'Why? Do they, like, get up to something illegal?'

He laughed. 'No, no, no. Not on my property. Any nonsense of that sort and I'd ban the lot of them.'

# 5

Georgina Dallymore, the Assistant Chief Constable in Bath, was unusually tense, gripping the edge of her desk with both hands as if she meant to heave it over and use it as a barricade when the enemy burst in. 'Shut the door, would you? This is for your ears only.'

Detective Superintendent Peter Diamond, not without tension himself, did as he was told.

'How is everything in CID?' Her standard question. It might mean anything.

'Humming, ma'am, humming.' His standard response. It meant nothing.

'Busy, then?'

He nodded. It is always wise to be busy.

'The jewel robberies?'

'Taking up a lot of time, yes.' Far too many of the rich and famous had their homes in and around Bath. A gang of thieves had been at work for eight months depriving them of some of their best items of jewellery. The gang used ladders and vans and they picked locks and neutralised security systems. Nothing remarkable in that. But generally even the top professionals give themselves away when they cash in. The marketing of stolen goods is messy and leaves trails.

'Are you personally involved in the investigation?'

'When you say "personally" . . .'

'Hands on.'

Careful here, he thought. 'I'm overseeing it, if that's what you mean.'

'Interviewing the people whose property was stolen?'

Hey-ho, had one of Bath's grandees complained that he hadn't doffed his hat? 'I've done a bit of that. They're VIPs, some of them, as you know. Can't send young constables to speak to people like that.'

'Understood. But you do have senior detectives like Keith Halliwell and John Leaman.'

'Absolutely.'

'I sometimes think, Peter, that you could delegate more.'

He said nothing. The use of his first name by Georgina was a cannon shot across the bows. The mention of delegating was a broadside.

'Halliwell and Leaman are old hands,' she went on, 'and as back-up they have an able detective sergeant in Ingeborg Smith.'

'Agreed.'

'Between them, they could round up this gang in the next week or so.'

'I wouldn't count on it.'

'You must have plenty of clues.'

'We don't, ma'am. This lot are good at what they do.'

'And so are we. Every contact leaves its traces.'

'But when the only traces are from disposable overshoes all we know is that they're experienced criminals. Or misguided health professionals.'

She didn't smile. 'Tyre tracks?'

'Nothing to speak of. Gravel surfaces, mostly.'

'And no CCTV?'

'They're wise to that.'

'I still think Halliwell and Leaman are capable of dealing with this.'

'I didn't say they aren't. We'll get there.'

'Without you breathing down their necks, I mean.'

He didn't like the way this was heading. 'With respect, I know how to get the best out of my team, ma'am.'

Georgina took a breath that tested the silver buttons on her tunic. 'I'm not criticising. My job – one of my jobs – is to manage, make the best use of resources. I don't think you're overstretched in CID.'

'Hold on,' Diamond said. 'I could go back to the office now and find I'm facing a murder. We have to be on our toes.'

Her eyes rolled upwards. Maybe he'd used the primed-and-ready-to-go argument once too often.

She glanced behind her as if someone might be at the window. *On the top floor?* 'What I'm about to tell you must not go beyond these four walls. I've been sounded out by a high source, the highest, in fact.'

Mental picture of Georgina dressed like Moses, with a tablet of stone under each arm.

'Headquarters?'

'Higher than that.'

'Federation?'

She shook her head. She was milking this. She wanted to impress him. He played along, curious and wary. How could it impinge on him if Georgina had been earmarked for promotion?

'ACPO?'

'No.'

'The Home Office?'

A twitch of the lips put an end to the game.

He waited for more.

'It's extremely sensitive.' Her face was screwed up now as if it was painful to go on. She lowered her voice. 'A certain police authority – not ours – has come under scrutiny.

Questions are being asked about their handling of an investigation that appears to have been flawed. As you know, each authority has its own professional standards department. Above that is the Independent Police Complaints Commission with their own investigators. But in exceptional cases the chief constable may request assistance from an officer of executive rank from another authority.'

'You?' he said, on cloud nine. He hadn't had a break from Georgina in years. 'Nice work.'

'It hasn't been confirmed yet. In matters such as this there's a vetting process, but I agreed to put my hat into the ring, so to speak.'

'They won't object to you, ma'am. You're a shoo-in.'

'Do you think so?' For a fleeting moment she looked quite kittenish. Then dignity was restored. 'We'll see. But if I do take this on, I'm going to need assistance.'

'They'll see you right.'

'Somebody I'm used to working with.'

His blood ran cold. 'Who's that?'

'Why do you think I'm telling you this?'

Anything. *Anything* but this. 'I'm not sure that's such a good idea, ma'am.'

'Why? You're a free agent. You have no family. You can spend a few weeks in another county.'

I'll say I can't leave the cat, he thought. He was as desperate as that. But the Home Office might not regard Raffles and his needs as a valid excuse. 'Which county is it?'

'I haven't been told myself. They'll put us up in decent accommodation.'

The thought of shacking up with Georgina. Sharing a table for breakfast in some cheap hotel. 'Just you and me?'

'At the beginning, while I get a sense of what is involved. We can get extra assistance later if required.'

'What would my role be?'

'The part of the job you really enjoy – rooting out the truth from all the people concerned.'

'To be honest, I'm not comfortable investigating brother officers.'

'Neither am I, but it's inescapable. There are bad eggs in every profession, Peter. They have to be found and ejected. I don't always understand your ways of working. I don't always approve of them. But you get results. And we already agreed who covers for you.'

'Did we?'

'This will do you good, get you out of a rut.'

'I hadn't noticed I was in one.'

'It takes an outsider to tell. You and I will make a terrific team. Dallymore and Diamond, troubleshooters.'

Dallymore and Diamond.

He was reminded of the story of a famous comic double act coming on stage at the Glasgow Empire, the toughest of all gigs. Mike Winters made his entrance and when his brother Bernie followed, a voice was heard to say, 'Oh Christ, there's two of them.'

Teaming up with Georgina would be a low point in his career, if not the pits. True, she was the assistant chief constable and he the head of CID, but in this partnership she was the detective in charge, he the plod, gofer and sidekick. Bound by his promise of silence, he said nothing to the rest of his team, but he was in no hurry to tell them anyway. They'd think this was hilarious.

That evening he confided in his friend Paloma and she laughed out loud. 'You and Georgina. Who would have thought it?'

'Now come on.'

'She's obviously got the hots for you.'

'That would really top it off, having to barricade my bedroom door.'

'It can't be a rational decision. You've always said she disapproves of how you run the show.'

'The truth of it is she wants me to do the door-stepping for her, grilling the wretched cops who messed up and don't want to talk about it and she'll take any credit that's going. That's her way.'

'Her privilege,' Paloma said. 'But there's always a flip side, isn't there?'

'Not obvious to me.'

'You're always saying you need to break free, get some sort of relief from the job. This could be it.'

'With Georgina for company?'

'You've got to admit it's different.'

# 6

Days passed with no progress on the jewel thefts. John Leaman, the anal retentive on the team, had spent days studying a map with the aim of profiling the offenders. The theory was that referencing the crime locations would pinpoint the likeliest area where the perpetrators had their base. If these had been one-man crimes, it might have worked. With a gang, the profile was never likely to provide the breakthrough. But the display board looked pretty decorated with push pins and pink strips.

'I expect they drive in from Bristol or London,' Keith Halliwell said. He'd long since given up sparing Leaman's feelings.

'If we had some idea where they'd strike next, it would help,' Diamond said. 'There are far too many big houses stuffed with valuables.'

'Our best hope is a tip-off.'

'Always is. But the snouts aren't helping – which gives point to your theory about Bristol or London.'

'The gang know seem to know what they're looking for. They take the major items and leave the rest.'

'And it's always a clean job. They must have a good look before they go in.'

'Planning.'

'But where do they get their information? How do they know who owns the rocks they steal?'

'*Bath People?*' Halliwell said.

'Which people?'

'*Bath People*. The magazine.'

'I get you.' The expensive glossy filled its pages with photos of the great and the good at local hunt balls, race meetings and glamorous fundraising events. The pages, that is, that weren't filled with advertising.

'All those women in posh frocks sporting the family jewels. Everyone is named. That's how it sells.'

Leaman spoke up from behind his computer. 'If you like, guv, I can look through the back issues and see if there's a connection.'

'What a good offer,' Diamond said, resisting the temptation of winking at Halliwell. It was another perfect bum-numbing task for Leaman. 'And I know where we can lay our hands on a stack of copies. Georgina buys it. In fact, she's in it sometimes, rubbing shoulders with the lord-lieutenant and the mayor.'

'Do you read it?' Halliwell said in surprise.

'Only at my dentist's.' He turned to Leaman. 'Georgina keeps her copies on one of the filing cabinets in her office. Be sure to ask before you borrow them.'

Halliwell looked at Diamond. 'Wouldn't it be better if the request came from you?'

'Me? I'm keeping my distance this week. She won't mind. She'll be tickled pink if we come across her picture.'

'Wearing the Dallymore tiara?'

'She's always in uniform.'

Leaman went off to try his luck with Georgina, never shy of speaking to one of the high-ups.

'He'll have my job one day,' Diamond said. 'See if he doesn't.'

'I believe you, guv. By then, we'll all be history except him. CID will be one man and his laptop.'

\*   \*   \*

The grotesque fantasy came closer to reality before the day was out. Diamond picked up the phone and it was Georgina.

'How ready are you?'

'For what, ma'am?' His mouth had gone dry.

'For what we were discussing.'

'The, em . . .?'

'We leave tomorrow morning.'

'Soon as that? I haven't made any arrangements.'

'You live alone like me, don't you? What arrangements?'

He didn't like to mention his cat. The neighbour would take over. Raffles spent much of his time in her garden anyway. 'I haven't spoken to Keith Halliwell.'

'Tell him he's in charge. You're away for an unspecified time on police business. No need to say any more.'

'I don't know any more.'

'Good thing. I've arranged for a driver. He'll call at my house and pick me up first and we should get to you about ten fifteen. Pack for at least two weeks.'

'Where are we going?'

'Peter, there's a very sensible rule in work of this sort called the need-to-know principle. I'm applying it. When it becomes necessary, you'll be informed.'

Pompous old trout. 'As you wish.'

'Until tomorrow, then. Don't sound so depressed. It could be quite an adventure.' Now she sounded like a character out of Enid Blyton.

He broke the news to Halliwell, as much as he knew. 'I don't need to tell you, it's not my choice.'

Halliwell couldn't hide the smile. 'You and Georgina? Someone at headquarters has a sense of humour.'

'It came from the Home Office. She has friends in high places. I'm tagging along as the dogsbody.'

'Have fun.'

'Make sure you collar the jewel thieves while I'm away.'

53

'Me and whose army?'

'You've got Ingeborg and Leaman and young Gilbert. All good brains. Get them busy and put this one to bed before I'm back.' He felt marginally better for saying that.

That evening he went for a parting meal with Paloma at the Ring O Bells in Widcombe Parade, almost a local for her. She'd got over her amusement and actually seemed sorry he would be away for a time. But their appetites weren't affected. They tucked into the char-grilled rib-eye steak with lemon, chilli and parsley butter, fries and salad (his) and vegetarian bake with salad leaves (hers).

'How long will you be away?' Paloma asked.

'It's open-ended. I expect we've got to look at evidence that was heard in court and find out what went wrong, who was lying, and so on. That's going to take ages.'

'You'll get some weekends off, I hope.'

'I'll make sure of that. God, I hope it's not the other end of the country, Durham or some such. She's not saying.'

'Is it a state secret?'

'The story hasn't broken in the press.'

'Does it still go on, one police force investigating another?'

'Less usual than it was. There's an independent commission that does the job these days, but certain cases still get farmed out to mugs like me and Georgina. Nobody is comfortable with it. We won't get a welcome from the locals. It's a pig of a job.'

'You'll see another part of the country. Travel broadens the mind.'

'Aren't I broad-minded enough?'

'No comment.'

'Right now, Bath offers all I desire,' he said, nudging her foot under the table. 'Your place or mine?'

*   *   *

He was at home in Weston next morning when the police Land Rover drew up outside.

'Don't let me down,' he said to Raffles, who had his head in the bowl lapping the jelly off a serving of ocean fish. 'No fights, no birds, no small mammals. And keep off the street at all times. Oh, and try not to shrink away when Mrs Monument goes to stroke you. Otherwise, it's life as normal. I envy you.'

He carried his holdall out and nodded to Georgina in the front passenger seat.

'Is that all you're bringing?' she asked.

'I'll get by.'

The driver had the hatch door open. It was not encouraging to see two jumbo-sized pink suitcases taking up most of the luggage space. As if this was not enough, various garments in suit covers were hanging inside the vehicle and when he got in he found he was sitting between a vanity case and a set of golf clubs.

*Golf clubs?*

'Don't sit on my hat. It's somewhere on the seat.'

They moved off, observed with indifference by Raffles, now perched on Mrs Monument's front wall.

'The first time I've seen where you live,' Georgina said. 'Quieter than I expected.'

'You should hear it at the weekend when the lawn-mowers are going.'

They joined the A4 and headed towards the city, which he took to mean that their destination wasn't the West Country. He wasn't going to ask, even though the need-to-know principle wouldn't be compromised now they were on the road.

'I don't suppose you heard the news,' Georgina said from the front seat without turning her head. 'There was another break-in last night. A large house in Upper Swainswick. The people were at the theatre. They got home to find the safe door open and an emerald necklace and matching earrings gone.'

'Another one? That's two in a week.' He could imagine the mayhem in CID.

'I don't doubt that this is the same lot. They disabled the security system and got in through a back door. And it seems they knew what they were looking for. I hope DCI Halliwell is up to this.'

'You were confident when we spoke yesterday.'

'I didn't expect he'd be tested as soon as this,' she said with a shake of the head.

This was too good an opportunity. 'If it worries you, ma'am, we can make a slight change of plan. We're heading towards the city. Drop me in Manvers Street and I can take a look at the scene and join you later.'

'Oh no, no, no, no, no,' she said. 'I'm not falling for that one, Peter. I know exactly how your mind is working. Phone messages to say more evidence has come up and you're delayed. I'm sorry, but Halliwell will have to cope. This mission has priority over everything. I need you at my side from the word go.'

As caddy? he thought.

The Land Rover cruised through the city and a short way along the London Road and then right at the traffic lights and over Cleveland Bridge, taking the A36. They were travelling south, through Wiltshire. The next place of any size would be Salisbury. He hadn't heard of any bent coppers there, but the Salisbury and South Wilts was said to be the finest downland golf course in the country.

'I hope you locked away your jewellery somewhere really safe, ma'am,' Diamond said, for his own amusement. 'You're chancing it, leaving Bath while this gang is operating.'

She puffed herself up. 'In the first place, I don't live in

a country mansion, and in the second I don't go in for expensive jewellery. The only valuables I have are personal items of no market value whatsoever.'

'I expect you've won a few silver cups in your time.'

'You noticed my clubs, then. It's a hobby. I don't win things. There might be the chance of a round where we're going. Do you play, Peter?'

'Not my game at all.'

'You go in for mind games, don't you? Pulling the wool over the eyes of your superiors. Superior in rank, not necessarily in guile. Can you swim?'

'If necessary, yes.'

'Not from choice? You don't go looking for opportunities to demonstrate your freestyle?'

'I'm a breaststroker.'

A volley of laughter escaped her as if she was a fourteen-year-old. 'Find me a man who isn't.'

Georgina in this skittish mood was a revelation, and not one he enjoyed. A foretaste of dreadful days to come? He didn't want to get chummy. He preferred her talking to him through the steel-mesh barrier of rank.

'The reason I mentioned swimming,' she added, 'is that you may get the chance of a dip, the place we're going.'

She made it sound like an invitation to sex. He would have told her he hadn't packed his shorts, but on present form she'd have an orgasm. Instead he said, 'I dare say we'll be busy with other things.'

'Possibly.' He'd given her the chance to volunteer something about the purpose of the trip, but she wasn't playing. With the talk of golf and swimming, he was beginning to wonder if the so-called mission was genuine police business at all. Could Georgina have flipped?

While they skirted Salisbury by way of Wilton, she pulled down the sun visor and adjusted the vanity mirror so that she could look at him without turning round. Was she just enjoying the power she had over him or did she think she was seducing him? She was humming some tune to herself.

Through all this, their driver remained silent, robotic, as he was trained to be. What he would tell his mates back in Bath when he was off duty was cause for alarm. Manvers Street was a rumour factory.

They picked up the A36 again and continued southwards along a dual carriageway through open country.

Finally, Georgina put an end to the waiting game. 'We'll be based in Chichester. Do you know it?'

He was cool, as if he'd known all along. 'Not really. I visited a couple of times a while back, that's all.'

'Sussex police requested my help. When I say "Sussex police" I mean a former colleague, Archie Hahn. And when I say "my help" I mean precisely that. We went through staff college together and got on rather well. They set us various aptitude tests and command tasks, such as getting across a wide stream using two planks and a barrel, and Archie always knew exactly what to do. A brilliant man.'

Diamond found it hard to imagine Georgina crossing a stream with two planks and a barrel. Whoever Archie was, he was a man to be reckoned with.

'Commander Hahn now. We haven't kept in touch, but I evidently made an impression on him because he thought of me when they had this spot of bother that needs attention from outside their own force. It's a police matter and they want it sorted by police, rather than putting it to the IPCC.'

'What's the spot of bother?'

'He hasn't explained yet.'

'It's got to be serious if he can't deal with it himself.'

'So one presumes. I'll find out this evening. He's taking me for a meal at Raymond Blanc's.'

Bully for you, Diamond thought. 'Does he know you're not alone?'

'You're wondering if you're invited? Sorry, Peter, but he doesn't know about you. You're my secret weapon.'

'That's a first for me.'

'So I suggest you come to my room when I'm back from my dinner date and I'll bring you up to speed.'

'Are we staying in the same place?'

'Oh, I'll make sure of that.'

'Did you book us in somewhere?'

'No, I left that to Archie.'

'But he doesn't know there are two of us. He'll only have booked one room.'

She smiled into the mirror. 'Don't fret, Peter. These days almost all the rooms are doubles. I'll squeeze you in one way or another.'

# 7

Georgina's reservation was at the Ship Hotel in North Street, Chichester. Elegant was the word for the building, in the Georgian style familiar to Bathonians.

Diamond and the driver lifted out the pink suitcases and other items and followed the boss inside. The receptionist greeted Georgina, asked for her name, checked the computer, looked up from the screen at the trio in front of her and said without blinking that the reservation appeared to be for one guest, and was that correct?

'Is another room available?' Georgina asked, and she didn't blink either.

The receptionist said she would check.

Diamond said at once, 'If it's difficult I don't mind staying somewhere else.'

'That would not be convenient,' Georgina said without a glance in his direction.

A room on the second floor was found and Diamond signed in and was given his key.

'Which is it? I'll need to know the number,' Georgina said.

Their driver took this as the cue to leave them to it. He said if he wasn't needed any longer, he'd return to Bath. He didn't say what he would tell Bath about the goings-on in Chichester.

\* \* \*

Not wishing for hotel food, Diamond went exploring that evening and found a pub serving burgers and chips. Chichester wasn't a total write-off, he told Paloma on the phone after he'd eaten.

'Chichester? That's a relief. Not so far as you feared.'

'A couple of hours by road. If I had my car, I'd be home by now, sleeping in my own bed tonight.'

'Better not. She'll think you've taken fright and deserted. Do you know any more about the job yet?'

'Not really.' He told her as much as he knew about Archie Hahn, the police college friend, and the request for Georgina's assistance. 'It could be just an excuse for them to get together again. She brought her golf clubs with her and enough clothes for a fashion show. He's taken her to some fancy restaurant tonight.'

'Weren't you included?'

'The bloke doesn't even know I'm here.'

'She wouldn't have asked you to come if it was only about linking up with a former boyfriend. There's got to be more to it.'

'I should find out later. She wants to see me in her room when she gets back.'

'What for? The woman's insatiable.'

He let it pass. If Paloma had heard some of the stuff that had been said in the car she wouldn't be joking. 'Don't you worry. I'll keep my distance.'

His room had a view across the roofs to the cathedral spire, floodlit by night. After an hour or so of reality television he sat by the window looking at pigeons and waiting for the call from Georgina. He assumed it would come about ten.

He was still there at eleven. The pigeons were all roosting.

At eleven thirty he decided she'd forgotten. The reunion

with her old college friend must have put everything else out of her mind. No point in waiting up indefinitely.

He was in the bathroom brushing his teeth when the call came at twenty to midnight. He let it ring. The ringing continued. He pictured Georgina, phone in hand, cursing him. He could lift the phone and cut the call, but she wouldn't give up. She'd ring again. In time she would come knocking on his door.

This time he picked the thing up.

'Peter?'

'Yes.'

'It's a little later than I intended. Archie wouldn't tell me anything over dinner because it was too public, so we went for a drive to West Wittering and had a moonlit stroll along the beach. There was a lot to catch up on. Are you decent?'

'Am I ever? Depends what you mean.'

'Dressed.'

'Not entirely.'

'Slight change of plan, then. Don't come to my room. We're making a six-thirty start in the morning. Off to the Isle of Wight.'

'What for?'

'Tell you tomorrow. I'll arrange for an early call for us both, but set your alarm as well, just in case. The sea air seems to have made me drowsy – or perhaps it was the wine. I'll sleep like a baby.'

Bully for you, Diamond thought. Personally, he was now anything but drowsy. His brain was hyperactive, trying to find some reason for visiting the Isle of Wight. All he could bring to mind was a childhood trip to Carisbrooke Castle where a donkey on a treadmill turned the wheel that worked the well mechanism. There had to be more to the place than that. Forced to dredge deeper, he was reminded of a postcard from someone on holiday depicting the so-called wonders of the island: Needles you can't thread; Ryde where you walk; Cowes you can't milk; Newport you can't bottle. And there was another wonder and annoyingly his brain wouldn't supply it. Repeatedly he went over the names: the Needles, Ryde, Cowes and Newport. Mentally, he did tours of the island: Bembridge, Shanklin, Sandown, Ventnor and Yarmouth. Then he was back to Cowes and Ryde. Infuriating. Relax, man, it doesn't matter, he told himself. But by now his brain was turning the treadmill like the bloody donkey.

He put the light on and watched a documentary about the *Titanic* disaster. Made himself tea. Went to the bathroom. Tried to sleep again.

Seaview was somewhere on the island, but that wasn't it. Seaview *had* a sea view. He was back on the treadmill.

At what hour of the morning he was spared and allowed to sleep he didn't want to know. Ten minutes after, it seemed, came the wake-up call. He heaved himself out of bed, tottered to the shower, failed – as he always did in hotels – to master the controls, got a burst of cold water, and remembered.

Freshwater you can't drink.

Two black coffees later he was downstairs, propped against the wall at the hotel entrance. Georgina appeared, spry and animated. It took a while for him to work out that she was in a black suit, the first time he could remember seeing her out of uniform. Apart from the silver buttons and insignia the look was the same.

'Archie arranged for a car,' she said, looking at her watch. 'It should be here by now.'

'Is he coming?'

'Absolutely not. Get this into your head, Peter. We're free agents, independent of his lot.'

'But using one of his cars.'

'It was either that or hiring one and I don't believe in burdening the taxpayer.'

The blue and yellow livery of the Sussex police car was too much for Diamond's tired eyes. He sank into the back seat, thankful he didn't have to drive and hoping the caffeine would soon take effect. Georgina got in from the other side, planted the seat buckle in his lap and said, 'I don't want you falling asleep and crushing me.'

They started the drive to the Portsmouth car ferry.

'You look queasy,' Georgina told him before they'd gone far.

'I'm all right.'

'Something you ate last night? If so, a sea crossing isn't going to help you. Personally, I had a wonderful meal.'

He hoped she would leave it at that.

She didn't. 'New season turbot and spring vegetables followed by baked Alaska, which comes as a dish for two.'

He thought for the first time that it was possible the Double Whopper burger he'd eaten may have had something to do with his sleepless night.

Georgina hadn't finished. 'Archie had the dressed Cornish crab and said it was excellent. Oh, and I forgot the starter. We both had the Burgundian snails. I don't suppose you're a snail person, but with the garlic herb butter they're as good a mouthful as you could wish. Do you eat snails, Peter?'

'Can we talk about what we're doing today?'

'By all means. We're going to meet a guest of Her Majesty.'

'A *prisoner*?'

'We're not visiting the island to make sandcastles.'

He should have remembered that Parkhurst and Albany were located there. For years they had been the 'places of dispersal' for dangerous convicts such as the Krays and the Yorkshire Ripper. A few years ago, the two prisons had been downgraded and treated as one, relabelled HM Prison Isle of Wight, a category B lock-up, which meant it housed prisoners 'for whom maximum security is not thought to be necessary, but for whom escape needs to be made very difficult'. Someone with a nice sense of irony thought that up.

'Anyone I know?'

'I doubt it,' Georgina said.

'Not someone I put away?'

'No, he was from here on the coast, a lifer by the name of Stapleton.'

'Never heard of him.'

'He claims he was wrongly convicted.'

'Don't they all?'

'This one could be telling the truth, and the truth he has to tell has come as a shock to certain people.'

'Your friend Archie?'

'Archie has an executive role. He isn't personally involved.'

'What's it all about, then?'

Georgina pumped herself up with one of those immense intakes of breath that meant she was about to say something that couldn't be questioned. 'If I were to tell you, it would only be hearsay. Better you learn the facts from the prisoner himself.'

'Can't wait.'

By the time they drove on to the car ferry, Diamond decided he'd need to be positive about the state of his stomach. This stretch of sea was Spithead, supposedly protected from strong winds and therefore a safe anchorage for the navy. Even so, the ferry passed close enough to a passing battleship to catch the slipstream and he felt his insides rebelling. Just as well he hadn't eaten breakfast. It was a forty-minute crossing to Fishbourne.

Promenading along the deck with Georgina (their driver was leaning over the side having a smoke), he concentrated on the view, wishing the blue haze of the island would become more solid.

'You're not much of a sailor, then?' Georgina said.

'Why do you say that?'

'You've gone a dreadful colour.'

And you're revelling in it, he thought. She didn't often catch him in a weakened state. This 'terrific team' of Dallymore and Diamond was already malfunctioning.

Back on dry land, he rallied physically and in spirit. A twenty-minute drive brought them to the gates of Parkhurst. Georgina told the officer on duty that they were expected and had documentation as well as IDs and this was confirmed, but they still had to submit to a pat-down search at the visitor centre. After a sniffer dog showed only passing interest in Diamond, they were escorted to a private interview room furnished with plastic chairs and a wooden table screwed to the floor. Notepads and pencils were provided.

'This will be a voluntary statement,' Georgina told Diamond. 'He's made it before and he's been told we're police officers following up on the facts.'

'Which isn't true in my case,' Diamond said.

'What do you mean?'

'I can't follow up on facts I don't know anything about.'

'You don't have to sound so tetchy, Peter. I'm not deliberately withholding information from you. Better you hear from the man himself than getting my second-hand version. Leave the questioning to me. Listen and make notes.'

The man brought in by a prison officer looked more like an advert for hearty eating than a deprived convict. He was at least a couple of sizes larger than Diamond. He grinned at his visitors and said, 'Danny Stapleton, at your service.' Turning to the warder, he said, 'You can go. I'll be safe. They look harmless.'

Georgina wasn't amused. She said, 'The officer stays.'

Stapleton spread his hands. 'Your choice.'

'Sit down, please.' She introduced herself and Diamond. 'We're from Avon and Somerset police.'

'Avon and . . . ?' The man gave another knowing smile. 'I get it. The local fuzz are tainted. You're not.'

'Enough of that.' Georgina took control. 'Any more back-chat from you, and you'll be straight back to your cell. I'm told you claim to be wrongly convicted.'

'I've been claiming it ever since I was slung in here,' Stapleton said. 'I'm an innocent man. You want to hear?'

'This is your opportunity. But understand this, Mr Stapleton. If any of what you say is false – any part of it – your credibility will be demolished and you won't see us or anyone else again. So you're not in court under oath, but you might as well be.'

'No problem,' he said. 'Honest to God, this is what happened. Seven years ago, I'm living in LA. D'you know it?'

Georgina blinked, thrown by the reference.

'Lil'Ampton, right?'

'Oh.'

'LA is what the locals call it. I call it run-down. Like most of these seaside towns, it's seen better days. You've still got the funfair and the beach, but you've also got poverty and loads of names ending in the letter z. The time I'm talking about I was unemployed, on the social, like half the town. OK, I get a little extra where I can, and it isn't declared. I'm a tealeaf, a good one, specialising in cars. I'm telling you this 'cause you'll have looked at my record. Doesn't mean I'm crap because I've done a few stretches in places like this, just a tad unlucky with alarms and cameras. Most times I get in, drive off and no one would guess. Never any violence. Until this stretch, my times inside amounted to less than three years, total. Do you understand me?'

'Get to the point,' Georgina said.

'Right. Well, my strike rate was suffering a bit on account of all the microchip stuff in modern cars. They have these smart keys and alarms. You need to be a computer nerd to nick one.'

'We know all this. What happened?'

'I took delivery of a box of tricks that would hack me into one of these new cars. Didn't get much luck at first. Then one evening I'm sitting on the terrace of my local, the old Steam Packet at the top of River Road, when a BMW 3 series draws up outside. Perfect for me to half-inch with my brand-new jammer and key programmer. A young guy gets out and walks off across the bridge and I do the business. In under five minutes I'm driving it away to get some new plates fitted.'

'Where?'

'Chichester. Geezer I happened to know, who did up cars for people like me. I get well clear of LA and stop to give Stew a call, tell him I'm on the way, like. That's all fixed and before moving off I open the glove compartment and – would you believe? – a load of money falls out. Used banknotes all over the floor. My lucky day, I'm thinking. I fill my pockets and drive on and almost get to Chichester when I hear this police car coming up behind me. Next thing I'm out of the car and being searched. They told me the Bimmer was stolen, which I knew, but they had no business to know.'

'What do you mean by that?

'The timing. It was far too quick, barely half an hour since I drove off. The kid who just parked it couldn't have known it was gone. Anyway, these cops found the money on me, two grand, I heard. later. I was bricking it by then and I told them a porky, said I'd sold a boat in Littlehampton and was on my way to Chichester for a night out. It wasn't true, OK? I admit it. I had to think of something to tell them. And then comes the bombshell. They open the boot and there's this body inside in a garden sack with a hole through his head. I swear I knew nothing about it. How could I, when I'd nicked the car half an hour before? Next thing I'm a murder suspect, handcuffed and bundled off to spend the night in a cell. I've been banged up ever since.'

'Your story wasn't believed,' Georgina said, more as a statement than a question.

'It didn't look good, me with all that money in my pockets. They said either I'd killed and robbed the dead man or I was paid the two grand to get rid of the body and was on my way to dump it somewhere when I was stopped. Nobody would listen. They found the tools I'd used, the jammer and the programmer, and said it was proof I'd nicked the car. Fair enough, but they were saying I'd nicked it the day before from a car park in Arundel. I swear I hadn't been near Arundel.'

'Couldn't anyone give you an alibi? The staff at the Steam Packet?'

'There was only the one barmaid on duty that night and she was Polish. By the time my lawyers got around to checking, she'd moved on and couldn't be traced.'

'Wasn't anyone else drinking?'

'None that I saw. I've had seven miserable years to think about this. The way I see it now, the car was already hot when I nicked it. That young guy was the killer. He was driving around with the stiff in the boot. He nicked the car in Arundel the day before. It was my bad luck to nick it from him.'

'Why would he have left it outside the Steam Packet?'

'The pub is right by the footbridge, isn't it? He was going to wait till dark and then move the body on to the bridge and drop it in the river. It's quiet there at nights. It is by day, come to that.'

'He'd have to be strong.'

'I told you he was young.'

'Did you get a good look at him, then?'

'It was how he was dressed, in one of them hoodie things the young tearaways wear – or they did do before I was banged up.'

'Did you see his face?'

'Not really. When he drove up I was looking at the car. And when he got out he had his back to me.'

'Why would he have got out?'

'To size up the situation. Work out the best place on the bridge to tip the body over.'

'You're suggesting he killed the victim in Arundel and stole a car to dispose of the body?'

'It makes sense. He wouldn't want to use his own car and get it loused up with DNA and all that stuff.'

'He chose to drive to Littlehampton and dump the body in the river?'

'Where the current would take it out to sea. The Arun is one of the fastest-flowing rivers in Britain. Six knots. Did you know that? I've done my research.'

'We do now we've heard it from you,' Georgina said.

'You don't have to look at me like that. If I was the killer, I wouldn't be driving to Chichester with the stiff, would I? I'd have tipped it in the river.'

'We've only got your word you were driving there.'

'No.' He frowned. 'You've got the word of the cops who stopped me.'

'It doesn't mean you were planning to go to Chichester. You could have been on your way to some isolated place where a body could be disposed of.'

'That's what they said in court, but it's not true. I was on my way to Stew to get the plates changed.'

'And then what? Drive on to your chosen place of disposal?'

'Fucking hell.' Danny Stapleton slapped his hand on the table between them. 'I'm here to tell you what happened, not listen to your crap theories.'

The prison officer grabbed Danny's arms and forced him against the chair.

'OK, OK,' the prisoner said.

'Do you want him cuffed, ma'am, or shall we end it there?'

Georgina had lost the thread. It was a long time since she'd interviewed a hostile suspect, so Diamond took over, flapped his hand at the warder and said, 'Let's get back to the facts. You were arrested that night and taken to where – Chichester police station?'

Released from the restraint, Danny picked up his story as if nothing had happened. 'They questioned me for hours, wouldn't believe what I was saying. Fair play, I'd made some of it up, about the money. It was in my pockets. My prints were all over it. I had to say something, didn't I? I made up the stuff about the car and where I was headed that night. But after I'd had the night to think it over, I came clean. I told them exactly what I've been telling you.'

'Which you can't prove.'

'Don't I know it? They called me a killer and all sorts. I didn't even know who the bloody victim was. That's how innocent I was.'

'You found out later.'

'They're not generous with their information, your lot.'

'So who was he?'

'For crying out loud, are you telling me you don't know and you're my best hope of getting out of here? I give up.'

Georgina started speaking again, more to Diamond than Danny. 'He was Joe Rigden, a self-employed gardener from near Slindon, one of the local villages. Shot through the head.'

'I've never owned a gun,' Danny said at once. 'Never

71

heard of Rigden before they told me his name. Never met him.'

Georgina added more details she must have got from her old college friend. 'Rigden lived alone in an isolated cottage. He had a van and took jobs over quite a wide area, visiting people about twice a month. Because his garden visits were irregular, governed by the weather, it was a couple of weeks before he was reported missing.'

'Living in a one-bedroom flat I didn't even have a windowbox, let alone a garden,' Danny said.

'You weren't charged with first degree murder,' Georgina said. 'There wasn't the evidence to convict you of that.'

'No, but they kept on at me for days, telling me I was in the frame.'

'Of course you were, and rightly so. You were the only suspect. You were found with the body. And you told the police a pack of lies.'

'Only when I thought I was being done for nicking the car. When it got serious next morning I told them everything I knew, but I wasn't believed. They decided they'd got their man. Talk about the third degree. It was brainwashing. I was having nightmares, dreaming I did it. I still get them. I'm psychologically damaged. When I get out of here I'm going to sue you lot.'

'Come on,' Georgina said. 'There were strong grounds for believing you did it. You were convicted of being an accessory.'

'A mandatory life stretch with a minimum of ten years before they even consider me for release. That's not funny.'

'The judge took the view that if you didn't carry out the murder yourself, you must have known who did it and were guilty of obstructing justice as well.'

'The judge was an arsehole.'

'Statements like that won't help your cause one bit. Do you know the identity of the murderer?'

'How could I?'

'Are you afraid of what might happen when you get out?'

'Bollocks.'

'I can easily terminate this, Mr Stapleton. You don't seem to realise you're ruining your chances. I was told you're well behaved, doing your best to get remission. It doesn't sound like it.' Georgina, fully restored, in headmistress mode – and for once Peter Diamond wasn't on the receiving end.

'I'm stressed,' Danny said. 'I shouldn't be here. They never went after the young guy. He was the killer and he's still at liberty.'

'Yes, you're under stress. Prison does that to people. Every inmate has a grievance. A lot of what you hear has no basis in reality.'

He leaned forward, gripping the table. 'There's more, isn't there? What's all this interest all of a sudden? Something's happened. Someone's been talking. I was left to rot until a week ago. Now I'm getting pulled out of my cell every other day to talk to coppers.'

'We'll end it there,' Georgina said. 'Your case is under review, Mr Stapleton. Be grateful for that. If anything of importance emerges, you will certainly be informed. Meanwhile, if you think of any detail of the case that wasn't aired in court, let the governor know, and we'll get to hear of it.'

# 8

The car left the prison and headed along a deserted road towards the ferry. Georgina was still acting as if they were dealing in state secrets.

'Are you going to fill me in?' Diamond said.

'First, tell me what you made of him.'

'Pathetic. No different from the thousand other small-time crooks I've come across.'

'But convincing?'

'He tells a good story. He's had plenty of time to work on it.'

'You didn't believe him?'

Staring out of the window at the bleak fields, he said, 'I haven't been told enough to form an opinion.'

'You don't have to sound so deprived, Peter. I'll brief you fully in a moment. To be fair to Danny Stapleton, what he said to us is no different from what he was saying when he was first interviewed. He insists he's a car thief and not a murderer. He seems to have made a living from it until the manufacturers went electronic with their security.'

'The man Stew, the plates man – does he exist?'

'Chichester police don't have any record of him, but of course if he was any good they wouldn't. The crooks in the stolen car business are very elusive.'

'He was Stapleton's best hope. Surely his lawyers would have pulled out all the stops to find him.'

'I'm sure they did. And I'm sure Stew moved on and covered his tracks as soon as he heard about the arrest. He'd know it would be the end of his activities.' Georgina seemed willing to swallow everything they'd been told in the prison.

'Wasn't the call Stapleton made traceable from the phone?'

'No phone was found.'

He gave a soft laugh.

She said, 'I expect he got rid of it when he was arrested. It was dark, remember.'

'They searched him.'

'He got rid of it earlier, then, at the time he made the call.'

'But after the arrest he needed to prove he was just a car thief and not a murderer. The phone was his best hope. If he'd slung it into a field he could have told his lawyers where to look for it. That's if he really made this call and if Stew the plates man wasn't invented just to enrich his story.'

'You really are a sceptic, aren't you?'

'From the way you're holding out on me, ma'am, I sense that the guy must have *something* going in his favour.'

'All right,' she said. 'I'll give it to you just as I got it from Archie Hahn last night. It was too much to hope that Stapleton's first-hand account might spark off a few original thoughts. You're obviously not at your best.'

He ignored the put-down. He'd had worse from Georgina.

She was in full flow. 'The murder of the gardener, Joe Rigden, was investigated by the local CID. As you heard, there was a couple of weeks' delay in identifying the victim, and in the initial stage of the inquiry the focus was very much on Danny Stapleton as the potential killer. The BMW was quickly reported as missing from a public car park in

75

Arundel. The owner was a man in his eighties, very absent-minded, who frankly shouldn't have been in charge of a wheelchair, let alone a powerful executive car. He may well have forgotten to lock it. I suppose we can be grateful that he noticed the blessed thing was missing and reported it. The car was thoroughly examined for traces of the perpetrator, of course, and various items were collected, including fingerprints and hairs, most from the owner, but several from Stapleton as well and from the victim.'

'Wasn't the body at the bottom of a refuse bag?'

'An open polypropylene bag of the kind gardeners and builders use. The policewoman who opened the boot got a few strands of Rigden's hair on her sleeve. There were also a number of additional hairs found in the interior of the car. As you may know, hair as such doesn't contain any nuclear DNA, but the hair follicles do and hair pulled from the head is OK for testing. There is also mitochondrial DNA in the cellular debris that forms a part of the growing hair shaft.'

Georgina showing off. Diamond preferred to leave the details of forensic science to the white-coated brigade. He'd once been nominated for a course at one of the Home Office labs and had DNA written on his personal file: Did Not Attend.

Georgina cruised on: 'Three individuals were isolated and DNA profiles obtained. Potentially this was vital evidence. Two were from males and one female. They didn't match anything in the national database and unfortunately the owner of the car was hopeless at remembering who had recently travelled with him. However, some good detective work identified one of the males as the mechanic who had last serviced the vehicle. On investigation he was eliminated from the inquiry and the other two profiles were kept on file. After that, the body was identified as Rigden and the whole inquiry shifted to his village and the various people who used his services as a gardener.'

'Any with a motive?' Diamond asked.

'Apparently not.'

'What was he like, this gardener? Ever been in trouble?'

'Far from it. I gather he had a spotless reputation locally. Always ready to help people out, shopping for the elderly, meals on wheels, looked after the graves in the churchyard for no reward.'

'Except in the life to come.'

Georgina shook her head. 'He was an agnostic. Didn't go to church. A total abstainer from alcohol. No philandering with either sex. Financial affairs all in order after he died. Sober, clean-living and honest sums him up.'

'Sounds a prime candidate for a shot through the head.'

'Now you're being cynical.'

'People like that don't make themselves popular.'

'Whatever the rights and wrongs of it, no suspect was found, even though the fact that Rigden was murdered was undeniable.'

'Did they discover where it happened?'

'No.'

'They must have searched his cottage for evidence of the shooting.'

'It was all in perfect order.'

'A perfect man living a perfect home life.'

'Apparently so. The people whose gardens he tended all spoke highly of him.'

'Not an easy case to crack.'

'Stapleton was offered the prospect of a lighter sentence if he'd name the killer, but he continued to insist he had nothing to do with it. He was brought to court as an accessory and was found guilty by a majority verdict and given the mandatory life sentence. After several months, the inquiry was wound down.'

'Until now, when someone wound it up again.'

'Yes – and this is the unfortunate part. Recently an anonymous letter arrived at Sussex police headquarters claiming that a DNA sample obtained in 2011 from a drunk and disorderly suspect matched the profile of one of the two unknown people whose hair was found in the BMW. The senior investigating officer on the original case was informed, but no action was taken.'

'Why not? It would have been simple enough.'

'It wasn't all that simple. The match was with the unknown woman.'

'The *woman?*'

'Yes, get your head around that, Peter. Two women get into a fight outside some nightclub in Portsmouth. They are arrested and held overnight. Their DNA is taken. One of them is the woman whose hair was found in the car used to transport Rigden's corpse.'

This required a rethink. Danny Stapleton had claimed he'd seen someone driving the BMW, and from everything he'd said he'd taken them to be male. Could he have been mistaken?

'Wearing a hoodie,' Diamond said as much to himself as Georgina. 'Danny didn't get a proper look, he told us. Could have been female, I suppose. Yes, it's easy to assume otherwise.'

'There's worse. The writer of the anonymous letter stated that the drunk woman was related to the senior investigating officer. She was the niece.'

A grunt of distaste came from deep in his throat. 'A family connection. That looks bad, I have to say. Is it true?'

Georgina nodded. 'The SIO has been suspended. The entire CID team is under suspicion of corruption. Do you understand now why it was necessary to bring us in?'

'I understand,' he said, 'but I don't like it. I don't like it at all.'

# 9

Diamond was silent for a long time, telling himself he'd been railroaded into this, knowing deep down that he hadn't. He recoiled from the idea of investigating a brother officer. To be fair, Georgina had been upfront with him the day she'd first mentioned the job and that was when he should have refused to have any part in it. She would have said he was insubordinate and disloyal, but he would have been true to his principles. As more details of the case emerged, his uneasiness was increasing. Already he felt sympathy for the hapless fellow officer under scrutiny and he hadn't even met the guy. He knew the pressure that comes in a long-running murder inquiry. As senior investigator you call the shots, and sometimes you call the wrong ones. If that wasn't enough to endure, when family gets involved in some way you're torn apart.

'How are you feeling?' Georgina asked during the ferry crossing.

'Ready to throw up.'

'It doesn't seem as choppy as it was on the way over.'

'It's not the sea, it's the job we're on. I don't mind hounding killers. Fellow police officers are something else. I should have made that clear at the outset.'

'You'd have disappointed me.'

'Not for the first time.'

'I knew you'd see it like that. I need you, Peter. We won't

be *hounding* another officer. When corruption is alleged, someone objective has to step in. See it as a professional duty.'

'Why didn't Sussex police sort it themselves?'

'It's gone too far for that. A possible miscarriage of justice. It might still end up with the IPCC, but the hope is that you and I can get to the truth. If a crisis like this ever happened on our own patch – God forbid – we'd look to another force to deal with it in an unbiased way.'

'The inquisition.'

'We can be civilised in our dealings. As I said to you before, I prefer to think of us as troubleshooters.'

'Dallymore and Diamond at your service.'

*Oh Christ, there's two of them.*

'They're lucky to get us.'

Trying to be philosophical, he said, 'So how do you want to handle it?'

He heard in her tone that she knew she'd won a little victory. 'We'll start by putting Danny Stapleton's story to the test, go to Littlehampton and find the Steam Packet.'

He went along. The way he was feeling, he needed a strong drink.


LA, as Danny had called it, was midway between the better-known seaside towns of Worthing and Bognor, a place with its own latter-day character, a top resort early in the last century when the British had taken their holidays at home and before boarding houses became known as guest houses. Some of those buildings now looked shabby and neglected even if the acres of safe sandy beach hadn't gone away and the swans still came in numbers to the riverside. Efforts had been made to tempt tourists with powerboat rides, the funfair in Harbour Park, a miniature railway, boating lakes, a golf course and a nature reserve, but the main asset was a natural one. Littlehampton scored over other seaside towns by having the outflow of the River Arun. With a history of boatbuilding and cross-channel ferrying, the town quay still functioned in a modest way as a commercial harbour, and more robustly with leisure craft and the fish and chip shops in abundance along the promenade.

They found the Steam Packet half a mile upriver, looking immaculate, red brick, with attractive hung tiles, hanging baskets and sky-blue boards advertising riverside dining. Clearly the Victorian building had been given a recent facelift, an act of faith in twenty-first century Littlehampton.

'Gorgeous,' Diamond said out of nowhere.

'What are you on about now?'

He pointed upwards, to the ship's figurehead projecting from the upper storey.

'*That?*' Georgina said with distaste. 'If that's your idea of gorgeous, I despair. Let's go in.'

They got some speculative looks from the drinkers inside. There was no denying the fact that they'd driven up in a police car, now parked outside. The man behind the bar asked what they'd like to order. Georgina went for a glass of the house white and Diamond for a pint of Directors.

'Was this restored recently?' he asked the barman.

'The place was closed six years. We reopened under new management in 2013.'

'With the same name. It's obviously got a history.'

'The cross-channel ferry service went from here to Honfleur in the eighteen-sixties.'

'How about that? And does your figurehead outside have a history?'

'If she does, she's not telling.'

'Smart lass. We want an outside table overlooking the river. And something to eat.'

'OK. Menu's on the board and table's through there.'

They found themselves on the small terraced area Danny had described. From their table they overlooked the road and a line of parked vehicles and beyond them the river.

'Presumably that's where the BMW pulled in,' Georgina said.

Diamond glanced over and said nothing, yet to be convinced.

Georgina added, 'The one car Danny was equipped to steal. He must have thought the gods were smiling on him.'

'If his story is true.'

'This is why I brought you here, to check the location and see if it fits in with what he had to say. Sitting here, I must say I can picture the events he described. It's exactly as he told us.'

'Is that surprising? He was talking about the place he lives in. This is his local.'

She smiled. 'So you don't dismiss everything he told us.'

'I'm willing to believe he lived here, yes. As for the rest of the story, the only thing we know for certain is that the BMW was nicked in Arundel the day before and was listed as stolen, which is why the patrol car stopped it.'

'Yes, we have independent evidence for that. Are you thinking it was Danny who stole the car in Arundel?'

He swirled his drink. 'It's the simple explanation.'

'In that case the driver in the hoodie and everything that's supposed to have happened here in Littlehampton would be a lie.'

He shrugged.

Georgina wanted it laid out more clearly. 'Why would he have concocted an elaborate story like that?'

'To put distance between himself and the murder.'

'Are you suggesting Danny is the killer as well as a car thief?'

'Impossible to say.' Playing his own words over in his head, he decided he was being a touch too rigid. 'On balance, it seems more likely he was brought in later as the disposal man. That would explain why he had the two grand in banknotes.'

'So when he was stopped, he was on his way to dump the body somewhere?'

'Well away from Arundel.'

Georgina plainly wasn't persuaded. 'At his trial, he didn't admit he had a minor role in the crime. He pleaded not guilty and denied all knowledge of it. If he'd cooperated, he would still have got the mandatory life sentence, but with a shorter term before being considered for release. Personally, I can't see him as the killer and I don't believe he knows the identity of whoever did it. These small-time criminals tend to stick to what they do. A car thief remains a car thief.'

'With rare exceptions,' Diamond said. He was keeping every option open.

The food arrived, sausages and mash for Diamond, lemon sole for Georgina. The big man's appetite was fully restored.

'Will Danny be told about the latest development – the DNA match?' he asked.

'Not yet.'

'And the niece?'

Georgina took a sharp breath as if she'd burnt her tongue. 'If he hears about her he'll take it as proof positive that we're corrupt.'

'He'll hear about it some way.'

'Not officially, not before we are certain it has some bearing on the case. All we know is that this young woman's hair was found in the car. There may be some innocent explanation none of us is aware of.' Georgina paused for inspiration. 'She could have travelled in the car as a passenger before it was stolen.'

'On a date with an eighty-year-old man?'

'Now you're being silly. Be serious, Peter.'

'OK. The presence of DNA doesn't prove anything.'

'Ah, but it might help to validate Danny's story. You pointed out yourself that the hooded youth he saw may have been female.'

'Has anyone questioned this young woman?'

She shook her head. 'She's gone missing.'

The last piece of sausage fell off his fork. 'Great! That's all we need. How recent is this?'

'She hasn't been seen for several weeks, according to Archie.'

'The niece of the senior investigating officer has done a runner? This gets worse. Hasn't any attempt been made to find her?'

'She's not a child any more. She may be travelling abroad.'

The drip, drip of information was getting to Diamond. At some point soon he would say so. For the present he suppressed his annoyance. 'I'm beginning to think we should take Danny's story more seriously.'

After they'd eaten, Georgina suggested a walk along the river bank towards the beach, but Diamond said he'd rather go over the footbridge. 'Let's see where the hoodie is supposed to have gone.'

They settled their bill. There was a general murmur of relief as they left the pub.

The river was wider than it appeared from the terrace. They'd walked over the metal bridge for half a minute before they were anywhere near the middle.

'This may be a sexist remark,' Diamond said, 'but I can't picture a young woman carrying a corpse all this way.'

'Come to that,' Georgina said, 'I can't picture your average young man managing it either. He'd need a helper – or a trolley. Even then it would be obvious what was happening.'

'I don't know about that. It's a quiet spot. We were the only people on the terrace while we were eating and I don't remember anyone coming by.'

'They wouldn't risk it in broad daylight.'

'Under cover of darkness they might.'

She gave a superior smile. 'It isn't only women who change their minds.'

'It's academic, isn't it? Even if Danny can be believed, the body didn't end up in the river. It didn't happen.'

But in his mind Diamond wasn't quite so dismissive. This *was* a quiet spot that might appeal to anyone wanting to get rid of evidence. Even now, at the height of day, nobody else was about, either on land or water.

'There isn't much room for boats passing underneath,' Georgina said, looking over. 'Anything with a mast would be in trouble.'

'The middle section rolls aside,' Diamond said. 'It's retractable. See the rails up ahead?'

'Now you mention them, I can. Do you want to go all the way across?'

She was inviting him to make the decisions, he noticed. This was no bad thing when he was used to giving orders. 'I wouldn't mind seeing what there is on the other bank. The hoodie was heading over there when last seen – so we were told.'

'Looks like a boatyard, some jetties and not much else,' Georgina said.

'I saw a car moving along there. Must be a road. Not sure where it leads. Let's find out.'

They reached the opposite bank and started along a narrow road between hedges.

'Desolate,' Georgina said. 'I can't think what he or she came here for, unless it was to meet someone.'

In a few hundred yards they came to some wooden buildings in a wire mesh fenced enclosure.

'The Arun Yacht Club,' Georgina read aloud from the sign outside. 'I imagine this is not your scene, Peter.'

'True.'

'But it's the only place the hoodie could have been making for if she turned in this direction.'

'If she existed.'

'Let's assume she did.'

'Well, I doubt if she was here for the sailing.'

They went through the gate. There was parking for cars at the back of the club buildings and mooring for boats at the front along the river bank, four pontoons with berths for about a hundred, enough to be called a marina.

'No use asking inside if anyone remembers her from seven years ago,' Georgina said.

A pretty obvious comment that he didn't bother to answer.

'I'm wondering why she came across the bridge at all,' she added.

'Leaving the car containing a body and two thousand pounds in cash and failing to double-check that it was locked. Yes, she had to be very careless or into some trickery I don't understand.'

'It was a risk.'

'A mistake.'

They were about to retrace their route to the bridge. Diamond hesitated. 'What if the plan wasn't to drop the body off the bridge? Wouldn't it be smarter to take it on a boat and get rid of it at sea?'

'That's the first intelligent observation you've made all day,' Georgina said. 'I do believe you're starting to function. Maybe she *was* here for the sailing.'

He'd come up with the theory, but he didn't like it. 'We'd need to find out if she can handle a sailing boat and if she had any connection with this place.'

'She could have stolen someone's dinghy. Well, borrowed it.'

'And sailed it over to the opposite bank and discovered the car was missing? It's all rather tenuous, ma'am.'

'I'm going to see if anyone is about.' Suddenly she was the boss again. She strode towards the clubhouse, with Diamond following.

Inside was a bar and lounge. A solitary drinker on a high stool turned to see who had come in.

'Good afternoon, we're police officers. Assistant Chief Constable Dallymore and DS Diamond.'

The man said, 'Pollux.'

'Well, really!'

'Yes, really.' He must have had the reaction many times before. 'Edward Pollux. Care for a drink?'

'Not at the present time. We're interested in a missing person, a young woman, who may have been a member of the club at some point.'

'Try me, then,' Pollux said. 'I've been a member twenty-three years. I've met just about everyone who came through those doors.'

'Mrs Jocelyn Green.'

The casual mention of a name he hadn't heard of was yet another rebuke for Diamond. How much more was Georgina keeping to herself?

'Sorry. Doesn't mean anything to me,' Pollux said. 'When was she supposed to have been here?'

'Seven years ago.'

'Do you have a picture?'

It wouldn't greatly have surprised Diamond if Georgina had produced one.

'Unfortunately, no. How is the security here? The boats, I mean. Is there any risk of someone stealing one?'

'Unlikely. We're not so vulnerable to casual visitors, being on this bank. It's the quiet side, as you'll have noticed. I was surprised to see you two walk in just now.'

'I expect it's busier at weekends.'

'True. Dinghy racing every Sunday through the summer.'

'At sea?'

'Oh yes. And there's an annual race upriver and back for the cup.'

'Upriver? Where to?' Diamond asked.

'The Black Rabbit at Arundel. They have lunch there and then come back.'

'Arundel? Is that far?'

'Half an hour, or less if you can handle a boat with any skill.'

'And with an outboard motor?'

Pollux gave him a pained look. 'We're a yacht club.'

Diamond was seething and not because of the put-down from Pollux. On the walk back he didn't trust himself to say anything until they'd almost reached the footbridge and then it was Georgina who cued the exchange that followed – and in a way that stoked his anger.

'Penny for them.'

'Mm?'

'Your thoughts. You haven't said a word since we left the club.'

'Isn't it bloody obvious?' he said. 'I'm not used to being treated like a ten-year-old.'

'Ah. You're in a strop because I knew the niece's name and hadn't told you. It hadn't come up. If it had meant anything I would have shared it with you. It's no big deal, Peter. You don't want to burst a blood vessel over something as trivial as that.'

He took a moment to contain himself. 'It isn't trivial. It's the name of someone involved in the case, someone who may turn out to be a suspect. I was entitled to be given her name.'

'You know it now.'

'I'll try and say this calmly, ma'am. If you and I are going to work together, there has to be respect between us. You outrank me, and I understand that. We've known each other a few years, long enough to tell that we're never going to be twin souls. But ours is a professional relationship, or should be.'

'Must be.'

'You asked me to work with you on this case. Your decision, and it's put an extra strain on that relationship. Back in Bath you give me the freedom to run CID in my own way. Here, with the two of us, I'm tagging along like Dr Watson.'

'That isn't remotely true,' she said. 'Let me remind you it was your decision to cross the bridge. I was all for a gentle walk along the promenade.'

A fact he couldn't deny. No point now in trading blows, reminding her that she had made the major decisions of the day, to visit Danny Stapleton in the prison and then drive out to Littlehampton.

'I've encouraged you to give your opinion and we've had some useful exchanges,' she said. 'I wouldn't call that "tagging along". My impression of Dr Watson is that he spent much of his time being awestruck by his companion's intellect. I haven't noticed much of that going on.'

He stared ahead, not trusting himself to speak.

'Have you had your say, because I'd like to raise a couple of matters myself?'

'Go ahead.' He was losing this battle of wills.

And now Georgina chose to play the card that always defeated him: the helpless woman. 'It isn't easy for me, dealing with someone of your force of personality. If I appear to pull rank sometimes, it's for my own survival. You can be a tidal wave at times. I've seen it often and stood back. Fortunately you aren't as destructive as a tidal wave, but you're very alarming, more so than you realise. I'd like to reach an understanding in the days to come. I didn't rise to assistant chief constable by sitting behind a desk fretting over the crime figures, as you mainly see me. I do have a human side. I want this investigation to be a partnership.'

'So do I, ma'am.'

'If you're serious about that, you can stop calling me "ma'am" – at least while we're alone. I won't insist you use my Christian name, but you may if you wish. In my family, I'm known as Georgie.'

His stomach clenched.

'I want to be comfortable with you, Peter.'

'Suits me.' He couldn't yet bring himself to call her Georgina, let alone Georgie.

This had become a heart-to-heart now. 'In the car yesterday, when I called you my secret weapon, I could tell it embarrassed you.'

'Surprised me, anyway.'

'I was more than a little on edge myself, trying to cut through the formality. The talk about sharing a room didn't come out as I intended. I wouldn't want you to think of me as a predatory female.'

'I wouldn't want it either.'

'The fact that you spoke just now about our relationship isn't going to throw me off kilter. We both know what you meant.'

'Of course.'

'We can work together without that kind of nonsense.'

'Absolutely.'

'Doesn't mean we aren't normal human beings, of course.'

'Goes without saying.' He walked a little faster. They were

both walking noticeably faster. They'd reached the foot-bridge and were more than halfway across. They'd soon be back at the car with their driver, who Diamond was begin-ning to think of as his chaperon.

'So let's both make an effort, shall we?'

'Right. Where do you suggest we go next?' He was tempted to add, 'Your place or mine?' but he couldn't risk the joke.

# 10

They returned to Chichester to read the file on the Joe Rigden murder. It couldn't be shirked. Georgina's knowledge was second-hand – from her college friend, Archie Hahn, in that moonlit stroll along West Wittering beach – and Diamond's was third-hand. He hated being under-informed. The original witness statements would give them both a better grasp. Georgina saw the sense in it. And there was another factor neither of them mentioned: they were at screaming point from being together so long.

In the circumstances, they didn't expect a warm welcome at the police station and it wasn't given.

'We were warned to expect you,' the desk sergeant said as if they were the flu virus. 'I'll tell them in CID.'

They were kept waiting ten minutes. 'This isn't good enough,' Georgina said loudly enough to be heard.

A young woman in plain clothes finally appeared and asked to see their IDs.

'We already produced them,' Georgina said. 'Who are you?'

'Pat Gomez.'

'Pat Gomez, *ma'am*. And we don't need to know your given name. Rank?'

'I'm on the civilian staff, ma'am.'

Pat Gomez showed them upstairs into a CID office not

unlike their own in Bath except that the faces looking up from computer screens might just have sucked lemons.

'Who's in charge here?'

Pat Gomez pointed to an open door.

They crossed the room and stepped inside. The bearded man on the phone behind the large desk continued talking into it and didn't even make eye contact.

'This is too much,' Georgina told Diamond.

'I wouldn't make an issue of it, ma'am.' Hearing a click from her tongue, he remembered too late that for him, at least, 'ma'am' was no longer protocol. Instead of calming her down, he'd added to her annoyance.

Georgina looked to be on the point of snatching that phone and jumping on it.

The call came to an end. 'We're short-staffed and busy,' the bearded man said. 'I take it you're the Bath contingent.'

'And what are you?' Georgina asked as if he was the lowest level of pond life.

'DI Montacute, currently running this department as a stopgap.'

'Standing in for the DCI?'

'Regrettably, yes.'

Georgina made a performance of introducing herself and Diamond. All it lacked was a twenty-one-gun salute. 'So in future when you speak to me, I expect to be addressed as "ma'am". We'll begin by examining the file on the Rigden murder from 2007.'

'I'll see if it's available . . . ma'am.'

'Why wouldn't it be?'

'It's been in Malling House for some weeks.'

'Where on earth is that?'

'Lewes. Sussex police headquarters. They took the decisions

over this. Actually we must have made a photocopy before sending it off.' He spoke into an intercom, then nodded. 'No problem. The original is back.'

Georgina said they would need the spare copy as well. They were offered the use of a stationery store as their base. She was outraged.

'Haven't you got anything better than that?'

Montacute shook his head. 'Like I said, ma'am, we're fully stretched. The briefing room is doubling up as an incident room for a murder inquiry and the interview rooms are constantly in use. It's been non-stop for weeks.'

They were shown the storeroom. Chairs could be brought in, they were told, and more space created by restacking boxes of envelopes. Georgina wasn't having it. 'There isn't even a window,' she said to Diamond. 'It's a glorified cupboard, that's all it is. We're being treated as pariahs because of what we're here for. I don't accept all this talk of being run off their feet. Have a look round and find us somewhere more suitable.'

He didn't fancy touring the corridors opening doors, so he had a quiet word with a uniformed sergeant he saw coming up the stairs. There really was pressure on rooms, he learned. A spate of serious crimes in recent weeks meant that resources were stretched to the limit.

'Leave it to me,' Georgina said, when told. She was in no mood to cave in.

She marched into Montacute's office. 'Are you overseeing the murder investigation as well?'

'I'm not the SIO, ma'am, but I see it as my responsibility to keep up with it, if that's what you're asking.'

'As well as these other serious crimes I'm hearing about?'

'Well, yes.'

'Multitasking?'

'Absolutely.'

94

'In that case, you can't be sitting behind a desk all day. That's no way to keep up.'

'Oh I'm on my feet a lot, ma'am. Anyone here will vouch for that.'

'As I thought. You're peripatetic. This office is under-used. We'll move a couple of extra desks in and make this our base.'

'You can't do that.'

'Of course we can't. I wasn't speaking literally. Get a couple of your team to shift the furniture. If you've got a problem with it, speak to Commander Hahn at headquarters. He'll want us treated right. We're doing you people a favour, coming here and taking on your little local difficulty. We'd like tea and biscuits as well.'

Georgina at her unstoppable best. Diamond almost felt proud.

They didn't take long to get installed. DI Montacute cleared his desk without another word and migrated somewhere else. Tactfully they avoided asking if it was the stationery store.

The desk beside the window with the view of the canal basin was claimed by Georgina. Diamond would be facing a wall on the far side of the room, but he didn't mind.

The case file and its duplicate were wheeled in on a trolley by Pat Gomez while they were finishing their tea. CID work had still been largely supported by paper records back in 2007. Diamond was given the bulkier of the two – three box-files of material – and it turned out to be the original. Enough reading to take care of the rest of this day and the next. Fortunately, whoever had dealt with all the documents had done an excellent job of arranging them by date and indexing them. Occurrence reports, witness statements, diagrams, photos, everything was so methodically sorted that you could be forgiven for thinking the case was solved and the killer sent down.

He supposed he should have started with the earliest stuff and worked through, but he couldn't resist looking at the most recent. Right on top was a handwritten note that caught his attention because it was headed *ACC Dallymore, Avon & Somerset*. It was on Sussex police headquarters notepaper.

A note for Georgina?

No, it was *about* Georgina.

Unlike everything else, it wasn't referenced or indexed. Someone must have received this private note and carelessly left it in the box. The paper looked and felt fresh, as if it had been written recently.

He glanced over his shoulder at Georgina. She had her glasses on and was already reading.

If the note had been written at headquarters in the last few days, it wouldn't be among the papers in front of her – which was just as well.

My recommendation is Dallymore. Many moons ago I went through Bramshill with her and she ended up in Bath as ACC crime management. Did all the right things, learned the drill, kept her buttons and shoes clean and never rocked the boat. Politically sound. Doesn't have a subversive thought in her head. If – heaven forbid – anything more damaging should emerge, we can rely on her to miss it altogether, or, at worst, bury it. What's more we can argue that being a woman she's the ideal choice for this one.

It was initialled in ink, AH. With friends like Archie Hahn, who needs enemies?

Diamond folded the note and put it in his pocket. He hadn't often felt sympathy for Georgina, but he did over this. She must never see it.

He couldn't fault the character sketch, but, as written down by her supposed old chum, it was a betrayal. If anything more damaging *did* emerge, he would make damn sure it wasn't missed or buried. The one point that intrigued him was the last. Why was a woman the ideal choice? Pure prejudice? The idea that women were put on this earth to rock the cradle and never to rock the boat?

Grinding his teeth, he turned to the earliest material, the statements by the officers who had stopped the stolen BMW that September evening in 2007 and found the body in the boot. Their accounts chimed with what he had learned from Georgina and Danny Stapleton himself.

At 9.43 pm, along the A259 approaching the Bognor Road roundabout, we spotted a car reported as stolen in Arundel the previous day. It was being driven by a male who identified himself as Daniel Stapleton. We searched him and found a large amount of money in banknotes stuffed into his pockets and socks. His explanation was that he'd sold a boat in Littlehampton and was on his way to Chichester for a night out. We then lifted the lid of the boot and discovered a dead body contained in a garden sack.

One of the statements added:

The suspect appeared to panic and insisted he had not looked inside the boot and had no knowledge of the contents and was unable to explain how the body got in there. He was cautioned and arrested and after we had radiocd for assistance he was taken to Chichester police station.

A signed statement from Danny the next day struck a different note, starting with the admission that he had lied to the arresting officers. He now claimed that half an hour before his arrest he had stolen the car from River Road in Littlehampton using an electronic jammer and a key programmer.

> The BMW was parked opposite the Steam Packet by a youth wearing a hooded garment, who then proceeded across the footbridge. I was unable get a close look at him. He was slight in build and appeared to have the movement of a young person.

The wording was unmistakable police-speak, but there was nothing sinister in that if the facts were essentially true and Danny had checked them and signed the thing. Faced with a statement form, many witnesses suffer from writer's block and need prompting.

Usefully, the next page was a transcript of the taped interview and Danny's authentic voice came through:

Q. Why did you lie about the money?
A. I was bricking it, wasn't I?
Q. Scared? Scared of what would happen when the boot was opened?
A. No, mate. I didn't know about that.
Q. You're lying again, aren't you? You knew the body was in there because you put it there. You were in deep trouble. That's what scared you.
A. Honest, I was as shocked as they was.
Q. You were shocked at being caught red-handed. You'd already shot the man through the head and robbed him. Then you had to get rid of the body, so you stole the BMW in Arundel—
A. Arundel? Did you say Arundel? No, you're wrong there. It was LA.
Q. Danny, this isn't funny. A man has been murdered.

A. LA – Littlehampton.

Q. The murder took place in Littlehampton? Is that what you're telling us?

A. No, that's where I nicked the car.

Q. Untrue. You've got to do better than this. It was definitely taken from the Mill Road car park in Arundel, opposite the castle.

A. Wrong. I know where I was.

Q. The car was reported stolen from Arundel. It's a fact. It's on record. That's why you were stopped.

A. Now you're confusing me.

Q. If you tell lies, you're going to get caught out. Let's have the truth of it.

A. I'm giving it to you. I don't understand what you're on about.

Q. Murder, that's what we're on about. When you were stopped you were on your way to dump the body some-where. Where were you taking it – the reservoir at Westhampnett? You were heading that way.

A. I wouldn't do that.

Q. You had other plans? Were you just going to leave it somewhere in the stolen car and hope it wouldn't be traced to you?

A. Jesus Christ, I'm saying I never killed this geezer. You got to believe me. I never touched him.

Q. You touched his money. Your prints are all over it. And you might as well know your prints are on the sack the body was wrapped in.

A. Oh shit. (Long pause.) That's because the cops in the car told me to drag the sack to the front of the boot so they could see who it was.

Q. They didn't say anything about that in their statements. You're at it again, aren't you – making it up as you go along? It's not clever, Danny. You keep tripping yourself up. Much better to front up and tell us what really happened.

A. I already told you.

Q. All that Littlehampton crap? You cooked a story up overnight to try and confuse us, but it hasn't worked. The car was stolen from Arundel. That's where the owner left it. All our patrols were notified the day before yesterday. You should have changed the plates.

A. I tried. I was too late.

Q. Well, that sounds like an honest admission at last.

A. I mean I was on my way to a plates man in Chichester when I was stopped. I told you about him.

Q. And we checked and there's no one called Stew on the trading estate.

A. He's not going to have a board with his name, is he? He's in a dodgy trade.

Q. He isn't there. He doesn't exist. Just imagine trying to get this story of yours past a prosecution lawyer. He'd eat you up.

Diamond flicked through more pages and found photos of the BMW and the body in the boot. Easy to understand the horrified reactions of the officers. You stop a stolen car and routinely open the boot and are faced with a sight like this. The wound to the head looked hideous: a bullet hole in front of the left ear and an exit wound that had blown a gaping hole the other side big enough for most of the brain to have been shot away. Yet the face was unblemished. As sometimes occurs after a shooting, the victim appeared serene, eyes closed, mouth slightly open and without strain.

A set of pictures from the autopsy was included, but Diamond had seen as much as he could take.

There were also mugshots of Danny looking bewildered, mouth in a tiny o and eyebrows arching. He had a God-given talent for appearing wide-eyed and misunderstood. In the same document sleeve were some more youthful photos projecting even more innocence. They must have been taken years earlier when he was caught stealing cars. Same expression, except he'd put on weight since then.

Various forensic reports stacked up more evidence implicating Danny. The tools of his trade, the jammer and the programmer, had been found in a carrier under the passenger seat, marked with his fingerprints and DNA. He had definitely handled the banknotes and the sack the body had been contained in.

The autopsy report confirmed the obvious – that the victim had died from a gunshot close to the head. No other injuries were found.

Diamond's grasp of events was being helped by the methodical filing by date. A full two weeks had passed before the dead man was identified. Meanwhile Danny had been in custody, charged with stealing the car. The more serious charge had waited while more evidence had been gathered.

The focus shifted to the South Downs village of Slindon after Joe Rigden was reported missing and duly confirmed as the victim. The reports showed that Rigden's isolated cottage had been searched and photographed, but no signs of violence or a break-in were found there and none of his property seemed to be missing.

A thick sheaf of statements showed how extensive the interviewing had been in Slindon. The murdered man had been well known locally and seemed to have led a blameless life earning an honest living. His skills as a self-employed gardener were appreciated and he wasn't short of work. Statements had been collected from the people he worked for and they read like testimonials. *Reliable and knowledgeable . . . often worked long past the time he was paid for . . . came in all weathers . . . brought his own tools . . . got rid of the moles that were ruining my lawn . . . advised me on my roses and came with me to pick the best specimens at the garden centre . . . I trusted him absolutely.*

Three weeks in, the detectives working on the murder had held a case review. Reading between the lines, they were frustrated by the lack of information. The investigation was hampered by the absence of any obvious motive. The early suspicions that Danny had killed for the two thousand pounds had been scaled down when it became clear that the money couldn't have been Rigden's. The gardener banked his earnings regularly on Saturdays and his bank statements confirmed he hadn't made any large withdrawals in the last three years. You might have expected a self-employed man paid in cash to have salted some of it away and avoided paying tax. Not so Joe Rigden. He kept accounts and was almost unbelievably straight with the inland revenue. Even his tips were declared. There was little chance that he had a large amount of cash in his house or on his person waiting to be stolen.

A month into the investigation, Chichester CID were forced to conclude that Danny had not acted alone and was not the prime mover in the murder, but an accessory. The money appeared to have been his payment for disposing of the dead body in a way that wouldn't connect the killer to the crime. As a professional car thief, he had been hired to steal a vehicle and either dump the body in some remote place or leave it to be discovered in the abandoned car. Unluckily for him, he had been caught.

The case against Danny as a paid accessory was always more likely to succeed than charging him as the killer. Substantial efforts were made to pinpoint the main perpetrator. Danny was repeatedly questioned and continued to deny all knowledge of the murder. He couldn't deny being in possession of the money and being caught with the body in the stolen car. And he was a self-confessed liar.

The Crown Prosecution Service took on the case and eventually it came to trial. Reading the summary, Diamond concluded that Danny had done himself no service by pleading not guilty and denying almost everything. The judge had come to the view that this habitual criminal knew the identity of the killer and was shielding him from justice. After a summing up stressing that the killing bore all the hallmarks of professional involvement and that Danny's part in it was for financial gain, a unanimous verdict of guilty was returned by the jury. The life sentence came with a minimum term of ten years before he could be considered for release.

If Danny's conviction drew a line under the case, it was only a dotted line. The team were conscious that the main man was still at liberty and reviews were held periodically, but each time they came back to the unanswerable question: why would anyone want to kill a popular working man who had never been involved in anything underhand? Without a motive they were hamstrung.

'How far have you got?'

Diamond was so immersed that he took a moment to register that Georgina had spoken. 'Ah. I'm up to the trial.'

'We've been here almost two hours. I'm starting to skip things and I shouldn't. I say we need a break.'

'Can't disagree.'

'I'll phone Pat Gomez and ask her for some tea.'

'Mine didn't taste too good. I don't know what they put in it. Fresh air would suit me better.'

'I can see the canal basin from here,' Georgina said. 'People are walking there and there's a café of some sort with tables outside.'

They found that the Canal Trust had its own shop and the tea was drinkable. Apart from a family of swans, there wasn't much activity on the water, but the path around it was ideal for a stroll and the locals were taking advantage of a fine afternoon. A group of schoolchildren had taken over a bench. There were cyclists and anglers.

'I'm not too impressed by these CID people,' Georgina said. 'Barely civil, don't you think?'

'I can understand how they feel, their regular boss suspended and a jerk like Montacute in charge. There were some grins when you turfed him out of the office.'

'I missed that.'

'And one of them must be the whistle-blower. There are going to be tensions in the team.'

'So you think the anonymous letter came from an insider?'

'Don't you? It was sent from here. It had to be someone in the know.'

'I expect you're right,' Georgina said. 'Yes, it would put everyone under strain.'

'Were you shown the letter?'

She flushed a shade deeper. 'I was told what it had to say. Brief and to the point, I gather.'

'You haven't seen it yourself, then?'

'I don't think anyone disputes the accuracy of it.'

'The SIO's career is at stake and we've been asked to investigate. I would say we have a duty to look at it.'

'Peter, we're not investigating the whistle-blower.'

'That isn't my point. This is evidence. We'd be negligent if we didn't ask to see it.'

She sighed. 'You're right. I'll speak to Archie.' She took out her phone.

When she got through, she got up from her chair and moved away from Diamond, along the towpath. A private call.

She soon returned and said, 'It's being sent by messenger. We'll get it before we leave.'

After that small victory, Diamond waited a few moments before saying, 'Up to now I haven't asked the name of this unfortunate SIO.'

'That's true.'

He waited and got nothing more and finally said, 'Who is he, then?'

'It's a woman, a DCI Henrietta Mallin.'

# 11

His thoughts were spinning like electrons, but he stayed silent and appeared unmoved.

He wasn't giving Georgina the satisfaction of seeing the shock she'd just delivered.

Ten years and more had gone by since he had worked with Hen Mallin on a case involving a Bath woman murdered on Wightview Sands, a south coast beach. The short, cigarillo-smoking DI from Bognor had been lively company on a complex, demanding investigation. Any woman heading a CID team had to be tough and vocal, and Hen was. Given a hard time when she was a rookie – more than her share of dangerous dogs, delinquent teenagers, abusive men and over-ripe corpses – she'd come through and risen in the ranks. With Diamond she'd formed an unlikely bond. He'd learned early on that she lived alone, a status that had been recently and painfully forced on him, and her strength of character had been an inspiration.

He couldn't believe Hen was the corrupt SIO.

Gulls were swooping over the canal, screaming a soundtrack to the mayhem in his brain.

'Yes, a woman,' Georgina added. 'Believe it or not, my half of the human race is as capable as yours of going wrong.'

She had misread his silence.

'Of course,' she went on, 'it pains me to investigate one

of my own sex who has reached high rank and misbehaved, but that won't put me off. Whoever she is, she needn't expect any favours from me.'

*Whoever she is?*

She was talking as if Hen was a stranger. What's going on here, Diamond asked himself. Surely she remembers.

He made a huge effort to get his brain functioning as it should, to recall that summer of 2003. Georgina had been in the job for sure. She was well established as the ACC by then. She liked to keep tabs on every investigation. She must have known about Hen. No one could forget a character like that. Hen had come to Bath at least once. He remembered questioning a suspect with her.

But had the two actually met?

Any conceivable reason why they hadn't?

A memory popped up, something to do with a cat.

A *cat?*

A cat called Sultan.

Georgina on the point of taking time off to go on a Nile cruise, all her thoughts focused on Egypt – except for the problem of what to do with her long-haired cat, Sultan. Diamond had come to her aid by finding her a house-sitter and – sod's law – Anna, the house sitter, had been allergic to cats. He'd ended up taking Sultan home.

By the time Georgina had returned from her cruise, the case was closed and Hen had gone back to Sussex.

So this wasn't loss of memory. She and Hen had never met.

Now she was filling the silence again. 'I didn't think you'd have a problem dealing with a woman under suspension.'

'I don't.'

'That's all right, then.' She smiled in a superior way.

But it wasn't all right. It was all wrong. He should declare an interest and extract himself from this mess.

He couldn't. He had a mental picture of Hen, her career in ruins, forced out of the job she loved and now about to be put on the rack by Georgina. Two formidable women. If each had the effect on the other he expected, Hen could only suffer more.

She needed support.

But was he the right person to supply it? How would she react to having him around at this low point in her career? She might take it as more humiliation than she could bear. He knew how *he* would feel. In time of trouble, he'd rather go to strangers than friends.

He could back off and be home tonight.

Except that he'd seen what Archie Hahn had written about Georgina. *'If – heaven forbid – anything more damaging should emerge, we can rely on her to miss it altogether, or, at worst, bury it.'*

Cruel, but true. Left to manage alone, Georgina would rubber-stamp everything headquarters had decided.

'Where does she live?'

'Chichester, I was told.'

'When do you want to see her?'

'Tomorrow.'

'At home?'

'It has to be. She's banned from the police station.'

'Better get someone to phone and let her know.'

They returned to their task of going through the files.

The anonymous letter was delivered by a despatch rider under instructions to hand it to ACC Dallymore in person and then return with it to headquarters.

Georgina opened the envelope and read what was inside before handing it to Diamond.

The message had been produced on standard A4 paper on a printer. It had been rubber-stamped *Sussex Police*

*Headquarters.* Someone had added a note and initials: *Received by post 3/8/14 . Chichester postmark dated 2/8/14 .* The initials were familiar: *AH*.

WITH REFERENCE TO THE MURDER OF JOSEPH RIGDEN IN 2007, A DNA SAMPLE TAKEN IN 2011 FROM A DRUNK AND DISORDERLY WOMAN, MRS JOCELYN GREEN, WAS CHECKED WITH THE NATIONAL DATABASE AND FOUND TO MATCH TRACES OF FEMALE DNA RECOVERED FROM THE CAR USED TO TRANSPORT RIGDEN'S BODY. THE MATCH WAS NOTIFIED TO THE SENIOR INVESTIGATING OFFICER, DCI MALLIN, CHICHESTER POLICE, AND NO ACTION WAS TAKEN. A MAN IS CURRENTLY SERVING A LIFE SENTENCE AS AN ACCESSORY TO THE MURDER. HE CLAIMS TO BE INNOCENT. JOCELYN GREEN IS THE NIECE OF DCI MALLIN.

'Pretty damning, wouldn't you say?' Georgina said.

'This is accurate?'

'That's why DCI Mallin is suspended and we're here.'

'Quite a professional job,' he said, trying to sound unmoved. 'Lays out the facts without any emotion, unlike other anonymous letters I've come across. I'm glad we've seen it. I'll photocopy it.'

Georgina took a sharp breath. 'I don't think we're entitled to do that.'

'No one said we can't. We may need to refer to it.'

'The rider is waiting to return it to headquarters.'

'He can carry on waiting.'

'That isn't what I'm saying, Peter. We saw this on the understanding that it was for our eyes only. Archie won't want us making a spare copy.'

Archie could go to hell, but he didn't say so. 'I'm not

going to show it to anyone. We've been asked to do a job, ma'am. They must trust us. Sorry about the "ma'am". It slipped out.' He crossed the room to the machine that served as printer, copier and scanner. 'Any idea how this thing works?'

If you want to be a Mr Fixit in the twenty-first century, it helps to be computer-literate.

Georgina sighed heavily, joined him and showed him how. Even so, it was a significant moment in their partnership. They made the photocopy and he folded it and put it in his pocket with Archie's damning note about Georgina. Then he sealed the original in an envelope addressed to Commander A. Hahn and handed it to the despatch rider.

Soon after, they finished reading the files and walked back to their hotel.

'Shall we meet for a meal in an hour or so?' Diamond said when they got there.

'I think not,' Georgina said. 'I've developed a headache. I'll have room service.'

She can't take any more of me, he thought with satisfaction. I'll find a pub that serves pie and chips.

# 12

Hen Mallin had a flat in a modern block near the Hornet, only a short walk from where they were staying. She wasn't the sort to be intimidated by senior officers, but she was likely to be keyed up. Difficult to predict how the session would go. At least she would be on home territory.

Stepping along a busy road that ran beside the ancient city wall, Diamond asked Georgina, 'How's your head this morning?'

'Why?'

'You weren't feeling so good last night.'

'I'm perfectly fit, thank you,' she said with a firmness that closed that avenue. 'I've decided it will be wise if you leave the questioning to me when we meet this woman.'

'Suits me.' He'd got the message. The skirmish over the photocopying had shaken the boss. She was nervous he would take over. And what a temptation it was to say she could do the whole shebang without him, but that would have been a cop-out. He needed to be there for Hen's sake.

'If I invite you to speak for any reason, I won't mind if you address me as "ma'am" in this situation.'

'Fine.' But he had to stop his stomach muscles twitching with amusement.

She added, 'I'm still agreeable to relaxing the modes of address when we're off duty.'

'Me, too.' Relaxing the modes of address – an expression

111

to savour. The old devilry made him add, 'Is it Georgina, Georgie or George?'

She almost tripped over her own feet. 'Is what?'

'What you'd really like to be called.'

She turned to look at him, eyes the size of sunflowers. 'I wasn't insisting you use my first name. On reflection I think I prefer nothing at all. Your "ma'am" sometimes comes over as insincere. But there's no need to go to the other extreme, absolutely no need.'

'That's OK, then.'

'It cuts both ways. If you don't like me using your first name from time to time, I won't.'

'You always have. It doesn't bother me. I'd draw the line at Pete.' And then the game became more serious as he remembered that Hen used to call him a variety of names from sport to sweetie and he'd found them all amusing. What on earth would she call him when he turned up at her front door after ten years? He didn't want Georgina finding out they were old buddies. A strategy was needed here. 'You did let this woman know we're coming? Is she expecting two of us?'

'I forget what I said. It doesn't matter.'

'You wouldn't have mentioned me by name?'

'Why should I? We'll introduce ourselves when we get there.'

They had to go upstairs to the top of the three-storey red-brick building and along an open passageway. And now the strategy came into play. Diamond made sure he was well to the rear when the door opened. Unseen by Georgina, he put a finger to his lips.

Hen must have seen the signal, but she still looked startled. Who wouldn't? Her reaction could be passed off as nerves, he decided. The main thing was that she didn't make it clear she knew him.

Georgina was going through the usual performance of

introducing herself. 'And this is my colleague, Detective Superintendent Diamond.'

The finger on the lips seemed to have worked. Hen had always been quick on the uptake. She nodded and asked them to come in.

Careworn, for sure. Easy to understand why she appeared more solemn than he'd ever seen her. Some silver hairs among the brown, but otherwise she appeared unaltered, small, stocky, with dark intelligent eyes. No obvious make-up. Black top and dark red pants.

Coffee was offered and declined. They were shown into a small, comfortably furnished living room smelling faintly of air freshener. Diamond chose a low armchair set back a little from Georgina. To his right was a bookcase filled with boxed CDs, all Poirot and Miss Marple, Hen's means of escape. She'd had them as tapes when he'd last met her. The technology moves on, but old favourites are for ever.

Georgina continued to set out her stall. 'You understand why we're here, I'm sure. We came by invitation because we are sure to have a different perspective on what has happened than your colleagues in Sussex. We've studied the file on the Rigden murder, so we know the essential facts and now we'd like to hear from you.'

Hen answered in a flat, resigned voice Diamond hardly recognised. 'I said it all before to Commander Hahn. I can't think what else you expect me to say. I messed up and got caught out. If you've looked at the file you'll know Joss – Jocelyn Green – is my niece and I should have pulled her in for questioning and didn't.'

'But why not?'

'She's family, that's why. My brother Barry's only daughter and a tearaway, you might say, but not a killer.' She hesitated, as if expecting to be challenged. 'The thing is, there was a falling-out over our father's will and Barry and I haven't spoken for almost twenty years. Daft, but that's how we are. I talk to my two sisters. They're older than me, incidentally, and thought I was crazy joining the police. Maybe I was, seeing how it all turned out. Anyway, I hear from my sisters what goes on in Barry's family. He's had trouble from Joss in spades. Do you need to hear this?'

'Certainly.'

'It's a wretched tale. She was a brilliant child who should have gone to university. Marvellous with computers and found she could earn a small fortune as an IT consultant, so quit school at sixteen and set up her own business. Word soon got around that Joss could speed up a system or find shortcuts that meant major profits for people. She was hugely in demand, visiting businesses or private homes. It was her kick, her whole existence. Unfortunately, it all happened too suddenly. She wasn't at all streetwise. The poor kid made a disastrous marriage to a city type when she was only nineteen that lasted about six weeks. This jackal got her into Class A drugs and messed up her head and her career and cost Barry a small fortune for the divorce. She was weaned off the drugs at more expense – one of those posh clinics – and took to drink instead. I suppose she's an addictive personality. Amazingly she avoided getting arrested until she was twenty-two. Then she got into some stupid fight outside a club in Portsmouth with another drunk woman. She was nicked, had her DNA taken and when it was put on the national database it matched the female DNA from the BMW that featured in the Rigden murder.'

'An enormous shock for you, I'm sure,' Georgina said in a rare eruption of empathy.

Hen gave a nod. 'Mind if I light up?'

'I beg your pardon?'

She mimed using a cigarette. 'I'm an addict, too. A family failing.'

114

Georgina paused for thought, then: 'It's your home. I don't see that we can stop you.'

Hen reached for the packet on the display unit beside her.

'Cigars?' Georgina said in disbelief.

'I don't inhale.'

'Everyone does, whether they're smokers or not.'

'Not what I meant.' Hen used a lighter and got the thing going. 'They last seven minutes. You said the news of Joss's arrest must have come as a shock.'

'I meant the DNA match.'

'Like being hit by a wrecking ball. I went through all the phases you do. Shock, disbelief, denial. Because of the family rift I hadn't seen her since she was a sweet little kid in a pink chiffon dress. She would have been eighteen when Rigden was murdered. I knew she went off the rails about that time, but nothing I'd heard from my sisters led me to believe she was involved in serious crime. My niece, my po-faced brother's genius daughter, caught up in a murder? It was unthinkable.'

'Did you tell anyone?'

'She's my own flesh and blood. You don't, do you? It was fortunate in a way that by the time the DNA thing came up she'd married and no longer shared a surname with me. My team didn't make the connection. But I still couldn't win. If I pulled her in, it would seem to my brother I was doing it out of spite.'

'Wasn't she already under arrest for being drunk and disorderly?'

'Portsmouth police kept both women in the cells to sober up and didn't charge them. First time up, it would have been hard. She got the usual caution. But of course she'd been arrested so she was in the system. I kept telling myself the only explanation for the DNA must be that she'd travelled in the BMW before it was stolen.'

'Was she a driver at the time?'

'I didn't really want to find out, but I made a computer check and she was, under her maiden name. She took the test as soon as she was old enough. A car was vital for her IT business. Yes, it's not impossible she drove the thing.'

'So she could have been the hooded driver allegedly seen by Danny Stapleton, the man now serving a prison sentence?'

A long pause. 'That's an unlikely scenario.'

'Is there another?'

'I just said it. She was in the car previously, for some unrelated reason.'

Georgina didn't disguise her scorn. 'A car owned by a man in his eighties? She was how old – eighteen? If you can think of a plausible explanation, I'd like to hear it. Did you interview the old man?'

'I thought about doing it. Discovered he was dead. He went within a year of the murder.'

'Did you speak to your niece? That was the obvious thing.'

She shook her head and said, tight-lipped, 'I took the decision not to pursue the matter.'

The crux of Hen's professional misconduct.

'On what grounds?'

'That there wasn't enough evidence to justify reopening the case. Nothing to suggest a link between the victim – a jobbing gardener who was a model citizen by all accounts – and my niece, who was a troubled teenager, but with no violence.'

'What do you mean – no violence? She was arrested for street-fighting.'

'I'm speaking of when she was eighteen.'

'But you didn't know her at eighteen. You hadn't seen her since she was a child.' Georgina folded her arms as if she'd made a telling point.

'I knew a lot about her. I was proud of her achievements.

My sisters kept me informed. She's a stunning redhead, and it's natural. As I just told you, Joss was a success, with a business of her own, lively, a bit naïve, but not evil.'

'Into drugs and alcohol.'

'The alcohol came later. We're talking about when she was still a teenager, before she married.'

'Just drugs, then,' Georgina said. 'As you well know, drug-dependent people resort to criminality to pay for their habit.'

'She had no police record at that time.'

'You know she's gone missing – just when we need to speak to her?'

'I do.' Hen's mouth tightened.

'She's evading arrest,' Georgina said.

'That isn't certain.' More puffs at the cigarillo. 'Listen, there's more than one way of looking at this. If Joss hadn't been my niece and I'd chosen to do nothing I don't suppose anyone would have got excited about it. I admit I ought to have followed up on the DNA match, particularly as she was a family member. When there's a personal link like that, there's even more reason to investigate properly.'

'We can agree on that,' Georgina said. 'You seem to be saying you disbelieved the new evidence regardless of who the suspect was.'

Hen drew in more smoke, thinking hard, then exhaled. 'Difficult to say for sure. I took it damn seriously, knowing she was Joss. And yet . . .'

'And yet what?'

'Put it this way: the only testimony we have for the hooded driver came from Danny Stapleton, a proven liar, who was convicted as an accessory, and he didn't once raise the possibility that this had been a woman. The judge and jury at his trial accepted the prosecution case that he was paid two thousand pounds by the killer to steal the car in Arundel and transport the body somewhere and dispose of it. Unless

Danny was wrongly convicted, I can't see where Joss or any other woman comes into it. So, yes, I chose to ignore the DNA as having no direct bearing on the case.'

'We spoke to Stapleton in prison yesterday,' Georgina said. 'He maintains he's innocent. He could have been out by now if he'd pleaded guilty and cooperated. If it turns out he *was* wrongly imprisoned, he may be planning to sue.'

Diamond had watched the to and fro of the interrogation. There was no question that Hen had been hit hard by this suspension. Ten years ago she would have given back as much as she took, and more. He wished he could find some way of letting her know that he still valued her, regardless of the issue.

She was drawing at the small cigar every few seconds and not much of it was left. Seven minutes would be an overestimate. She locked eyes with Georgina again. 'I suppose it's no use saying we were under extra pressure when the DNA report reached me?'

'Why?'

'All the missing people.'

'I don't follow you.'

'Haven't they told you? It's an ongoing thing. We've had this problem for months, if not years. A series of disappearances that can't be explained. You're going to tell me every police service has its list of missing persons. All over the country thousands of cases are reported. Believe me, these are different. We isolated as many as eight cases in the past four years where the victims were almost certainly murdered and their bodies never found. It's so prevalent in our part of Sussex that I asked my people to investigate and the scale of the problem became even more clear. I believe someone has set up a business disposing of bodies. There are hints in the criminal world that something like this is going on, but no one will say for sure.'

'A rogue undertaker?'

'We thought of that, of course, but it's unlikely. The official process of burial and cremation has too many safeguards written into it. This is organised crime. And the point of telling you is that it preoccupied me at the time the DNA details reached me. We'd had another peculiar case that same week. An obvious crime committed against someone who then disappeared. I was sure he was murdered and the trail was still hot. The last thing I needed was the news that Joss was in serious trouble.'

'In short, you're pleading pressure of work?'

Hen's lips tightened. 'I'm telling you how it was, not excusing myself.'

Georgina puffed herself up for one of her pious outpourings. 'We've all worked under extreme pressure, DCI Mallin. It's part of our job as police officers.'

Hen didn't bother to answer.

'You took no action. You didn't even get in touch with Jocelyn.'

'I said.'

'A few quiet words to see what it amounted to?'

The relentless censure was getting to Hen. She crushed the cigar butt into an ashtray. 'For Christ's sake, I don't go in for quiet words. It was all or nothing and I did nothing.'

'You didn't tip off your brother?'

'I told you how things are between us. He's so heavy-handed he would have turned a small coincidence into world war three.'

Georgina was quickly on to that. 'A small coincidence? How can you dismiss it so lightly – your niece linked to a murder?'

'Maybe because I'm dealing in murder on a regular basis. And this was little more than speculation.'

'It's nothing of the sort. There's a warrant out for her

now. She must have heard about the DNA match and made herself scarce.'

'Is that any surprise?' Hen said. 'Most of Sussex seems to know I'm being hung out to dry. Joss will have heard.'

'It isn't in the papers, is it?'

'Might as well be. The police service leaks like a sieve.'

'There's no need to be cynical.'

'It's well known.'

This was descending into a slanging match. Hen still had some spirit and Georgina was wading in as if she sensed blood. 'I won't take that sort of talk from any officer. We're trusted by the public to enforce the law and be worthy of that trust. If we can't take pride in the way we conduct ourselves, we lose all respect.'

'I don't know about pride,' Hen said. 'I'm content to do the job as well as I can, but I don't kid myself there's glory in it. There's more shit than respect.'

'Please!'

'I said at the beginning I messed up. You've got your views about policing. I've got mine. What else do you want to hear from me?'

'I haven't heard a single "ma'am",' Georgina said. 'That would be a start.'

Diamond's flesh prickled.

Hen rose to it, as he knew she would. 'God help us. Is that what you mean by respect? There was I thinking you were a fellow human being come to listen to my grubby little story when the truth is that you only came to hear me call you ma'am, and I missed all those opportunities. Well, I can put that right, ma'am, ma'am, ma'am, ma'am—'

'Hen!'

She stopped.

Diamond couldn't let her destroy herself in front of him. 'Get a grip.'

She seemed to have frozen, her mouth half open, eyes red-lidded.

'This isn't helping you or us,' he said. 'You asked what we want to hear from you and I'll tell you. We need to know how you acted at each stage and why: the Rigden murder investigation, the arrest and trial of Danny Stapleton, and the DNA report that brought Joss into the reckoning. We want to understand each decision you took and test it against the evidence.' He kept his eyes locked with Hen's. If Georgina objected to him interrupting, she could take it up later.

Hen said, 'Flipped my lid. Pressure.' She breathed in, clutched her hands and faced Georgina. 'If you looked at my personal file, I'm sure you'll have seen that. A hothead. Sorry for what I said. Truly . . . ma'am.'

Georgina was a beached whale. She, too, had lost it, but in another sense. Diamond was in charge now. He'd switched direction, offered Hen the chance to talk about something other than the mess she was in.

And it worked. She became the professional again, in control of her emotions, but speaking exclusively to him. 'The problem is that we couldn't find a motive. Rigden had no enemies.'

He nodded. 'We read the file.'

'You know, then. Everyone in the village liked him. We tried hard to find someone who would say a word against him. No one would.'

'To me,' Diamond said, 'this doesn't look like a village murder. The gunshot and the disposal in a stolen car is a professional at work.'

'That's how I saw it. But the idea that everyone's favourite gardener had any link with organised crime was beyond belief. We searched the house minutely, went through his papers, his address book, everything. Didn't even find an unwashed dish. He lived frugally, but cleanly. No one else had entered the cottage in weeks. He wasn't murdered there, that's for sure.'

This was more like old times, the two of them trading theories. 'And you got nothing useful from Danny Stapleton?'

'He claimed he'd never heard of Rigden.'

'He would, wouldn't he? But Danny is a professional car thief. He knew the local villains, obviously.'

Hen shrugged. 'So did we. Never got a sniff of a connection, from Danny or our usual informants.'

'The body in the car: was it clothed?'

'Same clothes he wore for his garden work. Sweatshirt and jeans. Socks, but no shoes. I expect you saw the autopsy report. Apart from the head wound, which was gross, no other marks of any significance. Nothing under the fingernails except garden dirt. He didn't fight for his life.'

Diamond turned in his chair. 'Anything you wanted to ask, ma'am?'

The tide was still out for Georgina. 'You carry on.'

He told Hen, 'You seem to have covered every angle except one.'

'What's that?'

'What we're here about.'

'Joss?'

'She may know something. We need to track her down. We've got to.'

'I understand.'

'Is her mother about?'

'Died when Joss was twelve. Brain tumour. It explains a lot about what happened after.'

'Did your brother find another partner?'

She gave a nod. 'Cherry. I've never met her. From what I hear, she's the quiet sort, a carbon copy of Jane, the first wife. Fits in with whatever Barry decides. He likes his women submissive.'

'Is he local?'

'Midhurst, a half-hour's drive away. You want their phone number? There's a Rolodex on the bookcase beside you. 'Look under Mallin.'

He made a note of it. Also under Mallin he found a card inscribed *My Mobile*, followed by the number, which he took down, unseen by Georgina. 'And if this turns out to be a wild goose chase, we'll be back to some of the people you interviewed.'

'Rather you than me,' she said. 'The folk round here who employ gardeners think they're God's gift, most of them.'

'I'm sparing no one, Hen. It may seem like a cold case, but there are high stakes here: a lifer who may be innocent and a damn good detective whose career is on the line.'

They left soon after. Georgina muttered something to Hen about hearing from them in due course and Diamond winked.

Hen widened her eyes a fraction.


On the walk back, Georgina said nothing until they'd gone more than halfway to the hotel. Finally she spoke. 'I suppose I ought to thank you, Peter.'

'What for?'

'Taking over when it all became too heated. She's a difficult woman. I don't have a shred of sympathy with her.'

'She lost her rag. She was out of order.'

'I'm glad you agree. You called her "Hen" more than once, I noticed, almost as if you knew her.'

'Relaxed the mode of address, that's all. Sometimes it gets results.'

She gave him a sharp look.

'At the end,' she said, 'you called her a damn good detective. That's more than I would have done.'

'She was in a state,' he said.

'So was I, by then.'

'But no one needs to say you're a damn good detective.'
She tilted her head and gave a sniff of satisfaction.

He moved smoothly on. 'So you didn't mind me picking up the baton? I hope I didn't say anything you weren't about to say.'

'I was coming round to asking questions about the Rigden murder just as you did, but her offensive outburst put me off my stroke.' She looked away, across the street. 'All in all, you covered for me rather well.'

'Thanks. I'm concerned about the niece.'

'Avoiding arrest, you mean?'

'It could be worse.'

'In what way?'

'I didn't say anything to DI Mallin when she was talking about the glut of missing persons almost certainly murdered. Joss is missing.'

# 13

Peter Diamond phoned Hen Mallin from his room in the hotel while Georgina was taking an afternoon nap.

'Me again.'

'Peter, are you alone?'

'She's on a siesta.'

'You're joking.'

'She's totally stressed out.'

'*She* is?'

'A rare admission of frailty. She tells me the minimum. I wish there'd been some way of tipping you off about the visit.'

'Did I look as if I'd seen a ghost? I was reeling and rocking.'

'You were fine.'

'Until I let rip. What a dumbo.'

'You aren't. She got what was coming. She's like that about rank. It comes from insecurity.'

'And she's your assistant chief constable?'

'Almost as long as I remember. You didn't meet her ten years ago when we worked together on that body on the beach case. She was away on a cruise.'

'A cruise? Siestas and cruises. Not a bad life.'

'It means I get a break sometimes.'

'How the hell do you cope?'

'We understand each other. I'm not easy to get on with either. Georgina has a good side I see occasionally.'

'She thinks I let down the whole of womankind. I saw it in her eyes.'

'Failing to investigate your niece? Women are allowed to show compassion.'

'Don't tell me. Tell your boss. Oh forget it. She's right. I screwed up. What do they call it, favouring your family?'

'Nepotism.'

'Right on. I admit it. Nepotist of the year. I don't deserve to stay in the job. Didn't I say it loud and clear to Dallymore?'

'You did – but something was missing.'

'What was that?'

'A little "ma'am" at the end.'

They both laughed.

Hen's voice improved. She wasn't back to her boisterous best, and might never be, but she made a try. 'Peter, my old cock sparrow, I don't know how you worked it, but I'm chuffed to have you on board.'

He let the 'old cock sparrow' wash over him. 'You can credit Georgina, not me. I tried to wriggle out of it – but then I didn't know you were the officer under suspension. Do you know who fingered you?'

'No.'

'Could it have been Montacute, who is now doing your job?'

'Too obvious.'

'Why – don't you get on with him?'

'He's a moaner, but he doesn't want me out of it. He might be forced to make decisions of his own.'

'Got to be someone with an agenda. Are the others loyal?'

'Does it matter? I've admitted to all and sundry I fouled up. I don't lose any sleep trying to guess who the whistle-blower was.'

'But you *are* losing sleep. I saw it in your face.'

'Is it as obvious as that? Joss was only eighteen when

Rigden was murdered. What was she doing to get her DNA in that bloody car, Peter? And where has she bunked off to, now the heat is on?'

'That's for us to work out.'

'You and Dallymore?'

'With any help we can get from you. Someone has to untangle this mess. We'll manage.'

'Find Joss. I don't care what happens to me.'

'You made that obvious. But I have a sense that your part in all this is going to seem small beer when everything is understood.'

'Commander Hahn may disagree. He'd like to see me roast in hell.'

'Hahn? He's got bigger things to worry about than you. He's spooked in case Danny Stapleton sues for wrongful conviction.'

'And he blames me.'

'Get this straight, Hen. You did your job with the investigation. Stapleton was caught with a murdered body in a car he'd stolen. His defence was paper thin. A judge and jury heard the case and convicted him.'

In the pause that followed he could almost hear her brain ticking over. Finally she said, 'You're music to my ears, darling. I was feeling lower than a snake's belly this morning. If Dallymore picked you for this mission she can't be all bad. I don't mind calling her ma'am. I'll call her your royal highness if she doesn't send you home.'

He hadn't made this call just to restore Hen's spirits, or his own. 'There was something you said this morning about recent cases you were working on.'

'You'll have to remind me. My head was in a whirl.'

'Missing persons. What's that about? Every police authority has missing persons.'

'Sure, and most of them turn up, one way or another,

127

dead or alive. This is serious stuff, Peter, and it's been going on some time. Far too many stay missing. They vanish. No one hears from them again.'

'Who are they?'

'Petty criminals mostly. The sort who mess with the local crime barons. In former times their bodies would be found riddled with bullets in a local quarry or some abandoned house. You expect it with rival gangs. Over recent years it's become more efficient. Plenty of victims still get taken out. We hear the same distress calls from their nearest and dearest. But the bodies aren't found. Death and disposal on an industrial scale.'

'And you were on to it? How far did you get?'

'Nowhere. Well, almost nowhere. I made a start. The first stage as always was to learn as much as we could from informants. The only message coming back is that someone has a foolproof method.'

'Of disposal?'

'A business operation.'

'Murder Inc – in Chichester?'

'Not just Chichester. All along this stretch of the south coast, from Brighton to Portsmouth. Forty miles, give or take.'

'So other forces are on to this?'

'I spoke to my CID oppos in all the main towns. Bloody hard convincing some of them anything is wrong.'

'These were informal contacts?'

'You bet. The top brass are going to take a lot of convincing. When the government judges us by the crime figures and the murder rates are falling, who in his right mind wants to know about killings that have gone unreported? I had to hammer the point home. When we put our information together it was bloody obvious this was too serious to ignore. So who do you think was volunteered to carry the thing forward?'

'You're a glutton for punishment. When did you start?'

'Two weeks before I was suspended.'

'And you say you got almost nowhere?'

'We'd barely started.'

'You must have some theories.'

'The obvious one – being so close to the coast – is that they take the bodies out to sea and dump them overboard. If so, they do it well. I can't find a single instance in the last two years of a murdered corpse being washed up or found floating.'

'Isn't the sea always supposed to give up its dead?'

'That's horseshit. No offence, my love, but it's one of those Biblical sayings that gets misquoted all the time. On the day of reckoning all the people who were ever drowned will come to life – that's what the good book says.'

'Didn't know you were a Bible-basher.'

'I'm not. So many people quoted it at me that I looked it up.'

'But there's an element of truth. Bodies don't stay under water indefinitely.'

'OK, a submerged body inflates with internal gases after a while and will rise to the surface, but if the disposal man is the professional we think he is he'll surely weigh the things down.'

'Have you talked to pathologists?'

'No help at all. If I could find them a body to slice up they'd give me all sorts of information. The whole point of this brain-teaser is that there ain't no evidence.'

'You've obviously thought of other methods?'

'There's no shortage of ideas. Everyone has a favourite theory, from acid baths to car crushers.'

'Old mineshafts?'

'Not in these parts. Mind, it wouldn't be much trouble to drive the bodies to Wales or Cornwall. Why are you so interested in this?'

'I was thinking if you were getting warm in your enquiries and the people behind this racket got to know, they would have wanted you suspended.'

'But they'd need a line into our investigation and it hasn't even reached the stage of *being* an investigation.'

He said nothing.

'Peter, that's appalling. Can't I trust my own colleagues? Who would leak it? I work every day with my team. They're solidly behind me.'

'All of them? You said Montacute moans about you.'

'Heat of the moment. We have a mutual disrespect. You know yourself CID isn't a love-in. But if there isn't loyalty, there's nothing.'

'Civilian staff?'

'They're OK. They don't get involved in office politics.'

'The only one I've met so far is Pat Gomez.'

'Pat who?'

'Gomez. She showed us upstairs and made the tea.'

'I know who you mean. She's only been in the job a couple of weeks. She knows nothing about my faux pas of three years ago.'

'You were in consultation with other stations. Can you trust all of them?'

'They're senior detectives.'

'So?'

A gasp came down the line. But there was amusement in her tone when she said, 'Peter Diamond, you're a rabid old cynic.'

'Tell me about it. Will Montacute have taken over from you as convenor of this unofficial group?'

'Nobody tells me anything. They seem to be under instructions to treat me as the enemy now.'

'Has it occurred to you that the villains could have won and your missing persons project might be kicked into the long grass? You were the prime mover. Is anyone else as keen as you to push on with this?'

She didn't seem to have an answer.

'Every chief constable wants falling crime figures,' he went on. 'Meet our targets, let the public think they're safer now than they ever were. You were threatening to spoil all that, uncovering lots of extra murders. Am I such a cynic?'

Hen gave a little murmur of impatience. 'Listen, matey, I appreciate your interest in my missing persons crusade, but right now I'd prefer you to concentrate on the case in hand – my runaway niece.'

'You want me to prove Joss had nothing to do with the body in that car?'

'That would be the perfect outcome.'

'I can't promise anything, Hen.'

After the call ended, he thought about what had been said and it didn't hang together. Hen preferred to think there was no connection between what she called her crusade and her suspension. But three years had gone by since she had chosen to ignore the DNA evidence that Joss was involved. She'd insisted she'd confided in nobody when Joss's name came up. Why had her dereliction of duty been raised at this particular time if it didn't have something to do with the stirring she was doing? She trusted her close colleagues in Chichester and couldn't face the realisation that one of them had betrayed her.

Trust is the mother of deceit.


Georgina knocked on the door and said she was ready to go again.

'Did you get some shut-eye?'

She glared. 'I wasn't sleeping. I was deciding what to do next.'

'Did you reach a conclusion?'

'I did. First, I want to get your impressions of DI Mallin.'

Difficult. This sounded like a trap. Georgina was no fool. She'd noticed him calling Hen by her first name. She could have used some of her siesta time to put a call through to headquarters and check whether their careers had over-lapped. He didn't want to be stood down. 'My impressions? Mostly favourable,' he said. 'At least she admits she was in the wrong.'

'She couldn't do much else.'

'She could have spun some story and fudged the issue. Pressure of work. Unfamiliarity with the Rigden case. She held her hand up and I can't fault her for that. It simplifies our task.'

'And . . .?'

'Do you want me to go on analysing her motives?'

'That's what I asked.'

'She's obviously under strain. The outburst towards the end.'

'More than an outburst. A personal attack,' Georgina said. 'I'm not used to being spoken to like that. I was tempo-rarily lost for words.'

'Yes, I hope you didn't mind me taking over.'

'You called her "Hen". What was that about?' She wouldn't let it go.

This time he was ready with his explanation. 'I heard it from you. Down by the canal yesterday, when you told me who we're investigating, you spoke her full name – Henrietta.'

'Did I? It seems a long time ago.'

'I once knew a Henrietta and called her Hen. The name sprang to my lips at the moment I needed to get this lady's attention. It seemed to do the trick.'

She said without much gratitude, 'Yes, you brought her to her senses. She made some sort of apology, I think. It's all a blur now.'

The blur was good news. Georgina wasn't often vague in her recollections. 'If she'd spoken to me in that way,' he said, 'it wouldn't have been just a blur. It would have been a red mist. You were gracious.'

'Was I?' she said in an interested tone, keen to hear more.

'I was proud of you. Can't recall exactly what you said, but I was grateful. Gave me the chance to move on and ask her some questions about the problems with the Rigden murder investigation.'

'I do have a memory of that.'

Better get back to the script then, he thought. 'And after that I asked about her missing niece.'

'Yes, and the family background. The mother who died young and the domineering father.'

'Brother Barry.'

'He sounds unpleasant. Do you think DI Mallin is in awe of him?'

'Hard to say.' He couldn't imagine Hen being in awe of anyone, but it wouldn't have been wise to say so.

Georgina wasn't the sort to be in awe either. 'We'd better go to Midhurst and meet this ogre.'

Their police chauffeur took them over the South Downs along a winding route through farmland and forest. Georgina had spoken on the phone to Barry's second wife, who had wanted to know if there was news of Joss and sounded genuinely distressed that there was none. She'd suggested they came at once. Barry would be there soon.

'Was he at work, then?' Diamond asked in the car.

'She didn't say. I've no idea what work he does.'

He looked out of the window. 'Management, I should think, if he can afford to live here.'

Midhurst is an affluent market town with a rich history and a low crime rate. Diamond assumed this branch of the

Mallin family had come up in the world, so it came as a surprise when the car pulled up at the edge of a field on the northern outskirts. There was a gate with a rutted approach that a tractor might have used.

'Are we there?'

'This is where the sat nav brought us,' their driver told them.

'Those things aren't infallible.'

'I can see something white through the hedge,' Georgina said. 'Take a look, Peter.'

He was wary. As a townie, he mistrusted fields. You never knew what they contained. Something white could be one of those enormous Charolais bulls. He thought about delegating the job to the driver who had brought them to this unlikely spot, but perhaps it wasn't enough to make an issue about. He stepped out and looked over the gate.

The white was a static caravan alone in the field. Grey breeze blocks had been used to stabilise it. A wooden set of steps was in place in front of the door.

The Mallin residence?

He opened the gate and went over.

A woman answered his knock. About fifty, blonde, over-weight, anxious-looking. 'You'll be from the police? Come right in.'

'Hang on. I'll fetch my boss.'

In this compact home they didn't need to be detectives to tell no one else was in. 'Barry won't be long. I called him,' Cherry Mallin told them after they'd made themselves known and perched on stools in the kitchen area. 'When you called I was hoping you might have news of Joss, but you say she still hasn't been found. We're at our wits' end.'

'Does she have a mobile?' Georgina asked.

'Turned off.'

'How long has she been gone?'

'More than five weeks.'

'Where does she live?'

'Here with us. I thought you knew.'

'We're not from the local lot,' Diamond said. 'Does she have her own room?'

She pointed to a door. 'It's poky, but we manage.'

'May we look?'

'Go on. The ones in uniform already went through it and took some stuff away, like the laptop. Nothing left, really.'

She was right. It was a minimal, impersonal space with a bed and hanging canvas storage space with six shelves which housed the rest of Joss's possessions, make-up, clothes, shoes, a few paperbacks. Diamond could imagine how Hen would feel if she saw this pathetic little collection.

'After the divorce, Barry insisted she moved in with us,' Cherry Mallin said. 'She wasn't able to support herself. We had a nice house in Pretoria Lane. We sold it and bought this box on wheels and paid for everything, the divorce, the rehab and the repayments. She'd borrowed heavily from loan sharks.'

'What's Barry's job?' Diamond asked, thinking the man couldn't be all bad.

'Pest control. He's out in the van all day killing things.'

'You need a strong stomach for that.'

'I don't know about his stomach, but Barry's strong-minded, that's for sure.'

'And is Joss his only daughter?'

'From his first marriage. He prefers Jocelyn, by the way.'

'Thanks. And what does she prefer?'

She gave a faint smile. 'Joss. Barry associates the word with joss sticks and the hippy life we want to wean her away from.'

Diamond added narrow-minded to his mental dossier on

Barry. 'I hadn't thought of that. She was quite a rebel as a teenager, I gather.'

'She had a difficult start, her mother dying when she was only twelve. Barry met me about a year later and we married quite soon, which wasn't easy for Jocelyn to accept.'

'I understand. Who'd choose to be a stepmother? How do you get on these days?'

'Reasonably well. She calmed down a lot after we all moved here.'

'It can't be easy, three of you in a confined space.'

'Everyone who lives in a caravan has to face that.' She seemed to have accepted the change in their lifestyle remarkably well.

'So what do you think it was that caused her to take off?'

'We're not sure. She didn't say anything to me. There wasn't an argument. The police seem to know what it was about – I mean the ones who searched her room – but they weren't saying much. Barry has heard since that his sister Henrietta is in some kind of trouble and it's connected to that. We can't understand why because Barry hasn't seen Hen for twenty years and neither has Jocelyn.' She stopped for the sound of a vehicle outside. 'This will be him.'

So much of Barry's reputation had preceded him that there was quite a frisson of tension while they waited for the door to open. Short, pale and skinny, he didn't live up to his billing until he spoke in a clipped, aggressive tone with a tilt of the jaw. 'What's all this, then? Any news?'

Georgina decided to assert herself. 'If you mean news of your daughter, no, we've heard nothing more.' She went through her usual ponderous introduction. 'Thank you for taking time off, Mr Mallin.'

'It had better not be time wasted,' he said. 'I've had it up to here with police people treating us as if we don't have a right to know why my own daughter is missing.'

136

'We're all agreed on the need to find her urgently,' Georgina said.

'So you issued a warrant for her arrest. What's that about?'

Georgina cleared her throat. 'Haven't you been told? Her DNA was found in a car used to transport a murder victim.'

'I was told that much. This happened all of seven years ago. Why this sudden interest in Jocelyn?'

'It comes from information that only recently came to light.'

'You're telling me her DNA was found in this car in 2007 and you've only just done anything about it?'

Peter Diamond was getting impatient. This was all wrong. Georgina shouldn't have been on the receiving end of the questions.

'There was a delay in tracing the DNA to Jocelyn,' Georgina said.

'Oh, come on. A delay of seven years?' Mallin said. 'How much confidence can be placed on evidence that's been lying around all that time?'

Diamond chose now to say to Georgina, 'If I may, ma'am.' And without waiting for an answer, he turned to Mallin. 'Let's deal with what concerns us all – your daughter's disappearance. Your wife has said Joss – Jocelyn – gave no hint to her that she was leaving. Just for the record, can you confirm the same?'

'I've been through this with your people already,' Mallin said.

'First, they're not our people. We're acting independently of the Chichester police. And second, be aware that you're assisting a high-level murder inquiry.'

The few choice words had a seesaw effect on the exchanges. 'You've got to make allowance. I'm under stress,' Mallin muttered and then said, 'Ask whatever you want.'

'I already did.'

'About Jocelyn leaving? We had no clue. I gave her a lift into town to the job centre and arranged to meet her at lunchtime and she didn't turn up. I waited almost an hour, tried calling her phone. Nothing.'

'How was her state of mind?'

'No different from usual.'

'Did you speak in the car on the way to Chichester?'

'Very little. She was listening to her iPod.' As if he'd given the wrong impression he added, 'It doesn't mean we're not on good terms. You can ask my wife.'

'So when did you report Jocelyn as missing?'

'The same day, about eight in the evening. There was a time when she would stay out unexpectedly, or come back very late, but that was years ago. When she came to live with us after the divorce, we came to an understanding. These days if she's not home by early evening there's cause for concern.'

'When you say "came to an understanding", you mean you made rules?'

'They were necessary.'

'But she doesn't always keep them, right?'

Mallin glanced at his wife. 'There was one incident about three years ago.'

'The fight outside the club?'

'An isolated event.'

'It must have been serious for her to have received an official caution. That's when the DNA was taken. And you're going to tell me you don't understand how it took three more years for her to be linked with the murder case. That's why the assistant chief constable and I were called in.'

'I was led to believe my sister Hen is implicated.'

'Who told you that?'

'One of the detectives who came here. He said she's been suspended.'

'We've spoken to your sister, Mr Mallin, and I can assure you she's as concerned as you are for your daughter's well-being. She's helping in every way she can. Getting back to Jocclyn, do you know of anyone who might wish her harm?'

He shook his head. 'We've thought and thought.'

'Her ex-husband?'

'That bastard? He married again and moved to some tax haven. If you ask me, he wouldn't be back unless there was money in it, and he got most of mine at the time of the divorce. One look at Jocelyn's present circumstances and you wouldn't see him for dust.'

Diamond had been watching Barry Mallin for any sign of what was really going on in his head. Here was a controlling man who had raised a daughter who had rebelled, got into trouble and turned his world upside down. He'd sold just about everything he owned to rescue her and pull her back into line. Now he was faced with another huge family crisis. How had he dealt with it? Was he responsible for the disappearance of Joss?

'Do you think she decided to go into hiding now that the DNA evidence has come to light?'

'What are you suggesting – that my daughter is a murderer?'

'I'm suggesting she's frightened of what might happen now.'

'She has no reason to be if she's innocent.'

'This is the crux of it, Mr Mallin. We don't know if she's innocent. The car with the body inside was stopped on a road ncar Chichester. The driver claimed he'd stolen it in Littlehampton and saw the driver walk away – a figure in a hooded jacket. Could that have been Jocelyn? We don't know, but we can't discount it. Did she wear hooded jackets at eighteen? A lot of youngsters did.'

'I can't remember that far back.'

His wife said, 'To be honest, she did go through a hoodie phase about that time.'

Mallin glared at his wife and said, 'So did a million other teenagers. It doesn't mean a bloody thing.'

'I expect you gave a description to the police.'

'We did. She won't be wearing the same stuff now.'

'She's five foot five and really slim,' Cherry Mallin said, at pains to be more helpful than her husband. 'She has red hair that she usually wears in a ponytail. And she always has a silver ring on the second finger of her right hand. It's not valuable, but it belonged to her mother.'

Her husband said, 'They're not interested where it came from.'

'Are you self-employed?' Diamond asked.

'What's this about? I pay my taxes, same as anyone else.'

'But you work for yourself?'

'Yes.'

'Dealing with all kinds of pests from fleas to foxes?'

'I don't see what this has to do with Jocelyn.'

'You carry your equipment in the van I see outside? The usual poisons, I suppose? Traps? Bait? Do you have a gun?'

Barry Mallin frowned.

'It's not unreasonable,' Diamond said. 'You'd need to kill gulls and pigeons. We can check for a firearms licence on our computer if you'd rather not say.'

'A twelve-bore I rarely use.'

'In your van?'

'Inside a locked cabinet of regulation size. Is that all right with you?' Mallin said in a spasm of anger. 'Now can we talk about what you're doing to find my daughter?'

'You haven't met your sister Hen in twenty years, I was told,' Diamond said.

'That's a family matter.'

'We're here to discuss family matters. Hen is under

140

suspension because she failed to follow up the DNA report linking Joss – sorry, Jocelyn – to the murder we were speaking of. You may not have been told this, but she put her job on the line for Jocelyn's sake. She can't believe her niece was involved in the shooting of a man everybody seems to have liked and respected. I'm telling you this because I think you should know she refused to let the family feud stop her from doing what she perceived as the right thing. Her employers perceive it as the wrong thing, of course.'

To his credit, Barry looked surprised, if not humbled. 'I didn't know that.'

'But my colleague and I have to keep an open mind, which is why we ask awkward questions. Here's another one: did you own a gun in 2007?'

He frowned. 'Long time ago.'

'Mr Mallin, I want an answer.'

Now he gave an impatient sigh. 'I was in a different job then, trading in antiques.' He paused. 'OK, there was good weekend shooting to be had at Goodwood. I can't afford it any longer.'

'So you kept a gun and your daughter might have had access to it?'

'That's ridiculous. She wouldn't have the faintest idea how to use one.'

'It's not rocket science,' Diamond said.

'This is not just ridiculous, it's offensive. She's done stupid things in her time, but she's not a murderer.'

'Pity she isn't here to tell us herself.'

# 14

Mel couldn't possibly tell the others. They'd cut her into small pieces if they found out. She'd had a suspicion ever since the first day back that something had gone hideously wrong, and now she was on the trail. Miss Gibbon was officially a missing person and she felt driven to find out more.

Logically, she needed to start in school. The problem here was that the person in the know was the head, who insisted staff matters were not to be discussed with students. No use asking her why Miss Gibbon had left. A more subtle approach was needed.

On Monday mornings the head actually did some teaching, the one fixed point on the timetable, RE to the year sevens. The memory of those dreaded lessons was seared on Mel's brain. It was all about discussing what the head called 'issues' and even the shyest children were expected to have an opinion and contribute. She'd suffered. When the finger pointed your way there was no escape.

But year seven's misfortune was Mel's opportunity. The school secretary, the well-named Mrs Bountiful, known as Bounty throughout the school, dealt with every enquiry she could while the head was teaching.

'I'm afraid she isn't available until later, dear,' she said when Mel looked into her office. 'Is it something I can help with?'

'That would be brilliant. I'm hoping to get in touch with Miss Gibbon, who taught me art, but she left.'

'Miss Gibbon?' Her face changed from the usual ever-present smile to a guarded, almost pained look. 'What's it about?'

'We didn't get a chance to thank her for all the things she taught us.'

'Well, that's a lovely thought, but it won't be possible now.'

'I was wondering if you could let me have her address.'

'I'm not allowed to give addresses to anyone.'

Mel needed a stronger reason. Think, think. 'She was especially kind to me.' In desperation she came out with a statement that was pure invention. 'She lent me a book on perspective and I didn't have the chance to return it.'

'What a shame.'

And now she had to embroider the lie if it was to serve the purpose she needed. 'It's a beautiful book signed by the author, who must have been one of her college lecturers, I guess, because it has a nice inscription, "To Connie". I think that's her name.' Under this pressure, Mel was discovering creative talent she hadn't dreamed she possessed. 'There's a personal message with it.'

'How unfortunate. Between you and me, Melanie, we don't know where Miss Gibbon is now, or I'd offer to send the book on for you. Let me see.' Bounty worked her keyboard. 'No, all I have is her last address and we know that isn't current because mail has been returned from there.'

'Could you let me have it?'

'I just explained. She isn't there any longer.'

'So you won't be breaking any rules if you pass it on to me.'

'What use is an old address?'

'Someone there may know. I feel so guilty hanging on to the book.'

Bounty sighed. 'This is in confidence, my dear. The head was faced with an impossible situation at the end of last term. Miss Gibbon left at short notice and hasn't been in touch since.'

'Should I speak to the head about it, then?'

'Absolutely not. That's the worst thing you could do. Don't speak to her or any of the staff.'

'What am I to do, then?'

'Take it from me, you're not going to find Miss Gibbon.'

'But it won't hurt for you to give me her old address. Please.' Mel started edging around the desk for a sight of the computer screen.

'What on earth . . . ?' Outraged, Bounty grabbed the screen and twisted it out of range, eyes blazing. This was a side of the so-called unflappable school secretary Mel had never seen before. 'Get out of here, girl, or I'll report you.'

The unpleasantness in the office left Mel shaky and troubled. It had been out of all proportion to the simple request she'd made. True, she'd overstepped the mark trying to see the address, but Bounty's reaction had been totally over the top. It only added to the mystery and made her more concerned about Miss Gibbon. What was the 'impossible situation' the head had been faced with?

One thing was clear: it was no use asking for help from *anyone* in school, staff or students. They were united in opposition to the poor woman.

Better think again.

Meanwhile the rest of the A-level group were still fixated on one topic.

'How old do you think he is?' No need for Ella to say who she was talking about.

'Under thirty.'

'That's obvious. I'd say twenty-six maximum.'

'Ask him.'

'Get real. You can't ask a teacher what age he is.'

'Does it matter?' Mel said.

'Of course it matters. We know almost everything else about him from his website, like where he went to art school and stuff, but there's nothing about his age.'

'Ask Ferdie, then. He won't mind telling us.'

'Perfecto. Great suggestion. He's friendly. I'll ask him Saturday.'

'While you're at it,' Ella said, 'ask him when the next party is.'

'He told me,' Jem said. 'It's when there's a full moon.'

'Like when the werewolves come out?'

A chorus of howling started up.

'He was winding you up.'

'He wasn't, I'm abso-fucking-lutely sure. He's honest. He tells you straight when you ask him.'

'What parties are these? I haven't heard about them,' Naseem said.

'They're not for the likes of us,' Jem said. 'Regulars only.'

'Why? Are they, like, doing drugs?'

Jem shook her head. 'When Anastasia told us about the parties I asked if they smoked pot and she was really shocked. Then for a laugh I asked if they were into orgies, and she was like, "If they were, I'd stay away."'

Shrieks of laughter.

'I'd stay away as well,' Mel said. 'Imagine an orgy with Geraint.'

'If it's not sex or drugs, that doesn't leave much to be secretive about,' Jem said. 'I guess it's just heavy drinking.'

'Do they think we don't drink?' Ella said.

'This is about Tom's job, most likely. He'd be in deep

doo-doo if the school got to hear we were drinking. I don't blame him. You can be sure one of us would get rat-arsed.'

'Ella,' somebody said at once, and got laughs.

Ella spun around. 'What do you mean? I can hold my drink.'

'Like you did at the last prom when you threw up over that boy's shoes?'

'Give me a break. That was yonks ago. Wouldn't it be wicked to crash one of the parties?'

Nobody spoke. Just because someone says jump in, you don't want to be the first.

Finally Jem said, 'Like put it on Facebook and get thousands of kids along?'

'That would be so uncool,' Ella said. 'I'm not suggesting we should be mean to Tom. I'm thinking just ourselves. After they've had a few drinks they won't care who turns up.'

'What would you wear?' Jem said. 'Your goth gear?'

'Naturally.'

'Count me out,' Naseem said. 'This could be *so* embarrassing.'

'How about you, Jem?'

Jem shook her head. 'It's not my scene.'

'Nor mine,' Mel said.

'We know that, scrubber,' Jem said, quick to deflect any criticism. 'Your scene is some greasy-spoon caff in the back streets of Bognor.'

No one was brave enough to come to Mel's defence. The put-down, like so many others, seemed to speak for everyone.

'What a load of wimps,' Ella said. 'Haven't you ever crashed a party before? Sounds like I'm on my own.'

# 15

'That man is capable of anything . . . anything at all,' Georgina said in the car on the drive back to Chichester. She'd been a dormant volcano in the caravan and at last she could send out sparks. 'I was watching him the whole time, those eyes like chips of ice. I wouldn't put it past him to be holding his daughter in some secret hideout.'

'Interesting thought,' Diamond said.

'Yes, but don't run away with the idea that this is for her sake. It's all about himself, always has been, as far as I can see. He couldn't deal with her teenage rebellion or her poor choice of husband. The only way to get control of the mess she was in was to fund the divorce, pay the debts, buy her back and make her dependent on him. So he sacrificed his home and his bank balance and thought he'd fixed the problem and now he's threatened with a worse scandal than ever.'

'So he locks her away and claims she's missing?'

'Or removes her from the scene altogether.'

Diamond blinked. 'Kills her, you mean?'

'I wouldn't put it past him.'

'His own daughter?'

'To me, he's a man at the end of his tether, single-minded, humourless, driven and dangerous. He has the means. That van is stuffed with lethal material, including a gun.' Georgina's eruption was in full flow.

'It comes down to pest control?' Diamond said.

She had to pause and think about that. 'In a manner of speaking, yes. Don't you agree?'

In truth, he was never going to agree. There were dangers in pinning a case on eyes like chips of ice and a job killing things. He couldn't rule out Barry Mallin as a potential perpetrator, but better evidence was needed. 'It would be unusual for a parent to kill their own daughter or son. The reverse happens more often.'

'All right, wise guy. You heard my assessment. What did you make of him?' she asked.

Diamond gave an oblique answer. He wasn't trading in character assassination. 'Difficult to see him as Hen Mallin's brother.'

'There's a resemblance in the face,' Georgina said. 'Something about the mouth and jaw.'

'But not in the way they deal with a crisis.'

He left it at that. He saw no point in discussing what the man might or might not have done. The potential for a serious crime was there, but no more needed to be said at this stage.

Fortunately Georgina went off on a different tack. 'I'm glad I left the bulk of the questioning to you. You covered most of what I would have asked. In fact, I can't think of anything you missed.'

'That's all right, then.'

Satisfied, she rubbed her hands. She almost clapped. 'We're a team that gets things done, Peter. Two interviews already, Henrietta Mallin and her brother, and both went rather well, with me setting the agenda, so to speak, and you following up on the detail. If people see us as Miss Nice and Mr Nasty, so be it. That's a well-tried method of interrogation.'

She meant good cop bad cop. Miss Nice and Mr Nasty was another nugget to tuck away.

'What's next?' he asked.

'More fact-finding. We mustn't lose sight of our main objective.'

'Which is?'

She blinked, shocked that he needed to ask. 'To discover the full extent of Henrietta Mallin's misconduct.'

'She already confessed.'

'True, but I don't take everything she says at face value. There could be more to come out.'

'Such as?'

'Don't forget she headed the original investigation into the Rigden murder. She charged Danny Stapleton and he was convicted. Was she aware at the time that her niece was involved?'

'The DNA result was four years after that.'

'Ah.' Georgina raised a cautionary finger. 'But what if she knew from the beginning about Joss and chose to shield her, chose even to pin the blame on Stapleton when she knew Joss was up to her ears in guilt?'

'Are you suggesting Joss murdered Rigden?'

'He was killed with a gun, we know that. And the girl knew where to get hold of one. Her own father keeps one in his van.'

'Is this part of our brief, to re-investigate Rigden's murder?'

She reddened and raised her chin. 'We're charged with examining DCI Mallin's conduct, and I take that to mean the way she led the murder inquiry as well as what happened later. It's inevitable that we look at the case again. And if we reveal a miscarriage of justice, so be it.'

'That's a far bigger job than I thought we were here for. We'll need to go over it in much more detail with Hen.'

'I wish you wouldn't keep calling her by that ridiculous nickname, as if she's one of us.'

'She's CID like me,' he said, annoyed with himself for the lapse, but finding it almost impossible to think of his one-time colleague as Henrietta, or DCI Mallin.

'Her conduct is under scrutiny,' Georgina said. 'Let's try and keep a proper distance, shall we?'

'As you wish.' His spirits had nosedived. A prolonged investigation would put intolerable strains on this so-called team effort. The prospect of being in Chichester with Georgina for days to come, if not weeks, was about as appealing as gangrene. 'We'd better not waste time, then. Shall we call at the nick and get things under way?'

'You can,' she said.

'Just me?'

'I'll drop you there. I'm going back to the hotel. Important calls to make.'

He didn't point out that important calls could be made from anywhere. Any break from Georgina was manna from heaven.

She insisted on telling him what to do, 'setting the agenda' as she liked to think of it. 'Speak to DI Montacute and find out if he was on the Rigden case and who else currently in CID was part of the team.'

'OK.'

'And when you get back to the hotel come directly to my room and tell me everything you found out.'

After school, Mel didn't go straight home. She walked down South Street and over the level crossing to where the police station was. Her calm personality could be deceiving. When she had a cause, she pursued it, regardless.

There was a sergeant behind the desk using a phone.

Mel waited, silently rehearsing what she would say. The fib about the borrowed book wouldn't work here. It would sound feeble in a police station.

'How can I help?'

'It's about a missing person.'

'OK. Who's missing?'

'I'm from Priory Park School. She was one of our teachers until the summer holiday and then she left suddenly. And now we've seen her name on your website, Miss Constance Gibbon.'

'So she's already notified as missing? That'll be the missing persons bureau you're talking about. It's a national website. And what's your name, young lady?'

'Melanie Mason.'

'Is there something you want to tell us about Miss Gibbon?'

'I was hoping you could tell me. We're worried about her. Well, I am, for one.'

'Constance Gibbon.' He typed the name in. 'Missing since mid-July. Thousands of people go walkabout for all sorts of reasons and most of them turn up later, so I wouldn't worry unduly about her. Missing children are another matter.'

'Someone must have reported that she'd gone.'

'Her family, I expect.' He checked on the computer. 'Yes, a sister in Limerick. Long way off. I reckon your Miss Gibbon isn't answering the phone. Do you know if she was depressed?'

'She could have been. I can't say for certain.' Mel stepped up the pressure. 'When do you start getting serious about people on that list?'

'Depends.' He hesitated. 'Hang on. There's someone upstairs dealing with local missing persons. I'll see if he wants a word. Take a seat.'

Mel found a chair and did some scrolling. The picture of Miss Gibbon on the missing persons website must have been provided by her family. She didn't look at all depressed. The photo had been taken in sunshine in a garden somewhere. Difficult to feel sorry for her.

\* \* \*

Diamond got out at the police station, showed his pass and went up to the CID room. Montacute had reoccupied Hen's office and had his feet on the desk. He didn't remove them.

'Yes?'

He had to fight off a huge urge to do a Georgina and pull rank. 'Not so busy today, then?'

'Busy enough. There's often a lull about this time. How's your day gone?'

'We visited your boss.'

'Ex-boss.'

'Boss. She isn't permanently suspended.'

'Everyone's saying she might as well be. The high-ups from headquarters have marked her card.'

'You want to be careful, coming out with stuff like that,' Diamond said. 'It can come back and bite you. One thing she mentioned this morning was an investigation into missing persons. Are you part of that?'

'I had a hand in checking the files and getting the word out to the snouts. But I can't see it progressing now that Hen is out of it. This was her baby. No one here wants to take on extra work with a senior officer short.'

'You can't shelve it.'

'It ain't shelved.' Montacute grinned. 'It's on the back burner.'

'Isn't this an inquiry spread over several divisions?'

Montacute stroked his beard as if contemplating how much information to give out. 'I'm being realistic. There wasn't a lot of enthusiasm from the other stations she contacted. To be brutally honest, it's better for the crime figures if missing persons stay missing.'

'Ah, the crime figures.'

'Do I detect a note of sarcasm?' Montacute said.

'Is there a file I can access, to see if Hen had uncovered anything?'

'I've been too busy to look at stuff like that.'

'Now is a good moment. Can you work the keyboard with your feet up?'

Montacute glared defiance, but removed his legs from the desk and set about accessing the file. With his attitude, he wouldn't have lasted five minutes in Diamond's team. Pity he had to be treated with kid gloves, being a key source of information.

Diamond wheeled a chair behind the desk and sat shoulder to shoulder with the obnoxious man. There was more to this than he'd expected. Hen had contacted the divisions at Eastbourne, Brighton, Hove and Shoreham, Highdown (covering Worthing and Littlehampton), Western (covering Bognor Regis and Selsey) and across the county border, Portsmouth, Fareham, Gosport and Southampton. Mostly she'd dealt with CID officers of her own rank, an informal exchange of emails to see what evidence there was of known criminals registered as missing. Some had written back to say nothing out of the ordinary had been noticed. However, she had received confirmation from several others of higher than average figures and their locations seemed to be significant. They were confined to a stretch of the south coast between Portsmouth and Brighton, under fifty miles.

The file also had the quotes Chichester CID had gathered from local informants.

*Better not put a foot wrong round here, or you'll not be seen again.*

*I don't know how it's done, or how much it costs, but I heard if you want to get shot of a stiff it can be arranged.*

*Two of my best mates vanished and they weren't the sort to go without telling anyone.*

*It's bloody efficient, whatever it is. No mess and no traces. Someone's making a career out of it.*

Diamond turned to Montacute. 'I'd like a printout.'

'What for?'

'Just do it. How long have you been here?'

'Me? In Chichester? I came in 2005.' He tapped the keys and a printer behind them jerked into action.

'So you were around for the Rigden murder inquiry. Were you on the team?'

'I was a dogsbody then, knocking on doors and taking statements from rich berks in Slindon who had him as their gardener.'

'He was well liked, I heard.'

'Pillar of the bloody community. Nothing was too much trouble. There was a lot of anger about the murder. I reckon if they'd got their hands on Stapleton, the killer, they'd have strung him up from the nearest tree.'

'Is there any question he was guilty?'

'Bang to rights, wasn't he? Caught in a stolen car with the body trussed up in the boot and two grand stuffed in his clothes.'

'Were you in on the interviews?'

Montacute shook his head. 'Hen and a DI called Austen did all that.'

'Is Austen still around?'

'Retired and died the same year. Surprising how often that happens.' He raised his eyebrows. 'Have you got long to go?'

Diamond treated the last remark with the contempt it deserved. This pain in the arse was pushing him to the limit. Exactly why, he couldn't tell. The guy had no loyalty to Hen. 'Is the Rigden investigation still on file?'

'Must be. If you want that printed out, we'll need a fresh ream of paper and more ink in the printer.'

'It's as large as that?'

'Took hundreds of man-hours just typing all the statements.'

'Get it on screen, then.'

Montacute glared and worked the keyboard with one finger to make clear it was all so much trouble.

'Now get the printing under way,' Diamond said. 'If you do need more paper, we'll deal with that when it happens.'

'You want the whole boiling lot?'

'All of it. Was Stapleton's story about stealing the car in Littlehampton followed up?'

'You bet it was. I was one of the mugs sent there to check on it. Couldn't find one sodding witness to back him up.'

'Where did you try?'

'The pub where he said he was sitting across the street from the BMW. Can't remember the name now.'

'The Steam Packet.'

A sharp look. 'It was, yeah. He was known there. Regular drinker, they said, but no one remembered serving him the evening this was supposed to have happened. Of course he claimed the pub was practically empty that night and the barmaid who served him had left the job. Convenient, eh?'

'He also said someone in a hood parked the car outside and walked away across the bridge,' Diamond said. 'Did you follow that up?'

Now there was a look of surprise. 'Have you been there?'

Diamond nodded.

'Well, you'll know there's nothing over the bridge except some seedy-looking boathouses and a yacht club. If the kid in the hood was going to the club, he would have driven there from the other side of the river, wouldn't he?'

'Did you make enquiries at the yacht club?'

'Yep.' He grinned. 'If a hoodie turned up there, they'd remember, believe you me. They didn't. Stapleton's story didn't stand up.'

'Except for the jammer and the key programmer he had with him when he was stopped.'

Montacute wasn't impressed. 'No one ever said he wasn't a car thief. Of course he had the tools. He half-inched the BMW from a car park in Arundel with the clear intent of using it to transport the corpse. This was the day before he was nicked.'

'He's maintained his innocence ever since.'

'They all do.'

The phone on the desk buzzed.

Montacute rolled his eyes. 'It never stops.' He reached for the thing and spoke his name.

Diamond waited while Montacute listened to the message coming through.

'Isn't there anyone else? I'm in conference here.'

Good name for it.

'All right, I'll come,' he said finally. He stood up and told Diamond, 'This is all I need. Schoolgirl who thinks her art mistress has done a disappearing act.'

'Another missing person, then?'

'It's hardly one for the serious crimes unit.'

'Never mind,' Diamond said. 'I'll join you.'

A constable appeared and showed Mel into a room with a table and wall-mounted recording equipment just like she'd seen on TV when suspects were interviewed. Two plain-clothes officers who looked important came in. One was bearded and watchful and the other was large, with a face that looked wrong for a policeman, as if he doubled as a stand-up comedian.

'Don't be scared,' the large one said. 'It's more private talking in here than out in the reception area.'

She was asked her name for the second time and had to supply her address as well. They introduced themselves as Detective Inspector Montacute and Detective Superintendent

156

Diamond. They didn't seem all that comfortable with each other.

'So you came in to report a missing person?' the bearded one, Montacute, said.

'Not really,' Mel said. 'You already know she's missing. She's been on the list since July.'

DI Montacute looked at a piece of paper the constable had brought in. 'This is Constance Gibbon?'

'Yes.'

'Art teacher at Priory Park?'

'Not any more,' Mel said.

'Right. She resigned at the end of last term. Have you got a new teacher now?'

She nodded. No reason to talk about Tom. This was about Miss Gibbon.

'I don't understand, then,' DI Montacute said. 'If she left, why are you bothered about her?'

Before Mel could answer, the other officer, DS Diamond, said, 'Let's cut to the chase, Melanie. What do you want to tell us?'

She hesitated. In truth, she had nothing to tell. She was there to gather information, not give it. 'I saw she's missing, but, like, nobody seems to care.'

'Nobody in school, you mean?'

'She means us,' DI Montacute said.

'Both. Well, I can't expect you to care. She's just a name to you.'

'Doesn't mean we're not concerned,' Diamond said. 'You like Miss Gibbon?'

'Not especially. Her lessons were pretty boring, to be honest. But I don't know why she left so suddenly.'

'Have you spoken to your teachers?'

'No one is saying. They clam up when I ask.'

'As if they know something you don't?'

'Maybe.'

'Did Miss Gibbon ever say anything about her life outside the school?'

Mel shook her head. 'Never. She was, like, stone-faced if anyone asked.'

DI Montacute took up the questioning again. 'Reading the file, it seems enquiries were made at your school after Miss Gibbon was reported missing by her sister and they weren't able to help.'

'I don't know about that.'

'The school couldn't get in touch. Letters weren't being delivered.'

She shrugged as if this was all outside her knowledge.

'You said she could be boring. Was there any open hostility to her?'

'I wouldn't say open, but after she'd gone, everyone cheered when we heard she'd left.'

'And you obviously feel different now.'

She spoke from the heart. 'It's like this. I don't particularly want her back teaching us, but I have, like, this really bad feeling something terrible has happened and I can't just ignore it.'

DS Diamond nodded. 'You've done well to come and talk to us.'

'I was thinking of getting it out on Facebook and the social media.'

He shook his head. 'I wouldn't yet.'

DI Montacute said, 'Christ, no. That's not the way to go. Leave it to us to make more enquiries.'

'What will you do?' Mel asked, far from convinced.

'Depends. We might speak to her sister, get more of a picture of her life. It may be that she lost her job and went away on some foreign trip without telling anyone and will surface again and wonder what the fuss was about. That happens.'

'I've remembered something. She did go on cultural cruises.'

'There you are, then. Could be as simple as that. But we're investigating, be assured of that.'

'You see the stuff we have to deal with?' Montacute said after the girl had left. 'If Hen's missing persons scare ever goes public we'll be snowed under. Runaway teenagers, confused old people.'

'I thought the focus was on known criminals.'

'Yeah, but we'd have to vet them all.'

'Miss Gibbon doesn't sound to me like a gang member. Will you speak to her sister?' Diamond answered his own question. 'I didn't think so.'

Montacute crossed to the door.

'Before you go,' Diamond said, 'I must pick up the printing.'

'You'll need a handcart.'

They returned to the CID section together. 'I'll also need the printout on the missing persons,' Diamond said.

'No problem. It'll be in the tray with the other stuff,' Montacute said.

'When I spoke to Hen this morning, she said there were eight cases that interested her. Eight in four years.'

'So?'

'Was that a deliberate choice, the four years?'

'Her decision, not mine.'

'Did it take long to check?'

'Hell of a time.'

'It was a practical decision, then? She might just as well have gone back eight years, or twelve?'

'She'd have had a bloody strike on her hands if she had.'

Diamond had the information he wanted. A scenario was taking shape in his brain.

'I notice you've started calling her Hen,' Montacute said.

'Same as you do.'

'Yeah, but you only met her this morning. You're investigating her. Shouldn't you keep it formal?'

'I need no lessons from you,' Diamond said. He scooped up the hefty printout and carried it out. Fortunately for his dignity he didn't drop the lot.

# 16

The deceased had been placed in a foetal position in a large cylindrical polypropylene bag of the heavy-duty type used for garden refuse, with stitched seams and webbing carry handles. He had been shot with a near discharge almost certainly from a rifle leaving a circular entrance wound 3cm above the left ear with smoke soiling, burning of the skin and some singeing of the hair. The cranium was severely disrupted, with some ejection of brain tissue.

Do I really need to read on? Diamond asked himself. He'd already skipped several sheets of photographs. He turned the page and found a list of the clothes worn by the victim, clearly working garments.

Then he took a deep breath and decided he'd better go back to the description of the corpse.

This was the moment Georgina chose to knock on the door.

'Homework?' she said, parking herself in the only armchair.

'The Rigden shooting.'

'A lot of reading.'

'Yes, I've made a start.'

'Anything of note?'

'One thing I hadn't appreciated was that the bag the body was found in was a garden refuse bag.'

161

'Is that important?'

'Could be.'

'Plastic?'

'No, that heavy duty synthetic material stitched at the seams. In other words, the sort of bag used by garden professionals. One of his own, I suppose.'

'That's grim, his own bag.'

'Not so grim as the pictures.'

'Had it been used before?'

'As a body bag?'

'I meant for garden refuse, grass cuttings and weeds.'

'Doesn't say so.' He picked up the report again. 'No, sounds like a fresh bag – at least until the body was dumped in it.'

'May I see?'

He handed over the sheets with those graphic images of the head wound printed in colour.

Georgina winced at each one and then tried to appear indifferent. 'Wasn't any DNA recovered?'

'Only Rigden's. Quite a lot of brain and gore.'

She turned the pages face down. 'I was about to ask if you've eaten yet, but I'm not sure I can face food now.'

Diamond wasn't sure he could face Georgina. He'd escaped shared meals so far. 'There's a mass of paperwork here to look through. I was thinking of seeing if room service do a burger or some such.'

A burger wasn't the suggestion Georgina needed at this moment. She turned ashen. Her eyes bulged and her cheeks puffed out. She made a beeline for the bathroom.

It became obvious Diamond would be dining alone.

Left to himself, he made a call, but not to room service.

'Yes?' In that one word Hen conveyed the misery she was going through.

'Chin up,' he said. 'It isn't the bank about your overdraft.'

'Peter? What's up now?'

'Is this a bad time?'

'Bad time, good time. To be honest, I'm feeling pretty low, so a call from you is a welcome distraction.'

'More problems?'

'It's finally sunk in that I can't rerun my big mistake. Like you, I sound off at regular intervals about the bloody job, but when it's taken away and you're hit with what you're missing, the future is bleak. I'm already thinking it was a mistake to fess up.'

'You were honest, Hen. That took courage.'

'Yeah, but my instinct is to fight my corner. I didn't.'

'Never been in trouble like this before, have you?'

'Christ, no. Once is enough.'

He understood and sympathised. His usual way of dealing with other people's troubles was to respect their fragile feelings by saying the minimum. This called for something different. He would share a confidence with Hen. 'Years ago, before we met, something similar happened to me. I messed up badly and quit the police.'

'I didn't know that.'

'I was out in the cold for the best part of two years, doing a series of temporary jobs to make ends meet, barman, security guard, Sainsbury's trolleyman, school assistant, even ho-ho-hoing it as Father Christmas. The hardship was self-inflicted, I may say. I'm hot-tempered now and I was worse in those days. Definitely not cut out to be Santa. Actually there were times when I felt like topping myself. But I got my CID job back eventually. I hadn't appreciated that a time would come when they needed me back to re-investigate a case I'd once been involved with. I won't bore you with it. I'm saying don't write yourself off. You have a wealth of experience and they'd be idiots to ignore it.'

'Peter, I appreciate what you're saying, but no one is indispensable.'

'You haven't been sacked, Hen. You're suspended. There's a difference.'

'Suspended pending an inquiry. But there's nothing to inquire about. I'm guilty as charged. Even you can't ignore the fact that I held up my hand to misconduct in public office.'

'I'm not ignoring anything. It's up to Georgina and me to look at all the circumstances.'

'That woman took an instant dislike to me. She has no sympathy.'

'She's not the dragon she appears. And she's only half the team.'

'If Danny Stapleton's trial turns out to have been a miscarriage of justice, nobody can help me.'

'We've been over that. There's no way you could have known about Joss's DNA at the time of the trial. I know it's difficult, but think about the positives.'

'Positives? What are they when they're at home?'

'You're going to be needed. You set up this inquiry into known crooks becoming missing persons when it's likely they were murdered, right?'

'That's putting it strongly. I wouldn't say I set up an inquiry. I was making enquiries, basically fact-finding.'

'OK, it was at an early stage, but you were in consultation with other CIDs.'

'Whatever gloss you put on it, the whole thing is a side issue, a red herring, matey. It has no bearing on the mess I'm in.'

'You may be wrong about that. It could have a big part to play. You asked the other CIDs to check their records of missing persons for the past four years, is that correct?'

A prolonged 'Mmmmm' came down the phone. She was plainly losing patience.

'Why four? Why not five, or ten? You don't know how long this may have been going on.'

'Listen, chuck. There's a limit to how much digging other CIDs are willing to do. Four years was stretching it.'

'You were being practical, so you said four?'

'I don't know where you're heading with this.'

'Let's suppose it's been going on longer, quite a lot longer, and no one picked up on it.'

'Peter, my old pal, you didn't used to be like this. You're starting to bore me.'

'What if the disappearances went all the way back to 2007, when Rigden was murdered?'

The line went silent while she took it in. Then: 'I don't know what you're on about. In the first place, Joe Rigden was no crook. He was Snow White's twin brother. Secondly, he didn't disappear. There was a body and it was his, no argument.'

'Found in a garden refuse bag in the boot of a stolen car. But who is to say that all the other victims weren't transported in bags in stolen cars to some place where they were disposed of? This one only came to your attention because it was stopped by two sharp cops on patrol.'

'That last bit is correct. The rest is horse-feathers.'

'Why?'

'Like I said, Rigden didn't swim with pondlife. He was Mr Nice Guy.'

'He was shot through the head and driven away in a stolen car. That's how it's done in the criminal world. The guy driving the car was a known crook. You've got to face the possibility that Mr Nice Guy got into trouble with someone in the mob who decided to have him taken out.'

'Unlikely.'

'Try this, then. Rigden happens to witness a crime. He's

so public-spirited that he decides he has a duty to report it. He makes no secret of it. He'd be a key witness, a marked man, wouldn't he?'

'But he wasn't. He was unknown to us as a witness or anything else. I appreciate what you're trying to say, but this is clutching at straws.'

'Did you come up with a motive for the murder?'

'No.'

'You tried, I'm sure.'

'Everything we could think of.'

'You spoke to all the people who employed him?'

'Every one. It's all on file somewhere in the system.'

'I have a printout here in front of me, all the statements, a large stack of paper.'

'Then don't waste time on the garden owners. They all said the same thing: what a lovely man Joe was.'

'It's possible he was up to something none of them knew about.'

'You reckon? Peter, I explored every corner of his life. Money, friends, family, his entire employment history, reading materials, phone calls, travel. A recruit for the secret service doesn't get a going over like that.'

'Growing cannabis? He was a gardener.'

'You're joking, I hope.'

He wasn't giving up. 'Getting back to Danny Stapleton, who *was* a villain with a record, we know there was organised crime involved in this. What was the prosecution case? Didn't they allege that Danny was taking the body to some place where it would be disposed of?'

'That was basically it.'

'And you, Hen? Did you form an opinion whether he was doing the dirty work himself, or delivering the corpse to someone else?'

'I'm of two minds now. In court, they portrayed him as

the driver and the disposal man. He had all that money, too much for a delivery job and nothing else.'

'And of course his defence was to deny all knowledge of the body, so they were free to cast him as the evil bastard on his way to tip it into a reservoir, or down a hole, or whatever?'

'Right,' Hen said. 'We couldn't pin the actual killing on him, so he was tried and convicted as an accessory after the fact.'

'And he still denies it all. He has his own version of what happened. He had the bad luck to nick a car containing a body.'

'And even worse luck to get caught.'

'So he would have us believe,' Diamond said. 'I'm tempted to have another go at him, see if we can break that story, but it won't be enough. Do you think Danny did the killing himself?'

'No.'

'Neither do I. He was a bit player. He may know who the disposal man is, but he won't say. It would destroy his story.'

'So you're stuffed.'

He ignored that. 'Rigden the gardener is the key to this. He may have led the life of a saint, but for some reason he got into dire trouble with one of the big boys. I've got to go over some of the ground you did seven years ago.'

'Waste of time.'

'Help me, Hen. There must have been someone close to him – closer than the rest, anyhow.'

'Seven years have gone by. No one's going to tell you anything new.'

'Give me a name.'

'Some are dead. Others have moved away. Actually, the one who seemed to know him best was the Reverend Conybeare.'

'A reverend? Wouldn't you know it?'

# 17

Just to be certain, she googled *full moon* for the fifth time that day and confirmed what she already knew. It was definitely tonight. If Ella had looked out of the taxi window she'd have seen the real thing emerging from behind a cloud, sharp, silver-white and symmetrical. This had to be the right night for Tom's latest party.

Her mum and dad were under the impression she was part of a sleepover at Jem's, a gathering of all the art group. They hadn't batted an eyelid when she'd appeared in her best goth outfit, the waist-clincher corset and crushed velvet miniskirt with lace trim her dad had disapproved of last time she'd worn it, saying it barely covered her backside – as if minis hadn't existed when he and Mum were teenage lovers. They had known each other since school and there were some seriously embarrassing photos in an album Mum kept, embarrassing because of the fashions and the fact that Dad in those days had longer hair than Mum's. But they hardly ever spoke about what Mum called their courting days and in all truth Ella didn't want to hear about such things. The notion of her parents making love was as distasteful as her own sex life would have been to them, not that it amounted to much. The really hot stuff was in her imagination.

She'd walked to the station and taken one of the taxis that lined up outside. This was about nine thirty, by which time she reckoned the party would be in full swing. Everyone would have had a few drinks and it would be no big deal when she made her appearance. Ought to be, anyhow. The only person she was worried about was Tom himself. His artist friends wouldn't care who was there. They were a laid-back lot and wouldn't know she'd invited herself. It was just possible Tom might disapprove and go into art-teacher mode – as he sometimes did when things threatened to get out of hand at school. Ninety-nine per cent of the time he was just one of the gang and you could say anything and get away with it, but just once in a while he reminded everyone of his role. Fair enough, in school. But here, in front of everyone, with Ella all white face and dark eyes, backcombed and in boots and her full-on gothic gear, a public slapdown didn't bear thinking about.

The other possibility – the one she had been fantasising about all week – was that Tom would not merely welcome her, but be amazed how stunning she was out of school and treat her as the woman she was, the gorgeous bird he was secretly longing to be alone with. If that happened, the rest of year eleven would drool with envy.

Being realistic, the best hope was somewhere between those two. Just let him be cool and allow her to melt in with the other partygoers.

Before leaving the taxi at the gate of Fortiman House, she asked the driver for his card and said she might call him later, depending on her plans. How could she tell? If everything clicked, and she pulled Tom, she wouldn't need a ride home.

Buoyed up with that thought, she stepped up the drive in her knee-high platform boots with the leather tassels flicking her knees while she told herself the big house up ahead didn't look the least bit spooky in the moonlight. Her insides were *not* turning to jelly. Once she'd broken the ice and got a drink in her hand, the rest would be a gas. She hadn't come unprepared. In one of her zipped pockets she had an ecstasy tablet she'd kept when one of the boys was handing them out at the last prom.

She couldn't hear any sounds yet, but it was probably a touch chilly for the party to be outside. Anastasia had said they moved into the studio in the winter months, so she headed there and as she got closer the comforting beat of rock music reached her ears.

Then she heard something else a few yards off.

'Hi, cutey.'

She froze.

The husky male voice had spoken out of nowhere. She looked left and right. It was difficult to see anything except vague shapes apart from a tiny glimmer of red that was possibly the tip of a lighted cigarette. She screwed up her eyes and made out a figure leaning against a tree trunk and wearing some kind of naval officer's jacket and cap.

He spoke again, 'Don't I know you? Yes, I do. You're one of the schoolkids.'

She was so annoyed that her nervousness evaporated. Great, she thought. I go to all this trouble and get an insult like that. 'I'm not a schoolkid. I'm a student,' she said. 'I have a name, you know. I'm Ella. And who are you?'

He took a step out of the shadow and she recognised his pot belly and still struggled to think who he was.

*Him?*

She hadn't expected Davy the model would be among the guests. He dropped the cigarette and trod on it. Then – in case she still didn't know him – he took up a posing stance with hands clasped behind his neck. 'Here's a clue.'

'Give me a break,' she said. 'That's so ridiculous. I can see who you are.'

'No probs,' he said, stepping still closer. 'It happens to

170

me all the time – in the street, in the pub, in buses and trains. People I've posed for stare at me and think where the hell have I seen that handsome guy before? They've looked at me for hours on end but it doesn't make a blind bit of difference. In the studio they see me as an object, not a human being. In my clothes and out and about I'm something different again. Try me.'

'I don't know what you're on about,' Ella said, getting scared and trying to sound unimpressed. She wasn't used to middle-aged men making a play.

'It works in reverse,' Davy said. 'If I was to see you without your kit on I'd be hard put to recognise you. Well, I say that. I wouldn't mind putting it to the test.'

'Get lost,' she said in a hiss that she hoped was pure goth. 'That's disgusting.'

'Chill, babe,' he said. 'I was only making a point. People look at a model, but they don't actually see him. I just proved it, surprising you.'

'You didn't. I knew exactly who you are.'

'Are you here for the party?'

'Isn't that obvious?'

'What's Tom going to say?'

'I don't care. It's not that kind of party, is it?'

'What – drugs?' He shook his head. 'Ferdie wouldn't stand for it and I don't think Tom would, either. I have to come out here for a bloody smoke – and it's not even whacky baccy.'

'Are they drinking?'

'Only wine and stuff. I've had my smoke. I'll go in with you.'

Her instinct was to tell him to get lost, but she reconsidered. This, she thought, could be helpful, being seen with Davy and not making a solo entrance. She'd dump him at the first opportunity.

She fluffed up her hair and followed him to the studio door. He opened it and the decibels hit them.

Brilliant, but terrifying. She got the shakes. She took the tablet of E from her pocket and gulped it down.

She needn't have worried about being conspicuous. The lighting was almost non-existent, a few candles in glasses at each end of the room and some sort of coloured lantern hanging from the ceiling. Davy shouted in her ear, 'Want a drink?'

'No.'

'It won't hurt you.'

'I said no.'

'Let's dance, then.'

She didn't fancy this fat slob one bit, but it was a reason to get away from the door and be a part of the action, so she allowed him to take her arm and move closer to the centre, where others were gyrating to 'Rumour Has It'. Making sure she kept out of range of Davy's pudgy hands, she let the music animate her arms and hips a little while her eyes got used to the near darkness. She thought she could see the elegant Anastasia on her right flicking a feather boa in time to the beat. And presently she heard a loud 'Hel–*lo*' in confirmation.

She nodded and smiled.

Cool. I cracked it, she thought. I'm in.

Anastasia drifted out of focus and in her place was the guy everyone called the Bish, making a much more frenetic movement, a sort of ungainly jig, frankly ridiculous. Tonight he wasn't in bishop mode. Instead of the clerical shirt he was in a kaftan, head back, eyes popping. He didn't recognise her, but by the state of him he wasn't recognising anyone.

She turned with the beat and saw a couple of people she thought she didn't know until she realised one of them

172

was Charcoal Charlotte, now scrubbed up and presentable in a pink frock, but with an equally stupid look on her face, eyes rolling. From what she could tell in the candlelight, the studio was packed, and most of the guests were well sloshed. None of them would bother about an uninvited guest. Every second that passed was adding to Ella's confidence.

The music merged into another Adele number and she made a sideways move to get out of Davy's range. Briefly he looked to be following, but then Anastasia took a step backwards, blocking his way without meaning to. Ella took her chance and squeezed into a space and zigzagged away. She didn't stop until she reached the far side of the studio where some non-dancers were standing, drinks in hand. She moved close to them and looked over her shoulder. She'd lost Davy.

She took out her smartphone and texted Jem and the others: full moon guess where I am.

'I know you,' a voice said.

Oops. She looked up and saw Tom's father Ferdie in a Hawaiian shirt.

'But only by sight,' he added. 'Which one are you?'

She thought about giving a false name, but thought better of it. This old guy was no fool. 'Ella.'

'Are the rest of the gang with you?' He sounded as if he hoped the entire art group had turned up.

'Em, not at this minute.'

'How nice that you came, Ella. I do like your outfit. Very dramatic. I'm supposed to be in charge of drinks. Would you care for one?'

'What have you got? I don't want anything strong.'

'It's mainly wine. Fruit juice for you?'

'Are they, like, alcopops?'

'Good Lord, no. Absolutely no alcoholic content.'

'What flavours do you have?'

'Pineapple, orange, cranberry?'

'Pineapple would be nice.'

'Don't move from here. I'll be right back.'

One of the group she'd joined turned to look at her. More accurately, he looked down. He was a head and shoulders taller. She swallowed hard, not because of his height, but because she'd met another goth. Black leather bomber jacket over a shirt with a werewolf design and baggy trousers with loops of chain hanging from them. And she swallowed even harder when she recognised Geraint, the scary one who painted with knives.

She managed to say, 'Hi.'

Geraint didn't answer. His eyes travelled slowly over her figure. Unlike her, he didn't need to wear make-up. The face was deathly pale and the eyes could have been drops of solder in black plugholes.

Under this withering scrutiny, she brought her left arm defensively across her chest and clasped her opposite shoulder. 'Ferdie's getting me a drink,' she said, to make clear that she wasn't available. 'He asked me to wait. That's the reason I'm standing here.'

Geraint muttered something she couldn't hear clearly through the music that could have been 'witch' or 'bitch'. In either case, Ella told herself, it didn't matter because it would be a goth term of approval. Then he turned his back on her and she felt the rasp of studs from his leather jacket against her arm. She wasn't sure if the contact was deliberate, but she suspected it was.

She took a step away and used her phone as a distraction: OMG just met geraint in goth gear.

Thankfully, Ferdie was soon back with a glass of pineapple juice. 'Does Tom know you're here?'

Her stomach clenched. She didn't want to be taken to

meet the person she'd most come to see. She'd rather approach him on her own terms.

'I expect so,' she said. 'I've already spotted a few people I know.'

It came as a relief when he changed the subject. 'You want to get some pictures with that phone of yours. Some of the guests look pretty wild.'

'I don't know if they'd like being photographed.'

'Too far gone to care, most of them,' he said. 'Ginned up to their eyeballs. Want me to take one of you?'

Good suggestion. Proof positive that she'd been here.

'Would you?' she said. 'I can show the other students.' She touched the camera icon and handed it to him.

'Smile, then.'

Smile? This old guy didn't have a clue what the goth subculture was all about. Ella stared like a judge.

'I'm not sure you're going to like it.'

'It's cool,' she said, checking. 'It'll do.'

'Pity the others didn't come with you,' he said. 'Bring down the average age. We could do with more young people to liven us up.'

'It seems lively to me.'

'It takes all sorts, I suppose, even among artists. We can't all live bohemian lives like Francis Bacon, although some make a stab at it.' He winked and tipped his head in Geraint's direction. 'But some are the opposite, rather staid, in fact. We had a teacher who was really prim and proper, but she stopped coming months ago.'

'Yeah?'

'The name's gone. Don't know why I mentioned her.'

'No problem.'

He raised a finger. 'Got it. Connie, her name was. In the drawing sessions she worked on large sheets of graph paper, measuring everything carefully.'

Ella almost gasped out loud. 'Connie who?'

'I never heard her surname. She taught art at your school, I was told – Priory Park, isn't it? – before Tom started there. That's what must have made me think of her.'

'I think I know who you mean. We called her Miss Gibbon.'

'Is that so? I'd better get back to the drinks table.'

Ferdie moved off and Ella whipped out her smartphone and texted her three student buddies: you wont believe this the Gibbon used to hang out here.

What a laugh.

She sipped the juice and considered her next move. She wasn't comfortable so close to Geraint. Just because he and she were both goths it didn't give him the right to hit on her. More and more she was wishing those wimps Jem, Mel and Naseem could have been here for support.

She decided to make for the far end of the room, but hadn't taken a step when her arm was grabbed and gripped.

Geraint's words were clear this time. 'Where ya going, bitch?'

Her worst fear.

'Let go of me. You're hurting.'

'What gives?'

'Nothing gives for you, Geraint. If you don't let go of me, I'll scream.'

'Be my guest.' He was grinning at the prospect. He had horrible teeth.

But his grip on her arm had loosened and she jerked free and spilled pineapple juice down his trousers. She dropped the glass and left him swearing. In panic, she weaved between dancers without even looking to see who they were.

'Ella?'

'Oh my God!'

Face to face with Tom.

This wasn't remotely what she'd planned.

He said, 'It *is* you. I saw you from a distance and thought I must be mistaken.'

All she could manage was a stupid twitchy grin.

'How did you hear about this?'

'One of the class.'

'And you thought . . .?'

She tried to make light of it. 'Just for a laugh.'

'A laugh?' He rubbed his chin, struggling for words. 'It's not . . . I'm supposed to be . . . Did any of the others . . . ?'

'I'm here on my own.'

He looked at the phone in her hand. 'But you've been texting.'

She bit her lip and said nothing.

'You have, haven't you?'

She nodded. 'They won't come. They're too scared. Please don't send me home.'

He placed his hand in the small of her back and steered her to a dark corner of the room where some of the easels were stacked. 'The thing is,' he said when they were as private as it was possible to be in that crowded room, 'it's a get-together for the artists and some other adult friends of ours. If I'd wanted you here—'

'You'd have invited me,' she said. She'd never stood so close to him before. They were practically touching. She felt a tingling sensation inside.

'Have you been drinking?'

'Ferdie brought me pineapple juice.'

'Are you sure no one gave you wine?'

'I know the flavour of pineapple, silly.'

'Where is it now?'

'I dropped the glass.'

'You don't look right. Are you feeling OK?'

'Sure.' She wanted to say she was feeling better than OK.

The warmth inside was coursing through her and her head felt kind of weird, but pleasantly weird.

'Have you taken something?'

She stared blankly at him and couldn't stop her lips curving a little.

'Ella, concentrate.'

There wasn't anything better to say than, 'It's a free world.'

'You have. Your eyes are huge. What have you taken?'

'One teeny-weeny relaxer, that's all.'

'Christ almighty. Are you hot?'

She giggled. 'Hot – you bet I am.' On the impulse she raised her hands to his face to pull him closer. She felt incredibly confident. 'How hot are you?'

He grasped her wrists and held them. So you want to play hard to get, she thought. She thrust her chest forward, but he swung her round and steered her between the dancers and towards the door. 'You need to cool down. What was it – ecstasy?'

She nodded. She didn't mind Tom being masterful with her. He could take her anywhere he liked.

Outside, the night air was pleasantly cool. Tom had his arm around her shoulders and was walking her across the yard towards the house. She was laughing to herself. Jem and the others would wet themselves if they knew what was happening to her.

'How many did you take?'

'Only one. That's enough.'

'Do you have any more?'

'Why? Would you like one?'

'I'm serious. It's dangerous stuff. How do you feel now? Are you any cooler?'

'Where are we going?'

'Ella, did you hear what I asked?'

'This is nice, you looking after me.'

'How did you get here?'

'Taxi.'

'Give me your phone.'

'Why?'

'Phone.' His schoolteacher voice.

She handed it to him.

They'd reached the house. He helped her up a couple of steps into a kitchen with a huge old-fashioned metal sink. Still with his arm around her, he moved her towards it and ran the cold water. It gushed and splashed.

'I'm not sick,' she said.

'You need to cool down. You get too hot after taking E and it can kill you. Lean forward.'

He splashed water against her face and neck. The shock was extreme at first, but she enjoyed the feel of his hands on her cheeks and neck. She didn't mind her make-up being ruined. Her hair was getting quite wet as well. He filled a glass with water and ordered her to drink.

She obeyed because it was Tom. She wouldn't have drunk frigging water for anyone else.

He handed her a towel and she dabbed her face. 'What do I look like?'

'You don't look normal, I can tell you that.'

'Don't want to look normal. I'm a goth.'

'When are you expected home?'

'Some time tomorrow. Sleepover.' She giggled. 'They don't know who with.'

He removed his arm from her and she swayed or the kitchen swayed. She wasn't sure which.

'Ella,' he said, 'you need to lie down. This can last some hours.' He steadied her and moved her out of the kitchen and across a hallway to another room.

'Are we going to bed?' she asked.

He didn't answer. Deeds are better than words, she

thought as he led her across a carpeted floor to a huge sofa. They were in a sitting room bigger than any she'd seen before. She sank among the cushions. He lifted her legs, so that she was fully stretched out.

A kiss would be a start, she thought.

Instead, he fetched some kind of throw and draped it over her.

'Have a sleep now. I'll look in later.'

# 18

'Why do you want to speak to this vicar?'

Georgina was back and letting Diamond know she was still on top of the job. She'd caught him emerging from the breakfast area after a full English and he'd been rash enough to say he'd like to interview the Reverend Conybeare.

The big detective picked his words carefully. 'He had more to say about Joe Rigden than anyone else. I was reading his statement last night. Went through it line by line. Hen Mallin interviewed him herself.'

'And?'

'I'm not sure she asked the right questions.'

Her eyes were the size of the two fried eggs he'd just consumed. 'Oh my word. Are you thinking she may have held back?'

'Soft-pedalled . . . possibly.'

The 'possibly' made no impression on Georgina. She didn't deal in uncertainties. 'Because she already knew her niece was involved in the murder? That's appalling.'

'I'm not a hundred per cent on this.'

'But you have your suspicions? Peter, you're absolutely right. We have a duty to look at this again. I'll join you.'

He'd guessed she would want to be in on the act. He said at once, 'Both of us taking this on might not be the best use of our resources. We really ought to step up the hunt for Jocelyn.'

She was unimpressed and flapped her hand to show it. 'That's all in hand. She's already on the PNC as locate-and-trace. Everyone has been informed – all the social agencies and car patrols, sea ports and airports.'

'So we're led to understand.'

Her antennae twitched – or at least her eyebrows did.

'The search is being coordinated from here,' Diamond added, 'from Chichester CID. Don't you think we ought to make sure there hasn't been soft-pedalling over this as well? Remember who was in charge.'

She caught her breath and mouthed the words *D.C.I. Mallin*.

'And they're still her team.'

If a sky rocket had shot from Georgina's lips it wouldn't have given a louder whoosh. 'That's unthinkable.'

He raised his eyebrows and said nothing and encouraged her to think the unthinkable.

'I'm taking an executive decision,' she said eventually. 'We shall divide our resources.'

And that was how Peter Diamond had the use of the police car for the morning.

'Slindon,' he told the driver. 'Do you know it?'

'I do, sir. I was brought up there.'

'I'm calling on the vicar.'

'That will be the rector.'

'If you say so.'

'Or the priest. Anglican or Catholic?'

'Two churches, are there?'

'The Catholics have always been strong in the village, even when it was dangerous for them. I'm going back in history, you understand. They had a secret chapel in the roof of a house at one time. Anyone looking for places to hide in Slindon is on to a good thing. Tunnels, priest's holes, they're two a penny.'

Diamond lodged that in his memory. Missing people weren't necessarily dead people. They could be in hiding. 'It must be the rector.'

'No problem. I'll take you to the rectory.'

'The Reverend Conybeare.'

'He's not the rector.'

'Then perhaps after all I want the priest.'

'His name isn't Conybeare either. And he doesn't live in Slindon.'

Why was nothing ever simple? 'The man I want to see definitely lives here.'

At Diamond's suggestion, the driver contacted Chichester police over the radio. The confusion ended. The Reverend Conybeare was a retired cleric from Dorset who lived in Baycombe Lane.

A postcard-pretty cottage with thatched roof, roses and a low doorway with a marked leftward tilt. The elderly man who opened the door had no tilt, but he was short enough to use the entrance without stooping, which made him not much over five foot. He was in a blue clerical shirt.

Diamond explained who he was and why he was calling.

'You'd better come in, then, Mr Detective,' Conybeare said. 'Mind your head.'

The interior was shadowy, requiring a moment or two for the eyes to adjust. Then some observation – if not detective work – was needed to work out that the tenant had an interest unusual for a man of the cloth. A display cabinet contained a top hat resting on its crown with white gloves displayed on the brim, a pack of playing cards fanned in a perfect arc, silk handkerchiefs, a coil of white rope, a silver revolver and a black wand tipped white at each end. Any uncertainty was dispelled by several posters for magic shows on the wall behind.

'It makes sense if you think about it,' Conybeare said in

a world-weary voice suggesting he'd said the same thing many times to visitors. 'A major part of my ministry was about miracles.'

'Isn't there a difference?' Diamond said.

This earned a smile. 'No magician worthy of the name admits to trickery.'

'I was thinking about the showmanship.'

'Ouch! That's a low blow. You're right, of course. There's no comparison. Shouldn't have made such a profane remark. I'm backsliding in my old age.'

'Well, I hope you have a licence for the handgun.'

'Caught again. I don't.' Without warning, Conybeare opened the cabinet, grabbed the gun, pointed it at his own head and pulled the trigger. There was no report. A spring-loaded flag popped out with the word 'BANG' on it.

Diamond tried to look as if he'd fully expected it. 'If only they were all like that. Do you give shows?'

'If pressed. But you're not here to see me perform.' Conybeare gestured towards an armchair. 'No need to check. It's not a whoopee cushion. I don't do practical jokes.' But could he be believed? This was a playful clergyman.

From the chair Diamond tried to sound a serious note. 'After Joe Rigden's violent death in 2007, you were interviewed by the police.'

'I was one of many, I believe.'

'You knew him better than most. At any rate, your statement was longer than anyone else's.'

'That may well be true. I tend to go on a bit.'

'He wasn't your gardener, I understand.'

'I couldn't afford him. I have to do battle with my own little plot, and a battle it is. "One is nearer God's heart in a garden . . ." doesn't apply in my case. I'd rather be doing almost anything else.'

'We understand each other, then. I'm no gardener either.'

'Fortunately there's nothing in the scriptures to say we should pull weeds.' He smirked as if he'd just thought of something improper. 'On the whole it would have been better if everyone in the Bible had avoided going into gardens. But you asked about Joe. I had a high regard for the man. His violent death was a mystery to us all. He led a good life, from all one could tell.'

'How did you get to meet him?'

'As a local volunteer. There are elderly folk in the village and they appreciate a helping hand with shopping, meals on wheels and so forth. Joe did it from the goodness of his heart. He was a lovely man. He didn't share my faith, but I have to say he was kinder to others than many Christians I could name.'

'What was his religion?'

'He didn't have one. He described himself as a realist. When someone says that to a clergyman it's a bit of a slap in the face.'

'But you still admired him?'

'Couldn't fail to. He was cheerful, honest, reliable, hard-working and mindful of others. He kept most of the Ten Commandments without having to think about them. It was only worshipping God he found impossible.'

'There are plenty like him.'

'Not like Joe. He lived by his principles.'

'It sounds as if you got to know him well. Did he talk much?'

'Not as much as me. We chatted, found our lives over-lapped in other ways.'

'Such as?'

'I used to visit several of the properties where he was employed. Garden parties and the like. Being a retired rev, so to speak, I'm on several invitation lists. I was able to admire Joe's handiwork, the stripes the mower made and the state of the flower beds. I'd make a point of complimenting him later.'

'Wasn't he there?'

'At the garden parties? No, in village society, gardeners are classed with hewers of wood and drawers of water.'

'How did he feel about that?'

'He didn't let it bother him. He was a teetotaller, anyway. Parties weren't his scene at all. I suppose he was a throwback to an earlier generation when working men were supposed to know their place and get on with life. Thinking about it, we had that in common as well. For some folk, the clergy are below the salt.'

Diamond didn't go down that avenue. 'Did you ever discuss your beliefs with him?'

'On a few occasions. Mostly we agreed to differ. I could tell it was no use trying to convert him.'

'So was he an awkward cuss?'

After a pause, Conybeare said, 'That's rather cynical if I may say so.'

'You'll have to make allowance,' Diamond said. 'I'm trying hard to think why anyone murdered such a saintly man.'

'It's a mystery to me, too.'

'Sometimes upright men antagonise others without meaning to.'

'Sadly, that is true.'

'You said he knew his place and got on with life. Was that because he felt inferior to the gentry, if I can call them that?'

'You mean the upper crust of the village? Inferior? Certainly not. He'd laugh about their vanities, just as I do.'

'But not to their faces?'

'He didn't go out of his way to be offensive.'

'If pressed – say if one of them accused him of doing shoddy work – would he stand up for himself?'

186

'Absolutely. He lived by his principles and defended them without fear or favour.'

'Did he have friends?'

'I'm not sure "friends" is the word I would use. People liked him, but he kept them at a distance. He wasn't ever seen in the pub in the days we had one and he didn't join things other than the volunteer group, who functioned mainly as individuals. You might think the horticultural society would have appealed, but Joe wasn't a member.'

'I expect he'd had enough of horticulture, doing it all day. Did he have a hobby, as you do?'

'The magic?' He laughed. 'That's peculiar to me and Joe thought it peculiar, too. In fact, he called it trickery. As a joke I once snapped my fingers and produced a bunch of flowers. Flowers for a gardener, get it? They're a paper effect, packed very small, and spring open. He wasn't at all amused. He threw them aside like a piece of waste. He liked his world to be solid and real.'

'Both feet on the ground?'

'Constantly. Well, he may have propped them up of an evening. He worked hard in the day and liked to relax quietly at home.'

'I was reading your original statement and it seems you were one of the last to speak to him.'

'Was I?'

Patiently, Diamond spelt out the facts. 'Chichester police stopped a car on the Tuesday evening and found it contained Joe Rigden's body and it was estimated he'd been shot some time in the previous twenty-four hours. He gave you a lift into Chichester, on Sunday, September twenty-third.'

'He was always doing good turns like that.'

'You attended morning service at the cathedral while he spent the time shopping. Do you still recall it?'

'I do. An excellent sermon on the raising of the widow's son.'

'I meant the drive in the car, in particular what was said.'

'Have a heart, superintendent. This was seven years ago.'

'But you remember the sermon.'

'It was the sixteenth Sunday after Trinity. The second lesson is always St Luke on the widow's son. I've preached on it many times.'

Diamond was beginning to wish Georgina had taken over this interview. 'You told DCI Mallin there was a difference of opinion in the car.'

'That must be true, then. DCI Mallin – yes, a lady. I remember her questions and very sharp they were. She interviewed me here and gave me the cue to fire my trick gun, just as you did. Good at her job. Firm, but friendly.'

'I'm asking about Joe Rigden.'

'I appreciate that.'

'What was this difference of opinion you had? It isn't clear from the statement.'

His expression changed. 'I'm sorry. It was a private conversation, of no conceivable relevance to your investigation. It did neither of us much credit and I prefer to remember Joe in a more positive light.'

'I'm sorry too, but this was the last conversation he's known for certain to have had with anyone. I need to know his state of mind.'

'He wasn't suicidal, if that's what you're thinking.'

'You're withholding information, sir. You may think it has no bearing, but I need to hear it.'

Conybeare gave an impatient sigh. 'If you must know, we had words about the sermon I'd heard, a theological matter, so you see it's of no interest to you at all.'

'The miracle of a man raised from the dead?'

'Yes, I told you. Now can we move on?'

188

'What was the issue?'

'Really, this is too much.'

Diamond was firm with him. 'It's not enough.'

Another sigh. 'If you must know, it was our old debate about magic. Joe said there was sure to have been a rational explanation for Our Lord bringing the man back to life – the usual thing one gets from disbelievers about people being pronounced dead and then resuscitated. I begged to differ, as I was bound to. I said this was only one of a number of miracles and I accepted it as fact, just as I accepted the feeding of the five thousand. He said as an amateur conjurer I ought to know a clever illusionist can do almost anything. He'd seen a man on television make the Statue of Liberty disappear. I insisted there was a difference between magic and miracles and he got very angry.'

'*He* got angry? I would have thought you had more right to be angry.'

He gave a faint smile. 'I was, to be truthful.'

'He was winding you up.'

'No, it wasn't like that. The concept of miracles unsettled him. He liked to believe everything had a rational explanation.'

'It sounds as if he was irrational, letting it get to him.'

'Sometimes it seemed like that. He told me – not for the first time – how much he disapproved of my hobby. He referred to it as conjuring, not magic, as I do. It was almost as if the word magic was too upsetting to speak aloud. I knew it was a sensitive point. I'm sorry our last conversation turned out the way it did.'

'Was there anything else on his mind, do you suppose?'

'What do you mean?'

'Well, maybe he was under threat.'

'From whoever shot him? I hadn't thought of that. All I can say is that he didn't seem himself at all.'

'Did you part as friends?'

Conybeare sighed. 'With less grace than I would have wished. I could tell he was troubled and I thought it was my fault. I thanked him for the lift and that was the last I ever saw of him.'

'You said you knew several of the people he worked for. Were there any who treated him shabbily?'

'If there were, he would never have told me. He was discreet.'

'Any with a reputation for violence?'

'You're clutching at straws now, aren't you? I don't deal in tittle-tattle any more than Joe did, never have.'

'Answer the question, please.'

'No, I can't think of anyone who would have wished him harm.'

This was getting nowhere. A different approach was wanted. 'Put yourself in my position,' Diamond said. 'Here was a good man who apparently worked hard and gave no offence to anyone, yet was murdered and his killer was never found.'

'I understood a man was put on trial,' Conybeare said.

'Convicted as an accessory after the fact. He isn't thought to have committed the murder. The killer may still be living here as one of your neighbours.'

'Oh, I very much doubt it. People here are convinced it was an outsider, a professional criminal, some armed robber who was challenged by Joe at one of the large properties where he worked. It would have been typical of Joe to face up to an armed man. His sense of justice quite outweighed the caution most of us would exercise in such a situation. The robber shot him and drove off with his body to cover up the crime. We don't lose any sleep thinking we're going to be murdered by one of our own.'

# 19

After the trip to Slindon, Diamond decided to visit Hen. Her black mood when he'd phoned the previous evening had been all too apparent. His efforts to shake her out of it hadn't made any difference. A face-to-face meeting – without Georgina looking on – might get a better result.

Up there on the third floor of her apartment block, he was surprised to find the morning's mail sticking out of the letterbox. He rang the bell and got no answer. Shame, he thought, but maybe it's a good sign if she's gone out.

Then he noticed some freshly splintered wood close to the latch. The door had been forced. At a push it swung open.

A chill spread through him.

Inside the small flat, he called her name.

Nobody answered.

The curtains were still drawn in the living room. There was no obvious sign of a burglary. His heart pounding, he stepped to a door at the end and crossed a small passage to the bedroom.

Drawn curtains again. He reached for the light switch.

Hen wasn't there. The duvet was half off the bed. On the bedside cupboard were an empty bottle of vodka, a glass tumbler and a used blister pack that had contained prescription capsules. He snatched it up.

Temazepam.

'Hen, what have you done?' he said aloud. 'Crazy.'

On his way out he was met by a woman with shopping bags.

She said, 'Did you want Hen? I live next door.'

'What happened?'

'She was taken off in an ambulance in the middle of the night. They had to break in. It woke us all up. She's been awfully down, poor darling. I think she lost her job.'

'Where will they have taken her?'

'St Richard's. That's the nearest.'

'Is that Chichester?'

'It's the main hospital. Off Spitalfields Lane.'

'I'll find it.'

He'd sent the police driver on his way, but he stopped a taxi in the Hornet and was at A&E reception inside ten minutes.

His ID didn't get him any favours. The receptionist confirmed that Hen had been brought in as an emergency during the night and he was told to wait with all the others.

Things have to be serious when the medics bar the police from going in.

With his own blood pressure rising to dangerous levels, he took his place in a crowded seating area among people in various states of unease and distress. A half hour soon passed. At one point his phone went and he got disapproving looks. He went outside with it and saw that the call was from Georgina. He wasn't ready to talk to his supremo about what Hen may or may not have done, so he switched off and returned to the waiting area.

He'd never understood why people topped themselves. Even in his darkest crisis after Steph's death, he'd not contemplated that way out. But you can't get inside people's minds. Depression is an illness. It's futile to judge.

A new face was now behind the reception desk, so he

had another try at explaining why he was there. He was told firmly to return to his seat. Twenty more palm-sweating minutes went by before his name was called.

'Are you Henrietta Mallin's partner?'

'Partner? No. I don't think she has a partner.'

'Next of kin?'

'No.'

'Then why are you here?'

Fair question, but he took it as an attack and snapped back, 'I keep telling you people. She's a police officer and so am I.' He brandished his ID again. 'I'm also a friend. I know her personally, is that good enough?'

She held up a finger. 'We're all under pressure here, sir. Let's not give way to it. Henrietta has been admitted. She's had some treatment and she's no longer critical, but she needs time here to recover. She's waiting for a bed now. You can go through and see her if you wish.'

Of course he wished. He'd been waiting almost an hour.

As he turned from the desk he heard the nurse say, 'She's probably sedated and if she isn't she'll seem that way.'

He found Hen on a trolley in the corridor, her head bandaged. She opened her eyes when he spoke her name.

After a moment's uncertainty, she said, 'Hell's bells.'

'It's me,' he said, 'Peter Diamond.'

'I can see who you are, dingbat. I was expecting another wet-behind-the-ears doctor. How did you . . .?'

'Never mind me. What happened? Did you fall?'

She screwed up her face. 'Don't ask.'

'I've been to your flat,' he said. 'I was able to walk in. The paramedics had to break in.'

'I was on the vodka – nuff said?' Hen in confessional mode again.

'You were depressed.'

'I'm not exactly jumping for joy right now.'

'We've all had a few drinks in our time.'

'Thought in my own home I could do as I liked. Woke up, needed the bathroom, stepped out in the dark and straight into a bookshelf. Hit my head and saw stars. It bled a bit. I thought I was all right and then I passed out. Tried standing up and it happened again, so next time I came round I crawled to the phone and called the ambulance. I don't remember much about it.'

'You did the right thing. You can't take chances with head wounds.'

'They say I'll survive. Brute of a headache. I don't know if it's a hangover or the bonk on the conk. They insist I spend some time in a recovery ward. Help me up, Pete. I want to be out of here now.'

'Take their advice. They won't keep you any longer than necessary.'

'I'm dying for a smoke. You don't happen to . . . ?'

'This is a hospital, Hen.'

'You could push this damned trolley outside.'

'No.'

'What a mess.'

'Did something else happen – or is it the situation you're in?'

'There's that, of course, and Joss.' She rolled her eyes. 'And there's Danny Stapleton. He was on my mind after you and the she-wolf came to visit. To be honest, I hadn't thought much about him in recent years. Out of sight, out of mind. I have to face the possibility that it wasn't a pack of lies he gave me about how he came into possession of that stolen BMW. I could have put him away mistakenly for a life stretch and I feel wretched about it, thinking of him in jail all this time.'

'If it was a mistake, it was a reasonable one,' he said. 'It convinced a judge and jury. We know Danny is a crook.'

'A small-time crook. You saw him in Parkhurst and he stands by his story after all this time.'

'Hen, I listened to him and he makes it sound plausible, but I was left in two minds. He'll say whatever he can to get another hearing. Any prisoner will.'

'I know, but as things are turning out, he could be on the level. He's on my conscience and it's doing my head in. That's why I took to the bottle last night.'

'The bottle – and the sleeping tablets.'

She blinked and looked more alert. 'Pete, I wasn't trying to kill myself, if that's what you think – else why would I have called the ambulance?'

'You didn't let them in.'

'You're right. I don't remember. I must have passed out again. You know what I hit my head on?'

'You told me – a bookshelf.'

'It's the one in the passage outside the bathroom. My Agatha Christie paperbacks.'

'The Queen of Crime strikes again.'

A nurse and a porter arrived and told Hen they were moving her to the ward. She tried to sit up, said she was ready to leave, but they insisted she remained and Diamond gave the nurse his backing.

'I'll keep her company and when you say she's OK to go home I'll call a taxi and go with her.'

'You don't have to talk about me as if I'm a pet rabbit,' Hen said. 'I can hear you. I'm fine now. I'll be all right.'

But she wasn't believed.

He passed twenty minutes seated beside the bed drinking lukewarm tea in a ward full of old ladies who stared at him.

Hen said, 'Where's the dragon?'

'Georgina? Still at the nick, I hope.'

'*My* nick?'

'That's where I sent her this morning.'

'You sent *her*?'

'I went to see the Reverend Conybeare and I didn't want her muscling in. She's sniffing out a possible conspiracy in your CID.'

She shifted herself higher on the pillow. 'Go on.'

'The search for Joss. I suggested they might be soft-pedalling.'

'God, I hope not. Why would they do that?'

'Out of loyalty to you.'

'I don't follow you. I don't want any soft-pedalling. I want Joss found as soon as possible, the same as everyone else. Her family are going spare with worry. We all are.'

'I know – and it won't hurt for Georgina to crack the whip.'

'You'd better watch it, chummy. She's not daft. She'll rumble you.'

'She often does.'

'I don't know how you stand it, Peter. I lost my cool with her, as you saw.'

'Practice. Georgina and I understand each other. In fact, I've got to know her a lot better since we came on this trip. I discovered she has a soft underbelly.'

The crossed swords of the Victory Arch in Baghdad were no higher than Hen's eyebrows. 'The mind boggles.'

'Oh, come on,' he said. 'A weak point. Insecurity.'

'I get you. Which you will now exploit.'

'I doubt if I will, but I can read her better.'

Now Hen's mouth curved at the ends. 'After all this time I do believe you're starting to understand the female psyche.'

'No chance.'

Each was silent for a while. Another patient on a trolley was wheeled past.

'So did you learn anything new from the sky pilot?'

'Conybeare? Well, you didn't tell me he's a member of the Magic Circle.'

'Why would you want to know? What the vicar does in his spare time doesn't have any bearing on the murder.'

'Ah, but it told me something interesting about the victim, Joe Rigden. He didn't approve.'

'Of the conjuring? How come?'

'For some reason it touched a raw nerve. There was an occasion when Conybeare performed a little trick, snapped his fingers and produced a bunch of flowers. They were only paper, but they unsettled Rigden so much that he slung them aside "like a piece of waste", according to the vicar.'

'Why? It was just a bit of fun.'

'His explanation is that Rigden liked his world solid and real. For the same reason he didn't have any time for religion – which you would think made problems for their friendship, but they seemed to respect each other's point of view.'

Hen shook her head. 'Peter, I don't know how you do it. You have this knack of rooting out information that goes over my head.'

'Well, you're only four foot something.'

'Bloody cheek.'

He became serious again. 'The same raw nerve twitched the last time the two of them were together. Rigden used to give the rector a lift into Chichester on a Sunday when there wasn't a service in the church at Slindon. The day before the murder, they had a strong argument on the way home. Conybeare didn't want to tell me anything about it. I had to prise the story out of him. He'd been listening to a sermon about one of the miracles in the New Testament, the widow's son who is raised from the dead. Rigden said there was probably a rational explanation.'

'Talk about a raw nerve,' Hen said. 'I should think that was a problem for the reverend.'

'Exactly – and it was. He felt bound to defend the story

197

and miracles in general and Rigden got very angry and when they parted at the end of the ride, they were both feeling frayed. It shows Rigden's state of mind was edgy not long before he was killed. Everyone speaks of him as a nice, obliging guy, almost saintly, yet here was a topic that got him rattled.'

'No sense of proportion.'

'You could put it that way. Whatever it was, I can see how it may have got him into trouble.'

'You're not suggesting Conybeare shot Rigden?'

'No. Like you, I've racked my brains for a reason why such a well-regarded bloke was murdered. Thanks to the vicar I now know there was a different side to him. Call it obstinate, or bloody-minded, he gave no ground when he felt the issue mattered.'

'I can see that, but I can't see how it helps unless the killer was an evangelist or a magician.'

He nodded. 'I agree it's not much to go on.'

A nurse came by and said to Diamond, 'Don't overtax her. She's supposed to be resting her brain.'

He waited until the nurse was halfway up the ward and said, 'One more question, then. Did you interview each of the people Rigden worked for?'

'Every one,' Hen said. 'No conjurers and no clergymen, I'm afraid.'

'How many?'

'That's two.'

He frowned. She'd lost him. 'Two employers?'

'Two questions. You said you would only ask one more. From memory, he worked in seven different gardens.' Hen's power of recall seemed to be unaffected by the injury.

'So which was the last he worked in?'

'It belonged to Mrs Shah, an Asian lady who has since died.'

'Of natural causes, I hope.'

'She was almost a hundred, poor old duck. She lived some miles from his place.'

'Alone?'

'That generation are very independent. According to Joe's Filofax, he was due there the day he was murdered, the Monday.'

'And did he come? Did the old lady confirm it?'

'No chance. She hadn't the foggiest. She never left the house. She relied on the phone and direct debits for all her needs. Joe would turn up and do the work, whatever he decided needed doing, and never see her.'

'You must have checked the garden.'

'I'm not a total beginner, Pete.'

'What's it like?'

'Big enough to be called an estate in my opinion. There's a wild section, an orchard, several lawns. We searched for evidence of the shooting and found nothing. Dragged the pond. The job took several days.'

'Did you find where he'd been working?'

'Even that was uncertain. The lawns weren't cut recently and the mower was in the garden shed along with a load of other equipment and the old padded jacket he used when the weather was cold.'

'He could have been weeding or pruning. This was September and gardens are still growing at that time of year.'

'I'm aware of that, ducky. If you take a trip there, you'll see what I mean, but don't expect to find anything.'

A young woman doctor came by and checked Hen's condition. 'She should be all right to travel now,' she told Diamond. 'Did you bring her day clothes?'

'Er . . . no.'

'She's in a hospital gown. She can't leave like that.'

'I came in a pink-striped nightie,' Hen said.

'They'll bring it presently,' the doctor said and turned to Diamond again. 'You can help her on with it.'

'Probably not,' he said. 'She might not welcome that.'

Hen said softly, 'Coward.'

From the doctor he got a look that said he was no gentleman and might well have been responsible for Hen's injury.

When the nightdress arrived and the curtains around the bed were being drawn, Diamond muttered something about calling a taxi and quit the ward at speed.

When he eventually got back to the hotel, it was after seven. He hadn't been in his room two minutes before the phone rang.

'There you are at last,' Georgina said in a voice drained of all tolerance. 'I've been trying to reach you on your mobile all afternoon. Was it switched off?'

He could so easily have said he'd been on hospital prem-ises and was keeping to their rules about phones, but he didn't want Georgina knowing of Hen's misadventure and putting the worst possible construction on it.

'Funny. I'll check.' He let a few seconds pass before saying, 'Ah, you're quite right. It was switched off. Sometimes I wonder if there are gremlins in this damn thing. You didn't need me urgently, I hope?'

'Fat use if I had,' she said. 'Come to my room and tell me what you learned from the Reverend Conybeare. And I want to know what else you've been up to. You can't have spent all day at his cottage.'

'Can you give me twenty minutes? I was about to take a shower.' Enough time, he hoped, to dream up some story that would satisfy her.

\*     \*     \*

200

After giving a detailed account of the Conybeare interview, he made a firm attempt to switch roles and invite Georgina to summarise her day. She was having none of it.

'You haven't told me where you were all afternoon.'

He'd told a few untruths in his time, but experience had taught him to stay as close to the facts as possible without actually revealing all. 'Not much to do in Slindon,' he said. 'I came back here and told the driver he wouldn't be needed again. I thought about joining you at the nick and then decided against it. You don't need me hanging on your coat tails. So I went out again. Fresh air and exercise to get the brain working. We haven't had a case conference since we got here, so I held my own, so to speak, reviewing what we've done and discovered.'

She said with suspicion, 'Where was this – in some pub?'

'No, no. I needed a clear head. Do you know Spitalfields Lane?' He was confident she didn't. 'That's where I ended up, if you want to know.'

'And did you come to any startling conclusion?'

'Startling? No.'

'But you thought of something important?'

'Maybe.' Anything to steer Georgina away from how he'd passed the afternoon. 'I was thinking of Danny Singleton and his story about the stolen BMW. Let's suppose it really happened just as he described: the car arriving outside the pub where he was and by good luck being the make his gizmo would unlock. I was asking myself why the car containing the body was parked in that particular spot in Littlehampton. The person wearing the hooded jacket got out and walked away across the bridge, right?'

'That's Danny's story – which has to be taken with more than a pinch of salt.'

'Let's go with it for a moment. The hoodie wouldn't run

the risk of leaving the car there and later returning. He'd leave it there because—'

'*She* would leave it there,' Georgina said. 'We're thinking Joss was the hoodie because her DNA was found in the car.'

'OK. Joss would leave it there because those were her instructions. There was an arrangement. After dark the body would be removed from the car by whoever it is who has been disposing of these missing persons. That was the plan. But Danny messed it up by stealing the car and driving off, unaware of what was in the boot.'

Georgina leaned forward. 'Peter, this is clever. I think you're on to something. I hadn't linked this case to the missing persons.'

'And if I'm right, we now have an insight into the method used.'

'How is that?'

'The location. The bodies are brought to this quiet spot by the river—'

'And dropped off the bridge?'

He was about to say, 'Nothing so crude,' and he stopped himself. 'It has to be smarter than that. My guess is that they're transferred to a boat and taken out to sea, probably weighted down and dropped overboard somewhere in coastal waters. The disposer – if we call him that – would make damn sure they'd stay submerged.'

'And officially they remain as missing persons. It answers a lot of the questions. Do you think it's still going on, leaving the bodies at Littlehampton?'

'Going on, yes, but I doubt if the location is the same. The Rigden case will have required a rethink. But from what we hear, people are still going missing all along the south coast.'

Georgina clearly liked what she'd heard. 'No one in Chichester CID has thought of this.'

'It's just a theory,' Diamond said.

'But not obvious. If you and I can find Joe Rigden's killer, we're more than halfway to collaring the ghoul who is making so many bodies disappear without trace.'

'Or there's another way of looking at it.'

'What's that?'

'Catch the ghoul first and he can lead us to our killer.'

She shook her head. 'Far too difficult. He could be anywhere along the coast.'

'He's known to the people who use his services, else how would they contact him?'

'Peter, I'm impressed. You've really thought this through. It wasn't a day wasted.'

Here was a perfect opening 'And how was your day, Georgina?'

This casual use of her name gave her a jolt. It practically gave her whiplash. Earlier on the trip she'd invited the liberty, but she hadn't expected him to take it up. 'My day?' she eventually managed to say. 'I was at the police station. I banged a few heads together, but basically they're doing all they can. Soft-pedalling? I wouldn't say so. Finding Joss is their priority and they've done all the right things, issued photos to the media, given a press conference, followed up on every lead.'

'But no success?'

'It's not for want of trying.'

'So DI Montacute can't be faulted?'

'He's not the easiest person to get on with, but I'm used to dealing with awkward detectives.'

Diamond grinned.

'However,' Georgina went on, 'I'm a little concerned about something that happened towards the end of the afternoon. It could so easily distract them. Well, it must, to some extent.'

He waited for her to go on.

'In my opinion, it's scarcely a CID matter at all. We deal with things like this all the time.'

'Like what?'

'A schoolgirl whose parents don't know where she is. You and I know there's nothing to get excited about when a teenager goes off the rails. In ninety-nine per cent of the cases they come back.'

His interest quickened. 'Which school?'

'Priory Park. She's only been missing a few hours.'

'Did you catch the name?'

'Melanie Mason. Everyone calls her Mel.'

# 20

Miss Du Barry, the headmistress of Priory Park, liked to be known simply as the head. She was a natural leader, dignified, decisive and calm in a crisis. She also terrified the students. Here, in her office, seated in the white leather executive chair behind a desk that could have doubled as Queen Victoria's funeral bier, she was ready to deal with anyone, police included. Gilt-framed portraits of previous headmistresses in academic dress adorned the wall behind her. She was in what she called informal attire, a charcoal grey suit and white blouse with a choker collar.

Peter Diamond, grey-suited as usual, on the other side of the desk in an upright chair a couple of inches lower than the head's, had an inkling of how any girl summoned here must have felt. A sharp aroma invaded his nostrils and added to the unsettling effect. He traced it to an arrangement of yellow and white chrysanthemums only an arm's length away, on the filing cabinet. Probably the school colours, he decided.

He'd come straight from the hotel. Georgina wasn't with him, having told him quite reasonably that this was a distraction, unrelated to their mission. Doubtless she thought it was another excuse to avoid a meal in her company.

'It's late in the day, I know,' Diamond said.

The head gave a thin indulgent smile. 'Not at all. My responsibility is twenty-four hours a day, seven days a week.'

'It's about the missing schoolgirl.'

'We call them students, superintendent.'

'The missing student, then.'

She gave a curt nod, familiar to anyone who has been through school, registering that a slow learner had got there without earning any credit. 'And if they fail to appear in school we say they are absent.'

He wasn't swallowing that. 'By our reckoning, if a girl hasn't been home all night and no one has heard from her, she's missing.'

'Do you have new information?'

'Not yet, ma'am.'

'Then why are you here?'

'I need information from you.'

She tried persuasion first. 'I have every confidence Melanie hasn't come to any harm. Young people of her age often go through a rebellious stage and give their parents a fright.' Then she covered herself. 'However, we're duty-bound to take it seriously.'

'So are we. Have you spoken to the parents?'

'To her stepfather, yes. He called me this morning, hoping one of her friends would know where she was.'

'And I gather they don't.'

'No. Melanie happens to be the kind of girl who keeps her life outside school to herself. Most of them are only too eager to share every trivial detail with friends and with the world in general, using the entire paraphernalia of the social media. Not Melanie.'

'Any reason for that?'

'Her situation. She's here on a bursary provided by the trade union her late father belonged to. He was killed in an accident at work. He was working-class, a road-mender, very different from the parents of most of our students. Any group of children is quick to notice an individual who is different. One can't do anything about it.'

What an admission. 'Have you tried?'

'It doesn't help the child in question. It's group psychology at work.'

'Mob violence.'

'That's overstating it. There was nothing physical involved. Some disapproval, a certain amount of teasing.'

'Mental cruelty, then.' Argument was futile, so he left it there. 'But the mother remarried?'

'To another working man.'

'When did they first notice she'd gone?'

'Don't you know?'

Sharp question. He tried not to react like the class slacker. 'I'm coming to the case rather late in the day.'

'Melanie was at home yesterday evening in her room,' the head informed him. 'She would appear to have gone out at some point without saying anything to the parents. They discovered this when they were about to retire for the night, towards eleven. She never fails to say goodnight to them. The scooter she rides is missing. People of their sort are either panicky or indifferent in a situation like that. They are clearly the former. I understand they phoned your police station about six.'

Explaining that Chichester wasn't his nick was just too complicated. 'Everyone has been alerted. Is there a boyfriend?'

'Not to the parents' knowledge. And her fellow students haven't heard of anyone either.'

'But you said she keeps thing bottled up, so we can't rule it out. Does she have any male teachers?'

Miss Du Barry shifted in her chair. 'I don't follow your reasoning here. If I do understand your question, I don't care for it.'

'It's got to be asked,' Diamond said. 'Students have crushes sometimes and teachers have been known to take advantage.'

'Not in this school.'

'There's always a first time. I assume you have some men on the staff?'

Her eyes slid upwards, letting him know this was all too impertinent. 'A few.'

'Getting back to my question, is Melanie taught by any of them?'

'Superintendent, there are more than five hundred students in Priory Park. I don't know the personal timetable of every one.'

'I'm not asking about them all. Just Melanie.'

'I can access hers if you wish.'

'That would be helpful.'

She opened a drawer, took out a laptop, worked the keys and said, 'One of her A-level subjects is art.'

'And is one of your art teachers a man?'

He was shadow-boxing and so was she. Of course she knew.

'Mr Standforth joined us at the start of term. He's from a good family and highly responsible in his dealings with the students.'

'What age would he be?'

'I don't see how that comes into it.'

'You must have some idea.'

'Quite young, between twenty-five and thirty, but that's not an issue.'

'Was he in school today?'

'He was.' She snapped down the lid of the laptop. 'I saw him myself.'

'Did you speak?'

'We passed the time of day, as one does.'

'Is he here now?'

'He will have left an hour ago.' She gripped the arms of her chair and took a deep breath. 'Superintendent, I don't seem to have made myself clear. There is no question whatsoever of Mr Standforth being implicated in Melanie's absence. He is fully aware of the sensitivities of being a male teacher in a girls' school. Like every new teacher, he went through the usual DBS checking process before we employed him. Aside from that, Melanie herself is one of the most mature students in the school, and the chance of her becoming infatuated with a teacher is so unreal as to be ridiculous.'

'I hear you, but—' Diamond said, and was stopped.

Miss Du Barry had cut in with: 'Thank you. There's a real danger in any teaching establishment of gossip and rumour spreading like wildfire. I won't allow unfounded theories to disturb the smooth running of the school. That would be deeply disruptive and mustn't happen.'

'I appreciate everything you say, ma'am,' Diamond said, 'but I have a job to do as well. We could be dealing with something far more serious than an absent student.'

She tensed. The bigger risk had got home to her at last.

Diamond said, 'If Melanie hasn't shown up by tomorrow, we'll step up the investigation. I'll come in and have a few words with your Mr Standforth.'

'I've vouched for Mr Standforth's character. Isn't that enough?'

He gave her the sort of look she gave her students.

She sighed. 'However you go about it, there will be consequences.'

'And while I'm here, I'll need to speak to some of Melanie's classmates.'

Her shoulders sagged. 'Oh dear. We'll never hear the end of this.'

'Let's hope she's perfectly all right, then.' He paused, watching her. 'I was impressed when I met her.'

Miss Du Barry blinked. 'You met Melanie?'

'Strangely enough, she came into the police station yesterday.'

'Whatever for?'

'She was enquiring about a Miss Constance Gibbon, who used to teach her art.'

'Melanie was asking you about Miss Gibbon?' The face turned pale. Almost immediately blotches of red started to appear.

'A missing person,' Diamond said. 'Officially missing, on the missing persons' index. Not absent, but missing.'

'There's no need for sarcasm. Miss Gibbon left the school last term, at the end of July.'

'And hasn't been heard of since. She hasn't been in touch with her family and they reported their concern.'

'I do know about this,' the head said in a more measured way, trying to recover her equilibrium. 'We had someone here asking questions. As far as we're concerned, Constance Gibbon handed in her notice and left.'

'May I see it?'

'May you see what?'

'Her letter of resignation.'

'There was no letter, I was using a form of speech, that's all. But I don't see what business it is of Melanie's.'

'If you're asking me, I'd say it's a credit to Melanie that she's troubled about this woman. I gather she wasn't all that popular.'

'Popularity isn't necessarily the hallmark of a good teacher,' Miss Du Barry said.

'Were there complaints? I'm wondering why she left.'

'No complaints I ever heard of.'

'Melanie said her lessons were boring.'

She gripped the desk and drew herself higher in the chair. 'I find this profoundly offensive, being asked to respond to student tittle-tattle.'

'It wasn't said out of spite. The teacher is on Melanie's conscience because of the way she was treated.'

'Superintendent Diamond, I assure you Miss Gibbon was

210

treated in the professional way every teacher is entitled to expect.'

'Don't get me wrong,' Diamond said. 'I'm not criticising you.'

'I should hope not.'

'And neither was Melanie. The problem with Miss Gibbon, as I understand it, was in the classroom. You may disagree, but I can't ignore what Melanie had to say. And now she, too, is . . . absent.'

'I think you'd better leave. Now.'

There was nothing to be gained by staying. At the door, he turned. 'This Mr Standforth. Is he a straight replacement for Miss Gibbon?'

'He is.'

'From round here?'

'He's a local man, yes, well qualified and with the right experience at this level. We were lucky to get him.'

'From a good family, you said. Do you know them?'

'I know *of* them. The Standforths have lived in Boxgrove for generations and contribute generously to all kinds of good causes. Tom Standforth has a studio that he opens regularly for local artists.'

'I look forward to meeting him – if it becomes necessary. Thanks for your time, ma'am.'

Back at the hotel, he ordered room service and spent some time on the phone. First he called Hen to make sure she was recovering well. She sounded like her old self, much amused by his account of the headmistress. She'd heard of the Standforth family and confirmed that they were well known locally, although she hadn't met any of them. 'Which is probably a recommendation, darling,' she added. 'You and I only ever get to meet the baddies.'

He also had a long call to Paloma, who didn't seem to

be missing him at all. Neither did his cat. Paloma had driven past the neighbour's house and seen Raffles blissfully asleep on a windowsill in a patch of sunlight.

'I'll be back as soon as possible,' he told Paloma. 'I'm trying my best to speed things up.'

'Don't you worry,' she said. 'Enjoy the hotel life while you've got the opportunity.'

Next morning, about a mile south of Selsey Bill, a small cabin cruiser was chugging through calm water. Aboard were two men in their seventies, friends for half a century, who had rented the boat for a day's sea-fishing. They didn't expect to catch much. They never did. The pleasure of these trips was being at sea, away from it all, with a hamper of good food and a bottle or two of wine, while their wives had a shopping expedition to Portsmouth's Gunwharf Quays. A good arrangement all round.

Jim Bentley, currently at the wheel, unexpectedly said, 'Something up ahead.'

'Give it a wide berth, then.' His friend Norman Hallows was relaxing in the cabin playing Klondike solitaire on his iPhone. 'It could be a marker buoy.'

'I don't think so. It's black. Low in the water.'

'Driftwood.'

'Maybe.'

'Is it moving? Not a whale, by any chance?'

'Wrong shape.'

'Use the glasses.'

There was an interval while Hallows made some moves in the game.

'I think it's an RIB.'

'A *rib*?'

'Rigid inflatable boat. Yes, I'm right. And it's anchored in some way.'

'Out here? Strange.'

'Can't see anyone aboard.'

'Give them a blast on the horn.'

'When we get closer.'

A few minutes later, Jim Bentley sounded the horn. Nothing came back.

'Be like that,' he said.

'They won't have a horn,' Hallows said.

'They could wave.'

'They're lying low. Shagging, I expect. Thought they were all alone in the ocean and we show up, giving them the fright of their lives.'

'It's early in the day for that. Seriously, I'm wondering if they're in trouble, engine failure or something.'

'They'd be waving to you by now if they are.'

'Not much sign of life. Suppose the guy has had a heart attack.'

'Serve him bloody right for being at it so early in the morning,' Norman said.

'I'm going closer, just to be sure.'

Hallows sighed. He wasn't going to get the game done. He stirred himself, got up and watched as they drew alongside the anchored inflatable gently bobbing with the waves. No one was aboard.

'The *Mary Celeste*,' he said. 'Another unsolved mystery of the sea.'

They both stared down into the empty boat. It was larger than most inflatables, with an inboard diesel that powered an outboard motor. The anchor chain looked sturdy.

'Should we do something?'

'Like what? Send up flares? A Mayday call? I wouldn't mind betting there's a perfectly good explanation for this.'

'Get a GPS reading. That's the least we can do.'

Hallows saw the sense of that. He checked their position

with the phone, picked up a pen and made a note of the coordinates on the back of his hand.

'You know what?' Bentley said. 'There's another line in the water as well as the anchor. See the red cord on the far side?'

'Where?'

'Going over the tube. From here it looks like part of the structure, but it's a line on a reel fixed to the hull.'

'I see it now.'

'I reckon someone's doing a dive and that's his safety line.'

'You could be right. What's the point of doing a dive out here, I wonder?'

'Something of interest below us, like a wreck. Divers make a thing of seeking out old wrecks. There are hundreds along the coast.'

'Treasure hunting, you mean?'

'Not really. Just knowing there's something down there to explore.'

'Dangerous, doing it alone.'

'Bloody stupid, if you ask me. Do you think he's all right?'

'How would I know?'

'Let's wait and see, just to be sure he's OK. He'll be coming up shortly. They don't stay down all that long, even with breathing equipment.'

'If you want,' Hallows said. 'But I think we should give him space, move off a bit. He *could* get a panic attack if he spots the bottom of our boat alongside his.'

Bentley started up again and took the cruiser some thirty metres south of the inflatable, still within hailing distance. 'Something to tell the ladies, eh, how we did the decent thing and made sure a diver was safe?'

'I suppose.'

'We could fish while we're waiting.'

'It had better not be that long.' Hallows sank into the

cushions, took out the phone again and went back to playing solitaire.

Several more minutes passed.

'He's up. I can see his head,' Bentley said.

Hallows joined him again.

Masked and hooded, the diver took a couple of overarm strokes towards the inflatable and flopped his arms over the near side. He had his back to the cabin cruiser.

'He hasn't seen us.'

'He looks OK. I'll give him a shout.' Hallows cupped his hands to his mouth and yelled, 'Are you all right?'

Now the diver turned his head and lifted the mask and they could see the pink oval of his face. After staring for a moment, he raised a thumb.

'He's fine. Well in control.'

They watched as the diver hauled himself over the side and into the boat. It was quite an effort with the cylinders he had on his back and he was no lightweight.

'Go in closer,' Hallows said. 'I'd like to know what's down there.'

The diver was reeling in the line. He seemed to have finished for the day.

Bentley took them closer. In this calm sea it was a safe manoeuvre.

Hallows took a souvenir picture. In the spirit of boating people across all oceans, he called out, 'Anything of interest down there?'

The diver turned his head and called back, 'Bugger off. I'm busy.'

'Suit yourself, mate,' Hallows answered. 'There's gratitude,' he said to his friend. 'We stop to make sure he's all right and he tells us to bugger off. I was about offer him some coffee from my flask. Full steam ahead, skipper.'

\* \* \*

Diamond couldn't avoid bringing Georgina fully up to speed. Soon after waking at six thirty, he'd checked with Chichester CID and the girl Melanie was still missing after two nights. There was a full-scale alert. The parents were distraught and a family liaison officer was with them at their home trying to see if there was some detail they'd overlooked. The fact that Melanie had visited the police station to enquire about the missing teacher earlier on the day she'd disappeared was a bizarre coincidence no one could understand.

He waited near the dining-room entrance, trying to ignore the tantalising aromas of breakfast. When the boss finally appeared at around eight thirty he put down the paper he was pretending to read and followed her in. She waited to be seated, oblivious that he was behind her until he spoke.

'Mind if I join you?'

She turned and frowned. Suspicion, more than pleasure, was her first reaction. 'I thought you liked to eat alone.'

He nodded. 'Table talk isn't one of my strengths, particularly in the morning.'

Her shoulders twitched. 'Don't feel under any obligation, then. We can ask for separate tables.'

'That's not what I meant.'

'Do you have something to discuss?'

'If that's all right with you.'

'A working breakfast? I'm all for that.'

They were shown to a table by the window. Georgina said she would have toast and coffee. After Diamond had collected a plate heaped with everything on offer at the hotplate, he explained why Melanie's disappearance needed following up.

Georgina saw the point. They were charged with examining Hen Mallin's conduct and if anything at all had governed her recent behaviour it was missing persons: Hen's niece, Joss, and the series of local criminals she had been

216

investigating and campaigning about. And now there were two people from the local school, a teacher and a student.

'The teacher went missing during the summer,' Diamond said. 'She left the school at short notice and vanished. Nobody knows the reason – or will admit to it, although she wasn't popular with her classmates.'

'Did DCI Mallin know about this?'

'She would have seen the report on the teacher, but she may have decided there was no link to organised crime, like some of the other cases on her radar. You can't get excited about every missing adult on your patch.'

Georgina raised the knife she'd been using to butter toast and brandished it between them. 'But consider this. What if the teacher – what's her name?'

'Miss Gibbon.'

'What if Miss Gibbon was involved in crime and Mallin overlooked it?'

'Miss Gibbon a villain? That's a new angle.'

Georgina looked pleased with herself.

'Not impossible, not impossible by any means,' Diamond said.

'What did she teach?'

'Art.'

'Ha.' Georgina clearly had a poor opinion of art teachers. 'If this had come into *my* in-tray, I'd have been on to it directly. Do we know anything about the company she kept?'

'Not much. She hasn't been an active line of enquiry.'

'That's got to change. We must speak to the head. Is there any suggestion of the teacher having an unhealthy influence on the girl?'

'I don't think it's been raised.'

'It should be.'

'They didn't go off together, if that's what you mean.'

Georgina replaced the knife on the plate. 'But you told

me the girl came to the police station to ask about Miss Gibbon. That suggests determination. Or devotion.' She glanced left and right, leaned forward and said in little more than a whisper, 'Peter, as a man, you may not fully appreciate the intensity some women feel for each other. I'm sorry this has to come up over breakfast, but it must be said. We can't ignore it.'

'A lesbian relationship?'

'Keep your voice down.'

Her prudery amused him enough to prolong it a little. 'Are you thinking Mel and Miss Gibbon . . . ?'

'I am.'

'Mel wanted to find her and now she has and they're together?'

'It has to be considered.' As if she urgently needed a break in the conversation, Georgina said, 'I'm going to get myself some cereal.' She was up from the table and away.

Diamond helped himself to a slice of her toast and waited.

When she returned with a bowl of cornflakes, she said, 'We need to know a whole lot more about Miss Gibbon.'

'I'm not sure who we ask.'

'The head – obviously.'

'Miss Du Barry? She's very guarded.'

'Leave her to me. I'll speak to her, woman to woman.' She hesitated. 'But I don't want you present in the room.'

'That's all right,' Diamond said. 'I've met Miss Du Barry anyway. I'll speak to some of Mel's fellow students.' He hoped he wasn't glowing in triumph, but he felt like it. The arrangement was ideal. While those two formidable women went head to head, he'd find out what really went on in this school.

Georgina couldn't resist saying, 'You see? When you joined me, you looked quite sorry for yourself and now you're relishing the day ahead. There's a lot to be said for a working breakfast. We must do it more often.'

Naseem, an Asian girl, had been sent for and asked to show Diamond to the art room. He tried chatting with her as they went through the corridors, but she gave one-word answers for the most part. He managed to find out that Mr Standforth was known to the students as Tom. At the mention of Miss Gibbon, Naseem didn't even speak. She nodded and looked away.

Tom Standforth appeared nervous when Diamond said he was a police officer. Tall, in his twenties, with quite a mane of loose black hair, the teacher crossed his arms defensively.

'It's about the missing student, Melanie Mason.'

'Mel?' Standforth said – and it was clear from the pitch of his voice that Melanie hadn't been foremost in his thoughts. 'Oh, Mel.' His arms relaxed and returned to his sides. 'Yes, I've already been asked. She hasn't been in for a couple of days.'

'She hasn't been home,' Diamond said. 'Her parents are very worried. We all are.'

'Sure – and so are we. She's a sweet girl and a talented artist, too.'

'Does she have close friends?'

He glanced around the room. About a dozen students were present. 'These are the girls who know her best. You met Naseem. And there's Jem.'

'Jemima,' a girl standing by the window said, 'Jemima Hennessy.'

Diamond was getting the message that no one here was keen to assist the police. Jemima was already looking out of the window again.

Speaking to the class in general, Tom Standforth said, 'Has anyone heard from Mel – a text, or an email?'

Nobody answered.

Diamond said to them all, 'Would you expect her to get in touch?'

The only response was a slight nod from Naseem.

This was hard work. He couldn't be certain if they were holding back information, or simply didn't know. From the direction of the looks being exchanged, one thing was clear: there was a dominant personality in this class.

He turned to the teacher. 'I'd like to speak to Jemima in private. Is there anywhere we could go?'

'The stockroom.'

Some sounds that could have been subdued giggles were heard, but not from Jemima.

Standforth said, 'Jem?'

The girl said, 'I can't tell him anything. I don't know where she is.'

'But you can give me some background,' Diamond said. 'I know very little about her. You'd like to help your friend, wouldn't you? I wouldn't be here if we weren't taking her disappearance seriously.'

Difficult to refuse. Without a word, Jem moved to the front and through the stockroom door.

Standforth told the rest of them to go back to what they had been doing.

Among the easels, blank canvases and stacks of paper of various colours and sizes, Diamond found two stools. Jem's feet didn't reach the floor. Short as she was, she looked unlikely to be pushed around.

'We're better off here,' Diamond said. 'It's not a good situation when all your classmates are listening, not to mention the teacher. I'm hoping you can give me some pointers as to why your friend is missing.'

'No,' she said.

Not a good start.

Can't?' he said. 'Or won't?'

'Take your pick. It comes to the same thing.'

He wasn't going to be shut down by a schoolgirl. 'Well, I'll tell *you* something instead. Mel came to see us at the police station the day she disappeared. I spoke to her myself. She wanted to know if we had any news of Miss Gibbon, who used to teach here.'

Jem's eyebrows arched. Resolved as she was to give nothing away, she'd been ambushed. 'Miss Gibbon?'

'The lady is on the missing persons' index.'

'I know that.'

'Then maybe you know why Mel wanted information. She was deeply concerned.'

Now she was frowning. 'She said nothing to any of us.'

'Yep,' Diamond said, ramping up the ill-feeling. 'I got the impression she was acting alone.'

'She's like that, telling nobody. You never know where you are with Mel.' Now that what amounted almost to a betrayal had sunk in, Jem's tongue loosened. 'The rest of us don't want the Gibbon back. She can stay missing as long as she likes. We're far better off with Tom. He's nice. We all look forward to art now instead of dreading it. He hasn't been here long and he's got us doing all kinds of really cool stuff.'

'Quite a change from Miss Gibbon, then.'

She nodded. 'He's an ace teacher. Even Mel will tell you that. She's doing a gorgeous mosaic with bits of glass from the beach for her extended personal project. We've all raised our game with Tom. All we ever did with the Gibbon was boring old perspective, more like geometry than art.'

'Did you give her a bad time? Not you, personally. The class, I mean.'

'She kept order.'

'But was it stressful?'

'For her, or for us?

'Her.'

'You'd have to ask her.'

'Where do you think she went?'

Jem shook her head. 'We were so pleased to see the back of her that we didn't give a toss as long as she stayed away for keeps. It was, like, only a couple of days ago we found out she was a missing person.' She remembered something and gave a gasp. 'And it was Mel who found her name on the website. Thinking back, she kept going on about why the Gibbon left so suddenly without getting a leaving present. Then we were out at Tom's one day—'

'At Tom's?' He was all ears.

And Jem was doing what she did best, sharing inside information. 'Fortiman House, where he lives. Didn't anyone tell you? Every Saturday we go to his studio and join a group of professional artists he knows. It's so cool. You can see the studio on his website if you want.'

'He has his own website?'

'He's an artist, so it's how he sells his work. In the studio – which is awesome – we get to see what his artist friends are doing and join in. They're so creative and they don't seem to mind us being there.'

'Where's this?'

'Out Boxgrove way. I take my car and some of the others come with me. Anyway, I was telling you about Mel. She's a law unto herself, the only one who ever wanted to talk about the Gibbon. She told us she was missing and her picture was online and we found it on our smartphones. But none of us dreamed Mel would go to the police. Did she find out something she didn't tell us?'

'Doesn't seem likely,' he said. 'She came to us for news, out of concern. What happens at these sessions at the house?'

'Art. I mean real, kosher art. It's a lot better than school.

The first time there were only three of us, me, Ella and Naseem, but now anyone from our class can go. Sometimes there's a model and sometimes it's still life or we do land-scape and stuff in the grounds. The garden is really big.'

'And Tom owns all this?'

A shake of the head. 'His dad Ferdie is the owner. He has a business growing orchids.' She laughed. 'The first time we mistook him for the gardener.'

'Does Mel enjoy going there as much as the rest of you?'

'She wouldn't come if she didn't. It's not compulsory. Secretly she may be shocked by some of the artists. She's working class and hasn't been about like most of us. They're a bit kooky, some of them, but what do you expect? And she hasn't had to draw a nude model like we did the first week. When I say a model, I mean a man.'

'You don't get that at school.'

'Oh my God, no. The head would have a blue fit. She doesn't know about the life drawing and we're not telling her.'

'When you say some of them are kooky, what do you mean exactly?'

'A *bit* kooky. They're not, like, out of their heads. They're artists, about ten of them, all ages. One is Charcoal Charlotte and by the end of the session she looks like she's been down a mine. There's a vicar they call the Bish and a creepy guy with starey eyes who paints with knives. Get the picture?'

'You're doing well.'

'It's a good laugh actually. Ella could tell you more.'

'Who's Ella? You mentioned her just now.'

'My best mate. She's a goth and she's up for anything.'

'Another friend of Mel's, then?'

'Sure.'

'Is Ella in today?'

'She is, but she's not at her best. She had yesterday off school and she's not saying why.'

'But you know?'

Her small mouth twitched into a smile.

'You have your suspicions?'

'I'm not grassing on my best friend.'

It's a little late for that, he thought. 'Is Ella likely to open up with me?'

'With a cop? No way.'

# 21

Georgina, white-faced and shaking, said she needed a strong coffee, so they found their way to the canteen, known in this aspiring school as the dining room.

'That woman! You could have warned me.'

'I thought I did,' Diamond said. 'Was it hard work?'

'Extremely.'

'Did you tell her your theory, about Miss Gibbon seducing the girl?'

'Please.' There was a prim intake of breath. 'There are children in this school.'

He was tempted, but he made no comment.

Georgina glanced about her and decided it was safe to continue. 'Yes, I was very frank and she hadn't even heard me out before she was telling me I had a mind like a sewer and how dare I sully the reputation of the school she'd worked so hard to lift to new levels.'

'What did you say to that?'

'To be truthful, Peter, one of my red mists came up and I'm not sure what I did say. I meant to remind her of that biblical text that says that if we say we have no sin, we deceive ourselves and the truth is not in us, but it may have come out as something more personal.'

'I bet you gave back as good as you got.'

'She treated me as if I was one of her pupils, and I wasn't having it.'

'Good for you. Did anything useful come out of it?'

'Not really. I was hoping she'd say more about Miss Gibbon and her sexuality, but she refused to discuss her. I suppose it's understandable. A teacher who takes advantage of her position doesn't reflect well on the school. I think the phrase you used about Miss Du Barry was that she's well-guarded, and I can endorse that now.'

'Most head teachers are.'

Georgina puffed out her chest. 'People in positions of trust need to be discreet. I – of all people – can appreciate that. We're privy to sensitive information. However, as one top woman speaking to another, I felt entitled to a frank exchange and I didn't get it.'

'Disappointing.'

'Very.'

'But you didn't have much to exchange.'

She shot him a fierce look. 'You'd better explain yourself.'

'Well, if you don't mind me saying so, your information isn't of much interest to Miss Du Barry. You need to trade something.'

'And, what, precisely, do you have in mind?'

'She thinks she knows everything that goes on in her school. She doesn't. It's not possible. Next time, you must go in armed with that bit of inside knowledge.'

'Do we have any?'

'We will. We only just arrived here.'

She seemed to understand. 'You may be right, Peter. I was so persuaded by my own theory that I failed to see how she would take it.' She ran her fingertip thoughtfully round the rim of her cup. 'At least I got rid of some of my pent-up frustration. Perhaps you noticed I haven't been functioning at my best.'

'Haven't you?'

'This fiasco with the head is an example.'

He sensed an embarrassing heart-to-heart coming on. 'Maybe you need a round of golf.'

'That isn't likely now,' she said after a wistful sigh. 'I rather expected I'd see more of Commander Hahn while we were here, but since that first moonlit walk along West Wittering beach he hasn't got in touch.'

For crying out loud, he thought, she's still smitten with Archie Hahn.

He had a clear memory of the note he'd found among the Rigden papers: *Did all the right things, learned the drill, kept her buttons and shoes clean and never rocked the boat . . . Doesn't have a subversive thought in her head.* He could have told Georgina she wouldn't be hearing much more from her old college friend. Good thing, too. What a toe rag. *If – heaven forbid – anything more damaging should emerge, we can rely on her to miss it altogether . . .* But this was one bit of knowledge she wasn't going to get, not directly. Against all usual practice, Diamond felt an urge to comfort and protect his boss. It didn't amount to putting an arm around her shoulders, but it was sincere.

The decent thing was to let her down gradually. 'I've been frustrated, too.'

'Really?'

'I get the feeling we've been dealt a losing hand.'

'How do you mean?'

'All these missing people. It would suit everyone down here if they stayed missing.' He'd discussed this with Hen, not yet with Georgina.

She blinked. 'That can't be true.'

'They're unsolved cases. With all the emphasis on crime figures the murder rate down here would rocket if bodies started being discovered.'

She sat back in her chair with a faraway look as if straining to hear some distant voice.

Diamond said, 'When Hen Mallin started to do something about the missing people, she was suspended.'

She reacted as if he'd nudged her in the ribs. 'No, no, no. That wasn't why she was suspended.'

'Officially no. Officially she was suspended because an anonymous letter was sent to headquarters. It was received within two weeks of her starting to rock the boat. Isn't that convenient timing? The offence she's charged with – favouring her niece – happened three years before, in 2011.'

There was a pause for thought. 'Now that you put it like that . . .' As Georgina's voice trailed away, her look sharpened.

Diamond went on in the same reasonable tone, 'With Hen suspended, all the impetus has gone out of the missing persons inquiry. You and I were brought in to deal with the problem over Joss, which is sorted, basically, because Hen admits to it. We're not supposed to make waves about missing persons.'

She gave a nervous, angry sigh. 'This is appalling if true. Who would have sent the anonymous letter?'

He spoke as if each word was a pain. 'To be really cynical about the whole exercise, it may have been concocted at headquarters.'

'Oh, Peter! That's impossible.'

'I'm thinking they may have known about the misconduct ever since 2011, only because Hen is a good detective they took no action. But when she started agitating about missing persons, she became expendable. She couldn't be gagged, so she had to go.'

Georgina wasn't having it. 'I can't accept that. It would show Sussex headquarters in a terrible light.'

'It may not be the whole of headquarters.'

She said as if she was miles away, 'I see.'

She didn't see, yet. He left the thought to take root. At some stage she would make the connection with Archie Hahn.

'Meanwhile,' he said, 'I've met Miss Gibbon's replacement, a young man called Tom Standforth.'

'A man?'

'A more popular choice with the art students. Their word for him is cool. T-shirt and jeans, hair to his shoulders and his own website.'

'How can that be? I can't imagine Miss Du Barry approving.'

'He seems to have worked his charms on her. He's local, lives with his father at a place called Fortiman House, near Boxgrove.'

'Where's that?'

'About four miles from Slindon.' He snapped his fingers and for a moment his brain was in overdrive. 'How do I know that? Yes. One of the gardens Joe Rigden looked after is out there.'

'Not Fortiman House?'

'No, a place belonging to an old lady who was over a hundred. A Mrs Shah. She's dead now.' He smiled. 'It's likely she would be, seven years on.'

'I don't remember hearing anything about this,' Georgina said.

He'd almost given the game away. He remembered he'd learned about Mrs Shah while visiting Hen in hospital. 'Must have been among the statements I was reading.' And it could have been, so it wasn't an out-and-out lie. 'Anyway, young Standforth has a studio of his own and invites other artists there, including some of the Priory Park students.'

'And Miss Du Barry knows about this arrangement?'

'Apparently, yes, but she doesn't know they sometimes have a nude male model.'

'Hm.' She had a gleam in her eye. 'That would test her liberal principles.'

'I gather it brings on the drawing by leaps and bounds.'

'I'll take your word for that.' She drank the last of her coffee. 'While you were in the art room I was speaking on the phone to DI Montacute. They've gone public with the missing girl. He's holding a press conference about now. It will make the national news and her picture will be all over the local television and newspapers.'

'High time. Is he linking this to Miss Gibbon?'

'Apparently not. There's too long an interval since her disappearance. And the media would be sure to turn it into an abduction story. They like nothing better than teachers going off with their students. Other lines of enquiry might get overlooked.'

'Is he handling it right, do you think?'

She held up a warning finger. 'We're not going to interfere.'

'I've met the girl,' he said. 'It becomes personal.'

'Don't even think about it. Our brief is to pin down the facts about DCI Mallin and her misconduct.'

'And that involves her niece Joss,' he said, 'who has also gone missing.'

'But it isn't our job to find these young women, Peter. We're on a fact-finding mission.'

'We won't get the full facts until Joss is found, and Montacute hasn't given me much confidence so far. He'll be even more distracted now.'

'You're like a dog with a bone.'

'I didn't come here to sit around and do nothing.' He looked at the clock above the door. 'Break's over. I must

get back to my fact-finding. There's another girl to see –
Ella the goth, who knows more than anyone.'

'Ella the what?'

'The goth. It's a cult.'

'You be careful.'

'Oh, I will. They say she takes no prisoners.'

# 22

When Diamond returned to the art room and asked to speak to Ella, he was told apologetically by Tom Standforth that she wasn't there.

'I was told she was in today.'

'That was earlier.'

'Is she allowed to leave midway through the morning?'

'Uh-oh,' one of the class said. 'Someone else goes missing.'

'It's not funny,' Jem said, swinging around in her chair. 'Mel could be dead for all we know.'

'He's talking about Ella.'

Standforth said to the class in general, 'Cool it, people. Did Ella tell anyone where she was going?'

Silence.

'You could try the yard,' he said to Diamond. 'That's where her project is. It was too large to assemble in here.'

'And too smelly,' Jem added, to general amusement.

Asked for directions, Standforth gave some and added, 'Look for the big black construction. You can't miss it.'

Diamond's law decreed that whenever those last four words were used he was doomed to lose his way. Downstairs at the back of the main building he found a yard where the bins were kept and surplus desks and chairs had been left to take their chance with the elements. It wasn't promising until, against expectation, he saw that for once he'd picked the right route. Rising above the school furniture was a strange creation in the form of a scaled-down mansion with gables and turrets mostly covered in foliage. The onion-shaped cupola at the top of the main tower must have been more than fifteen feet above ground. In outline the whole thing was so dark that it was like a silhouette, undeniably creepy.

On getting closer, he saw that the entire structure was a rickety collection of lobster pots and creels piled on top of each other and lashed together with nylon rope. The cupola was formed from two beehive-shaped pots joined at the base. A creative imagination beyond his own had envisioned this. True, it smelt strongly of bad fish and was better appre-ciated out of doors, but as a concept based on limited materials it spoke eloquently for its designer. Pity she wasn't around to be congratulated.

He circled this amazing artefact and examined it from several angles. If this was the result of Tom Standforth's teaching, the young man deserved the head's high opinion of him. Yet here it stood in a scrapyard among rubbish bins and unwanted furniture.

He was about to leave when he noticed a movement. A black cat was inside, among the lobster pots, preening itself. Seeing him, it gave a plaintive cry that anyone except a cat owner might interpret as distress. Raffles sometimes got attention the same way. The thought of his own cat touched a sympathetic chord in Diamond and he crouched and offered his hand to nuzzle against.

'Leave her alone,' a voice behind him said. 'She likes it in there.'

He stood up and turned. 'Would you be Ella?'

She was in her own clothes rather than the school uniform worn by the junior kids, a black dress cut low to display more cleavage than a seventeen-year-old is entitled to possess and worn over baggy black trousers. Untidy dark hair. Eye shadow, probably in defiance of school rules. This young lady didn't strike him as the sort who would pay much attention to rules. She ignored his question.

'If you *are* Ella, I heard you created this,' Diamond went on. 'I'm impressed.'

'Are you, like, visiting the school?'

'I work for the police.' He could have been a window-cleaner, the offhand way he spoke. 'Where did you get all the pots?'

'Fishermen.'

'You went to the beach?'

'Loads of them are lying about broken. Pots, not fishermen. They're, like, only too pleased to get shot of them.'

'Your idea – building this wonderful thing?'

Flattery is a sure persuader. She started telling him about her work of art. 'It wasn't planned. I talked to those guys and learned some cool stuff about pots, like they have eyes, did you know?'

He shook his head slowly.

'Where the poor old lobsters go in, soft or hard eyes, depending if it's net or wire. If it was me, I'd call them mouths, but the fishermen don't. I had this thought about doing a sculpture, making a statement about emptiness. Have you heard of de Chirico?'

He shook his head again.

She didn't need any prompting. She was away. 'Doesn't matter. When I stacked them on top of each other, the different types, old-fashioned beehives and boxes, some on end and some flat – well, D-shaped – they stopped being lobster pots, right? I thought what I was producing was shaping up to be an abstract, but then, like, this structure starts to appear and I talk to Tom and he agrees with me it could be a building with towers and I'm away. Do you think the seaweed works?'

234

'As the creeper? I'm no expert, but it took me in.'

'It's not meant to be a creeper. It's fungus, tiny fungi hanging from the eaves in a kind of web. '

Fungus or a creeper. Did it really matter? To humour the girl, he nodded sagely. 'I see it now.'

'I want it to look right.'

'It does, believe me.' Her flow of words had stopped. She needed another confidence boost if he could provide it. 'So this is your A-level effort, is it?'

'Extended personal project.'

'It's big. Hope you don't have to send it in to be marked.'

'We can send images.'

'When you do the photography try not to get the bins in the shot.'

'Don't know about that,' Ella said. 'I'm thinking the symbolism is stronger with them in the background.'

'You're the artist,' he said. 'Is it gothic, this building?'

'Don't you recognise it?'

'Em . . .' He didn't want to be discouraging.

'Have you heard of *The Fall of the House of Usher*?'

'The horror film? Never actually seen it.'

'It's a story by Edgar Allan Poe.'

'I've heard of him, but I'm not much of a reader.'

She almost stamped her foot, she was so put out. 'If you don't know what I'm talking about, this must look like a heap of old tat.'

'Not at all. It's spectacular. Now you've said what it is, I'm lost in admiration.'

He was subjected to a long, penetrating look. 'Well, now you know what it's meant to be, the House of Usher, an ancient mansion in a state of decay. Poe says, like, it gives you a feeling of insufferable gloom, right? The walls are bleak and the windows are like vacant eyes. If you know about lobster pots having eyes, there's an extra layer of meaning. They're mostly broken, too, so that's in keeping with the story. But I've got a problem. The house is supposed be beside a tarn, a dark, lurid tarn. Do you know what that is?'

He shook his head. 'I'm pretty ignorant about this kind of stuff.'

'A lake. In the story, after Roderick's twin sister Madeline is left for dead and he and his friend bury her in a vault downstairs, she comes alive and terrifies him and they both die and the house collapses into the tarn. I haven't worked out how to show the tarn.'

'Tinfoil?'

'Wouldn't work.' But she seemed grateful that he'd tried. 'How did you know about me and my gothic interest, then?'

'Stands out a mile, doesn't it?' Diamond said and moved on smoothly to what he hoped would be a more productive topic. 'One thing I was told is you're the expert on Mr Standforth's – Tom's – artist friends.'

'Someone was having you on. I've only met them a couple of times.'

'Let's say you know more than the other students.'

'Why? Why do you say that?' Her mood had changed. She was wary of a trap.

'I'm going by what I was told. It could be that the professional artists sense you're one of them, a rare talent.'

She wasn't falling for that. She grasped a stepladder and moved it right up to the House of Usher. 'I can't stay talking.'

Art had never been one of Diamond's talents, but thinking on his feet definitely was. 'What you could do for the tarn,' he said, 'is transport the whole thing to some place that has a large pond and position it there, close enough to catch the reflection. Is it possible to move all this?'

'I'd need a bloody great truck, wouldn't I?' She was up the steps and rearranging seaweed.

'Is that impossible?'

'For crying out loud, where would I get a flaming truck?'

'Is there a pond at Tom's place, Fortiman House?'

'A pond? You're joking. It's more like a lake.'

'Ideal, then.'

It seemed this possibility hadn't occurred to Ella. She continued with her task while she considered. 'I could ask Tom,' she said finally. 'He might agree.'

'Does he own any heavy transport?'

She laughed. 'Like his little old MG?'

She'd dropped a strip of seaweed. He stooped and handed it up to her. 'If you have to dismantle the house and reassemble it, the artists might help. Are they there most days?'

'Saturdays. Now I think about it, they do have quite a large van. His dad grows orchids commercially and it's used to deliver them, I suppose.'

'And you only go there Saturdays, you say?'

'Except when they have a party, and they wouldn't want to help with my project on party nights.'

'Do they all get drunk, then?'

'No worse than the average party. There's wine and fruit juice if you want it, pineapple or . . .' She had stopped in mid-sentence, making it all too clear that she'd given away more than she intended. She added limply, 'The drinks are handed out free. I was told, anyway.'

He didn't miss an opening like that. 'And I was told you've been to one of the parties.'

She gripped the ladder with both hands. 'Who said that – Jem?'

'In fact, no. I talked to Jem earlier and she didn't mention parties. But you've been to one, haven't you?'

'What if I have? It's no big deal.'

'I knew if anyone was bold enough, it would be you. Are

they wild, these parties? Soft drinks don't sound all that wicked.'

'They're not. There's dancing in the studio, but it's not what I'd call a rave. They're middle-aged, most of them. The music is crap. There's a vicar and some ladies older than my parents. More your age, really.'

'Thanks. I must see if I can get invited. When were you there?'

'Night before last.'

*The same night Mel had disappeared.* This, surely, was critical. Keep the girl talking and find out all you can.

'As recently as that? Did any of your friends go with you?'

She made a sound of scorn. 'No chance. They're a bunch of scaredy-cats.'

'You're certain of that?'

'Positive.'

'I bet they all wanted to know about it, though.'

She nodded. 'Isn't that typical?'

'How do you know you were the only one of your class there? That happens to have been the night Melanie went missing.'

'Mel wasn't there.'

'Can you swear to that?'

'You don't know her, or you wouldn't even ask. She's not into parties.'

'Unlike you.'

'I'm up for anything funky. It's just a shame it was a let-down.'

'Not funky?'

'I didn't let the others know it was a turn-off when I texted them.'

'You texted them from the party?'

'Naturally. Crashing it was a top result and I wanted everyone to know.'

'All of them, including Mel? Did you get a message back?'

'From Mel? No.'

'Going by what you just said, she didn't miss much. Did anyone spot you as a gatecrasher?'

'Tom, obviously, and he was OK with it.' She appeared to decide enough had been said about the party. 'Can we talk about something else? I'm getting bored with this.'

'Do you have any idea where Mel might be?'

She shook her head. 'What a dumb question. I'd have told someone by now, wouldn't I? And now, if you don't mind, I've got work to do.'

'She hasn't texted you?'

'She hasn't texted anyone for two days.'

'Each hour that passes makes it more likely she's in real trouble. You'd help me if you knew anything, wouldn't you?'

'Of course. I want you to find her.'

He believed her. For all the posturing, she had integrity.

Back in the art room, he was keen to question Tom Standforth about the party.

The young teacher was on the defensive straight away. 'Who's been talking? Ella, I suppose.'

'I was thinking that as Ella turned up uninvited, Mel may have had the same idea.'

'Hold on,' he said. 'You're not suggesting I have anything to do with Mel's disappearance?'

'Asking, not suggesting.'

'Well, she most certainly wasn't there. I wasn't pleased when Ella gatecrashed. The parties are for my adult friends. We don't need schoolgirls barging in.'

Students, he thought, but didn't voice the thought. 'She didn't seem all that impressed.'

'What did she tell you?'

'That the parties might suit someone my age. Cheeky.'

He grinned. 'I'm not angling for an invitation, but it would be useful to meet your artist friends. Will they be at Fortiman House tomorrow, being Saturday?'

Tom frowned. 'I don't know why you need to meet them.'

'We're following up all the contacts Mel has made recently. She comes to your Saturday sessions, so she must have met the artists.'

'They're not kidnappers.'

'Did I say they were?'

'They wouldn't appreciate being questioned by the police.'

'No one ever does. What time do you get under way?'

He seemed to accept the inevitable. 'Eleven.'

'Don't worry. I won't ask what they smoke.'

'I had the feeling those schoolgirls were running rings round me,' he confessed to Georgina back at the hotel.

'They probably were.'

'I wouldn't want to be their teacher.'

She smiled. 'Don't worry. You'd never get the job.'

'They're smart. They seem to be chattering nineteen to the dozen, but I'm certain what I'm getting isn't the whole story. There's more to come out. They're selective in what they tell me.'

'How do you know?'

'The way they have of shutting me down when I'm getting warm, particularly the goth girl, Ella. Suddenly I'm told not to be boring. She's only seventeen and she's capable of making me feel like a schoolboy.'

'Peter, you should be grateful. Thanks to this assignment of mine, you're getting an education yourself.'

'How, exactly?'

'Into the ways of women. I don't suppose you've ever been exposed to such a line-up of females: the devious schoolgirls; their overbearing headmistress; the highly inflammable Hen Mallin; her downtrodden sister-in-law, Cherry; not to mention me, bossing it over you twenty-four hours a day. And you haven't even started on the artists. It's a wonder you've survived as long as you have.'

# 23

Before visiting Fortiman House next morning, the police car took a route through a wooded area near Boxgrove that even the driver wasn't familiar with. It was so quiet along these back ways that the local wildlife didn't expect to be disturbed. Several pheasants and a rabbit came close to premature death and a territorial fox stood its ground in the middle of the lane until the last seconds.

'The sat nav makes us close,' the driver said without much confidence.

They were looking for the one-time home of the centenarian, Mrs Shah, who had once employed Joe Rigden as her gardener.

'This has got to be the boundary fence,' Georgina said.

A line of split hazel hurdles extended along the lane. After a short distance the driver braked in front of a low iron gate. Chained to it was a dusty and faded enamel nameplate with the words holly blue cottage and a picture of a butterfly. The two detectives got out. Being in such a remote spot, the cottage probably had as much land as the owner would wish to cultivate. Whether you could term it a garden any longer was questionable.

The front was as overgrown as the ancient wood they'd just passed through.

'The one that got away,' Diamond said. 'A gardener hasn't been near this place since the old lady died.'

'Sad,' Georgina said.

Between enormous shrubs crying out for a clipping, the cottage came into view, not quite the House of Usher, but showing signs of neglect. Slates were missing from the roof and the windows hadn't been cleaned in a long time.

'Last night I did some checking on the present owner,' Diamond said. 'It's a company known as Mombasa Holdings Limited.'

'Exotic,' Georgina said.

'Kenyan Asian, I would guess, like the late Mrs Shah. Clever people, making money and expanding into property.'

'This doesn't look clever to me. Who'd want to live here, way out in the country?'

'Mrs Shah did.'

'I don't know how she managed when she was so old.'

'She paid people to come to her, like Joe Rigden.'

'Whoever is here now isn't employing a gardener. Is it inhabited, do you think? Doesn't look like it. You'd think they'd want to collect some rent and make it profitable.'

'Maybe there are plans to develop it.'

'It's remote, Peter.'

'It's not all that way out, just difficult to reach. Five miles from Chichester, probably. We're townies, you and me. Plenty of people like the country way of life.'

'Desolate. I'd pay money *not* to live here. Do you still want to look round?'

'We made the effort to find it, so why not?'

Georgina seemed to have made up her mind why not. Seven years after Joe Rigden had pulled his last weed, nothing helpful to their investigation would be found here.

Diamond wasn't giving up. Mel's disappearance troubled him and he was leaving no stone unturned. To be certain no one was at home, he tried the doorbell and the knocker.

Junk mail had been pushed through the letterbox and was heaped inside.

'No one is going to object if we explore.'

'I expect it looked presentable at one time,' Georgina said. 'Joe Rigden wouldn't be happy to see the grass this high and all these thistles.'

'Spinning in his grave. Let's go round the back.'

The ground was sodden after overnight rain. Georgina looked down at her smart brogues. 'Do we really need to?'

'There ought to be a garden shed.'

'And what do you hope to discover there? A rusty mower?'

'If someone hasn't nicked it already. Look, here's a path.' By shifting some groundsel with his foot he'd found a moss-covered paved area that skirted the cottage.

He stepped out confidently. Georgina, muttering, followed.

The back garden had once been laid to lawn and was now a crop of hay asking to be harvested. A solid-looking trellis and pergola arch showed above the swaying seedheads. Beyond that, a red brick wall about nine feet high marked the end of the garden. And, as if Diamond had ordered it, a dilapidated shed stood in the shadow of the wall, its felt roof torn and gaping.

'If you think I'm going to fight my way through this jungle, you've got another think coming,' Georgina told him. 'I'm not dressed for it. I'll see you back at the car – if you're not eaten by a tiger.'

She had a point. It *was* a struggle and his trousers were sodden before he'd gone more than a few yards. Worse, they snagged on brambles and the thorns got through to his flesh. But he persevered. Up to now, Joe Rigden had been elusive, a vague figure from witness statements and court records. This, at least, was one of his workplaces. Seeing the inside of the shed and his tools would make some kind of connection.

Thrusting his way through and ignoring the damage to his clothes, the big man presently reached an area where the grass was shorter and less abundant and he could make his way more easily. And now mushrooms or toadstools – he wasn't sure which – appeared underfoot, slippery when crushed. The moist conditions must have encouraged them. So many were there that it was impossible not to trample some. If he hadn't been brought up a townie, he might have foraged for lunch, but he had no idea if they were edible.

He had no difficulty forcing open the padlocked shed door. The wood was rotten and the screws came out like drawing pins from a cork board.

He stepped inside.

Eerie. The first thing he saw was a dark green wax jacket draped over the back of a plastic chair. On the floor was a flask. These items could only have belonged to Rigden. If you ignored the cobwebs and dead leaves, you could kid yourself that the owner had sat there a short time ago drinking tea. Then the sun had come out and he'd stepped outside to do some digging.

No. That couldn't be right. Surely the man wouldn't have padlocked the door if he was still at work. Yet if he'd gone home, why had he left the jacket and flask behind? He was supposed to have been methodical and tidy.

The rest of the contents were predictable: the motor mower, several sets of shears and clippers, saws, trowels, hoes, spades and forks, buckets, a sieve and plastic sacks that probably contained fertiliser or compost. On a low table were the remains of seed packets shredded at the edges by mice.

He lifted the jacket and held it up. These all-weather garments had more pockets than anyone ever needed. Was it too much to hope something of interest might have been left behind? He resisted the urge to start looking. He'd take the thing with him. Time to move on and meet the artists at Fortiman House. A shake of the jacket and a large spider hit the floor and scuttled for shelter.

Outside, Diamond hadn't taken two steps when his heel slipped on some of the fungi he'd already trampled. His feet went from under him and he fell heavily, his backside hitting the ground first.

'That's all I need.'

He wasn't sure whether he'd injured himself, but bar some bruising and the indignity, he would be OK. Rigden's jacket had fallen with the arms crossed as if the owner was saying, 'Serve you bloody right.'

'Get real,' he told himself. 'He's got no use for it.'

He hauled himself up, grabbed the jacket and stumbled back to the car.

'Look at the state of you,' Georgina said.

'I don't particularly want to.'

'What happened?'

'I tripped over a toadstool.'

'Can't you ever be serious?'

'Actually I slipped.'

'Is that the only suit you have? Didn't I say you should have packed more clothes? You'll need a dry cleaner's now.'

'Don't fuss. I'm all right.'

'I'm not thinking of you. I'm the one turning up at Fortiman House with a scarecrow in tow. Remember who we are.'

'Plain-clothes police.'

'Plain doesn't mean scruffy.'

'Artists don't dress up.'

'They're as fashion conscious as anyone else, if not more. And what's that disgusting garment you're carrying?'

His tolerance was being stretched. He explained.

'Keep it away from me, then. It will be home to a million unspeakable things.'

He tossed the jacket in the boot and slammed down the lid. Yesterday's burgeoning sympathy for Georgina was just about used up. He wasn't sorry she chose to sit beside the driver.

On the map, Fortiman House looked extremely close, but to reach it they had to thread their way back through the woods to a busier road.

'Remind me why we're visiting this place,' Georgina said.

He said through his teeth, 'To meet the artists, Tom Standforth's friends.'

'But why?'

'Because of the missing schoolgirl, Melanie. She comes to the house on Saturdays to draw, so she'll be known to them. A couple of nights ago there was a party. Her friend Ella gatecrashed it and texted her friends, including Mel, to boast that she was there. It's not impossible Mel was tempted to do the same.'

'Did you question Ella about that?'

'She claims Mel isn't a party-goer and wasn't there.'

'But you think she could be mistaken – or lying?'

'I ask myself is it just a coincidence that Mel disappeared on the night of the party? She rides a scooter. She could have got there quickly.'

'All right. I suppose it's worth looking into. I can only think of one set of people less reliable than schoolgirls and that's artists. Kidnapping might be someone's idiotic idea of performance art.'

The Standforth property was in a far better state than Holly Blue Cottage. The grounds appeared well managed and the house they drove up to must have been one of the grandest in the district. Unseen by his superior seated in the front,

Diamond rubbed his muddy shoes against the backs of his trousers.

Other cars and vans in a variety of makes and conditions from a rusty Renault to a brand-new Lamborghini were already parked in front of the house. The police vehicle drew up beside the red MG Ella had mentioned and the first person they saw was its owner. Diamond suspected he had been waiting for them.

'You *will* respect the reason my friends are here?' Tom Standforth said as he escorted them to the barn that doubled as his studio. 'These sessions are meant to be laid-back and some of them can get a little touchy if they feel their space is invaded.'

Georgina was quick to answer. 'Don't think of us as invaders. We're used to mingling with strangers, aren't we, Peter?'

'It's our job,' he said, his toes curling. *Mingling with strangers?* Like at a cocktail party? Pity he couldn't have thought of some alternative mission for Georgina.

'I must apologise for the state of my colleague's clothes,' she said to Standforth. 'We had a diversion involving a trek through a quagmire.'

'I hadn't noticed.'

The studio was abuzz with people chatting over coffee. Three of the Prior Park schoolgirls glanced across and immediately went into a huddle. Ella, Jem and Naseem were alert for every twist in this drama.

'There's no need for an announcement,' Georgina told Tom Standforth.

'Sorry, you've lost me.'

'To explain who we are and why we're here. I dare say they'll find out soon enough.'

'I wasn't aiming to say anything. I'd rather keep it low key.'

'So would we.'

'In fact,' the young man said, 'I'm wondering if you'd like to join us.'

'We intend to,' Georgina said. 'We'll introduce ourselves as we go round.'

'That isn't what I mean. Would you like to do some drawing?'

'Actually put pencil to paper? Oh my word, I hadn't thought of that. I suppose we *could* appear to be sketching. In fact, it might be rather a clever move. Peter, what do you say to that?'

He was speechless. They hadn't come here to make fools of themselves.

'In which case,' Georgina said, 'we need drawing materials.'

'Not a problem,' Standforth said. 'Help yourselves to coffee and I'll fix it.'

'I can't draw,' Diamond said after their host had moved off.

She was without pity. 'Anyone can make marks on paper. That's all it is. Go to any gallery and you'll see aimless scribbles passed off as masterpieces. Art is ninety-nine per cent bluffing.'

'Are you any good at it?'

'As a matter of fact, I won the art prize at school. I'd offer to show you the basics, but we'd better split up when it starts, don't you think?'

'I need a strong coffee.'

All too soon, Standforth clapped his hands and addressed everyone. 'Let's start the first session, shall we? You'll be pleased to hear Davy is back with us today.'

'Who's Davy?' Diamond asked, jumpy as frying popcorn.

'How would I know?' Georgina said.

The floor squeaked to the sound of easels and stools

being dragged into position. Two of the men pushed a low wooden stand into the centre.

'What's that for?'

'The dais,' Georgina informed her colleague from the depth of her experience. 'To support the arrangement.'

'What of?'

'Come on, Peter, this is art. Still life. The usual thing is a bowl of fruit or a potted plant. Personally, I prefer apples or oranges. They're easier to copy.'

Standforth handed them drawing boards with large sheets of paper clipped to them. 'I recommend charcoal if you haven't done much before. Take as much as you like from the box on the table at the end. And help yourselves to easels. Back of the room.'

'Do we really need easels?' Diamond asked his boss.

She was implacable. 'Thank you for offering. Place mine next to the gentleman with the clerical collar.'

The easels were heavy and paint-spattered. By the time he'd manoeuvred one to where Georgina wanted it, a circle was forming. He noticed some people weren't bothering with easels at all. They perched on high stools or at a lower level astride donkey stools. A tall black man in a Rasta hat was standing with a sketchbook. One of the stools would do for Diamond.

'I'll be on the other side,' he told Georgina.

She didn't answer. She was staring over her shoulder at a large man in a black silk dressing gown standing beside the dais, barefoot and bare-legged. The apples and oranges would have to wait for another day.

The next hour was a new low in Diamond's career. He had the rear aspect of the nude model, Davy, and he wasn't interested in committing it to paper. No one spoke. The concentration in the room was absolute. The whole point in being here was to get acquainted with the artists, but it wasn't possible. He could only look around and try to get an impression of them as people.

The only consolation was the sight of Georgina with her full-on view of the model, having her artistic credentials tested to the limit as Davy faced her, hands on hips. Each time Diamond glanced her way she swayed like a boxer out of sight behind the easel. Mostly she managed to hold a fixed stare at Davy's head and shoulders as if the rest of his body didn't exist. There was one exquisite moment when the tension became too much, her charcoal snapped and a piece rolled across the floor and stopped six inches from the dais. She didn't go after it.

Finally Tom went over and drew chalk marks around the model's feet to allow him to move and ease the strain on his muscles. Everyone relaxed. And then, with the grace of a true gentleman, Davy stooped, picked up the charcoal and handed it to Georgina. She turned geranium red, took a step back and knocked over someone's easel.

Diamond didn't have long to savour the incident. The woman beside him said, 'Are you having trouble?'

'Trouble?'

'With the pose. You haven't made many marks. I'm Drusilla, by the way.' She held out a slim hand. Her voice was sharp, but she looked friendly enough, a slim woman about his own age dressed in some kind of ethnic sweater and frayed jeans.

'Peter,' he said, shaking hands, 'and it's no use pretending I can draw. I'm a fraud, as you can see.'

'An interloper?'

'In a way, yes. A police officer, volunteered for this by my boss.'

'The lady hiding behind her easel?'

'Right. She thinks we should join in and not be too obvious.'

'She's more obvious than she thinks. Are you supposed to be undercover? If so, you're not very good at it. What are you hoping to find out? We may look a suspicious bunch, but I don't think we're lawbreakers – except Manny, the West Indian. He had a short spell inside for dealing in cannabis, I was told, but he served his sentence and made use of the time to become a brilliant cartoonist.'

'Good for him.'

'Tom and Ferdie employ him as the gardener. They're like that, open-minded, willing to give a man a fresh start. You should ask to see his cartoons. He'll do one of you if you ask. He might have done one already. There's character in your face, if I may be personal. But if you're going undercover—'

'If I was undercover, ma'am, I wouldn't have told you I was in the police.'

'My dear, you can tell me anything and it stays in here.' Drusilla tapped her forehead. 'What are you investigating?'

'One of the schoolgirls who has gone missing.'

'I saw on the TV. I was hoping it was just a tiff with the parents. Isn't there any news?'

'Nothing yet.'

'Have you spoken to her friends? I suppose you will have.'

'They don't know either. There was a party here a couple of nights ago – the night she went missing. Did you go?'

She nodded. 'They couldn't keep me away if they tried.'

'Was Melanie there?'

'If she came, I didn't spot her. I thought only one of the schoolgirls came and that was Ella, the tall one over there, looking amazingly grown-up and different in her gothic get-up, and she didn't stay long. When she got a little woozy, Tom removed her from the scene. It was the right thing to do. He's a responsible young man.'

He nodded, trying not to seem over-interested. 'When you say woozy, are you talking about alcohol?'

'She wouldn't have been offered the wine, I'm sure. She's far too young. Most of us stick to soft drinks, anyway. Pressed fruit in various flavours.'

'That's restrained for a bunch of artists.'

She laughed. 'This is rural Sussex, my dear, not Soho in the sixties.'

'But you don't expect to stay sober at a party, do you?'

'Personally, I can get high on good company and music, but I can't speak for everyone. A few I could name knock it back, but I'll spare their blushes. We're all rather hyped up by the end of the evening.'

'Does anyone do drugs?'

Drusilla laughed. 'Good God, you *are* a suspicious policeman. Get that idea straight out of your head. I wouldn't have anything to do with drugs, I assure you, and neither would most of the others – including Manny, who learned his lesson the hard way.'

'But you just said by the end of the evening . . .'

'I meant something much more innocent. Haven't you ever been to a pop concert? Just listening to the music gives me an adrenalin surge. Coming back to young Ella, I saw Ferdie taking her a glass of fruit juice.'

'When you say Ferdie . . . ?'

'Tom's father, the unofficial barman. It's thanks to his generosity that we come here at all.'

'So you didn't see Mel that night. You're certain Ella was the only girl from Priory Park who showed up?'

'You'd better ask around if you doubt me. Ella's the only one I saw.'

His theory was looking shaky. He didn't get a chance to ask around because the model had just stepped up to the dais again and people were back behind their easels.

'I'm ducking out of this session,' he told Drusilla. 'I've done all I can.'

He glanced across at Georgina. With her easel in a prime position, she would find it impossible to extract herself without everyone noticing. Stuck between the clergyman and a tall man making slashing movements with a palette knife, she looked as if she'd rather be anywhere else on the planet.

But Diamond escaped.

As if in sync with him, a wintry sun emerged from behind the clouds, throwing shadows and patches of bright green across the landscaped estate. What better than fresh air and exercise? Well, there was something better if the exercise had a purpose. Somewhere was the lake Ella had spoken about and that he'd speculated would be the ideal place to set up her lobster-pot House of Usher. Ella was a useful contact. With time in hand before lunch, the least he could do was to check. Down a gentle slope to the left was a beech copse turning gold. Logic suggested the lowest point on the landscape where the wooded area flourished would be where the lake was sited. He started walking.

One thing he hadn't expected until he got close and felt it underfoot was a gravel driveway running directly across the lawn, not so much in the direction of the copse as off to the right. From the size of the tracks it appeared to be in use by heavier traffic than cars. He couldn't at first understand why. There was nothing worth driving towards, just the tall brick wall that bounded the garden. Then he noticed a point where the wall angled sharply inwards and formed a square-shaped enclosure, presumably a walled garden. He wouldn't have picked it out from the background unless he'd asked himself where the road headed. Now it made sense. He could just see the roofs of buildings inside the walls that evidently housed the orchid collection. The driveway across the lawn would be needed to transport the orchids by van to the main drive.

His thoughts moved quickly from orchids to lobster pots. How simple it would be for the Standforths to transport Ella's House of Usher from the school to its new location by the lake – provided they liked his suggestion.

He crossed the drive and continued down the slope. Before reaching the copse he saw the gleam of water between tree trunks. All doubt was removed when a pair of mute swans glided across. He picked his way down a steeper incline and reached the bank where the water lapped. He was impressed. Two hundred to two-fifty metres to the far side, he estimated. The depth was anyone's guess, but this was much more than a pond. In his estimation it qualified as a lake. The dark reeds at the edges would blend in superbly with Ella's creation.

No question: it would pass for Edgar Allan Poe's sinister tarn.

The find was pleasing. There hadn't been much to celebrate lately. He stood a little longer, enjoying the view, thinking if Tom and Ella agreed he would have contributed to a small success.

In the act of turning to go back, he spotted a movement on the far side. The lake almost lapped the wall there, but a narrow path existed because someone was walking slowly from right to left.

Impossible to tell if it was male or female. Well covered in black beanie hat, brown overcoat and trousers. Not particularly tall and moving in a preoccupied way, with head down and arms folded. Maybe one of the artists had got the same idea as he, and escaped. Whoever it was hadn't seen him and was too far off to hail, or wave to, so he turned and retraced his route.

# 24

Diamond had plenty on his mind as he toiled up the slope towards the house so perhaps it was excusable that he failed to spot Georgina striding towards him.

She was not at her most sunny. 'What do you think you're playing at?'

'Didn't see you coming, ma'am.'

'Answer me, Peter.'

'I went for a walk.'

'Went for a walk in the middle of the session, when everyone else was in the studio?'

'It goes completely silent when the drawing starts, and that's useless to us. Can't talk to anyone, can't overhear other people talking. So I stepped outside. A chance to look round.'

'With what result?'

'I found the lake.'

Her eyes rolled upwards. 'Have we ever discussed a lake?'

'You and I? No. Young Ella needs it for her A-level extended project. She also needs transport and I think there's a chance of getting some.'

Georgina looked ready to strangle him. 'Have you gone soft in the head? You're not here at the beck and call of schoolgirls. You're assisting me in a serious investigation.'

'Point taken,' he said in the same untroubled tone. 'I'm on the case. I need to persuade Ella I'm on her side. A rather odd incident happened at the party that she hasn't told us about. She started behaving as if she was drunk or drugged and Tom Standforth led her away.'

'Where to?'

'Don't know yet.'

'Did he take advantage of her?'

'That's not a question I can answer yet. I doubt if Tom will tell me, but if I win Ella's confidence, I might get it from her.'

'Who told you this – about Tom taking her off some-where?'

'Drusilla. One of the artists.'

She frowned. 'That is disturbing.'

'If true, yes. Drusilla is a vocal lady. These things can grow in the telling.'

'There's a danger here of getting sidetracked. Even if you discover the truth, how does it help us find the missing schoolgirl?'

'Get Ella talking and she might tell me more about Mel.'

Georgina didn't, after all, strangle him. She didn't even grab him by the throat. His explanation may have caused her to reflect a little. She sounded slightly reassured. 'So you're going to speak to her now?'

'When I can prise her away from the others. She won't open up while they're around.'

'You haven't got long. They're still in the studio, I believe. It's a short break for lunch.'

He needed no better cue to escape from Georgina. 'I'll get straight to it, then.'

She nodded, and then announced in a voice that didn't encourage debate, 'I shan't be doing any more art myself. Charcoal is a messy medium.'

He was tempted to say something, but he didn't.

\* \* \*

Jim Bentley always watched the lunchtime news at home in his Emsworth bungalow with his wife Sheila. First the national and then the local, by which time he'd finished his tomato soup and started on the banana. This was the routine right through the year except for the days he went fishing with Norman. Even the flavour of the soup never changed. For a man of his age he was enviably slim.

*Points South* were screening an item about swans.

'Hey-ho,' Jim said, 'this could be close to home.'

But it wasn't. They were the swans at Christchurch, some way up the coast.

'They want to come here,' he said. 'Ours take some beating.'

'You're so competitive,' Sheila said.

'There's nothing wrong with loyalty to your own home town. If they came to film our swans they'd probably show the town quay. I'd like to see my boat on the telly.'

'You and that boat.'

'She's given us some good times, you have to admit.'

'You're speaking for yourself, I hope. I don't go to sea.'

'But you make the most of it when I do.'

'In what way, may I ask?'

'In the shops – Debenham's, Jaeger, The White Stuff. Shall I go on?'

The news had moved on to a man speaking to a collection of microphones. Seated to his left were a man and a woman. The woman's eyes were red with weeping.

'Poor soul. Why do they put them through this?' Sheila said.

Jim had picked up the latest *Practical Boat Owner* and was leafing through it. 'Through what?'

'It's a missing child. He's a policeman and they're the parents. I hope they don't force the mother to speak. She's too distressed. You can see.'

It was the father who spoke. 'If you're watching this, Mel,

please, please get in touch some way and let us know you're alive. We're here for you as always and we're missing you dreadfully.'

Sheila said, 'It can't be a kiddie if they're asking her to get in touch.'

'Runaway teenager probably,' Jim said. 'They aren't young, those two. I'd say they're knocking on fifty, both of them. Trying to bring her up to old-fashioned standards, I bet. It doesn't work in the modern world.'

'They don't look particularly strict,' Sheila said. 'It could be nothing to do with the parents. Some boy could have put ideas in the girl's head.'

'Let's hope that's all it is,' Jim said. 'If I was in charge of the case I'd take a close look at the family. Nine times out of ten it's what they call a domestic.'

'They aren't faking,' Sheila said. 'Believe me, they're out of their minds with worry, those two.'

Now the detective in charge was speaking again.

'He's trying to sound positive,' Sheila said, 'but look at his eyes. You can see he doesn't really think she's alive. We'll turn the news on tomorrow and they'll say they've found a body. I've seen it all before.'

The weather girl came on, pointing at the map.

'I wouldn't bank on it,' Jim said. 'She may never be found. Real life isn't like these soaps you watch. It isn't all storylines that get tied up neatly, so you know exactly how things turn out.'

'There's an end to the story of every one of these poor people who go missing,' Sheila said. 'Even if they're never found, they must end up somewhere. Sometimes they're all right and survive and sometimes they don't. But they all have a story.'

'What I'm saying,' Jim said with deliberation, 'is we don't always find out.'

'It doesn't matter tuppence if you and I never find out,' Sheila said, 'but for the families, it must be slow torture not knowing.'

The weather forecast had come to an end. Cold air from the north was coming in.

Jim said unexpectedly, 'I'm going to call Norman.'

'What for? You're not planning another fishing trip? She said there could be gales.'

'It's about something else.'

The studio was pandemonium, a theatre bar between acts in a Beckett play, with everyone needing a break from the tension. Drawing from the model required strong concentration. Most were holding baguettes and drinks. Diamond squirmed through to the table at the end where the food was set out and a silver-haired man was presiding.

'May I?'

'Help yourself. Smoked salmon and salad to your left and bacon, lettuce and tomato here. The bacon is still warm, I think.'

'I can smell it. I'll go for it.'

'I'm Ferdie, by the way, Tom's father. Don't know you.'

'Peter Diamond, interloper, as one of your guests put it.'

'A first-timer, then? What will you drink – hot or cold?'

'CID, in fact, making a nuisance of myself asking questions about a missing schoolgirl. As I'm working, a coffee will suit me nicely.'

'Instant, I'm afraid,' Ferdie said, pointing to the urn. 'Help yourself. We're all extremely concerned about the young lady. I'm at your disposal.'

'You're not an artist yourself, then?'

'One in the family is more than enough. I try to make myself useful as the catering manager.'

Diamond took a bite of the BLT. The bacon was still crisp

and warm. 'These are good. Do you cater for Tom's parties as well?'

'They're easy to put on,' Ferdie said. 'Plenty of alcohol and savoury biscuits.'

'Nothing stronger?'

'What do you mean?'

'I was thinking a bunch of artists wouldn't be above dropping something extra into their drinks.'

'Never seen it happen,' Ferdie said. 'I wouldn't allow it in my house if they tried. Tom knows that.'

Diamond nodded. No one was going to admit to a police officer that drugs were being taken, but Ferdie seemed to mean every word. 'I guess most of them are past that sort of carry-on.'

Ferdie smiled. 'They're a lively crowd after a few drinks. You should see them.'

'I'd like to, but they may not appreciate a policeman showing up. Did you see the students at the latest party?'

'I saw only one, with the wild hair, wearing black. A goth, she calls herself.'

'That's Ella. The missing girl is Melanie Mason, known as Mel, shorter, with dark hair. She hasn't been seen since that night.'

'I know who she is, from the art sessions. She definitely wasn't at the party.'

'Ella was taken ill, I heard. Can you tell me what happened? She had to leave the party, I believe.'

Ferdie sighed and shook his head. 'She shouldn't have been here. You'd better speak to Tom about that. All I can tell you is that she spent the night on a sofa in our main sitting room. He drove her home next morning. I offered a cooked breakfast, but she couldn't face it.'

They were interrupted by a woman with charcoal smears on her face wanting a coffee. Diamond picked up his plate and mug and moved off. He definitely needed to speak to Ella.

He was crossing the room to where the three Priory Park students were in conversation when his path was blocked by a tall, gaunt man in a butcher's apron holding a knife. Sunken eyes and a mouth like a gash from the blade.

'You want to be careful with that,' Diamond said.

'You want to be careful where you fucking walk,' the man said. He pointed with the knife.

At knee level was a small armoury of knives and daggers spread out on a donkey stool. Diamond would have crashed into it if he hadn't been stopped.

'Thanks. Didn't spot them.'

'Fine fucking detective you are.'

'You know about me, then?'

'Everyone knows.'

'And you are . . . ?'

'Geraint.'

'So you use the knives in your art?'

'Fucking obvious, isn't it?'

'May I see your work?'

Geraint didn't answer, but stood back from his canvas, making just enough room for Diamond to step around the knives.

The painting looked like a skid pan at the end of the day, riven with intersecting tracks. Many colours had been worked into a thick khaki mess in which the broad shape of a man was just about discernible.

'What do you think?' Geraint said.

'I'm lost for fucking words,' Diamond said and moved on.

The three students turned their heads like meerkats.

'Good to see familiar faces,' he said. 'This is better than school, I bet.'

Not one of them answered. In truth, it wasn't much of an icebreaker.

He tried again. 'I started doing some drawing and gave up when it came out looking like the Michelin man.'

None of them smiled, but Ella couldn't resist saying, 'Show us.'

'I tore it up. Didn't want the model thinking I see him like that. I came over to ask if anyone has heard from Mel?'

'We'd tell you, wouldn't we?' Jem said.

'I was hoping she might have texted one of you.'

'She's not much of a texter,' Ella said. 'Not like Jem and me.'

'But she owns a phone?'

'Natch. Doesn't everyone?' Jem said. 'Ella's right. Mel keeps a load of stuff bottled up in her head. Even her best friends don't know.'

'And who are they?'

'Ella, for one. Me and Naseem.'

'Does she get on with her parents?'

'I suppose. They're stuck in their ways, like most parents. When I say "parents" I mean her mother and stepfather. She's their only child and that makes it all a bit heavy for her, but she doesn't complain. She'd hate to see them upset like they were on TV.'

'What's your theory, then?'

'About Mel?' Jem said. 'I think she's dead.'

'Oh, Jem!' Naseem said.

'Some psycho tried it on and she fought back and he killed her.'

'That's horrible.'

'Murder is horrible. Isn't that the truth?' She turned to Diamond.

She was trying to shock, and he didn't play along. 'It may not be in this case. Let's hope there's another explanation.

She left her house unexpectedly on the same night as the artists' party.'

'Pure coincidence,' Jem said. 'Mel wasn't a party girl. She didn't like hanging around with blokes. She wasn't even a drinker.'

Naseem said, 'I wish you wouldn't talk about her in the past tense. You don't know she's dead.'

'None of us knows for sure, but if she just ran off because of a row with her parents, she wouldn't last one night on her own. She's a home lover. Correction: she *was* a home lover.'

'She went out on her scooter,' Ella said. 'She definitely had some place in mind.'

'Well, it wasn't here,' Jem said. 'She wouldn't go near one of Tom's parties. She'd pay money to stay away. Am I right?'

'Unless she came for another reason,' Naseem said.

'Such as?'

'The texts we were getting from Ella.'

Ella turned accusingly and made a snorting sound – and it was clear that a confidence had been broken.

Diamond, inwardly alert, didn't alter his expression.

Naseem refused to be cowed by Ella. 'Were you texting all three of us, including Mel?'

After a moment's consideration, Ella nodded.

'So she would have got that message about Miss Gibbon, saying she was here,' Naseem went on.

'That's not what I texted, dorkbrain.'

'What was it, then?'

Suddenly all three had their phones out, checking stored messages. Diamond watched and waited with mounting interest. This could be vital information.

'Found it,' Naseem said and held out her phone.

They all looked at the message, including Diamond.

you wont believe this the Gibbon used to hang out here

Ella was quick to comment. 'Is that clear enough for you? She *used to* hang out. Past tense, get it? I didn't say she was at the party.'

The main force of these remarks had been directed at Naseem. She wouldn't be silenced. 'But we all know Mel was forever going on about Miss Gibbon and how we never had a chance to say goodbye and stuff like that.'

'That's true,' Jem said, and added in a complete about-turn, 'What if she read Ella's text and made up her mind to crash the party just to talk to people and find out for herself? Mel's very single-minded. Once she gets an idea in her head, it won't budge.'

'So what are you saying?' Ella said. 'She got on her scooter and drove here and met some psycho—'

'Like Geraint,' Jem said. 'And he cut her throat.'

'Please!' Naseem said. 'That's so gross.'

'He's creepy enough.'

Suddenly Ella was looking murderous herself. 'You're blaming me because of the text I sent? How mean is that?'

Diamond didn't want this to end in a spat. He'd been content to listen up to now. 'Hold on, young ladies. This is all supposition. We don't know what was in Mel's mind that night. Ella, did you send more than one text?'

'She did,' Naseem answered for her, 'and I can show you.' She brandished her phone with all the ceremony of Moses on Mount Sinai. 'This was the first.'

Diamond read the message:

full moon guess where I am

'And then this one,' Naseem said.

OMG just met geraint in goth gear

'So what?' Ella said. 'They're texts, that's all. I was being sociable, reporting what I saw.'

'I would have done the same,' Diamond said in a show of sympathy, wanting to tease out all the information that was going. 'How did you find out about Miss Gibbon?'

She was recovering her poise. 'From Ferdie. He was doing the drinks and talking to me about the artists and he goes, "They aren't all weird like Geraint. Some of them are prim and proper, like the art teacher who worked on graph paper, measuring everything".'

'Could only be the Gibbon,' Jem said.

'Yeah, silly old cow, and he goes, "Her name was Connie and she used to teach at Priory Park," so I knew it was her straight off. Constance Gloria Gibbon. We found her name on that missing persons' website. It makes sense really, her joining the local artists.'

'Did he say any more about her?' Diamond asked.

'Only that she stopped coming months ago.'

'Are you sure of that?'

'Those were his words. You can ask him if you don't believe me. He's still here. I was glad to have him talking to me at the party. I asked him to take my picture and he did.'

'With your iPhone? May I see?'

'If you want.' Ella surfed through several pictures. 'Here.'

The image of the young girl in her goth outfit with a fixed stare gave him some impression of her strength of purpose that night. In poor light in the background some shadowy dancing figures could be made out.

'Can you zoom in?'

'On me?'

'On the people behind you.'

'You won't see Mel, if that's what you're thinking. She wasn't there.' She used her fingertips to enlarge the background.

'That looks like the Bish. He was mental. The black guy in the hat is Manny. And the woman could be Anastasia or Drusilla. Just about everyone was there.'

'Except us,' Jem said. 'I've got to hand it to Ella. She was the only one with the guts to crash the party.'

'Unless Mel turned up later,' Naseem said.

'Let's hope she didn't,' Diamond said, to draw a line under all the speculation. He turned to Ella. 'If you wouldn't mind stepping outside, I can point to the lake we were talking about as the setting for your project. I had a walk down there and it looks ideal to me.'

Ella's eyes widened. She was hooked.

Outside the studio, and alone with Ella, he pointed down the hill towards the copse and added the promising news that large vehicles of some kind seemed to travel the estate. 'I think you could safely ask Tom if you can bring the House of Usher here and whether they can provide the transport.'

'It's a good thought, but I couldn't ask him.'

'Why not?'

'After I crashed the party, I'm not exactly the flavour of the month.'

'Want me to have a word with him?'

'About my project? Would you?'

'If you don't ask, you don't get.'

She gave him a rare smile. 'Thanks.'

'And now will you tell me what happened to you at the party?'

The smile vanished. 'To me?'

'Did you take something that made you ill? It's OK, you can be open with me. I'm not the drugs squad.'

'Who told you?' she said, fired up again. 'Tom?'

'Doesn't matter. One of the others. They saw the state you were in and Ferdie told me you spent the night on the sofa and couldn't face breakfast in the morning.'

The mood changed. She was resigned to Diamond knowing. 'I took one tablet of E and it went to my head.'

'Who supplied it?'

'No one.'

'That can't be true, Ella.'

'Someone at another party, ages ago. I've had it in my room ever since and I brought it with me. Tom was pissed off with me, but he acted really kind, helped me across to the house and made me comfortable on the sofa. I said some cringe-making stuff to him. I think I even tried to kiss him. In the morning he drove me home in his MG. Not quite home, because I didn't want my parents finding out, so he put me down at the end of the street and I walked the rest. That's it. End of story.'

'Have you told the others?'

'Not yet. I'd really like them to know I rode in the MG, but it's kind of embarrassing, me spending the night there and not sleeping with Tom. I'm supposed to be the most liberated girl in the school. They'd give me a hard time if they knew.'

'He'd get a worse time. He'd lose his job.'

'I swear to God he didn't touch me.'

'I believe you, Ella.'

'Unlike some of his friends. They treated me like I was some kind of slag.'

'Who do you mean?'

'That Geraint, for one. He's evil. I just happened to be standing near him and he scared me, the way he looked at my body. He called me "bitch" and grabbed my arm and squeezed really hard. I mean, just because me and him were both in goth gear it doesn't give him the right to hit on me. I only got away by spilling pineapple juice down his trousers.'

Diamond managed not to smile.

'And worse than that was Davy.'

'The model?'

'He was coming on to me even before I reached the studio. He stopped me outside, where he was having a smoke. I couldn't avoid him. He's middle-aged and he was, like, "Hey, babe, I wouldn't mind seeing you without your kit on." That fat old freak wanting to me to strip for *him*. I nearly threw up on the spot, I was so disgusted. Just because everyone has seen him nude he thinks he can get away with murder. Well, not murder, but really bad behaviour.'

'But you managed to escape?'

'This is going to sound bad. You've got to remember I crashed the party. I told you I met Davy outside the studio when I arrived. I decided it would be easier going in the door with someone else than on my own, so I took control. I walked into the studio with him as if we were an item and dumped him after one dance.'

'Have you spoken to him since?'

'No, and not to Geraint either.'

'Two men got their marching orders in one night. You're formidable.'

She grinned.

'And you didn't see much more of the party because the ecstasy tablet made you ill? Was it still in full swing when you left?'

'Absolutely.'

'So it's not impossible that Mel turned up later – after getting the text about Miss Gibbon – and you didn't see her?'

Denial was written all over her face. She didn't want to be blamed for sending the text. 'There's no evidence of that. Nobody saw her. That was just a dumb idea of Naseem's.'

Diamond wasn't letting it go so easily. 'Remembering

what happened to you – meeting Davy outside the studio – it's just possible Mel did try to gatecrash and was met outside and never got in.'

She caught her breath. 'Who would have met her – Davy?'

'As you say, it's a dumb idea.'

# 25

The life drawing still hadn't resumed when Diamond returned. Davy the model was standing outside the studio in his dressing gown, smoking, no doubt pleased to be earning a fee for doing nothing. Inside, the noise level had reduced and the food and drinks had been cleared away. But some of the artists were restless.

'Something holding you up?' Diamond asked Drusilla.

She rolled her eyes upwards. 'We can't start without Tom. We need him to set the pose.'

'Where is he?'

'Over at the house. There's some kind of flap going on. The police arrived.'

He moved fast. Two response cars and a large yellow van marked SPECIALIST SEARCH UNIT had drawn up in front of the house. Georgina was there among a group of uniformed officers doing her best to appear in control of events.

'So there you are,' she said when he approached, and made it sound like a rebuke.

'What happened?'

'Isn't that obvious?'

'But what brought them here – a tip?'

'Better than that,' Georgina said. 'Good information. One of the many responses to the TV appeal. On the night of the party a Boxgrove businessman was returning late from

271

London in his car when he passed someone on a scooter in the lane only half a mile from here.'

'A scooter?' The hairs on his neck stood up. 'Mel?'

'He said she looked young and female. This was about eleven to eleven fifteen. The report was processed with all the other possible sightings and this morning Chichester CID linked it to information from the parents that Melanie came here on Saturdays for the art sessions.'

His throat had gone dry. 'Is Montacute with them?'

'With the Standforths in the house. He knows all about the party.'

'He won't know *all* about it. He won't know about the texts Mel was getting.'

Georgina said with a petulant sigh. 'What's this – something else you've been keeping from me?'

He was far too troubled over Mel to get into a spat with Georgina. He simply told her what he'd heard from the schoolgirls.

'How long have you known this?' she asked, still suspicious he'd failed to share vital information.

'A few minutes.'

He could have joined in with her as she spoke the thoughts forming in her brain:

'These text messages may have been the trigger for Melanie going out that night, especially the one about Miss Gibbon being a member of the art group before she went missing. We know how keen the girl was to trace Miss Gibbon. She must have got on her scooter and come straight here to find out more.'

He nodded. Speech was difficult right now for him.

'You'd better inform Montacute. He's in charge of the hunt for the girl. Our enquiries, such as they were, have been overtaken.'

'He won't welcome being told.'

'Why not? It's relevant.'

'You said he's with the Standforths. They're starting to look like suspects. You don't reveal all you know in the presence of people who may be involved. I can fill him in later, when he's alone.'

She saw the sense in what he said. 'Fair point. Better not barge in there.' Her thinking was still transparent. 'Everyone who was at that party is a suspect if harm came to the girl that night.'

'True.'

'And there are some very odd people among them.'

He didn't wait for her to list them. 'Have you spoken to the search team?'

'Not yet. They're standing by, awaiting instructions.'

'I'll have a word.' He marched over to the van and introduced himself to the senior officer, with a sergeant's stripes, seated in the cab. 'You got a shout, then?'

'It's the missing schoolgirl, sir. DI Montacute says she could have been coming here.'

'So what's the game plan?'

'The map shows a stretch of water at the edge of the property.'

'I've seen it. Quite large. Muddy water, too.'

'We're used to that. Britain ain't the Caribbean, more's the pity.'

Diamond pointed down the slope to where he'd visited the lake. 'I've been there. There's a gravel path you can drive down.'

Montacute emerged from the house and came over. 'You got here fast,' he said to Diamond in a brusque aside, before briefing the dive team. 'We're in business, gentlemen. The owners have no knowledge of the girl coming here the other night, but she's been here previously as part of an art class and will know the place. She's familiar with the grounds. The lake is in the north-west corner, wherever that is.'

The sergeant pointed. 'Down the slope behind the trees. Superintendent Diamond has seen it.'

With all the gratitude of a dog whose bone is snatched away, Montacute swung back to Diamond. 'You've been there already?'

'Took a stroll earlier this morning.'

'Someone tip you off, then?'

'I was taking a break between art sessions.'

There was a pause for thought. Unable to decide whether he was having his leg pulled, Montacute vented his annoyance on the sergeant. 'What are you waiting for? Get to it.'

While the van disappeared down the slope, Diamond did the decent thing and updated Montacute on the text messages Mel had received. The DI didn't need reminding Mel was the schoolgirl who had come to the police station.

'At the time, I didn't give this lass high priority.'

'Nor me,' Diamond admitted. 'Gets more personal, doesn't it, when you've met her?'

'Believe me, we're pulling out all the stops. Headquarters will go berserk about all the overtime, but I intend to find her. And so does Tom Standforth. He's her art teacher and he's bloody upset.'

'What's your next move?'

'We timed this well. Most of the people who were at the party happen to be here today. I'll take statements from them all. They can carry on with their drawing and I'll pull them out one by one.'

'Hoping there was a sighting of Mel?'

'If they were in any state to notice. What about you? What are you planning to do?' Montacute asked and added with a leer, 'Finish off your masterpiece?'

'Got a few questions for Tom Standforth. Have you finished with him?'

'He's in the clear.'

'You think so?'

'You don't piss on your own doorstep.'

With that sage dictum to reflect on, Diamond returned to Georgina. 'The art is about to get under way again,' he told her.

'You're not going back in?'

'It's a chance to speak to Tom.'

'In that case, I'll find out how the divers are getting on,' she said. 'I've seen more of that model than I ever wished to see.'

Jim Bentley called his fishing friend Norman while Sheila was watching one of her daytime soaps.

'Is this a good moment?'

'If you really want to know, it isn't,' Norman said. 'I was having my afternoon nap. Sometimes I think I'll take a hammer to that phone.'

'You could try turning it off.'

'Now I'm awake, what do you want?'

'Don't know if you saw the news item about the missing schoolgirl.'

'May have done. Can't remember.'

'Melanie, from Priory Park School.'

'What's she got to do with me?'

'Nothing at all,' Jim said. 'Keep your hair on. She's been gone several days now and they had the parents on, making an appeal for information.'

'I still don't see—'

'Listen, Norman. The police guy clearly thinks she's dead. They're hoping someone can give them a clue about what happened to her. I've been thinking back to our last trip.

Remember the inflatable we found that you said was like the *Mary Celeste*?'

'Except it wasn't,' Norman said. 'It belonged to that dickhead diver.'

'But what was he up to? He didn't say when you asked. He told us to bugger off.'

'We caught him out, that's why. Treasure-hunter, if you ask me. Found some wreck in the middle of nowhere and hopes it's stacked with gold. If they make a find, they never tell anyone. They bring it up secretly, piece by piece.'

'There wasn't anything like that in the inflatable and he didn't come up with any. I was thinking something else. Instead of bringing stuff up he was taking it down.'

'What – hiding it? The schoolgirl?'

'Her body.'

'That's far-fetched, isn't it? If he wants to dump a body at sea he can heave it overboard. End of.'

'But he chose that particular spot. He was anchored there. You thought there could be a wreck down there, right?'

'I still do.'

'What's the depth out there? Not all that great.'

'Forty metres probably. Enough water to cover a pretty big ship.'

'OK, there are hundreds of wrecks along the south coast and divers like exploring them, but they don't go alone. They dive in groups, for safety. This guy was alone and he was bloody annoyed when we found him. He was up to no good, Norm. We agree on that.'

'Sure.'

'Getting back to my theory, if you dump a body in the sea, it gets washed up eventually – unless it's trapped. If there's an unmarked wreck down there, it's not a bad place to hide a body, tuck it into a hold where it can't get loose and rise to the surface.'

'I'm not convinced,' Norman said.

'Tell me what he was up to, then.'

'I haven't the foggiest.'

'Well, I take it seriously enough to report it, just in case. Then it's up to the police and it won't be on my conscience.'

'Is this what you woke me up to tell me?'

'No, I woke you up to get the GPS reading. I asked you for it at the time, remember? You made a note of it.'

'On the back of my hand,' Norman said.

'Bloody hell. What use was that?'

'There was a pen, but no paper.'

'It's gone, then?'

'Believe it or not, I wash my hands several times a day,' Norman said.

'And I don't suppose you memorised the numbers?'

'Come on, Jim, get real. Do you know how many digits there are in a GPS reading? Nine for latitude and nine for longitude. These days, I can barely remember my phone number.'

'Thanks a bunch. I thought I could rely on you.'

'You're serious about this, aren't you?'

'I can't ignore it.'

'I took a picture with my iPhone.'

'Of the guy sitting in his inflatable. I remember. But it's not much use when we can't say where it was.'

'Got a pen and paper handy?'

'What? You *do* remember the reading?'

'No, my friend, I just told you I took a picture. I photographed the back of my hand before I washed it.'

In the studio, Tom had set the pose and the artists were already at work. He agreed to speak to Diamond. 'Are you working together, you and Inspector Montacute?'

'Sort of.'

'He wants to question every one of my art group.'

'About Mel.'

'The thing is, he won't set foot in here. They're having to step outside one by one. Do you think he's shy?'

'Of a naked man? I expect he doesn't want to be overheard, and neither do I. Can we move to the far end?'

They faced each other on two stools where the refreshment table had been set up, far enough away to speak without the artists hearing them. Tom could still supervise the session from there.

Diamond was torn. His thoughts were of Mel and what might have happened. He wanted to be at the lakeside watching the search, but he wasn't needed there. This interview could be critical to the case. To make it tougher for himself, he knew he shouldn't go for the obvious.

'I won't go over the ground DI Montacute covered with you,' Diamond said. 'Let's talk about young Ella.'

A guarded look slammed down like a visor. 'Ella? I thought you were interested in Mel.'

'This is a bit of a cheek, outside my brief,' Diamond said, as disarming as he could be under stress. 'When I went looking for Ella yesterday at the school, I was really impressed by her artwork in the yard. A fantastic effort. She told me what it's supposed to be.'

'The House of Usher.'

'What a terrific idea, all put together from old lobster pots and seaweed. And the size of it. She was explaining that it doesn't have to be sent to the examining board. She can send them the image.'

'Correct,' Tom said, still wary of where this was leading.

'I commented that the school yard isn't the ideal setting, with the rubbish bins and the broken desks as a background.'

'She can edit those out.'

'But to anyone familiar with the original story, the Edgar

Allan Poe' – Diamond made it sound as if he was a world authority – 'there's one major element missing, and that's the tarn.' He looked for a reaction and got it. He'd guessed that the word would be unfamiliar. 'The lake the house was built beside, and which swallows the building when the collapse comes. I suggested mocking it up with tinfoil, but Ella didn't think much of the idea. Ideally, she needs to get her House of Usher erected beside a real lake. After all the effort she's put in already, it must be worth trying. It would lift her grade, I expect.'

'She'll get a top grade anyway.'

'But to get into art school, she needs it to look as good as possible. She can show this as evidence of her talent. It's a unique creation, and I know you helped inspire it. This morning I went for a walk around your grounds and found the lake beside the beech trees and thought what a perfect setting that would be for Ella's house.'

Tom had visibly relaxed as the talk stayed off the party. 'I hadn't considered it.'

'So I'm putting in a word on her behalf. If we can find some transport, and you don't object, we'll be treated to a spectacle that will have Poe himself rubbing his hands with glee.'

'He's been dead more than a hundred and fifty years.'

Diamond managed a daft grin. 'He wrote horror, didn't he? I wouldn't rule it out, would you?'

Tom didn't get it.

'Seriously,' Diamond said, 'is it on?'

Tom tugged at his mane of dark hair. 'We'd need to look at the logistics. I don't know how well she lashed the pots together.'

'I couldn't help noticing commercial vehicles have been using the track across the lawn that passes quite close to the lake.'

'That's my dad's horticulture business. He'd let us use the van for sure. It's just a question of whether the House of Usher would survive the trip.' He reached a decision. 'Why not? If Ella's willing to risk it, we'll try.'

'She'll be thrilled,' Diamond said and moved smoothly into more contentious territory. 'She was nervous about asking you herself in view of what happened at the party.'

'What do you mean by that?' Tom's whole physique tensed.

'It's more a matter of what Ella meant by it. She told me she took an ecstasy tablet and it went to her head and you helped her to the house. She doesn't have much memory of what happened after.'

'If you think it was anything inappropriate . . . '

'Did I say so?'

Tom spaced each word of his response. 'She spent the night on a sofa. In the morning I drove her home, or near to home. Nothing improper happened. To be frank, I was bloody annoyed with her for gatecrashing the party and even more pissed off that she took the drug.'

'You didn't tell me any of this at the school yesterday.'

'I wasn't going to volunteer it, was I? I could lose my job.'

'Did you know she was texting her friends, including Mel?'

'I saw she had the phone with her. I took it away when I knew she was spaced out, but I gave it back next morning.'

'One of the messages she sent was about Miss Gibbon, their former art teacher.'

'OK,' Tom said, but his expression didn't say OK. He looked like death.

'It said, in effect, that Miss Gibbon was one of your Saturday group.'

'She was. She left.'

'Something else you didn't volunteer. So was that how you learned there was a vacancy for an art teacher at Priory Park?'

He nodded. 'Jobs are hard to come by. They needed someone at short notice. I put in my application before they advertised the post.'

'Did you find out why she resigned?'

'I heard there was a row with the head.'

'About her teaching?'

He shrugged. 'Things like that are kept confidential.'

'But they leak out.'

'I don't know anything for certain.'

'Put it this way: were you asked to take a more relaxed approach than Miss Gibbon?'

'That's my style. I *am* relaxed' – he tried to show it with a twitchy smile – 'except when the police are grilling me.'

'Did you find out what Miss Gibbon was planning to do after she resigned?'

'I don't think anyone knew, except possibly Miss Du Barry.'

'And you haven't heard from her?'

'From Connie Gibbon? Why should I?'

'As one of your Saturday artists.'

'She wasn't the sort to send a postcard, if that's what you're thinking.'

'I'll tell you what I'm thinking, Tom. It's about Mel. She was troubled about the way Miss Gibbon left the school and even more troubled that she became a missing person. The others weren't particularly bothered, but it became a personal issue for Mel. She even called at the police station in Chichester to get the latest information.'

A pause.

Tom said, 'I didn't know that.'

'It's likely Ella's text about Miss Gibbon was the trigger for Mel leaving her house. To the girls, it was new information. They didn't know their former teacher was in your art group. Mel, who I said was eager to know more of what really happened, must have thought she would get answers at your party, from you or the other artists.'

'She was wrong about that. I couldn't tell her anything and I don't think anyone else could.'

'Mel didn't know that.'

'She didn't come here. Ask anyone.'

'There was a sighting of someone on a scooter a short distance from here.'

'I know, and that's why you lot want to search the place, but I don't expect you to find anything. They're looking at the lake. Why would she go anywhere near the lake? The party was going on here, not down by the lake.'

'What time did it finish?'

'Not all that late. It wasn't an all-night rave. Most of these people are middle-aged. We packed up by midnight.'

'Another question: back in 2007, a man from Slindon, a gardener by the name of Joe Rigden, was murdered. He worked on a garden not far from here, a place called Holly Blue Cottage. I'm wondering if he did any work for your father. You were living here then, weren't you?'

'I was born here. But you'll have to ask my dad about Rigden. If he ever he came here, I didn't meet him.'

'Where can I find your dad?'

'Right now? Over at the house. He'll be clearing up the kitchen.'

Diamond was halfway across the yard when his phone went. He tugged it out and put it to his ear.

'Peter?' The voice was Georgina's.

'Speaking.'

'I need you here at the lake – fast.'

'Have they found something?'

'Get here as soon as you can.'

# 26

His legs were starting to feel as if they didn't belong to him, but the steep descent helped him run the final stretch to the wooded area where the van was parked.

Already the dive team had a small inflatable on the lake. The sergeant driver he'd spoken to earlier was alone on the bank, smoking. Georgina wasn't in view.

Strong as he told himself he was from his rugby-playing days, he had to take several gulps of air before saying, 'Seen my boss?'

The cigarette was taken from between the lips and put to use as a pointer. 'She spotted someone and went after them.'

*Georgina in pursuit?*

'Did you get a sight?'

A shake of the head.

'Could it be one of your people?'

'They're all here. I was told to give you a message.' The driver took another long drag.

'Tell me, for Christ's sake.'

'She said go the other way round and head them off.'

Suddenly the lake looked ten times as large it had before. And the superfit legs were stiffening up. There wasn't much more running in them. 'I've got a better idea. You go instead.'

A slow shake of the head. 'It may not look like it, but I'm on duty here.'

'No problem.' Diamond pulled rank. The man was only a sergeant. 'I'll take over.'

'With respect, sir, it has to be someone who's done the course. Dive team protocol.'

Strongly tempted to tell the sergeant what to do with his dive team protocol, he took out his phone.

At first he thought Georgina wasn't going to take the call.

'You took your time.' There was a pause for breath. She was obviously jogging or at least striding out as she spoke. 'Did you get my instruction?' Pause. 'I'm almost at the opposite side now.' Pause. 'Can you see me?'

He shielded his eyes and stared across the water. 'From where I am, no, ma'am.'

'You can't be looking in the right direction.'

'I think I see you now.' There was a speck of blue moving steadily in a clockwise direction along the path on the far side. The colour showed up well against the red bricks of the boundary wall. He assumed it was Georgina. Deplorably for a detective, he couldn't recall the clothes she was wearing.

'Don't hang about, then. Go to your right, round the other side,' she told him in short bursts of words. 'We'll catch them in a pincer movement. But hurry.'

*Them?* 'More than one?'

'Just the one. I don't know if they're male or female. I'm not even certain what colour they're wearing.'

You and me both, Georgie, he thought, as he forced his aching legs into action again. The boss was right. This had to be done. This person needed to be identified. Presumably it was the same individual he'd spotted before lunch going in the other direction.

The path was an obstacle course. There was a choice between thick mud at the water's edge and exposed roots on the more solid ground. He was in danger of tripping every yard of the way. With eyes down for safety's sake, he noticed the occasional footprint, but didn't celebrate it as a Man Friday discovery. The owner and his guests no doubt took an occasional walk here.

Cursing every few seconds, Diamond picked his way through the mud at the best speed he could. His head ached and his throat was dry.

So who could the lone walker be? All the artists were at work in the studio and Ferdie was in the house clearing up after the meal. There shouldn't have been anyone at large on the estate.

He forced himself forward, wishing he were fitter. If Georgina could keep going, so would he. But it was damned hard work.

Ten minutes in, he was startled by the shriek of a moorhen and saw it take flight from the reeds beside the bank and skim across the water. Something must have disturbed it.

He froze.

Then a twig snapped.

Someone was definitely coming towards him.

He stepped behind a tree.

Now he could hear dog-like panting and it wasn't his own. This person wasn't in condition.

No need to tackle them physically, he decided. It was reasonable to have a few civilised words with someone you met out walking in the country. He waited for them to draw level.

As they did, he had a sense of solid physique, shorter than himself. But a woman. Definitely a woman. At the moment he stepped into view, she made a sound like a train going through a station.

His 'Good afternoon' – completely inaudible – came out feebly in the instant he realised who she was.

Georgina.

'You?' she said with disgust.

'I thought you were—'

'You could have given me a heart attack, leaping out like that.'

He hadn't leapt. He'd appeared unexpectedly, that was all, but there was nothing to be gained by pointing it out. All he could do was wait for Georgina to stop hyperventilating. She reached for the trunk of the tree and grasped it.

After some time she said, 'Where the devil did he go? I was in pursuit. Has he passed you?'

'No chance. Was it definitely a man, then?'

'Definitely? Can't say, but that's the impression I got. I assure you I wasn't chasing a shadow.' She stepped away from the tree, closer to the water, and looked along the bank in both directions. 'I can't understand it.'

'Did he know you were following?'

'Unlikely. I was never that close. Are you certain he didn't get past without you noticing?'

'Not if he kept to the path.'

'There's no rule that says he should,' Georgina said. 'He must have gone off at a tangent, turned away from the lake and made a getaway through the wood.'

'Seems so,' he said, ready to admit defeat.

But Georgina wasn't. She had that implacable look he knew from Bath Central whenever she demanded to see his budget report. 'He wouldn't get far on this side. There's a nine-foot wall. He's in the area still. He must be.' She turned away from the lake and started striding through the wood, with Diamond following. 'I've ruined a good pair of shoes. I'll be damned if it's all for nothing.'

They hadn't gone more than a few steps before a patch of red brick showed ahead in the autumn sunshine. 'You see?' Georgina said. 'There's a wall. There's no escape. He's got to be here somewhere.'

It was the boundary wall marking the limit of the estate.

'Shall we split up again?'

'No,' she said. 'We stay together now.' Already she was marching off to the left, following the course of the wall. The ground here was soft and moist, but the grass wasn't so thick. Brown-capped fungi sprouted in profusion.

'Mind you don't slip,' he said. 'I came a cropper this morning.'

She didn't answer. She had more on her mind than slippery mushrooms.

'Ha!' she said when they'd gone another two minutes. 'We might have guessed.' They had come to a wooden door set into the wall. 'This has got to be the way our elusive friend went.'

'Is it bolted?'

She tried the handle and the door opened.

They both went through and found themselves in an overgrown, neglected garden. Waist-high grass the colour of hay. Looping brambles. A roof in the distance covered in moss and with a number of tiles missing.

'Familiar?' Diamond said.

'Not to me.'

'You didn't come this far in. It's Mrs Shah's garden.' He was sure of it. He forced his way forward a few steps and spotted the top of the trellis and the garden shed.

'Holly Blue Cottage?' Georgina said, as if they'd landed on the moon.

'How dumb is that?' he said. 'I knew both places were in this area, but I didn't appreciate they were either side of the same wall.'

'Didn't you notice that door in the wall this morning?'

He shook his head. 'There wasn't much time and I was more interested in what was in the shed. Shows how easily you can miss things.'

Georgina looked right and left across the tall grass. 'Where's our fugitive, then? If he came in the way we did, he can't have gone far. I'm no Indian scout, but hasn't someone forced his way through this?'

She was right. Some of the long stalks were bent and broken – and it wasn't the track Diamond himself had made earlier in the day.

He went ahead. Not that he was any more of a scout than Georgina, but it was pretty obvious where they were heading. The garden shed.

The lone walker could be inside.

They reached the mould-scarred building, stood for a second in front and exchanged glances, saying nothing. Then Diamond kicked the door. It swung inwards and revealed Hen Mallin, seated in the chair, holding a cigarillo to her lips.

'Manners,' she said. 'Always knock before entering.'

For once even Diamond was lost for words. Not for one moment had he thought they'd been pursuing his old colleague.

Georgina was already in a foul mood. These two would never hit it off, but she couldn't be blamed for the fury she put into the word, 'You?'

Hen shrugged.

'Just what are you doing here?'

'What does it look like?' Hen said. She reached down and picked up a transparent bag containing a few fresh mushrooms. 'Resting my limbs after a forage around the lake . . . ma'am. It's the mushroom season, in case you hadn't noticed, but I'll be checking my Observer book of fungi before I sample them. You can't be too careful with these little varmints.'

'You're under suspension.'

'Not under house arrest. No one said I can't go out.'

'This is private land. You're trespassing.'

'Aren't we all?'

Georgina had all the fire power, but was coming off the worse. 'Here – of all places – where there's an investigation going on. You were instructed to stop doing police work of any description.'

'I have,' Hen said. 'I'm collecting mushrooms. Haven't interfered. Haven't spoken to a soul. I'm not obstructing you in your duties.'

'There's a major alert, a child gone missing. We should be hunting for her, not you.'

Diamond agreed with that. Much as he admired Hen, this had been a fool's errand. All their efforts should have been geared to finding Mel.

'Your choice,' Hen said. 'There was no need.'

'We know that now,' Georgina said. 'What possessed you to come here?'

'Family loyalty,' Hen said. 'It's no secret that the investigation has shifted here. All your interest has shifted to the missing schoolgirl, but I'm still worried sick about Joss. Are they diving for bodies in the lake?'

'We're not discussing the case with you.'

'As you wish,' Hen said. 'I'll shut up, then.'

Georgina may have taken this as a small victory, but Diamond didn't. He'd noticed a gleam in Hen's eyes suggesting she'd been on the point of sharing something. For the present, he didn't take it up. Georgina was calling the shots.

'You'd better leave,' she told Hen. 'Did you come by car?'

'It's in the lane in front of the cottage. I wasn't going to park it in front of Fortiman House.'

'So you knew about this place?'

'Came here when I was on the Joe Rigden murder, didn't I?' She reached for a flower pot and flicked ash into it. 'I'll be on my way, then. Leave you serving officers to get on with your vital work.'

They had to step out of the shed to make room. Holding her mushrooms in front of her like a trophy, Hen stepped outside and waded through the long grass without looking back but with a definite swagger, a small, defiant figure in no way contrite.

'I've lost all sympathy,' Georgina said to Diamond.

He was under the impression she hadn't any to lose, but didn't say so. 'We've solved the mystery of the solitary walker.'

'But at what cost?' she said. 'You're a physical wreck. I feel like a scarecrow. We're senior officers. It's degrading.'

'We found the connecting door. That's progress.'

Georgina wasn't consoled. 'I've had enough. I shall tell Commander Hahn we've gone beyond the call of duty to examine that loathsome woman's misconduct and I'm recommending her immediate dismissal. I know you're sympathetic, but in my book there's nothing to be said for her.'

He didn't take the bait. 'Shall we return to the real action, then?'

'Certainly.'

'Want me to call our driver to pick us up?'

'No. We walk.'

'As you wish.'

They closed the shed and returned through the connecting door to the Fortiman estate. At once it became obvious that Georgina expected more from him on her hard-line decision. 'I mean, isn't it transparently clear, Peter, that she's not fit to lead a criminal investigation department?'

'The jury's out on that one, ma'am.' He was speaking to her back as he trailed after her along the path beside the lake.

'You don't have to "ma'am" me now we're alone. It's

beginning to sound more like a term of derision – especially the way she uses it.'

'I won't, then. If we're talking about Hen Mallin's fitness to lead, I have to speak up for her. Having seen her at work, I have a lot of respect.'

'More than she ever demonstrates.'

'That's her style. She's not employed to show respect. She was upfront and honest about what she did wrong, failing to investigate her niece. The question we should be asking is whether that disbars her from ever working again. I don't know of any other failings.'

'Oh, for God's sake! She's insubordinate.'

'Under strain – and she's under plenty at the moment. She's a good investigator, a whole lot more likely to succeed than Montacute, who is trying to do her job now.'

'That's beside the point. I don't care for him either.'

'As I said to you before, I believe Hen Mallin was suspended because she rocked the boat.'

She stopped and wheeled round. 'Tell me, Peter. Is there something going on that you haven't shared with me?'

It would have been so easy to tell her about Archie Hahn's memo, but it would break her. Difficult as she was, he couldn't do that to her.

They were standing toe to toe like boxers, so he sparred with her, just as he had the day before in the school dining room. 'We've been over this, but I don't think you believed me. Hen started getting interested in missing persons, contacting police stations all along the south coast to see if there was a trend – if someone was disposing of bodies on an industrial scale. The figures bore it out. She proposed coordinated action. This was the development that alarmed the high-ups. The murder rate in Sussex and Hampshire was about to rocket. By sacking Hen, they snuff out the problem.'

'I can't accept this.'

'They want you to rubber-stamp her dismissal, so everything goes back to normal.'

'Peter, that can't be true. Don't forget I was invited personally by my old colleague Commander Hahn. Archie, of all people, knows I wouldn't be a party to anything dishonourable.'

He swallowed hard. 'That goes without saying.'

'Well, then.'

'Commander Hahn asked you to investigate Hen Mallin's behaviour, and no more. Hen shot our fox by admitting straight off that she'd favoured her niece.'

'She did.'

'That's all they need from us. Job done.'

She frowned. 'It isn't as simple as that . . . is it?'

'I'm glad we agree on that. Blame me for throwing it open and asking awkward questions. Bad things have been happening here and you and I are rooting them out. If we give up now, they may never see the light of day.'

She tilted her chin higher, always a promising sign. 'That is possible.'

Encouraged, he went on, 'From all I know of you, Assistant Chief Constable Dallymore, you're not going to turn your back on serious malpractice. You'll get to the truth, however inconvenient it may be.'

'We'll see it through, the two of us,' she said, quite fired up. And then she turned her back and continued the trek around the lake, brisk and business-like.

Plodding in her wake, Diamond thought about Paloma and home and Raffles the cat, and tried to reconcile himself to at least one more night away.

They continued as far as the dive team and stopped to ask if anything of importance had been found.

The van driver shook his head. 'This could be a long job,' he said, lighting another cigarette.

*   *   *

292

Up at the house, DI Montacute had finished interviewing the artists. 'Waste of my bloody time,' he said, when Diamond asked. 'Not one of them saw Melanie. I'm starting to ask myself if she was ever here. Just because one of the schoolgirls decided to gatecrash the party, it doesn't mean her friend did. Out of all those people, someone would have noticed, wouldn't they?'

'Is your information reliable, the sighting of the girl on the scooter?'

'You put your finger on it. We've had dozens of possible sightings since I put out the appeal. This one had to be followed up because of the scooter. We know she owned one, a 125cc sports scooter, very distinctive, purple, and she certainly went out on it that night.'

'Did the witness see the colour of the thing?'

'You don't get that lucky.'

'What time was this?'

'He reckoned about ten thirty. This rider was only five minutes away from here and the party was still going. But nobody from here saw the girl or her scooter.'

'You interviewed the artists. Have you spoken to the owner, Ferdie Standforth?'

'Saw him first, with his son. Another blank.'

'There's someone you won't have questioned.'

'Who's that?'

'Davy the model. He was at the party.'

'You're right,' Montacute said, wide-eyed. 'He's been in the studio all afternoon. Easy to miss. I'd better catch him before he leaves.'

'Have you searched the lane where the girl on the scooter was seen?'

'Of course. Nothing.'

'But your informant was reliable?'

'He wasn't an attention-seeker, if that's what you mean.

We've had a few of them. Pathetic, aren't they? Want to be part of the action, so they call you up and tell you a load of bullshit.'

'How do you know they're making it up?'

'The same people call every time. And they're generally the first to get in touch. Fantasists. They convince themselves they're helping. My team are good at spotting them, thank Christ. The calls that come in later are more likely to be genuine. We're still getting them. I've got a guy coming to the nick at five thirty, reckons she may been dumped in the sea off Selsey Bill.'

'That's a lot of sea.'

'He took a GPS reading. I'll have to put him off till tomorrow. Got to see the model while he's still here.'

'I can interview your Selsey Bill man,' Diamond said.

# 27

When DI Montacute got back to his office in Chichester police station at the end of his demanding day, he found Peter Diamond in occupation. Nothing is more certain to induce insecurity than finding someone seated in your office chair.

'Don't stand on ceremony,' Diamond said with all the warmth he could muster for this dislikeable detective. 'Come on in. I've finished, anyway.'

'Doing what?'

'Chatting to your helpful member of the public, the boatman who reckons all the missing people are at the bottom of the sea.'

Montacute must have forgotten already. 'Oh, him.'

'I knew you wouldn't mind if I brought him into your office. So much more homely than the interview rooms.'

'Is it?'

'Jim Bentley is from Emsworth. Nice man. Retired civil servant. Owns a small boat and goes fishing with his friend Norman, an ex-lecturer. Not one of your fantasists, I'd say. His information is reliable, such as it is.'

Montacute gave the grimace of a policeman who wants it known that he will not be suckered. 'He saw a body being dropped overboard?'

'No. He saw an empty inflatable anchored in the sea and

a diver coming up, a lone diver who told Jim and Norman to sail into the sunset, or words to that effect.'

'Is that all?'

'They took a photo, fixed the spot with the GPS and did as they were asked.'

'And he thinks that's worth reporting to us?'

'It's a personal tribute to you. He saw your sparkling performance on TV and felt compelled to respond.'

'Oh, yeah?' That grimace again.

'And how did you get on with Davy the model?' Diamond asked.

'Same as all the rest. He didn't see Mel at the party. Not one of them did.'

'And did the dive team find anything?'

'No.'

'It's a big lake.'

'They searched the obvious area closest to the house.'

'Maybe they should try the less obvious parts.'

'I've laid them off now. It's bloody obvious we've wasted our time at Fortiman House. Someone out of all those people would have seen the girl.'

'Didn't you learn anything at all?'

'I'm in the wrong job, that's what I learned. I'd do better as an artists' model. Did you see that yellow Lamborghini on the drive? It belonged to Davy. I watched him drive off in it at the end of the day.'

'If he owns a thing like that, he doesn't need to model.'

'It gives him pleasure.'

'The modelling or the car?'

'The modelling. He enjoys being looked at. As he put it to me, he's an average bloke with an average body who doesn't get noticed by anyone when he's in his clothes. This way, he's the centre of attention.'

'Strange. Rather him than me.'

'It takes all sorts. And now if you've finished with my office . . .'

Diamond didn't move.

'Where's your boss?' Montacute asked, making it sound like a threat.

'Back at the hotel, taking a shower and arranging for her clothes to be dry-cleaned. She got in a mess stomping around the lake chasing a trespasser who turned out to be *your* boss.'

'Hen?' he said with disapproval. 'What was she doing there?'

'She heard the art group were under investigation. She's anxious to find her niece, Joss. Is there any news?'

Montacute shook his head. 'All the focus is on the school-girl. Hen's off the case. She'll get into worse trouble if this gets back to headquarters.'

'It won't, will it?' Diamond said.

'Why not?'

'Because you're going to forget I told you. You're a hard man, but my reading of you is that you wouldn't shaft your own boss.'

In the privacy of his room back at the hotel, he called Sussex police headquarters and asked to speak to Commander Hahn.

'It's Saturday,' the duty officer said.

'I know that.'

'He isn't here, I'm afraid.'

'For the whole weekend?'

'He'll be in Monday.'

Excellent. If Diamond hadn't been holding the phone he would have rubbed his hands. 'Unfortunately I can't wait for Monday,' he said, launching into one of those hectoring speeches he could make without trying. No duty officer could withstand them. 'I'm speaking on behalf of Assistant Chief Constable Georgina Dallymore, working on a top-level assignment at Commander Hahn's personal request. How shall we do this? I don't suppose you want to call him on his mobile and I guess you won't let me have the number. Are you empowered to take executive decisions?'

'Depends what they are.'

'My chief needs to use the search and rescue unit for a sea search tomorrow morning. A dive about a mile off Selsey Bill.'

'Not possible, I'm afraid. The SRU aren't available. There's an ongoing operation.'

Gotcha. Diamond smiled to himself. 'Not ongoing any more if it's the one at Fortiman House. I just spoke to DI Montacute at Chichester. He no longer needs the dive team. So would you ask them to get in touch with me at the Ship Hotel and we'll arrange a time and place?'

An hour later, Diamond was stretched on the bed waiting for someone from the dive team to call. His neck started itching. He flicked it with his fingertip and felt a faint contact and realised he'd disturbed a living thing, an insect of some sort, now wriggling on the quilt. He sat up fast.

A ladybird, upside down, its little legs going like pistons. Invading ladybirds are easier to forgive than most other bugs.

He righted it, took it to the window and released it.

A second one was crawling up one of the window panes.

'It's an invasion,' he said, letting the little creature move on to his finger. 'Where are you guys coming from?'

He had the answer the moment he turned back. The old wax jacket from the garden shed at Holly Blue Cottage was draped over the armchair in the corner. He'd given the thing a shake before bringing it indoors, but it must have contained some tiny hostages. It wasn't impossible that some less attractive wildlife was harboured there, so he decided to check.

The jacket was in a bad state. His intention had been to go through the pockets, but he didn't fancy putting his hands inside now that insects were on his mind. The answer, he decided, was to turn the pockets inside out. It was just possible that Joe Rigden – if he had been the owner – had pocketed something of interest. So he started methodically pulling out the linings. Most were empty and probably had never been used.

Some green garden twine fell out of one of the large side pockets along with a copper coin turned green and some bits of black organic material, dry and shrunken, that might have been the remains of fungi. The opposite pocket yielded some walnuts, surprisingly well preserved. All in all, nothing likely to explain the unanswered questions about Joe Rigden and his violent death.

Then the phone rang.

# 28

Georgina wasn't happy missing her Sunday breakfast to be on the road by 6.30 a.m. All the way to Selsey she emitted short, disapproving sighs as if every turn in the road was a pain. And when a sea mist crept over the fields, she said she might as well have stayed in bed. 'What's the point of making a search in these conditions?'

'The mist makes no difference,' Diamond said. 'We know the GPS reading and the search is under the water.'

They met the dive team – four of them, led by a giant of a man called Dave Albison – beside the launch ramp for the lifeboat, the main feature of a long narrow stretch of pebble beach. But they weren't using the ramp. A large rigid inflatable was on the stones ready to go.

Georgina gave it a suspicious look and said she'd been expecting a proper boat – not the most tactful of starts. The senior man said it was their main marine vessel and they were proud of it. He added that she might want to put on waterproofs. They had spares with them.

For Diamond, the spectacle of his boss in bright yellow and with her ample chest augmented by a life jacket was an amusing sideshow.

'Does it bounce?' she asked.

'The sea doesn't get much calmer than this,' Dave Albison said – which didn't exactly answer the question.

Screaming seagulls added their own comment.

The team loaded so much diving equipment into the front of the vessel that Diamond found himself wondering if there would be room for everyone as well. But the professionals didn't seem to have any doubts. They boarded their two passengers in the shallows and then three of them gave the craft a hefty push to get it afloat. They leapt on board, the motor spluttered and roared, a beacon light flashed and the search mission was under way.

Did it bounce much? It did, but there wasn't any point in protesting, because you wouldn't have been heard. The thing fairly raced towards the deeper water. Diamond had a suspicion that this was the SRU's payback time. There was really no reason to be hurtling across the water at maximum speed unless it was to intimidate the passengers. The same team had spent a fruitless day at Fortiman House and now their Sunday morning was spoken for as well.

In the mist, it was extremely exciting or extremely scary, depending on your state of nerves. Diamond made sure he didn't lock eyes with Georgina. She was being brave. He'd insisted she came on the trip, pressing her at least as hard as he'd pressed that duty officer. She would regret not being there, he'd said. This was the most promising shout they'd had. A sighting at sea was one thing; a sighting with a GPS reading was a gift from the gods. Even the SRU lads had been impressed by that.

What seemed a long ride took under ten minutes in reality before Albison eased the throttle. One of his team took a reading. They were close.

It was weird to be fixing a position in open water with only sea and mist on all sides. The Selsey shore had vanished. With Albison using his iPhone to call the fine points, they used paddles to manoeuvre before taking the decision to lower an anchor. One of the crew, already in a drysuit, was being prepared to dive, making checks to valves and seals.

When Diamond saw a tin of powder being used, he tried to lighten the mood a little.

'Is that talc you've got there?'

'It is.'

'Does the suit chafe, then?'

'It's to help the hands through the wrist seals,' Albison said. He wasn't receptive to chafing jokes.

'Will he take a camera down?'

'That's the plan. You won't see much if he doesn't.'

'So can we look at the images up here?'

Albison said in a voice as unfriendly as the sea, 'Would you mind letting us get on with our job?'

Fair enough, he thought. Diving is risky at the best of times. There were safety procedures to be gone through in a small space and the experts could do without some land-lubber demanding a running commentary. Instead, he asked Georgina how she was doing. She had her arms clasped tight below the life jacket.

'Do you want an honest answer? My hair is ruined and I wish I was wearing thermals.'

'It should get warmer when the mist lifts.'

'Good God, I can't wait that long.'

He was shivering himself, even under the waterproofs. For once his two-piece suit hadn't been the ideal choice.

She asked him, 'Is Commander Hahn aware of what we're doing?'

'He doesn't work over the weekend.'

'I was thinking he'd want to be informed.'

Diamond nodded, privately thinking Archie Hahn would hit the roof if he was told they were on the trail of missing people.

A line had been put overboard for the diver to use. The youngest of the team, he was finally ready to go, full-face mask and fins on, gas cylinders attached and a dive video camera strapped to his chest. He seated himself on the side, gave a thumbs-up and dropped back-first into the water. A splash, a glimpse of fins and he disappeared.

Already his colleagues were fully occupied with something else, as if the diver entering the water wasn't important. They were giving their attention to a flickering monitor.

Diamond gestured to Georgina and they both edged closer for a view.

For some seconds there was nothing on the screen you could call an image. Then the interference stopped and they could see things moving, definitely the contour of the seabed. A crop of the weed known as dead men's fingers sharpened into focus. Something like a sheet of newspaper rippled and rose from the mud.

'Skate,' Albison said.

The diver's movement disturbed more flat fish. This was all quite involving for those above, sharing in the search, in spite of their discomfort.

Diamond wasn't comfortable with the underwater images. They reminded him of a dream he'd been getting lately, of being trapped in deep water.

'For some reason, his intercom isn't functioning,' Albison said. 'I may have to bring him up to fix it.'

Georgina exchanged a glance with Diamond – and not with the diver's welfare in mind. This could be a long morning.

More swaying weed and no sign yet of anything you wouldn't expect to see down there. The quality of the picture was good. They had a glimpse of the line the diver was using and some bubbles from his regulator.

'Making a turn,' someone explained.

'Is he OK?'

'He appears to be.'

'Has he spotted something?'

'Don't get your hopes up,' Albison said to Diamond. 'Horizontal visibility isn't great today. He's surveying the area. Doesn't look like there's much of interest to you, but he'll be thorough.'

'The GPS marked the place where the suspect surfaced, not necessarily where he was below water,' Diamond said.

'We're aware of that, sir,' was spoken in a tone that might as well have said the team weren't total novices.

'Perhaps this man you're calling the suspect was innocently filming the life below, just as our diver is,' Georgina said.

This wasn't what anyone wanted to hear.

Doubts had been introduced and Georgina started to act and look like the player with the winning hand as the methodical process continued. Weed, mud and the occasional fish. The first thrill of seeing submarine life on the screen was wearing off. There is only so much seaweed you can find interesting.

The diver glided to a new section and his left hand loomed large on the screen and then reduced in size as he stretched towards the seabed. He was agitating the mud, creating clouds that fogged everything for some seconds.

They waited for the cloudy mud to clear.

With agonising slowness, some of the silt dispersed and they saw the diver's hand again, this time with a raised thumb.

'He's found something,' Diamond said.

'You wish,' Georgina said.

More seconds passed before the image sharpened enough to be apparent. Where there had been mud there was now a cleared patch that was level, so level that it could only be man-made.

'Looks like a floor.'

'The surface of something or other.'

'A ship's deck – assuming the rest of it is buried?'

Diamond's stomach clenched. He wasn't down there with the diver, and he had to keep telling himself he wasn't.

The diver moved on a couple of yards and repeated the process, clouding the screen again. When it cleared, another level section was revealed.

'All right, I'm willing to believe there's a wreck down there,' Georgina said. 'I expect that's what the mysterious diver found and why he was annoyed at being seen. They like to keep these finds a secret in case there are valuables to be salvaged.'

If that was truly the case, Diamond thought, the man must have been disappointed. 'It looks metal rather than wood. It can't be all that old. A lot of shipping went down here or hereabouts in the war.'

'Quite a discovery, even so,' Georgina said. 'I believe divers are very competitive. Are you satisfied? Mystery over?'

While they were talking, the diver had progressed several more yards.

'He's found something else,' Albison said.

'Not another strip of deck?' Georgina said. 'He's made his point, hasn't he? Can't you call him up?'

But the 'something else' was being revealed, fast filling the screen: an area of blackness that was actually a void.

Diamond stared at the screen. This was so involving that he clasped his hand to his mouth.

They were looking at an opening in the deck, a square hatch.

Albison said, 'He'll get some light on it.'

A right angle defining one corner of the hatch entrance slid across the screen. This wasn't edited television, it was disconcerting and jerky, but compelling. The diver was preparing to go inside. His free hand grasped the crosspiece. He'd switched on a lamp attached to his helmet.

'A hold of some sort,' Albison said.

Diamond didn't need the commentary. Everyone could see what was being revealed.

The diver had dipped inside and now visibility was restricted to what appeared in the light-beam.

First there was more mud. The interior was silted to a level of several feet, but above that some large objects were coming into shot, stowed between the mud and the underside of the deck.

'What's he found?' one of the team said.

'Looks like a plastic sack with something inside,' Albison said.

The ray of light moved slowly along a row of such sacks, some partially immersed in mud, as if they had been in position longer than others.

Diamond said, 'If this is what I think it is, we've found what we came for.'

The diver reached towards one of the sacks and poked the thing several times. It remained securely tied. He worked at it without result. Every action underwater is subject to resistance. He pulled back briefly and his arms disappeared from the screen. When they came into view again, he was holding his knife.

No one spoke.

The knife was seen to penetrate the plastic. The diver made a slit and widened it with a sawing motion. Abruptly, he withdrew the knife. The opening in the sack gaped as if something was straining to get out. After a couple of seconds, it slipped out and hung below the bag.

'God help us,' Georgina whispered.

They were looking at a human hand.

# 29

Back on solid ground – the beach at Selsey – they dragged the inflatable clear of the water and removed their waterproofs, still barely exchanging a word. A staggering sense of shock gripped them all. These officers were used to dealing close-up with death, but none had experienced anything on this scale. The young diver had counted eleven body bags and thought more might be concealed in the mud that partially filled the hold. Little else was said after he surfaced. Everyone needed some silent reflection to come to terms with the gruesome discovery.

Diamond respected the dead as sincerely as anyone else, but things needed to be said, so he gave a briefing of sorts, there on the pebble bank. 'Listen up, all of you. This is going to be huge, obviously, but there's work to be done before the media get hold of it. For one thing, we need to nick the toerag who put them down there before he knows we're on to him. And as soon as the story breaks, the ordeal for the victims' families will be horrendous. They must told in advance. It's essential we leak nothing to anyone and that includes your wives, girlfriends, close mates, even other officers. Silence rules – is that understood?'

Dave Albison looked down and shifted some stones with his shoe. 'Two days' work, I reckon, recovering that lot. They'll fill the mortuary – and some.'

'So?'

The big team leader raised his eyes. 'We can keep it to ourselves, no problem, but that's no guarantee it won't go public. You can bet your life as soon as we start bringing them ashore, someone from round here is going to see us. There's sure to be some gawper. People get suspicious, take pictures, and then we'll have the TV, press and sightseers camped here watching every trip we make.'

The defeatist tone infuriated Diamond. 'For Christ's sake, you're the locals, not me. You don't have to bring them ashore here. You must know which beaches aren't much visited. If you can't stage a secure recovery operation you don't deserve to be called a specialist unit, or whatever is on the side of your van. When you get the go-ahead from Chichester CID – which I expect to be this afternoon – you need to have your plan in place.'

'This afternoon?'

'What are you about to tell me – that it's a day of rest?'

'It's a complicated operation, sir. We'll need a bigger boat and more divers.'

'So get them.'

'Ah, but you just said we don't want to alert the scumbag responsible for this.'

'Is that a threat? Are you saying you can't organise yourselves without leaking information?

'That's not what I meant. Isn't it a question of priorities? Nicking this guy comes first, right?'

'I'm confident of an arrest in the next two hours.'

After a stunned silence, Albison said, 'Christ. Do you know who he is?'

'We do.'

A stifled sound of surprise came from Georgina.

Diamond brought the briefing to a close. 'So call up your reinforcements, make your plan and stand by for further orders.'

As he and Georgina toiled up the shingle bank, he expected a blasting, but she surprised him. 'I endorse everything you said, Peter. It would be calamitous if this got out prematurely. You and I must decide who needs to know.'

'Montacute,' he said.

She rolled her eyes. Clearly she had someone more senior in mind. 'Can we trust him with it?'

'We have to. He's the senior investigating officer.'

'He'll hate being told, particularly by you and me. He was pretty dismissive about the missing persons, wasn't he?'

'He told me the inquiry was on the back burner now Hen is suspended. But this is Montacute's patch. He's running the CID, so he must deal with it.'

'I'm not impressed by the man.'

They had reached the narrow walkway above the beach. The car was a short walk away, in the parking area beside the fishermen's huts.

'I've had a few dealings with Montacute,' Diamond said. 'I wouldn't want him in my CID, but he's doing his best in a stressful situation. I sensed hostility when we first met him. I actually suspected him of sending the anonymous letter that got Hen into trouble at headquarters. I don't think so any more. He was resentful of us because his cushy existence had come to a sudden stop. He's a natural second-in-command. It suited him to have Hen as the boss. So I don't believe he undermined her.'

'But is he capable of dealing with this new emergency?'

'Not in the long term. If Hen was right, and it involves other police forces like Hampshire and Dorset, they'll need someone of higher rank.'

'Exactly. I'm thinking we should go straight to headquarters with this.'

Not if I have anything to do with it, Diamond thought. 'They'd just about shut down for the weekend when I tried

309

calling them. We need immediate action, a swift arrest. I'd sooner work with Montacute. I can pull his strings. Headquarters will get to hear soon enough.'

A small sigh escaped from Georgina's lips. 'I suppose you're right. The arrest is more of an operational matter than an executive one. I was thinking Commander Hahn ought to be informed.'

Give me strength, Georgina, he almost said aloud.

But she wasn't quite such a lost cause. A smile tiptoed over her lips. 'It will come as a massive shock to him. He wasn't at all keen on DI Mallin's inquiry.'

'You're right,' Diamond said, grinning back. 'He won't be pleased. So let's spare him today.'

He called Chichester CID and arranged to meet DI Montacute at the police station in twenty minutes.

Beside the car park was a children's playground. Children off school today were enjoying the slides and swings while their parents drank coffee at the tables in front of the refreshment stall, untouched by the horror out at sea.

As soon as they were back in the car, he could sense Georgina preparing to broach the question they had not touched on. 'Were you bluffing when you said you know who put the bodies down there?'

'No, ma'am.'

After a pause, she said, 'I thought we were a team.'

'We are. You said so.'

'You haven't shared your reasoning with me.'

'There isn't any reasoning. It was handed to me. Jim Bentley's friend Norman took a photo.' He dug into his jacket pocket and took out the print he'd been given.

She said, 'Him? Oh, my word.'

The man pictured in the diving suit was Davy the model.

# 30

'Do we know his surname?' Georgina asked.

'Clitheroe. I asked Tom Standforth.'

'How long have you had this photograph?'

'I met Jim Bentley late yesterday afternoon and he gave it to me along with the GPS reading.'

Her mouth tightened. 'You didn't show it to me.'

Tricky. The news would have gone straight to Archie Hahn.

'It could so easily have been a red herring,' he said.

'What on earth do you mean by that?'

'There was no certainty the police diver would find anything. Davy could have been diving for his own amusement. I made sure you came along this morning and I had my fingers crossed that it wasn't all for nothing.'

'You should have told me. We're in this together.' She wasn't exactly sulking, but she was making her annoyance clear.

Some guile was wanted here. This was mainly about massaging Georgina's ego. 'Knowing you as I do, ma'am, I strongly suspect you had more than an inkling of what was going on.'

A flush of comfort came to her cheeks, and she indulged in some guile of her own. 'I won't deny I had my private theory.'

'I wouldn't mind betting your thoughts were ahead of mine.'

'Not necessarily.'

'Along the lines of people disappearing all along the south coast and the common factor being the closeness of the sea?'

After a moment's consideration her lips curved a little. 'That did rather stand out.'

'There being so many wrecks in these coastal waters and if bodies were being buried at sea without any risk of coming to the surface, they'd have to be stowed away in a hold, or some such?'

'It takes a woman to think of practical things like that,' Georgina said.

'And I daresay the name of Davy didn't pass you by: Davy Jones's locker, eh? That's the name he goes by, but his real name is Stanley.'

'Deep inside, I knew something was wrong about the man.'

'Intuition – another feminine talent.'

She raised a warning finger. 'Peter, don't overstep the mark.'

'Far from it. You'll have asked yourself how an artists' model could possibly afford the Lamborghini.'

'Now that *is* the sort of thing a lady notices.' She let a few more bends in the road go by before saying, 'I'll be interested to see what kind of house he has. I expect he lives in style.'

'Very likely.'

'Do you think he's our murderer?'

'No. My assessment is that he disposes of bodies and that's all. He'll be known in the underworld as the man they go to. And he makes them pay – handsomely.'

'So – going back to the start of our investigation – was Joe Rigden's corpse intended to be buried at sea with the others?'

'Without a doubt. It was loaded into a stolen car and driven to an agreed spot in Littlehampton and left there beside the river for Davy to collect.'

'Elaborate.'

'Davy's cover arrangement. The driver, Joss, wasn't to see him. It's likely she didn't know what she was carrying either. She did her job. Then things went wrong. Danny Stapleton, the man we saw in prison, happened to steal the car before Davy made the pick-up.'

'Stapleton is innocent, then?'

'Guilty of car theft, that's all.'

'And he went down for life.'

'He'll get the sentence quashed, but he'll sue, no doubt. Right now, let's focus on Davy. He has enough information to put several murderers behind bars.'

'He'll want to do a deal.'

'I don't think so.'

'A safe house, a new identity. Of course he will.'

'Davy won't risk it. Our best hope is that there are names on his computer, or his phone, or his bank statements.'

'He's smart,' Georgina said. 'I doubt if it's so simple.'

Diamond couldn't disagree with that.

At the police station, DI Montacute was grudging in his admiration. 'I don't know how you fingered Davy. He wasn't on our radar at all.'

'But you found his address, I hope?'

'He doesn't have one.'

'No fixed abode?' Diamond said in disbelief.

Georgina chimed in with, 'This man owns a Lamborghini. He must have an address.'

'He lives on his yacht in the marina.'

'"On his yacht"?' Georgina's rising voice suggested she was ready to revise her opinion of Davy.

'On his ill-gotten gains,' Diamond said. 'The marina – where's that?'

'South of the city. Want to come? We're about to pick him up.'

It sounded so straightforward that Diamond found himself wondering what could go wrong. Had Davy and his yacht already left the marina? Could he have escaped in his inflatable? Or his Lamborghini? Was he sipping champagne on the French Riviera?

Two patrol cars and a minibus full of uniformed officers sped out of the police station and across the A27 bypass. In the holiday season it's a crawl to the coast along the A286, but today the road was almost clear. The leading driver still used his siren and flashing light when necessary.

Diamond, squeezed into the back seat of the second car between Georgina and Montacute, said, 'Is it far?'

'A mile or so.'

'Tell them to cut the blues and twos. It's supposed to be an ambush. He doesn't know we're on to him – or shouldn't.'

The order was given over the radio.

'Will he be armed?' Montacute asked.

'No idea. Have you issued weapons?'

'You bet I have.'

'We want him alive. He's no good to us dead.'

'Relax. We're professionals here in Sussex.'

They swung right on to the narrow road to the marina running alongside the canal. Montacute told the driver to pull over and stop.

'It's still half a mile off,' he explained, 'but we don't want to be obvious so we'll let the leading car go ahead and find where the yacht is berthed.'

'Do we know the name?'

'The *Michelangelo David*.'

314

'That's a work of art, isn't it?'

'Just about the most famous statue in the world,' Georgina said. 'A perfectly proportioned nude male figure. Davy the model must have delusions of grandeur.'

'Or a sense of humour.'

'Men don't joke about their own bodies,' she said. 'I've never met one who did.'

No one argued with her.

Parked at the roadside, they were close enough to see some masts rising weirdly above the hedge in the flat landscape.

Static was heard from the intercom, followed by: 'We've located the yacht, sir. It's at pontoon H, on the right as you drive in. Over.'

'Can you see the suspect?'

'Not at present. It's a big ship, about the biggest here. Over.'

'We'll join you.'

'A ship?' Diamond said. 'Do they mean that?'

Georgina treated them to more of her worldly wisdom. 'A ship can carry a boat, but a boat can't carry a ship.'

They covered the short distance to the marina entrance. The facility was on a scale Diamond had not anticipated, at least the size of the lake at Fortiman House, with berths for several hundred craft of all sizes. Support buildings, restaurants, boatsheds and a chandlery were ahead.

'We may have got lucky,' Diamond said and pointed to the Lamborghini, parked opposite one of the berths for the largest vessels.

All attention switched to the *Michelangelo David,* moored at the end of pontoon H, a tri-deck monster that dwarfed all the others. No one was visible on deck or in the wheelhouse.

'I thought only Russian oligarchs owned things like that,' Diamond said.

Georgina nodded. 'He didn't buy it from his modelling fees.'

Montacute was with a uniformed sergeant deciding on a strategy. The problem was that the boarding ramp midway along seemed to be the only means of access. The gleaming white hull rose at least fifteen feet above water level.

Georgina then surpassed herself by saying, 'You're looking at the wrong end. As I remarked, a ship can carry a boat. Any decent hundred and fifty footer has a tender garage. Go aft and you'll find it. That's your way in to all the decks.'

Where had that piece of expertise come from? Diamond had no idea how his boss had become familiar with the design of luxury yachts. There were areas of her life she'd never spoken about.

Deliberately, no doubt, the yacht was moored with its aft end overhanging the open water, but Georgina was right. A boarding party could reach it by using some kind of dinghy, and there is no shortage of them in a marina. It didn't take long to commandeer one from a neighbouring boat owner.

They sealed off pontoon H and the approaches to it.

Montacute took two officers up the boarding ramp while another half dozen approached by water. A short interval followed to allow them to get aboard and find positions. Diamond and Georgina remained in radio contact in the car. Waiting passively didn't come naturally to Diamond, but this was Montacute's operation. The locals had to be trusted to get on with it.

One of the three on the ramp yelled, 'Armed police. We're coming in.'

No reaction.

They stepped over the gunwale. It wasn't like battering a door down.

Watching from the patrol car, Georgina said, 'Let's hope he's home.'

'And hospitable,' Diamond added. 'Something's got to happen shortly.'

The heads and shoulders of armed men could be seen moving on the open areas of each of the decks.

Shouting carried to them from the ship, but it wasn't combative shouting, more like a repeat of the first announcement.

At least another minute went by – and felt like ten.

Then the radio crackled.

'Mr Diamond, you'd better come up.'

'Have you got him?'

'Yes and no.'

What sort of answer was that? He turned to Georgina, eyebrows raised. She spread her hands.

They left the car and ran along the pontoon and boarded the yacht. Officers with drawn guns waved them along a stretch of deck to the main salon, a carpeted space with a marble inlay bar, L-shaped leather sofa and chairs and a fold-down plasma TV. Forward was the dining area, with a walnut wood table capable of seating twelve. Another police officer directed them down the steps of a companionway and into a spacious cabin where Montacute and two others were standing beside a king-size bed with a black duvet.

Georgina said, 'Tarnation.'

Face down and naked on the duvet was a male body all too familiar to the two novice artists. Davy would not be posing for them again. Nor would he be answering questions.

Diamond said, 'This wasn't in the script.'

# 31

The cause of death appeared obvious. A cocktail of drugs and champagne had killed him. Two empty Bollinger bottles and some used blister packs that must have contained sleeping tablets stood on the bedside shelf.

Self-inflicted? Almost certainly. If you had resolved to take your own life, this method beat most others.

Georgina said, 'Damn you, Davy!'

Diamond's anger was focused elsewhere. 'Some idiot tipped him off. I thought I could trust that dive team.' He snatched up one of the blister packs and looked at the label. A sedative, one of the benzodiazepine group.

Montacute was shaking his head. 'I can't understand his thinking. If he'd cooperated, he'd have got a short stretch.'

How naïve was that? 'Cooperated by naming his clients, you mean?' Diamond said. 'A short stretch is right. He'd have been found dead in his cell in days. These are major criminals with as much clout inside jail as out.'

'Well, if he'd stayed silent and served a full term, he'd have survived.'

'He wouldn't. If he'd stayed silent as a bag of feathers the mob would still have killed him. He was too much of a risk. He knew if ever he was caught, his number was up. When his business was thriving, the killers came to him and paid him well. One failure and he was dead meat.'

All the talk was negative. Montacute tried to be upbeat. 'We'll check everything he used, phone, iPad, computer.'

'Don't build up your hopes. In a high-risk job like his, you don't leave a trail. It's all too easy to drop things overboard.'

The optimism was all used up. 'I thought this was the breakthrough.'

'You're not the only one. We're stuffed.'

But Diamond knew better than to dwell on it. Out at Selsey, the dive team were standing by to begin recovering bodies. He called Albison. Any recriminations about leaked information would have to wait. He told him tersely to launch the boat.

The man couldn't resist saying, 'About bloody time.'

'Where are you starting from?'

'Selsey beach – where we were before.'

'I thought you decided Selsey was too public.'

'Doesn't matter where we start from, does it?' Albison said. 'Like you said, it's where we land them that counts.'

Fair comment. 'So have you chosen somewhere else?'

'Pagham Harbour. It's quiet and should be getting dark by the time we return.'

'Call me the minute you bring the first one up.'


'One good thing about being from another force,' he remarked to Georgina when they were being driven back to their hotel. 'The crime scene is someone else's problem.'

'I'm not sure about that, Peter.'

'Why?'

'We can't cut ourselves off from it. As you said on the beach this morning, the press will have a field day when those bodies are brought to the surface. I keep wondering how Commander Hahn will react. It won't play well in terms of public confidence. Rightly or wrongly he's going to suspect we exceeded our brief. I entered on this mission from the best of motives, willing to help another force.'

No you didn't, he thought. You wanted to cosy up to your old flame and get out on the golf course.

She went on: 'He's going to wish Davy's grisly trade had never been exposed.'

She was right about that.

And then a smile flashed across her features like a flick knife and Diamond realised that his boss had seen the light at last.

In the hotel entrance, Georgina said, 'After the morning we've had, we deserve a late lunch.'

'No offence,' Diamond said, 'but I need to make a personal call.'

'How long will that take?'

'Depends. Don't wait for me if you're hungry.'

'I'll find a table for one, then.'

This time, he felt a twinge of guilt. After that smile at Archie Hahn's expense, she didn't deserve to eat alone.

The call he made wasn't on the phone as he'd implied. He left the hotel and walked round to Hen's flat. The morning's discoveries would affect her profoundly and he wanted to break the news to her in person.

In a tracksuit and flip-flops, she appeared smaller and more vulnerable than he'd seen her before. 'Come in, love of my life,' she said. Whatever you thought of Hen, you couldn't call her standoffish.

He'd been trying to think of a way of telling her about the bodies under the sea. She was certain to fear Joss was down there with the others. Family ties overrode everything. The fact that she had been proved right to agitate about missing persons would not be high in her thoughts.

He set out the facts as calmly as he could, explaining

how Jim Bentley's information had led him to the discovery of the wreck containing the bodies and to Davy's suicide, but he could see the increasing alarm in Hen's eyes.

'They're starting to bring them up,' he said. 'It's not a job they can hurry. It may be days before the identification can start.'

'So I should prepare for the worst. I can't go on denying it,' she said. 'The truth has been staring at me for days. Joss knew too much. She may not have known at the time it was a murdered corpse she was delivering to Littlehampton, but she found out later when the plan went to buggery and started a murder hunt. Poor kid must have been bricking it – and with her own daffy aunt heading the inquiry.'

'Don't knock yourself, Hen.'

'Thanks to my incompetence no arrest was made at the time. The whole thing went on hold. After years went by, she must have hoped she was in the clear. She didn't know about the DNA match. Finally it all got out because of that whistle-blower I prefer to call a rat fink. I was suspended and Joss – now known to the police – put in danger of her life.'

'You think she knew Rigden's killer?'

'Must have got her orders from someone, mustn't she?'

'How would she have got into this in the first place?'

'With her history as a druggie? Obvious, isn't it? When you're in deep, you meet bad people and get asked to do bad things. They don't make life easy for you. I must face it. She's going to be one of those bodies.'

'She could have gone into hiding.'

'Pete, I know you mean well, but this won't have a happy ending.'

He tried stressing the positive result of the morning's discoveries. 'You've been proved right about the people who went missing. That's something Georgina and I can tell headquarters when we make our report.'

'Do they really want to know? I'm a thorn in their flesh.'

'With your job on the line, as it is, I'm going to make damned sure they know what a good cop you are.'

'You're pissing in the wind, Pete. They want me out.'

'We'll see about that.'

She insisted on making coffee and sharing a pork pie she'd been saving for lunch. He realised that, like Georgina, he'd got hungry. While watching those images from the ocean floor, he'd thought he wouldn't be able to face food for the rest of the day.

With Hen busy in the kitchen, he stepped into the living room and tried calling Dave Albison for the latest news of the recovery operation. Without success. He left a message and used the word urgent twice over. As a non-diver he had no way of estimating how long it would take to retrieve the first body.

Facing Hen across her small kitchen table, he said, 'I still haven't worked out a motive for Rigden's murder. Everything stems from that. Find the motive, find his killer and we'd be motoring.'

'And the best of British luck,' she said.

'Did he have any connections to the underworld?'

'Joe Rigden? You're joking. The angels formed a guard of honour when he went through the pearly gates.'

'Was mistaken identity a possibility?'

'Crossed my mind, but I never got anywhere with it.'

'You see what I'm driving at? The planning that went into his disposal suggests it was organised crime, same as the others you were on about, but he wasn't a known criminal.'

'Did you say organised? A large part of his head was blown away with a shotgun. Downright messy for professionals.'

He nodded. He, too, believed the killing had been clumsy.

Hen's thoughts had moved on. 'I don't like to think what they did to Joss.'

'Don't go there, Hen.' He changed tack. 'Yesterday, in Mrs Shah's garden, after Georgina and I found you sitting in the shed, I caught your eye at one point and you seemed to be on the point of saying something important.'

'Was I?' Her thoughts were still elsewhere.

'Shortly before you left,' he said. 'Georgina was ranting about you wasting police time. Fair enough. She *had* got herself in a mess pursuing you around the lake next door.'

She managed a slight smile. 'She wasn't dressed for a hike.'

'She was in a strop and she ordered you to leave. That was when I thought you were ready to share something with us.'

'Got you.' Attention was fully restored. 'But I don't know if it's still worth sharing. When I first parked my car and looked inside Holly Blue Cottage, I thought I saw someone.'

'In the cottage?'

'Yes.'

'It looked derelict to me,' Diamond said. 'We knocked and got no answer and when I looked through the letterbox there was a heap of mail on the floor.'

'I saw that, too. Like you, I took it that no one was at home, but when I went round the side I saw a large black cat creeping through the long grass for all the world as if it thought it was a panther in the jungle. I must have startled it, because it turned into a moggy and dashed to the back door and straight through a cat-flap. Made me think twice because it was obviously used to going in. I went right up to the kitchen window and looked in and I'm sure there was a movement inside.'

'The cat?'

'No. This was a figure framed in the doorway.'

'Male?'

'Couldn't tell you. They darted out of sight immediately. I tapped on the window. After all, I was on someone else's property and you don't march through without so much as a good-day, do you? Whoever they were, they had no wish to meet me.'

'A squatter?'

'That was my thought. Empty place. It's a temptation.'

'You've got me interested, Hen. On Saturday, when the artists were doing their stuff at Fortiman House, I took a walk down to the lake and I definitely saw someone on the far side walking the bank. Beanie hat, long, brown coat and boots. They were in front of the wall, which we now know is shared with Holly Blue Cottage.'

'Are you sure it wasn't one of the artists?'

'They were all in the studio. I thought I was alone out there until this person appeared. Could be your squatter.'

'Don't blame them on me, squire. I'm in trouble enough.'

'Whoever it was could have come through the door in the wall, thinking they wouldn't be seen. I'm going to take another look.'

'Good call.' Her eyes glinted. 'There's something else you ought to know. I thought a lot about Holly Blue Cottage and its situation.'

'So close to Fortiman House, you mean?'

'And so neglected. I decided to make some enquiries about the owner. Got on the internet and accessed the Land Registry. It took persistence and a couple of phone calls as well, but finally I got some information. After Miss Shah died it was bought by a company known as Mombasa Holdings Limited.'

'I know. I did a check myself. Makes sense – the Indian connection.'

'So you would assume. So anybody would assume. But did you check the directors' names?'

'No.'

'I did. I got on to Companies House and got the names. There are two directors: Ferdinand and Thomas Standforth.'

'Ferdie and Tom? How odd.'

'That's what I thought at first. I don't know how these deals are done, but it looks as if they took over an existing company that owned the place while Mrs Shah was alive. Buying the property next door makes sense if they plan to expand.'

'But they've done nothing to it.'

'And now they seem to have a squatter. You want a lift to the cottage? I'm up for it.'

# 32

Georgina wasn't on the trip. If Diamond had learned anything in recent days, it was the wisdom of keeping two strong women apart. Almost certainly she would have vetoed more trespassing at Holly Blue Cottage.

Hen drove while Diamond talked, making sure he kept off the topic of the bodies under the sea. Small talk didn't come naturally to him. He treated her to his opinions on films of the nineteen-forties, notably *Odd Man Out* and *The Wicked Lady*, and for some reason she was amused. She was still chuckling when she stopped the car in front of the cottage.

He got out beside the nameboard. 'Daft name – Holly Blue. The only holly I've ever seen is green, with red berries.'

'Shows your ignorance, city slicker,' Hen said. 'It's a butterfly. Look at the picture underneath.'

'But why give a butterfly a name that makes no sense?'

'It's blue – a gorgeous silver blue, much more delicate than the picture.'

'I get that part.'

'And it feeds on holly leaves. Satisfied?'

'How the heck do you know about the holly leaves?'

'Are you questioning my countryside cred? I'm a Sussex woman. I get about, go for walks, notice things and look them up when I get home. Townies like you spend all your time indoors watching old films. You wouldn't know a holly blue from a silver-spotted skipper.'

'The clouded yellow,' he said, 'I know that.'

'Cripes! There's hope yet.'

'Jean Simmons and Trevor Howard, 1951.'

'God help us, not another old film.'

The cottage looked every bit as derelict as when they'd seen it last. They decided to try the back door. Hen stepped out confidently without any pretence of subterfuge. Diamond, a couple of paces behind, could only admire this forthright little woman, the set of her shoulders and the head held high. This was the DCI Mallin he knew, on the case and primed for action.

She stopped. 'Did you hear something?'

'My phone?' His hand went to his pocket. It was high time Dave Albison called. But nothing had come through.

'Voices,' Hen said.

He shook his head.

'I'm not making this up.'

'Inside the cottage?'

'No, in the open. From next door, I expect.'

They waited a few seconds. Whatever Hen had heard wasn't repeated, so they pressed on, tangling with spiders' webs, brambles and overgrown shrubs to get to the back door.

'This was the window I looked through,' she said.

He put his face close to the dusty glass. 'I don't know how you saw anything.'

'Outlined in the doorway.'

'The door's closed.'

'Get away. It wasn't when I was last here.' She peered in, shading her eyes with her hand. 'Well, there's a thing. Someone *was* inside, or I've gone squiffy.'

He approached the back door. 'Let's see if we can get in.'

'Notice the catflap,' Hen said. 'I didn't imagine that.'

327

'I can't squeeze through there. You might manage.' He tried the handle, but the door was locked. It was a simple, old-fashioned mortise lock set into the wood. He bent to look through the keyhole.

'Wouldn't you know it?' He stepped back and felt in his pocket. 'There's a way of picking a lock like this.'

'Tell me about it, Houdini. I don't think the credit card trick is going to work. All you'll do is damage your card.'

'Do you have a nail file?'

'Do I look like a woman who carries a nail file?'

'I may have to use brute force.'

'Before you do,' she said, 'look under the doormat.'

After giving her the look that said even in rural Sussex keys under doormats were a thing of the past, he stooped to lift a corner of the filthy old coconut mat. Underneath were a few dead earthworms and a large family of woodlice. He lifted the whole mat. More wildlife. No key. He dropped the mat, making his feelings clear.

'Try the ledge above the door.'

Swearing under his breath, he felt with his fingertips and touched something that moved, fell and hit the mat.

A rusty key.

'How did you know?'

'Old cottage, old custom.'

He used the key and it worked. 'Hen, I owe you a beer.'

'Make that Sussex Pride.'

They stepped inside the kitchen and saw at once that it had been in use not long ago. A bowl of fresh cat food was on the floor to the right. The sink was damp and there was a mug with the dregs of some coffee. Diamond found the fridge and opened it. The interior light came on.

'They have a power supply.'

They also had eggs, butter, milk, yoghurt, an opened tin of apricots and some grapefruit.

He said, 'I'm starting to feel like Goldilocks.'

She eyed his scant hair and said, 'No comment.'

He crossed the room and stepped through a door.

It's strange how violence announces itself. For a split second he sensed imminent danger. He ducked, but couldn't stop something heavy and hard impacting with his head. A starburst was followed by oblivion.

Somebody was speaking his name. He tried to respond and couldn't. His voice wasn't working.

He felt the chill of water splash his face. He shook his head and opened his eyes. Focusing was difficult. A shape materialised and sharpened. A face close to his.

'Get a grip for God's sake, Goldilocks.'

Only one person ever spoke to him like that.

He managed to whisper to Hen, 'What happened?'

'You got taken out with a frying pan.'

It took an effort to work out that he was lying on the floor. A cushion had been placed under his head. It felt like a cement block. He tried to move.

'Keep still,' Hen said. 'Don't force it.'

'Who . . .?'

'Can't tell you. They're not here any longer. Belted out through the front. I didn't get much of a look. He must have been poised right here with the frying pan. Can't really blame him. We're intruders.'

'You didn't give chase?'

'Seeing to you was more urgent.'

'Am I bleeding?'

'You'll have a bump the size of a plum.'

'How long was I out?'

'More than the official count. It was one hell of a crack. Do you want a drink now? I can prop you up a bit.'

'I'd rather get after him.'

'You're in no shape.'

'Never was.' He propped himself up on one elbow. The head was sore, but clearing. 'I'll be all right. I took harder knocks in my rugby-playing days.'

'Not with a three-pound frying pan you didn't. Feel the weight of that.' She held out the offensive weapon, black and solid-looking.

'I'll take your word for it.' He sat up fully. 'Let's at least take a look outside. He can't be far off.' He braced his legs, grabbed the doorpost and hauled himself up. Briefly he thought his balance was going, and then he stood firm.

'Crazy guy,' Hen said. 'You're not ready.'

The fresh air helped his head. In the hayfield that had once been a garden, they looked for signs of disturbance. The beaten paths to the front gate, the garden hut and the door in the wall were the obvious routes his attacker might have taken.

'Stay here while I check the back. Give a yell if you see him,' Hen said. She was in charge and he was in no shape to argue.

The front gate wasn't far off, and he didn't feel quite so bad, so he stepped out on those shaky legs to get a better view. Hen's car stood in the lane. No other vehicle had been in sight when they arrived, making it unlikely anyone had escaped on wheels. He managed a few more steps, looking to both sides. There weren't many places for his attacker to hide.

As he was turning to go back he thought he heard a sound like someone clearing their throat.

He stopped to listen. It may have come from the woods fringing the road. Possibly a deer or a fox. Hen, the countrywoman, would know one animal sound from another. She'd laugh if he'd been taken in.

He started to move on, then felt unsteady, so he stopped

by the car and leaned his back against it, thinking Hen had been right. He should have waited longer before trying to move.

He felt in his pocket for the phone. Albison still hadn't called. Had the thing been damaged when he fell? He checked and it seemed to be functioning normally. No calls had been received.

Then a disembodied voice said, 'Are you all right?'

He turned.

A woman stood up on the other side of the Fiat. She must have been crouching out of sight behind it. Middle-aged, with owlish round glasses and her dark hair in a coiled plait, she was in a jumper and skirt – unsuitable for outdoors on a cool autumn afternoon – so he had to assume she was the squatter.

'Was it you in there?' he asked.

She clutched both hands to her chest. 'I'm *so* sorry. You frightened me, coming into the cottage suddenly like that.'

He returned the phone to his pocket, trying to decide how he should deal with this.

'You're terribly pale,' she said. 'You ought to lie down.'

As if he wasn't confused enough, his attacker was troubled about the state of his health. 'What were you doing in there?'

'I'm living there. Who are you?'

The question he'd been on the point of asking her. Saying he was from the police would surely panic her. He didn't trust his legs to go in pursuit. 'You don't know me. My name's Peter.'

'Did Tom send you?'

So she knew young Standforth. And well enough to call him by his first name.

She expected an answer, so he gave one. 'Not exactly, but I know him. Shall we talk in the cottage?'

'I don't wish to talk.'

331

He took a small step to his left, meaning to move around the car, and she took a step of her own the other way. They were like a pair of kids playing chase – a game he certainly couldn't win.

Keep her talking, he told himself. Hen will be back shortly. 'You're living in a cottage that doesn't belong to you.'

'Is that any business of yours?'

She had to be told. 'It is – because I'm a police officer.' He turned his head and yelled, 'Hen, we're over here, by the car.'

Instead of running off, she put her hands to her face and sobbed, shaking convulsively.

When Hen appeared round the side of the cottage, he was already steering the distressed woman towards the open door.

'Christ, Peter, did you give her a clout?'

'I told her we're police, that's all.'

She took the woman's hand and helped her inside. 'It's all right, my love. He's not going to do you for cracking him over the head. He'd be a laughing stock. I've often felt like clonking him and you've beaten me to it. Let's all have a friendly chat in the front room.'

'Friendly' would have been overstating it and the chat had to wait some minutes, but Hen dusted off three chairs and brewed some tea and the woman dried her eyes.

The homely touch was working.

'He's Peter and I'm Hen and we're not here to evict you or anything. What shall we call you?'

She hesitated before saying, 'I'm Constance.'

'Then I know who you are,' Diamond told her. 'You're the missing schoolteacher – Miss Constance Gibbon.'

She blinked twice and said nothing.

'So do we call you Connie?' Hen asked as she filled the three mugs.

'No one calls me that,' Miss Gibbon said with disdain.

Connie or Constance, it didn't bother Diamond. He'd worked out her identity. And he felt more comfortable seated. 'So this is a sort of grace and favour home for you, is it?'

'I wouldn't call it that,' she said. 'It's more of a refuge. I'm not ungrateful, but that's what it is.'

'You didn't want anyone to know you're here?'

'That was the intention. I've been in a dreadful state of mind for weeks, close to a breakdown. I needed privacy, a place to shut everything out and Tom kindly suggested here.'

'So you leave the mail on the mat to make it look as if it's still empty?'

'Nobody except Tom knew until you came along.'

'Something must have gone badly wrong for you.'

'That's an understatement. I was lured into a situation that was dishonest and impossible to cope with. I was so cruelly treated that I almost lost my sanity.'

Almost lost it? Diamond was asking himself if she'd already gone beyond. 'What happened?'

She closed her eyes for some seconds as if the memory was too painful to recall. Finally, she spoke in an expressionless voice. 'It goes back three years, to a time when I was unemployed. I'm a trained teacher, but there weren't any jobs where I was, in Fulham. I lived alone in a bedsit. It was so depressing. I was in debt, but I just had to get out sometimes and go for a drink. When I say "a drink" I mean exactly that, a single glass of red wine. I'd visit a gay and lesbian bar in Soho – that's the way I am, in case you hadn't realised.'

Diamond wasn't in realising mode. He had given no more thought to Miss Gibbon's sexuality than to her size in shoes.

'One Saturday evening,' she went on, 'I met this woman called Olivia who unexpectedly took an interest in me. She was strong and attractive and I thought she was out of my league. She was dressed in the latest clothes and wearing jewellery that was clearly the real thing. She didn't seem to mind that I couldn't pay for drinks. She took me to a club I'd never heard of and we danced and had more drinks and spent the night together. She paid for everything. In the morning I thanked her, thinking that would be the end of it, but to my astonishment she said she'd like to do the same thing the following weekend. I told her I felt uncomfortable not paying my share, but she brushed that aside.'

'Had you told her your situation?' Hen asked.

'Oh, yes. But she didn't say much about her own, simply that she had a well-paid job and money to burn. She charmed me. I had more compliments from Olivia the first two evenings we were together than I've had in the whole of my life. I was flattered. Who wouldn't be? I'm not promiscuous. I've been with two other women – brief affairs – and I'm almost forty now.'

'How old was Olivia?'

'Forty-seven. She didn't say, but I found out later. To be fair, she looked marvellous. She went to beauticians and the best hairdressers and of course her clothes were superb. My worry was that I was so drab beside her. I had one black dress, basically, for nights out, and the only changes were scarves and shawls I bought from a trader in the North End Road market. Olivia didn't complain. That second weekend she gave me a present, beautifully wrapped in a giftbox, and it was . . . clothes.'

'Intimate clothes?' Hen said.

Miss Gibbon turned sunset red.

Diamond stared into his tea.

'They were exquisite. Our Saturday meetings in the West End went on through the spring. Blissful, but soon both of us were finding it a strain meeting only at weekends. We

334

wanted to be together all the time. Then Olivia asked me to move in with her. She said she had plans for me. I felt I knew her so well by then that whatever she was thinking of could only be something wonderful.'

'A civil partnership?'

'It crossed my mind, but I didn't like to ask. She made the decisions in our relationship and I wanted it to stay that way. It's my nature.'

'Did you take her up on the offer?' Diamond asked.

'I did. I moved in at the end of the week. She had a large house in Bosham overlooking the harbour.'

'Down here?'

'It's a lovely spot.'

'I know it well,' Hen said. 'Bit different from the gay scene in London.'

'Different from a Fulham bedsit, too,' Constance Gibbon said. 'I loved it as soon as I saw it. She made me very welcome. The house is palatial inside, Scandinavian in style and beautifully furnished.'

'Did you discover where her money came from?'

'She said it was from a legacy, but I found out later it wasn't. Anyway, I had no intention of being a kept woman, so I thought I'd look for a teaching position in a local school, in the hope that there were some openings here in Sussex. I went online and started actively searching, wanting to surprise Olivia by announcing that I'd joined the employed once again. It was midsummer and the schools were recruiting for the new session.'

'Were jobs more plentiful here than in Fulham?'

'Not really. The government is always saying there's a shortage of maths teachers, but when it comes to finding a school that wants one, it's a different story.'

'Maths?' Diamond said. 'But you teach art.'

She sighed and shook her head. 'That's where I went

wrong. I was persuaded to teach art, but no, all my experience is in maths. Where was I? I'm telling this in the wrong order. Olivia caught me leafing through the *Times Educational Supplement* one morning and asked what I was up to, so I had to tell her I'd put several applications in, but hadn't been shortlisted. She gave me a hug and said she had been secretive, too, but now she was compelled to tell me the plan she'd mentioned before I moved in. To my utter amazement she told me she was the head of a private school for girls in Chichester.'

Diamond jerked forward, almost spilling the tea. 'Which school?'

'Priory Park.'

'Miss Du Barry? You and Miss Du Barry are lovers?'

'Do you know her?'

'I've been to the school and met her. I didn't have an inkling of this. Didn't suspect it for a moment.'

'She's brilliant at keeping things to herself,' she said. 'In London when we talked about my difficulties finding a teaching post, she never once mentioned that she was a school head, so when she came out with this I was dumbfounded. Nothing I knew about her seemed to suggest she was in the same profession as me, but it was true. She kept her personal and professional lives completely apart. Her plan, she said, was to offer me a teaching position to start in September. There was a vacancy on the staff and how would I feel about teaching art?'

'What did you say?'

'I was speechless. I knew almost nothing about the subject, but Olivia seemed to believe it was not only possible, but a breeze, to use her word. She said when an opportunity came she would find me a post teaching maths. Art was the one subject any experienced teacher could cope with because it's so individual. Each student has to develop her own creativity. The teacher is there mainly to encourage and inspire, not to work through a curriculum as you do in most other subjects. I could take them round galleries or look at images on the internet and teach them about the theory of composition, which is closely related to maths.'

'The golden mean,' Diamond said with all the authority of a man who had lasted one hour in a life class.

'Exactly. She showed me a syllabus and persuaded me I could handle it. In short, I agreed to take it on – the worst professional decision I ever made. You can't bluff your way through, you really can't.'

'Did the other teachers know you were living with the head?' Hen asked.

'Absolutely not. Olivia didn't want anyone to find out, so we travelled to school separately. She drove in and I took the bus. It's only a short ride. I was introduced as a new member of staff from London and no one questioned me. I'm quite a private person anyway and others seem to respect that.'

'Facing a class must have been an ordeal.'

'Any teacher fills in for absent colleagues from time to time, so it wasn't terrifying. I tried my best. I believed, and still do, that one can analyse the structure of a picture in geometrical terms, but it failed to excite the students. The ones who choose art are more interested in flouting the rules rather than observing them. I was trying to constrain them while they wanted to take risks and break out.'

'Did you have trouble keeping discipline?' Hen asked.

She shook her head. 'It's not that sort of school. There were a few mischief-makers, but there always are. I can handle them. My difficulty was that I had no confidence in myself as a teacher of the subject. In desperation I decided to join a recreational art group to experience practical art.'

'Tom's group?'

'Yes, I made enquiries and heard that they were the best. The Saturday mornings fitted in nicely with my teaching. So I came to Fortiman House. The standard was depressingly high. They're professional artists, some of them, and I was just a beginner, but several gave me tips. Tom was particularly generous with his advice.'

'Did Miss Du Barry know what you were up to?'

'I had no reason to be secretive. She thought it sensible. I didn't have transport, so she gave me a lift in and left me at the gate. Later, one of the others who also lived in Bosham – a nice woman called Drusilla – took over the ferrying.'

'I've met Drusilla,' Diamond said. 'I did a session with the artists myself.'

Hen gave him a disbelieving frown and then turned back to Miss Gibbon. 'Did it help you at the school?'

'Helped my confidence, a bit. I was hanging on, hoping a position would arise in the maths department. Two whole years went by. I kept saying to Olivia that I felt a fraud, but she insisted I was a success and they'd get through their exams. Most of them did in the first year, but no thanks to me. It was down to their own talent.'

'What went wrong, then?'

She lowered her eyes. 'Our relationship. A silly, embarrassing thing was blown up out of all proportion. She asked me to get a tattoo. I'm not a tattoo person. I don't care for them.'

'What kind of tattoo?' Hen asked.

'Her name between a red rose and a heart.'

'Olivia?'

'All of it – Olivia Du Barry.'

'The full moniker. Where was it to go?'

Miss Gibbon blushed deeply again. 'My lower back. She said once it was done I would never see it unless I used a mirror. She made an issue of it. She told me if I was unwilling to have her name tattooed on my flesh it must be because I didn't intend to stay with her. It wasn't that. And it wasn't the pain of having it done. What upset me was that it was like being branded, being marked as her possession. She said if I couldn't do that simple thing to please her, I was selfish. She kept on about it.'

'Did she offer to have your name tattooed on her own butt?'

'It was never suggested.'

'Does she have tattoos?'

'No. And what's more, she won't allow any of the Priory Park students to have them. One girl came in with a tiny heart design on her face and was asked to leave.'

'Double standards.'

'That's what I thought, but I didn't say so.'

'You were right to stand firm,' Hen said. 'You *didn't* get the tattoo, I hope?'

'I almost did, just to end the friction between us. In fact, I got to the point of enquiring about tattooists in Chichester. Our relationship was under such a strain that I thought about getting the wretched thing done in secret and' – she gave an embarrassed cough – 'letting Olivia find it. The sense of relief would have been wonderful. One Saturday on the way home in the car I asked Drusilla – who seems to know everything – if there was a reliable tattoo artist she knew. For some reason this amused her and she asked what I was planning and it was a critical moment. I needed desperately to confide in someone other than Olivia, so I told Drusilla all about my relationship and my reluctance to get the tattooing done. To my surprise, she pulled the car over and stopped at the side of the road and said I'd be mad to go through with it. She'd known Olivia when she was at school and her name wasn't Du Barry. It was Dewberry. She was plain Olive Dewberry then.'

Diamond could scarcely hold back the laughter. Olive Dewberry – he loved it. But he couldn't risk upsetting this solemn woman at the climax of her story. Miss Gibbon hadn't paused. She was very wound up.

'She'd started calling herself Olivia Du Barry after she won the big prize on the national lottery. That was where her wealth came from. I'd been led to think it was inherited and the Du Barrys were an old Sussex family. I'd been completely taken in and she wanted me permanently labelled with this false name – as if it confirmed her status.'

'Did you take it up with her?' Hen said.

'Certainly I did. I was more angry than I can say. The hypocrisy didn't seem to register with her. She didn't deny any of it. She called me vile names I can't repeat and turned the whole thing round and accused me of latching on to her because she had money and position. It was deeply wounding. She told me to leave at once, and I said I had no intention of staying. I gathered my things, only the things I'd bought myself. I left behind all the clothes and presents she'd given me. I filled the one suitcase I'd arrived with and walked out without saying goodbye.'

'Where did you go?'

'I took the bus to Chichester. I thought of returning to London, but I had nowhere to stay. At times like this you need the help of friends. I thought about trying to contact Drusilla, but it was awkward. She'd been shocked to learn that I was lesbian. You don't need antennae to tell you when somebody disapproves. I'm not sure how she would have reacted if I'd asked her to let me stay with her. Instead I thought of the one person who had shown me kindness throughout – Tom Standforth. I got on the phone and blurted out to Tom that I was homeless and could he possibly put me up for the night at Fortiman House. He didn't hesitate. He came to collect me from the bus station. He

340

must have seen my pitiful state at once because he said I was to stay there as long as I wished. I spent the first night in a spare room in the main house and the next day he showed me this cottage and said his father owned it and asked if I'd like to live here while I got myself together again. It's ideal for me. I just wanted some time out from the world. He brought over fresh bedding and food and cleaned the main rooms and he's made sure I've lacked for nothing ever since. I can't speak of him too highly.'

'You wanted nobody else to know where you were?' Hen said.

'It was a breakdown, or whatever they call it these days – post-traumatic stress. My emotions had been shattered. Even speech was difficult for me. I needed time to shut out the world and rest up. I stayed indoors for weeks. Only in the past few days have I ventured outside for a walk around the lake.'

'In a beanie hat,' Diamond said.

'You saw me?'

'A long way off.'

'I'm much better than I was. If you thought I was living here illegally, I promise you I'm not. Tom will vouch for that. He's visited me every day and got shopping in for me.'

'Seen anyone else?' Diamond asked. He slipped the question in casually, as if it had just occurred to him, but the answer mattered hugely.

'How would I? It's private here.'

'I was thinking of one of the Priory Park students who may have come here looking for you on the night the artists had their party.'

'Looking for me?' Her face was a study in disbelief.

Diamond nodded, willing her, almost begging her, to break through the black cloud of uncertainty that hung over them.

'Who on earth are you talking about?'

'Mel.'

'Melanie Mason, the quiet one?' She widened her eyes. 'What would she want from me?'

'You may not know it, but Mel was troubled that you'd left the school so suddenly, and when she discovered you're officially a missing person she decided to try and find you. She learned that you'd been one of the Fortiman House art group and there's reason to believe she came here that evening in search of more information. She didn't return home and she hasn't been seen since.'

She clutched at her hair. 'That's dreadful. I can't believe what you're saying.'

'Believe me, it's true. She came to the police station to see what was being done to find you. I spoke to her myself. Are you certain she didn't come here?'

'How would she know I was staying in the cottage? I heard nothing. No, that isn't correct. The sounds from the party carried a long way. I could hear the beat of the music on this side of the wall. And some time after midnight they let off some fireworks. Several loud bangs woke me up. I hate sudden noise.'

'Fireworks?' Diamond exchanged a shocked glance with Hen. 'We weren't told they had fireworks. The party was over before midnight.'

Hen asked her, 'Could it have been shooting you heard? Did it go on for long?'

'No, it was soon over. Two or three loud bangs.'

'Gunfire must be a possibility.'

'Oh, don't say that. This is deeply disturbing – and so much more so if Melanie came here looking for me. Please God nothing dreadful has happened.'

# 33

Diamond tried phoning once more. And had to stop himself from flinging down the phone and kicking it.

Dave Albison was still not taking calls. The recovery operation at sea must have been under way for three hours or more. No sense in thinking these guys on a gruesome mission would be using phones.

The waiting was hell to endure.

The shadows of early evening were spreading across the neglected garden as he left Holly Blue Cottage with Hen. He'd counted on hearing something by now.

'Is it back to Chichester?' Hen asked.

It was not. 'I want to take a look next door. I'm curious about those voices you heard. Were they male or female?'

'Both, I thought. Whoever it was has gone by now. It's so quiet you can hear the snails saying their prayers.'

He gave her a look. 'Where did that come from?'

'My grandma. She had some quaint expressions. If you want to go trespassing I'll collect the torch from my car.' Which sounded like another of Grandma's sayings.

Left alone, he assessed his fitness for the task. If he was ever going to crack this case, it would be tonight. The back of his head felt sore, but he was steadier on his feet now. And his brain was sharper than it had been all day. He needed to steel himself for horrible discoveries. Things said and things noticed were coming together and making sense, and none of it was good.

His phone buzzed. He tugged it out.

'Yes?'

'It took longer than we thought.' Albison at last. 'The wind got up. A real blast. The seagulls were flying backwards.'

'Where are you now?'

'Pagham.'

'Well?'

'We managed to bring two up. They'd be the most recent.'

He took a sharp, short breath. 'And?'

'Female, both of them. And both with bullet wounds. One is almost certainly the missing schoolgirl. She's wearing the motorcycle jacket in the description, purple and black, with reflective panels.'

A stark, pitiless statement from a bearer of bad news who in fairness had no reason to feel pity.

Diamond had been hit by a wrecking ball. The last hope that Mel had somehow survived was dashed.

Cruel.

A huge lump came to his throat. He wanted to give vent to his sorrow, but this wasn't the moment and Albison's wouldn't be a sympathetic ear. 'And the other?'

'Older. In her twenties. A redhead. Slim build. Silver ring on her right hand. Black leather jacket and trousers. The killer must have been so confident they would never be found that he left them in the clothes they had when they were shot.'

The second body was almost certainly Joss. The silver ring had been mentioned by her mother. The age, build and hair colour were right. Devastating for those troubled parents. And for Hen.

'So the plan is to take them to the mortuary now and see how many more we can bring up tomorrow.' Albison made it sound like baggage-handling. But who could blame him? On a job as horrific as this you have to find some way of insulating yourself from personal reactions that would overwhelm anyone else. 'Do you want calls about all the others as we find them?'

The words hadn't penetrated Diamond's jangling brain.

'The others,' Albison repeated. 'The bodies.'

Mentally, he put himself on autopilot. 'DI Montacute will need to know. Best report to him as you go along. These are the two I wanted to know about.'

Mel and Joss. The two he *least* wanted to know about. The grieving, the long sleepless nights of self-doubt, lay ahead.

He pocketed the phone. Hen was already through the gate on her way back, jaunty and confident as she habitually was. In his present emotional state it wouldn't be right to blurt out the bad news. He would find a way of telling her before the day was out.

'How's your head now?' she asked him. 'Jesus Christ, you're looking groggy again. Don't you think we should call it a day and get you back to the hotel?'

'I'm better than I look.' He was lying, but so what?

'Men have been saying that to me all my adult life and it just ain't true. What is it you expect to find here?'

He ignored the question. 'Let's get to it, Hen.' Stepping out briskly to leave no doubt that he was fit again, he took the route around the cottage and along the well-trodden path towards the connecting door in the high brick wall. Tom must have come this way regularly to deliver supplies to Miss Gibbon. Where the grass grew sparsely in the shadow of the wall, it was wise to watch for the mushroom hazards. A repeat of yesterday's slip-up wouldn't be clever.

'Did you make a meal of those mushrooms you collected?' he asked.

'I did – and very tasty they were in a two-egg omelette.'

'You said you'd be checking them for safety.'

'Of course. Chucked out a couple of liberties. They're really abundant in this garden.'

'Liberties?'

'Liberty caps. In my state of stress I don't need that sort of trip, thank you.'

They'd reached the door. He turned to face her.

'When you say "trip" you don't mean slipping over like I did the other day.'

'Correct, my innocent. "Trip" as in psychedelic experience. The liberty cap is the good old magic shroom beloved of hippies.'

Diamond said a simple, 'Ha' – but he might as well have said 'Eureka!' The mystery he'd been wrestling with for days was solved. Surrounding them on the shadowy ground were clusters of the delicate helmet-shaped fungi on long stalks.

Within his recent memory freshly picked hallucinogenic mushrooms had been openly on sale, although their psychoactive constituents were deemed class A drugs under the Misuse of Drugs Act. The police had a thankless task deciding whether they had been 'dried or altered by the hand of man' and were therefore illegal. But in 2005 the act had been tightened to include fresh mushrooms of the liberty cap variety. In the eyes of the law they were as dangerous as heroin and cocaine.

Hen added, 'Cutesy critters, aren't they, with their pixie hats? Have you tried one? The trip is similar to LSD, but not so powerful.'

'I hope you're not serious. I've had enough head-blasting for one day,' he said. 'It's going to be dark soon. If we don't get a move on, we'll see nothing.'

'All right, all right. Only joking.'

They tore their thoughts away from dangerous drugs.

Diamond opened the door to the grounds of Fortiman House.

And what a change of scene. Not a mushroom in sight and not a blade of grass more than a centimetre high.

A faintly purple October mist was settling over the lower levels, but the main features of the garden could still be made out: the house and outbuildings to the left and the striped lawns down to the lake. Nobody was in sight.

'Something's different,' Hen said.

Diamond couldn't think what she meant.

'By the lake. What are they building down there?'

He looked where she was pointing and was able to make out a tall skeletal structure outlined against the silver water. Recognising it, he smiled. Good things happened, even on bad days. 'That will have been the noise you heard. They were rebuilding the House of Usher. It's not finished, but they've made a good start.'

'Looks more like the House of Lobster,' Hen said.

'Yes, it's basically lobster pots lashed together. Ella's A-level project. I suggested they moved it here from the school. The voices you heard must have been some of the girls with Tom.'

'Good man, giving up his Sunday afternoon.'

Diamond was silent.

'One mystery solved, then,' Hen said.

'Hm?'

She said in a tone that left no doubt he was acting in an absent-minded way, 'We've worked out who the voices belonged to.'

'I'm going down there.'

'To the lobster pots? What for?'

'Come with me and I'll tell you as we go.'

'They all say that, and I fall for it every time.'

They stepped out sharply towards the lake.

'You reminded me earlier that you're a countrywoman,'

Diamond told her. 'Answer me this if you can. How do mushrooms travel?'

'Is this a riddle? They go "Shroom, shroom" and cover the ground. Here's one for you. Why does the mushroom get invited to all the parties?'

'It was a serious question, Hen.'

'What do you mean – how do they travel?'

'Is it root systems spreading through the ground?'

'It's spores. Don't you know that, dumbo? The mature mushroom reaches a stage when it ejects these tiny cells of almost no weight at all that are carried by the wind and reproduce somewhere else.'

'Then they colonise a place?'

'Like Holly Blue Cottage. Some spores must have been blown there in the first place.'

'That's the reason I asked. And if you've spent years culti-vating a garden, you won't be over-pleased when mushrooms start popping up all over it. This must have happened back in September, 2007, to Joe Rigden's pride and joy. He wasn't a happy man.'

'They're a natural phenomenon, Pete. You can't control spores.'

'I'm not sure about that. Magic mushrooms aren't all that common, are they?'

'No, but they grow naturally in this country.'

'And they could be cultivated.'

'That would be illegal and very risky.'

'Rigden, as a horticulturist, would have known what these were,' Diamond said. 'He found some growing in Mrs Shah's garden. As a man of principle, clean-living and all the rest, he would have disapproved of them on moral grounds as well as finding them a bloody nuisance.'

Hen screwed up her nose in a way that said she wasn't fully persuaded.

Diamond saw it and said, 'Now think back to a man you and I both interviewed at different times – the Reverend Conybeare, not quite a buddy of Joe's, but the nearest thing he had to a buddy. Do you recall what he said about the word "magic" being like a red rag to a bull when Joe was around?'

'Go on,' she said. 'You're starting to interest me.'

'The vicar was an amateur magician, a member of the Magic Circle, but Joe insisted on calling him a conjurer because he had a thing about magic.'

'And you think there's a link with the magic mushrooms? Joe tasted them and got addicted?'

'No. He wasn't the sort. They were getting to him in a different way, making him mad because they were spreading over the garden. I found his old coat in the garden shed and in one of the pockets there were dried-up remains of some sort of fungus that I now believe to have been liberty caps.'

'Why would he put them in his pocket?'

'To keep them separate from other garden waste. He didn't want them spreading.'

'No offence, but this is all rather iffy, Pete. A few shrivelled bits from his pocket. You'd need to get them checked by a scientist.'

'That may not be necessary.'

They'd entered the copse beside the lake. Ahead, at the limit of the solid ground, two columns of the House of Usher were in place and a third had been partly constructed. A stack of loose pots nearby showed that the work was only half done, but it was already possible to see how spectacular the completed house would look in the new setting. In this fading light it had an eerie look. If Diamond had read the story – which he had not – he would surely have recognised that 'sense of insufferable gloom' Edgar Allan Poe had noted.

'Help me with this,' he told Hen as he grasped one end of the incomplete column, four large creels fastened end to end with stout fishing cord.

Between them they lifted the pots as one object about eight feet long. For two people it wasn't all that heavy, but it would be awkward to carry.

'I can't think what you have in mind, matey,' she said. 'It's a good thing I've got a modicum of trust that you're not completely barmy.'

With Diamond leading, they bore the thing back up the sloping lawn towards the dividing wall. There they stopped.

'My little legs are going to be black and blue,' Hen said.

'You'll survive.'

'Are we nicking it, or what?'

'That's not the plan. Are you game to go on?'

'How much further? Through the door in the wall?'

'Past that by fifty yards – as far as the walled garden.'

'The orchid collection? You're not aiming to take it in there? It's locked and alarmed. He doesn't want his precious orchids contaminated.'

'We're going to use this as a ladder.'

'To scale the wall?'

'If possible.'

'Better be, after all this effort.'

They hoisted the column and moved off again, staying close to the wall.

'So why *does* the mushroom get invited to all the parties?' Diamond asked, to keep her on side.

'Because he's a fun guy. Get it?'

'If I stop to laugh, I might drop it.'

They reached the outside of the walled garden and took another brief rest. The short transition from daylight through dusk to night was almost over. They couldn't see back as far as the lake.

'Mind if I smoke?' Hen said.

'Be my guest.'

Her lighter flared. 'What's phase two of this crazy adventure?'

'I'm going over the wall.'

'Leaving the little woman to mind the lobster pots? I guessed as much. The world has moved on, Pete. We gals want a slice of the action. I can get over this wall as well as you, probably better.'

'Oh, I don't—'

She interrupted. 'Yes, you do. In your state of health you need protecting more than the pots.' She produced the torch and switched it on. 'Let's see if this is doable.'

They propped the column of pots against the wall. It was some feet short of the top, but it made a serviceable ladder, using the trap-holes as steps.

'Me first,' Hen said. Before Diamond had a chance to argue, she handed over the torch and started climbing, still with the small cigar between her lips. Reminding him of a koala scrambling up a eucalyptus, she reached the top with ease. 'It's going to be OK,' she said. 'There's a shed this side and we can step on to the roof.'

He followed her up, but more ponderously. Supporting his less sure-footed ascent, the ramshackle structure rasped several times under his weight. He got one leg over the wall, hauled himself up and recovered his breath.

Hen was already standing on the felt-covered sloping roof she'd mentioned and she helped Diamond to join her. From its size, the building appeared to be some kind of office or packing shed. Three much larger long metal sheds without windows filled most of the space, running from end to end.

'What now, action man?'

'We come down to earth.'

'And not before time.'

A stack of filled compost sacks lined most of the wall Diamond and Hen had climbed over – which was helpful, providing a cushioned landing.

'Bigger than I expected,' Hen said, when they were standing on a wide concrete path that ran the length of the nearest shed. 'Looks like a business enterprise. I had the impression the orchids are just a hobby that pays well. If you can grow them successfully, that is. My efforts with the two or three I've been given over the years were disastrous. I kept them about two weeks before they gave up the ghost – and they were supposed to be hardy specimens anyone can grow.'

'Keep your voice down,' he said. 'We may not be alone.'

'It's after dark. Who's going to be here now?'

'Let's see if we can get inside.'

Using the torch-beam, they walked half the length of the shed before coming to a large sliding door. Something was written on it. 'That'll be about closing the door after you,' Hen said. 'They hate draughts. I do know that much.'

In fact when they shone the torch, the sign said: entry only by authorised persons. controlled humidity and temperature.

'Same thing really,' Hen said.

Without debate as to whether they were authorised persons, Diamond grasped the door handle and slid it open, triggering a rapid, high-pitched beeping.

'Jesus, what's that?'

'Step inside fast.' He pushed the door back and the sound stopped. 'Just a reminder . . . I hope.'

Hen wasn't listening. She stood in awe of what was revealed. For one thing, the interior was brilliantly lit, and for another there wasn't an orchid in sight. Ranged as far as they could see were trays containing slender cream-coloured mushrooms in their thousands. Above the trays were strip lights and a spray system. Compared with the cool of the evening outside, the warm, moist atmosphere felt tropical.

'Did you ever see anything like this, countrywoman?'

'Awesome. Enough to supply every ageing hippy in Europe.'

'With the two other sheds, they'll have the capacity to dry them or freeze them and I expect the one we climbed on to was the packing shed.'

'The scale of it. You can't call it a crime scene, Pete, it's a crime spectacular – and in my manor. I didn't dream such a place existed.'

'Just to be certain, they *are* liberty caps?'

'Every one a class A drug,' Hen said. 'Are you as drop-dead flabbergasted as I am? You don't look it.'

'I had my suspicions about the walled garden, but I wasn't thinking of magic mushrooms until you mentioned them.'

'I didn't think past orchids. They can be grown under glass, but growing rooms like this are often preferred because you have complete control of the lighting and humidity.'

Diamond walked up one of the three aisles between the tables of trays and examined the crop. The spindly mushrooms were being grown in phases. The youngest were pale and sticky-looking, while the taller they got, the browner they had turned. The most mature were four inches tall and chestnut brown. They were dryer, too. The spraying must have been phased as well.

'There's huge investment here.'

'And huge returns,' Hen said, from a different aisle where she was getting her own perspective on the crop. 'They'll have cornered the market in the south of England.'

Diamond couldn't disagree with that. 'Before the law was strengthened, there was a flourishing mail-order industry in fresh ones. You could buy them openly, even in my snobby city of Bath. All that stopped overnight.'

'But how did it lead to murder, Pete?'

'This is high risk.'

'Can't argue with that.'

'My reading of it is that some spores escaped. Next, Joe Rigden started noticing rogue mushrooms in Mrs Shah's garden and decided to take it up with the people next door. He wasn't the sort to turn a blind eye to law-breaking and he did some snooping. And when he learned the truth and took it up with his neighbours, he signed his own death warrant. I don't know if there was panic or if it was a cold-blooded shooting, but Joe got taken out.'

'And they arranged for Davy to dispose of the body?'

'That was the plan.'

'The plan that misfired. I can see how Davy came into the equation. He did his modelling here. Presumably his disposal business was known about. But how did Joss get involved?'

The subject of Joss's fate had been coming like a train down the line and Diamond knew he couldn't talk about her without breaking the dreadful news to Hen. 'Probably it was like this. She was into drugs herself, right?'

'At one stage, no question.'

'Magic mushrooms?'

'Among other substances, yes. She tried them all, my sister told me.'

'Then if she was a customer of Fortiman House, some kind of deal was struck, such as a supply of liberty caps in exchange for driving a stolen car to Littlehampton. I doubt whether she knew what was in the boot. And she didn't meet Davy, so his part in the operation was concealed.'

He was steeling himself to reveal that Joss was dead. But it wasn't to be. A heavy trundling sound interrupted him. He swung around and saw the sliding door moving.

Hen had seen what was happening and ducked. That piercing electronic beep was sounding. All too clearly it was linked to an alarm system.

In different aisles, Diamond and Hen had taken cover under the tables bearing the trays of mushrooms. Clearly they were in danger of their lives. Any doubt about that was removed a moment later.

'OK, I'm armed. I know you're here,' a male voice shouted, echoing through the long building. 'You have five seconds to show yourself, or you get it.'

Not much scope for negotiation there.

Heart thumping, Diamond stayed out of sight and silent under the table and Hen did the same. He had a view of her hunkered between the trestles two aisles to his left. If the gunman came along either aisle they'd be easy targets. Any fool would know they'd taken cover.

What now? Wait here passively or do something? Diamond wasn't the passive sort. The difference between survival and a bullet through the head was all in the timing. The obvious move was to create a distraction. But how, without getting shot?

The gunman had entered by the same door they had, so he wasn't all that far away. After the chilling first threat, he'd gone silent. His feet weren't making any sound, very likely because he was wearing trainers. Diamond held his breath and strained to listen for the softest footfall.

It came, a steady padding along the aisle he was in. He felt in his pocket for his mobile phone, the one solid object he had apart from his shoes. His heart thumped faster than the advancing footsteps. Get this right, Peter Diamond, or you're history, and so is Hen Mallin.

The gunman slowed, as if he sensed someone nearby.

Diamond waited.

Two short steps closer and already he could see the feet

and the faded blue jeans. They'd stopped again. The legs angled forward a little as if the gunman was stooping for a better look.

Diamond didn't move a muscle.

The front shoe lifted at the heel and advanced almost to within touching distance.

Now.

Diamond slung his phone as far and as fast to his right as he could, aiming below the tables. It didn't get far before it clattered against one of the metal trestles. It still should have been enough to create a diversion and draw fire.

But instead of loosing off a reaction shot, the gunman hesitated.

This wasn't supposed to happen.

After five agonising seconds came a blast of what sounded like rapid machine-gun fire.

*A machine gun?*

Diamond rolled into the aisle, grabbed the gunman's legs and brought him down. Surprise is a weapon in itself.

At the same time a heavy object clattered against the ground and slid under the table.

A brief bout of wrestling, and Diamond grasped an arm and yanked it upwards behind the man's back. He had him in an armlock.

He didn't need to shout to Hen. She was already on her feet, dashing between the tables to snatch up the weapon.

A chainsaw.

What Diamond had taken to be machine-gun fire had been the saw on full throttle.

With his weight bearing down, he hadn't much of a sense of who he'd captured, except that he was large and strong. There was something he hadn't expected. Instead of the solid feel of back and shoulders, his chin was up against a

356

padded surface that felt like wool. He pulled back for a better view.

A Rastafarian crocheted tam.

The chainsaw man was Manny, the cartoonist gardener.

# 34

The blast from the chainsaw had deafened Diamond temporarily.

He didn't relax his hold, even though Hen was standing over them, gripping the chainsaw as if she meant to use it. There was no struggling from Manny, just swift, shallow breathing. All resistance seemed to be over.

Hen said something inaudible, probably meant for Manny.

After almost a minute, Diamond decided it might be safe to move. His legs were shaking when he put weight on them, but he didn't want to show frailty, so he propped himself against the nearest table edge.

It took a while for his hearing to return. He caught the last part of something Hen was saying: '. . . to tie him up with.'

Good thinking. Manny was disarmed, but he also needed to be disabled.

In a horticultural building this size there should be some twine or wire lying about.

'Thank Christ for a man who dresses well,' Hen said – and he heard her clearly this time. 'Take off your tie, sunshine.'

Needs must. It was his Bath rugby club tie – but he could buy another. He secured Manny's wrists. Then he removed the laces from his trainers and bound the ankles together. Hen was still ready for action, gripping the chainsaw handle with her left hand and the pull-cord with her right.

Diamond told her it was OK now. 'He's not the main man. He's only the gardener.'

'I don't care who he is. He was dangerous. This thing can inflict horrific injuries.'

Manny said from the floor, 'No, lady. I mean to scare, that's all.'

'Shut up.' To Diamond she said, 'Is your phone broken, squire?'

'Who cares?' He was doing his best to appear cool.

'I do. Mine's in the car and we need armed back-up.'

His phone was in pieces in the next aisle. He shook his head.

'He'll have one in his pocket.' Hen was never short of a suggestion.

Diamond used Manny's phone to call Chichester police.

'What we do now is sit tight,' Hen said. 'We can't go looking for suspects with a chainsaw.'

She'd summed it up. This resourceful and quick-thinking officer would be a huge loss to the police if Archie Hahn had his way and her dismissal was confirmed.

Diamond was steeling himself to tell her about the recovery of Joss's body. No time would be right, but he had a duty to break the news. He chose to do so now, as sensitively as he was able. 'Let me tell you about—'

Her eyes had the sudden force of a blowtorch. She understood at once where he was going with it. 'They found her?'

'I'm afraid so.'

'Brought her ashore?'

'This afternoon.'

She turned as white as paper and the veins showed in her face and neck, but she didn't shed a tear as he went through it.

\*　\*　\*

Hen's private grief was allowed to last about three minutes before a noise outside galvanised them. The door started to slide open. Diamond snapped back into full alert. The police reinforcements couldn't have got here so soon.

This time, he and Hen didn't duck out of sight. Empowered by the chainsaw, they stood their ground and waited. Two men stepped through: Tom Standforth, followed by his father. Ferdie had a rifle under his arm. But it wasn't levelled and threatening.

'Let me deal with this,' Diamond muttered to Hen. He shouted across the shed, 'It's all over, isn't it? We've called the police. Drop the gun, Ferdie. Nobody wants to add to the bloodshed.'

Ferdie didn't take long to make up his mind. He did as he was told.

Tom spoke first. 'How did you—?'

'Over the wall.'

'No, I mean . . . find out about this?'

'The magic mushrooms? You've been next door, the same as we have. They're taking over.'

Ferdie said to his son, 'What does he mean?'

'You haven't been in there lately, Dad. There are more than there used to be.'

'Growing wild,' Diamond said, 'in the garden a certain Joe Rigden once had in his care.'

'Why do you say that?' Tom said.

'Because Rigden objected to them and was shot dead.'

Tom couldn't have looked more bemused if Diamond had spoken in Serbo-Croat.

Now Ferdie joined in, his voice more regretful than angry. 'If it hadn't been for the bloody man interfering, complaining, threatening to expose me to the drugs squad, he would be alive today and—'

'And so would your two other victims, Joss Green and Mel Mason.'

Stopped in full flow, Ferdie put his hand to his throat. 'That's an extraordinary claim.'

'Not really. Their bodies were recovered this afternoon.'

Tom switched his disbelieving stare from Diamond to Ferdie.

'He's bluffing,' Ferdie said. 'Ignore it, son.'

'I saw them today,' Diamond said, 'out at the wreck where Davy hid them.'

Tom swung round to face his father. 'Davy? Does he mean our Davy? The model?'

It was already obvious that Tom was only on the fringe of the major crimes committed here. He knew about the mushrooms, but little else. The main man was Ferdie – the ever-obliging, self-effacing Ferdie.

'I can't take this in,' Tom said. 'Davy hides bodies at sea?'

Diamond said, 'On an industrial scale. But he won't any longer. Davy is dead of an overdose. We found him on his yacht at the marina.'

Father and son were lost for words.

After the news had sunk in, Diamond said to Ferdie, 'Let's have the truth about Rigden in 2007. You eliminated him because he threatened to expose you.'

'I had a profitable business.'

'Still have, by the look of it. How did you get into it?'

Ferdie glanced at his confused and troubled son as if to check whether he objected to the story coming out. Tom was in no state to decide.

'I used to cultivate orchids here and did quite well, but I couldn't see the business expanding,' Ferdie said. 'Then as a sideline I experimented with a few of the so-called magic shrooms. This was before liberty caps were demonised by the Home Office. They're a challenge to grow, but I persevered and found a way to do it and made it profitable. By degrees, I phased out the orchids. The growing requirements are not all that different. I already had these growing rooms in a secure place behind high walls.'

'It took over completely?'

'I'm the main supplier in the south of England. No one else would take the risk after liberties were made class A drugs. When Rigden came calling one afternoon he told me straight that he was going to report me. He was one of those bloody-minded, holier-than-thou people you couldn't argue with. I would have been banged up for fourteen years, minimum. Maybe life. Really. They can give you life for doing this commercially.'

'You shot him.'

'You know I did.'

'And arranged to have his body disposed of.'

'Yes. By then I had contacts who knew about such things.'

Ferdie seemed resigned to the truth coming out, but Tom had put his hands to his face and covered his eyes.

'And the plan backfired,' Diamond said.

'Thanks to bloody Davy. His method was supposed to be foolproof. He wanted big money up front, but those in the know spoke well of him, so I approached him.'

'And you wish you never had.'

'His system was too elaborate. I had to provide a driver and a stolen car. The driver wasn't to know what she was transporting.'

'This was Joss?'

'Yes, she was only eighteen at the time, but bright and up for anything. I knew her through the dealing she did in shrooms. She did what I asked, stole the BMW and brought it here. I loaded the body into the boot, just as Davy had insisted, making sure Joss didn't know what she was carrying.

There was two grand in used notes to cover the disposal of the car. She drove to Littlehampton and parked exactly where Davy wanted it. Then the plan went belly up. Some idiot nicked the car before Davy got to it and was stopped and arrested and ended up doing time.'

'A life sentence.'

'His own stupid fault.'

'You were content to let him rot in jail.'

'Him or me, wasn't it?'

The callous comment ignored the horror Ferdie had expressed a minute before at the prospect of doing a life sentence himself. Empathy is a state of mind unknown to killers.

'And for a time,' Diamond said, 'your crisis blew over. You thought you'd got away with it. Seven years passed before you heard any more. Out of the blue came the news that a senior detective was suspended for failing to follow up a DNA match linking her niece to a car theft and murder in 2007. The niece was Joss, your driver. I don't know if she came to see you of her own volition or if you got in touch and asked her to come. Either way, she was now linked to a murder, and so were you. Joss was a threat to your freedom. She knew too much and had to be silenced.'

'She was unstable,' Ferdie said. 'All druggies are. Sooner or later she would have shopped me.'

Listening to this, Hen observed a brave silence. She must have been desperate to wade in on behalf of Joss, but she left Diamond to deal with Ferdie as he had asked.

'How did you do it?'

'She came here, as you said, and she was in a state, swinging from blame to panic. I could see there was only one way to deal with her. She and I were alone here at the time. Tom was teaching and Manny had the morning off. I shot her on the driveway after she left the house.'

A shudder ran through Hen and she shut her eyes, but managed to maintain her stoic silence.

'And you handed the body over to Davy.'

'Not directly. He always safeguarded himself by collecting them from a neutral vehicle. And this time the system worked – or seemed to.'

Diamond paused for a few seconds out of respect for Hen's feelings. Then he said, 'And now we need to know what could possibly have possessed you to shoot an innocent schoolgirl.'

Ferdie sighed and shook his head. 'That was deeply unfortunate. There was a party here. Tom holds them regularly for his artist friends. It's been going on for years. I help with the drinks. But something went terribly wrong.'

Tom looked up and said, 'Ella gatecrashed.'

'One of his students,' Ferdie said. 'She was texting her friends, showing off, I suppose. Only later did I realise the havoc she caused. She was soon spaced out on Ecstasy. She'd brought some with her. Full credit to Tom, he hooked her out of the studio fast and settled her in the house.'

'By then she was too far gone to take home,' Tom said. From his stunned appearance he might have been on a drug trip himself while listening his father's revelations.

'The party didn't go on all that late,' Ferdie said. 'I always clear the drinks after, so I stayed on in the studio for a bit, then turned out the lights and was making my way back to the house when I spotted someone riding a motor scooter across the lawn straight towards the walled garden and my growing rooms. My immediate concern was that one of the party guests meant to break in and see what was there and maybe help themselves. I was angry. It was abuse of hospitality. More alarming than that, it was a breach of security. I'd killed two people to keep my business a secret. It could all unravel if they managed to get in there and saw my crop.

I fetched my gun from the cabinet where I keep it. All these thoughts were rushing through my head as I went in pursuit.'

'It didn't cross your mind that there might be another explanation?'

'What else could there be? It was obvious it was an attempted break-in. As I got nearer I saw that the rider was off the scooter and at the door of the walled garden. It has a combination lock and they seemed to be trying the numbers.'

'Couldn't you tell it was one of the schoolgirls?'

'I wasn't close enough. There was a full moon, but she was in the shadow of the wall. I couldn't even tell if the figure was male or female. At that stage she still had the crash helmet on. I fired a warning shot into the air and that created panic. Instead of getting back on the scooter, she made a run for it, trying to stay in the shadow of the wall. She took off the helmet, for ease of movement, I suppose, and sprinted away at a rate I knew I'd never match. You may not have noticed, but along that wall there's a door that connects to the next garden.'

'We used it today,' Diamond said.

'You know what I was thinking, then. I could see she would escape, and I was alarmed, telling myself I shouldn't have fired the shot because it showed I had something of value to protect. But as I'd pulled the trigger once, it wouldn't hurt if I fired another.' He stopped and dragged a hand through his silver hair. 'It's hard to explain why I did what I did next. You have to be in charge of a gun to know the strength of the impulse. A moving target is compelling, asking to be hit. I took aim and fired. She went down straight away. I think I hit her in the back. When I caught up, she was lying still, making no sound. I didn't know if she was alive or dead. To me, in that situation, she would be better off dead, so I put another one through her head.'

In the stunned silence, they could all picture the scene, Ferdie like a huntsman despatching his quarry.

'Didn't you recognise her as Mel?' Diamond asked. 'You must have met her.'

'After she was dead I did.'

Tom's eyes were like searchlights. He'd listened in mounting horror. Now he faced his father. 'How could you be so callous? She was just a kid, one of the sweetest I ever taught. I'm revolted, sick to the stomach. My own father. I trusted you. I thought the worst you were doing was growing illegal shrooms and I was willing to turn a blind eye. I brought my students here in the belief they would benefit. They should have been safe. But you shot Mel, little more than a child. She died because of my pathetic loyalty to you. You and your disgusting greed, preserving your dirty profits at all costs. Three killings – it's obscene. You deserve all that's coming to you.'

Ferdie gave a nod and looked away. In the distance, a police siren was wailing. It sounded like a lament.

# 35

On the short drive back to Chichester, nothing was said for some time. Both detectives needed to reflect on all they had learned. As the glow from a streetlamp passed across Hen's face, the tears were trailing down her cheek. She reached for a tissue, and Diamond had the sense not to comment. His gritty companion would have hated that.

He left a reasonable gap before saying, 'That was a day and a half.'

'I'll go for that.'

'But you got through.'

'With difficulty.'

'I can understand.'

'I'm not new to murder, as you know,' Hen said. 'I've been a copper long enough to know there are no happy endings in our line of work. There's always a loser. But this was family. Poor kid, she had a wretched life. I'll visit my brother and Cherry in the morning.'

'They'll have been informed.'

'Yes, but . . .' Unable to go on, she swallowed before starting up again. 'Sad, isn't it, that it takes a tragedy like this for us to come together and forget old feuds?'

'If something positive comes out of it . . .'

She hadn't taken that in. 'I can't begin to imagine their feelings. And as for Mel's parents . . . Little more than a child.'

He murmured his assent. He, too, was feeling a profound sense of loss. He grieved for Hen and her family and he also grieved for Mel. Meeting her that afternoon at the police station had made it harder. He would forever ask himself whether Mel would have survived if he'd handled the meeting differently. She'd been sent away without much reassurance that the police really cared about Miss Gibbon's disappearance. At the time, a missing teacher mattered less than a valued colleague in danger of losing her job. An unsolved murder, corpses being disposed of . . . Miss Gibbon was never going to be high priority. Yet Mel had persisted and got herself killed. And the irony was that Miss Gibbon had survived.

'What makes it worse,' Hen went on, 'is the piffling reason why these killings were done – to allow that despicable man to go on selling his illegal mushrooms.'

'He was living in fear, Hen. He had a monopoly in growing the things. Made him a small fortune, but it also tied him into every drugs syndicate worthy of the name. He was dealing with hard men who think nothing of murder. One false move, one name leaked, and he signed his own death warrant.' Before Diamond had got the words out, he realised they were a mistake. He'd meant to ease Hen's pain by stressing that the motive wasn't trivial, but it came out sounding like an apology for Ferdie.

'I refuse to waste any sympathy on him.' She put her foot down and the engine roared. 'You asked how I feel, matey, and I told you.'

Half a mile on, she relented a little. 'How are *you* feeling?'

'At this speed? Uncomfortable.'

She slowed to just above the speed limit. 'What's next?'

'If I survive this car ride? A night's sleep and some unfinished business tomorrow.'

'The business that brought you here?'

She meant her own suspension. He needed to take the

heat out of the topic. 'I had mixed feelings when this caper was dumped on me.'

'Which caper?'

'Investigating a bad egg like you.'

'Get away, you enjoyed it.'

'The only thing I enjoy – apart from seeing you again – is this bit: riding away and leaving someone else to clear up the mess. Poor old Montacute will be doing overtime with Davy and Ferdie and their crimes and a major drugs operation to unravel.'

'Don't fret about Montacute, Pete. It's his chance to shine. He'll take any credit that's going.'

'And get promoted?'

'He won't want that. As you said the other day, he's a natural second-in-command. He isn't after my job.'

'Who do you think is?'

'You're still on about the whistle-blower, aren't you? Forget it, like I did. It's not as if that anonymous letter was a lie. Hahn read it out to me before I was suspended and every word was true.'

'I've seen that letter, too,' Diamond said. 'In fact, I made a copy.'

'There you go, then. I did know about the DNA result and I made my choice not to investigate Joss. I can't argue. I must face the music for what I did – or, rather, what I didn't do.'

'How many of your present team were working for you when it happened?'

'At the time the DNA result came in? Five I can think of, all trusted friends.' She sighed. 'I don't know why you keep on about this, cocky. It's a blind alley.'

'Perhaps you're right. I'm coming from the wrong direction. I'll try a different way in. The team knew you well. Could it have been someone who didn't know you well?'

'You've lost me now.'

'A newcomer.'

'That's daft. It had to be someone who knew about the DNA result.'

'And you said you spoke to no one?'

'Not a word. The DNA report came to me via headquarters from the lab. Put yourself in my position. You don't blab about it when you bury bad news.'

'Who were the latest to join your team?'

'In CID? Nobody in the last year. You know how it is with all the cuts. They're not recruiting these days.'

'Civilian staff?'

'Only Pat Gomez – but she knows nothing. She arrived from headquarters a couple of weeks before I was suspended.' They had reached the first roundabout for Chichester town centre. 'Where to, Grand Inquisitor? Your hotel?'

He looked at his watch. It was close to midnight. 'I suppose.'

'Will Dallymore be waiting up for you?'

'Sure to be.'

'You've got plenty to tell her. What's *she* been up to? Has she written her report on me?'

'Not when I last saw her. If she has, she's wasted her time.'

She managed a hollow laugh. 'How can that be?'

'You'll find out, Hen.'

Next morning, Diamond and Georgina checked out of the hotel and loaded their luggage into the official car. With difficulty Diamond squeezed himself into the back seat among the golf clubs and pink suitcases.

'We need to call at Chichester police station first,' Georgina told their driver. 'And then county headquarters in Lewes. After that, you can return us to Bath and your duties will be over.'

'They do themselves proud down here,' Diamond said as they eventually approached Malling House, the executive home of Sussex police, an elegant seventeenth-century building in red, grey and orange brick. 'Makes ours look like a bus station.'

'Old doesn't mean better,' Georgina said. 'We're not going to be intimidated.'

'No way.'

'You haven't met Archie. He's no lightweight.'

They were shown up a superbly carved oak staircase to Archie's suite on the second floor.

'Commander Hahn is aware that you're here,' his personal assistant told them. 'Please take a seat and he'll see you presently.'

'The age-old trick,' Diamond said to Georgina. 'Part of the process of making us feel servile. Don't forget to curtsey when we go in.'

She gave him a look. She was getting nervous of how he would behave in there.

They didn't have long to wait.

'Georgina!' Hahn, all silver buttons and badges, got up from behind his desk as if meeting a long-lost sister. But instead of a hug, her one-time heart-throb gave her the social double kiss with the minimum of contact. Georgina's remark in the car had been true: he was no lightweight. He was a featherweight. In fact, he was not much more than a cotton bud.

Georgina introduced Diamond by name and rank. Hahn barely gave him a look. Evidently he didn't shake hands with mere superintendents. He showed them to a black leather sofa and offered coffee, which they declined.

Diamond was distracted by a movement beside his leg. A little dog with a sandy, long-haired coat had appeared from nowhere and was sniffing his shoes.

'That's Nipper,' Hahn said in a voice suitable for reading from a charge-sheet. 'He's being friendly, but keep your hands out of range. He seems to be interested in the splashes of mud on your trouser leg.'

The remark was surely meant to undermine. The attempted clean-up of the suit before breakfast hadn't been entirely successful. There is only so much you can do in a hotel room with a toothbrush.

Georgina said, 'I asked to see you, Archie, because we've concluded our work here.'

Hahn gave a confident nod. 'And very grateful I am. Perhaps you can give me the gist of it before you write the report.'

'That's why we're here.' She turned to Diamond. 'Peter?'

Hahn couldn't avoid looking at his second visitor now.

Diamond folded his legs, wanting to discourage Nipper, who was getting to be a nuisance. 'We've spoken to DCI Mallin more than once and she's entirely frank about what happened. She admits she was in error for failing to investigate her niece when the DNA evidence came to light. It amounted to misconduct.'

'That's the crux of it,' Hahn said, bringing his hands together. 'There was no justification. Policing has to be scrupulously impartial. Anything that smacks of corruption can't be tolerated.'

Diamond added, 'There's no question that the niece, Jocelyn Mallin, as she was then, before she married, drove the car containing Joe Rigden's body to Littlehampton.'

'It's good to have this confirmed independently.'

'And it became clear as we investigated that this was part of an ongoing conspiracy within the criminal community to dispose of murdered corpses.'

This was the first thing Archie Hahn didn't like. He shifted in his chair. 'But that's not part of your brief.'

Diamond had his own opinion. 'I'm sure news has reached you that the person behind this was found dead yesterday on his yacht, apparently from an overdose.'

'I saw a report, yes – but until the matter has been investigated, his activities must be a matter of speculation.'

'There isn't much room for doubt, commander. As we speak, corpses in refuse sacks are being brought up from a wreck a mile off Selsey Bill. The man known as Davy, actually Stanley Clitheroe, was photographed recently in diving gear with his boat anchored over the point where the wreck lies.'

'I'm not sure where you're going with this. You'd better confine your remarks to DCI Mallin.'

'Very well. Before she was suspended, DCI Mallin had taken an interest in the conspiracy. She suspected a significant number of missing persons along the south coast were murder victims and had been disposed of—'

Hahn broke in so abruptly that Nipper started yapping. 'Georgina, will you tell your man to address the matter in hand. This is outside the scope of your inquiry.'

Georgina didn't get a chance because Diamond had no intention of stopping. 'She took the initiative of contacting CID colleagues right along the coast. It must have created quite a stir here at headquarters when news of what she was doing reached you. Just when there's pressure from government for improving crime statistics there's a real danger of your murder rate rising astronomically. She had to be stopped as a matter of urgency.'

'That's outrageous.'

'How convenient that you had something on her, something you'd been content to ignore three years ago when it first came to light.'

Hahn was on his feet. 'Get this man out of my office, Georgina.'

'That wouldn't be wise, commander,' Diamond said. 'I'm sure the chief constable will be willing to listen and, if he isn't, there's the police and crime commissioner.' He glanced down. 'Nipper, basket.'

The tone of voice must have done it. The little dog gave a whimper and ran to the corner of the room and into its basket. And Archie stopped protesting, too.

'The DNA match that implicated Jocelyn in 2011 was sent here first from the lab and then to DCI Mallin. She showed it to no one and took no action, as we know. Here in head-quarters nobody was unduly perturbed. The possibility that a man was in jug for a crime he didn't commit didn't trouble you. Danny Stapleton was a career criminal anyway. But someone here was sharp enough to note that Jocelyn Green had been Jocelyn Mallin before she married. The informa-tion was noted. Why don't you sit down? You're making the dog nervous.'

Hahn had turned as pale as moonlight. He had started pacing, arms folded, fury personified.

Diamond continued. 'Three years on, when Hen Mallin became interested in missing persons, the alarm bells started ringing here and, I dare say, in the neighbouring police services. She had to be stopped. The difficulty is that she's stubborn, unlikely to listen to a warning from high. She knew she was on to something.'

Georgina said, 'Please sit down, Archie. We can deal with this in a civilised way.'

Hahn said to her, 'Are you associating yourself with this unfounded rubbish?'

'I happen to know it isn't rubbish and it isn't unfounded either.'

Diamond picked up his thread. 'A plot was devised to

stop her. You had the dirt on her, but you had to use it cleverly. You didn't want anyone knowing you'd been sitting on it for three years. So the whistle-blowing couldn't appear to come from headquarters. Instead, you thought up the dirty trick of having an anonymous letter sent from Chichester, apparently written by one of her team.'

'Outrageous.'

'Yes, it was,' Diamond continued smoothly, 'so it had to be done with all the skill of a spy operation. Communications between divisional police stations and headquarters are mostly electronic, as we know, but there's still a regular pick-up of paperwork collected physically by despatch rider. The idea was for someone at Chichester to make sure the letter was included with the other material – and for that you needed a plant. We've just been speaking to her: Pat Gomez. It emerged that she was transferred from headquarters to Chichester two weeks before Hen Mallin was suspended. A tried and trusted civilian clerk with family in Chichester, who was pleased to be assigned there.'

'Don't blame her, Archie,' Georgina said. 'Through no fault of hers we worked out that she acted as the so-called whistle-blower, but she was just the messenger. She did all that you asked.'

The 'we worked out' was bending the truth somewhat. Diamond had got there by questioning Hen the evening before.

He let it pass. 'Pat Gomez had been given a sealed letter to slip in with the other documents for delivery to headquarters. We questioned her closely and that's as much as she knew. It all went to plan and on receipt the letter was officially stamped and dated and you had the pretext to suspend Hen Mallin and put a stop to her missing persons inquiry.'

'Which is where we came in,' Georgina said. 'You didn't

want it going to the Independent Police Complaints Commission, but you needed an inquiry of some sort to get her sacked, so you approached me as a high-ranking officer from another force. The case was watertight. Even I, with my reputation for leaving no stone unturned, would be sure to endorse the dismissal.'

Georgina's reputation wasn't quite as she imagined. Diamond recalled the note Archie Hahn had carelessly left in the file. *If – heaven forbid – anything more damaging should emerge, we can rely on her to miss it altogether, or, at worst, bury it.* But he'd long ago decided she should never be told.

'I must inform you now that I'm not going to endorse it,' Georgina went on, at her barnstorming best. 'Yes, DCI Mallin was guilty of misconduct, but that was overtaken by far more deplorable misconduct at a higher level.'

'What?' Hahn gaped at his college buddy as if she was a ten-tonne truck advancing on him.

'And there isn't much doubt who I'm talking about. This may be a matter for your chief constable, or your PCC, or the Home Office. That rather depends on you. We're going to insist that DCI Mallin is reinstated as head of CID at Chichester with immediate effect. You need her there as a matter of urgency. She's a fine detective and she was right to start the inquiry into missing persons. She must follow it through to its conclusion, regardless of your damned statistics.'

A cloud of misery had descended on Archie Hahn. He'd stopped pacing. He sank into the chair, defeated. 'Whatever you say, Georgina, whatever you say.'

Some way into the journey home, Georgina took out her phone and called Bath police station to find out what had been happening in her absence. 'That's good,' she said a number of times. And when asked a question, she said, 'Oh, highly satisfactory. It was of a sensitive nature and it must remain confidential. It's safe to say that we solved their little local difficulties.'

She ended the call and turned in her seat. 'I was speaking to your deputy, Keith Halliwell.'

'Really? How's he coping?'

'Admirably, by the sound of it. They rounded up the jewel thieves you were so concerned about. Caught them red-handed. Purple-handed, in fact. The old trick with the anti-theft detection powder.'

'They'll be crowing about that.'

'Didn't I say they'd manage perfectly well without you?'

'I believe I remember something of the sort.'

'It's no bad thing, Peter. It could free you up to work more closely with me from time to time. Dallymore and Diamond, detectives.'

He gritted his teeth and said nothing.

Peter Lovesey was born in Middlesex and studied at Hampton Grammar School and Reading University, where he met his wife Jax. He won a competition with his first crime fiction novel, *Wobble to Death*, and has never looked back, with his numerous books winning and being shortlisted for nearly all the prizes in the international crime writing world. He was Chairman of the Crime Writers' Association and has been presented with Lifetime Achievement awards both in the UK and the US.